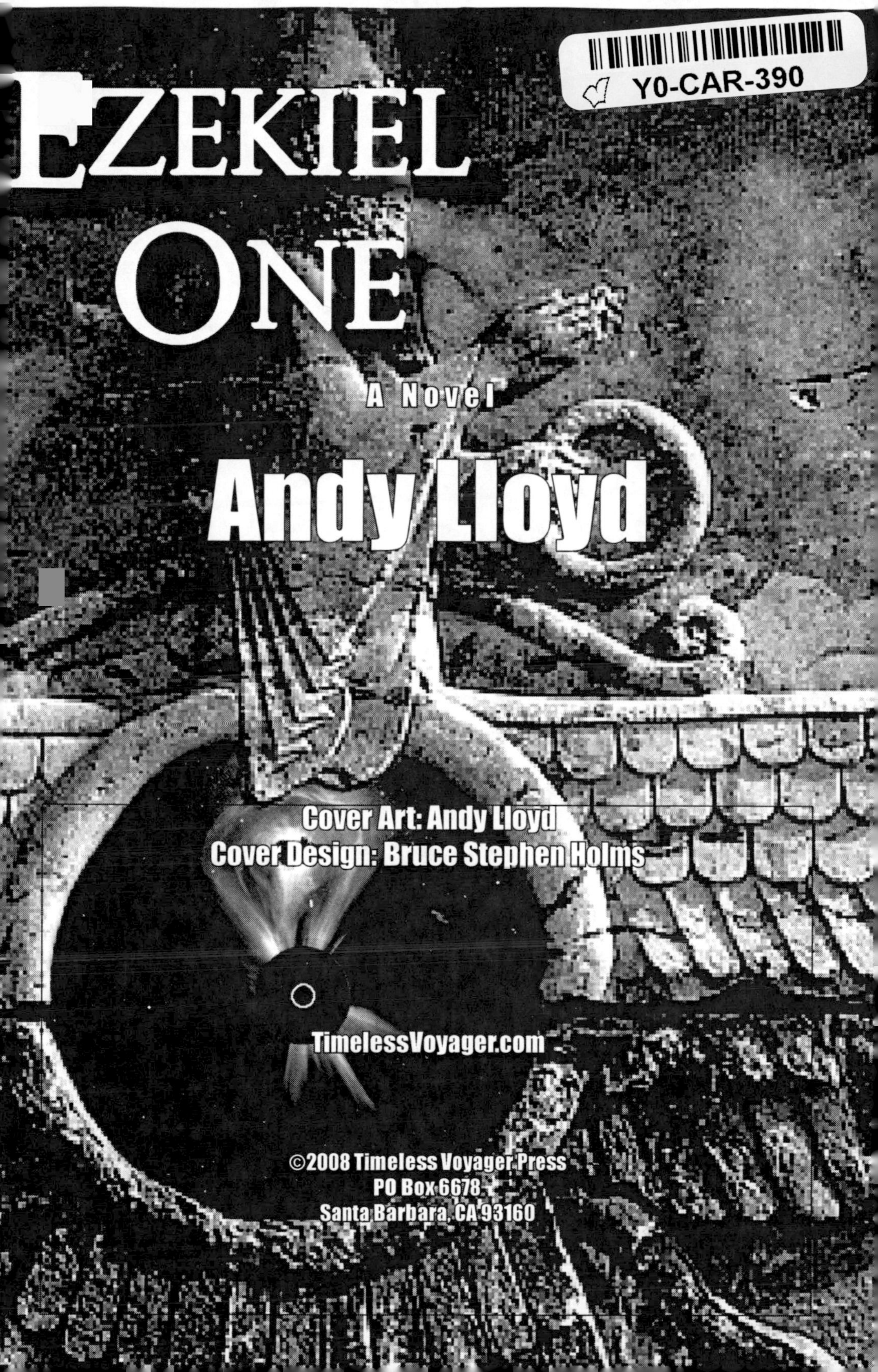
EZEKIEL
ONE
A Novel
Andy Lloyd
Cover Art: Andy Lloyd
Cover Design: Bruce Stephen Holms
TimelessVoyager.com
©2008 Timeless Voyager Press
PO Box 6678
Santa Barbara, CA 93160
Y0-CAR-390

EZEKIEL ONE

ISBN: 978-1-892264-25-1

TIMELESS VOYAGER PRESS
PO Box 6678
Santa Barbara, CA 93160
1-800-576-8463

Acknowledgements

I'd like to thank my publisher, Bruce Stephen Holms, my other editors and proof-readers, Monika Myers, Lee Covino, and my wife, Fiona.

Thanks also to Mattia Galiazzo for his astronomical knowledge, to Martin Horwood M.P. for the tour of the Palace of Westminster, and to Joan d'Arc for publishing the article which acted as a prelude for this fictional work.

This book is dedicated to my father, Peter Lloyd, who is steadily working his way through his local library. He'll read this book in an afternoon, and remember it forever.

Table Of Contents

CHAPTER ONE

On the fifth day, of the fourth month in the thirtieth year, while I was among the exiles by the river Kebar, the heavens opened and I saw a vision of God.

It was much too pleasant a day for a funeral. A light, autumnal breeze scattered masses of dead leaves across the road in front of Bill's car. He sat at the driving wheel, watching the sunlight pick out yellow and red highlights amongst them; a pretty display for a sad day.

Bill Bainbridge was in his mid-forties, with a bald patch and a middle-age spread both bigger than he would have wished. His soft, urban features and casual suit complimented a relaxed face whose laughter lines outnumbered the creases criss-crossing his brow. His eyes shone with deep intelligence.

It had been a long drive from London to Cheltenham, and it had taken a while to find Prestbury Church. It had taken almost as long to find somewhere to park the car. Prestbury was a small village on the outskirts of the town, and the main car park served a pub. It was full. But as Bill had driven past he had noticed that the pub itself was almost empty. He had concluded that the car park was filled with mourners' cars. This was not surprising, Bill thought, given the age of the deceased. The church was likely to be packed.

Bill reached into the glove compartment of the car and pulled out a plain buff envelope. His home address, without his name, was written on the front. The postmark was Gloucestershire. The envelope could have been sent from the village post office in Prestbury, Bill thought. It had come full circle. He took out the now familiar document within. It was a photocopy of a memo, but there was no addressee, and neither was it signed.

The letter was dominated by the familiar NASA logo, and below this was a typed list of 12 names. Underneath this was an almost illegible handwritten note in black biro, and below that a neater line written in pencil. The pattern of the words in the two sentences matched, almost like the second line was a tidy version of the first. But the handwriting was entirely different.

Putting the document back into the envelope, and then into his pocket, Bill stepped out of the car and locked the door carefully. He looked up at the church tower in the middle distance and consoled himself with the thought that the exercise would probably do him some good.

The mass of mourners in the graveyard obscured the coffin almost entirely. Bill stood below a tree, which helped to shield his eyes from the afternoon sun. Several other mourners stood close-by, talking quietly amongst themselves, or sobbing gently. Bill didn't know any of them. This was unsurprising; he had never visited Cheltenham before, not even for the famous Gold Cup, held at the nearby racecourse in middle of March.

"It's starting to get chilly. The evenings are setting in early now", sounded a male voice to Bill's right. The accent was unmistakeably Gloucestershire: a broad, farming dialect more appropriate to workers in the fields than the urbanites of Georgian Cheltenham. Bill turned to face his new companion. The man looked to be in his fifties, an unfashionable cigarette set into the corner of his mouth. He was a large man, with a sizeable beer belly.

"Yes, I must admit it feels colder than I expected. I should have brought a coat with me", Bill replied.

The stranger suppressed a laugh. "Oh, that'll be the ghosts of Prestbury sending a chill down your spine. This place is haunted, you know. A lot of people feel cold in this graveyard. Hell, I do every time I walk through it to the pub. Even on a summer's day." The man tilted his head slightly and frowned. "Your accent's odd. You're not from round these parts, then?"

"No, I'm from London."

"How did you know Lyn, then? She's lived around here for donkey's years."

"I went to university with her back in the eighties. I haven't actually seen her since then, believe it or not. We've kept in contact over the Internet for the last few years. My name's Bill, by the way."

"Hmmm. Tony." The men shook hands while Tony took a long puff on his cigarette. "She must have meant something to you if you drove all the way over here. Mind you, she *was* quite a woman. Alan's absolutely distraught. And Christine…well, it can't be easy at that age, can it?"

The large gathering around the burial was noticeably quieter, and Bill could hear the soft tones of the vicar echo across the graveyard. Several of the peripheral attendees started to move towards the crowd, pressing in to watch the proceedings. Tony stayed where he was, and continued to smoke his cigarette. He offered one to Bill, who declined.

"I can't for the life of me figure out how she ended up being buried in Prestbury graveyard", Tony whispered under his breath.

"Why do you say that?"

"Lyn was not exactly a churchgoer, and neither was Alan to be honest. So how did he manage to wangle a plot in the graveyard for her?"

"Maybe they had a family plot, or something like that."

"I doubt it. Do you have any idea how hard it is to get a burial plot nowadays? Particularly in a haunted graveyard?" Tony raised an amused eyebrow at his own joke. "They must have connections high up in the Church."

Bill shrugged. But his mind was already racing. Tony half-turned towards him.

"So what's your line of work down in London?"

"I'm a journalist."

Tony smiled. "That would explain why she never met up with you. Can't imagine the Firm would have liked that – her consorting with a hack."

"The Firm?" Bill feigned ignorance. "She never discussed her work," he lied.

"Not surprising, I guess. Lyn used to work at GCHQ. Well, before she had to retire on the grounds of ill health, of course. I couldn't tell you what she did. Don't know myself. She used to joke that she did the gardening up there, but I don't suppose there are many shrubs in the Doughnut."

"The Doughnut?"

"GCHQ is that massive doughnut-shaped building off the A40. It's Britain's main spy-base. Take a look at it when you drive back towards the motorway. You can't miss it."

In fact, Bill had already seen GCHQ on the way into Cheltenham from the M5. It was a strange looking circular building, with a large hole in the middle, and had apparently cost a small fortune to build. Or rather, it had cost a fortune shifting the computers from the old building.

Spying was big business in Cheltenham. It was a town full of spooks, but a different variety from the ghosts of Prestbury. The spooks of GCHQ provided the British Government with signals intelligence from across the globe, in the never-ending war against terrorism.

It was rumoured that every electronic communication in Britain was filtered through their vast array of super-computers....and possibly those of the rest of the civilised, and less civilised, world too. The members of staff who worked there were themselves monitored, in classic Big Brother style. It was George Orwell's nightmare written large in a rural Cotswold town.

Lyn had always been careful to cover her tracks, Bill thought. Until recently, anyhow.

"Paranoia without end. Amen," he muttered under his breath. Tony, still smoking, either didn't hear him, or ignored his remark.

The burial service was reaching its inevitable conclusion. The emotional devastation on the faces of the mourners was more evident now, although the proceedings remained dignified. As Bill watched the grief-stricken community before him he unexpectedly made eye contact with a woman, standing near to a strange-looking tombstone in the shape of a pyramid. Although her face was half-covered by a scarf, Bill momentarily recognised her.

Quickly, she looked away, and then began to shuffle uncomfortably on the spot. She seemed to be whispering to a tall man stood next to her. He wore a long trench coat hiding a smart, tailored suit. He was an obviously handsome man in his mid-forties with blond hair swept back from his face. His skin was unusually pale, giving him a Scandinavian look. Bill thought he caught the man surreptitiously looking at him. Then Tony spoke again.

"Well, maybe I'll see you back at the house. Will you be paying your respects?"

"Er...yes. But I'm parked about half a mile away, so it'll take me a while to get over there. And then I'll have to find somewhere to park..."

"Why don't you park in my drive? I'm one of Alan's neighbours. That's how I knew Lyn. My house number is 72, in the same road. You know how to get there?" Tony extinguished his cigarette by treading it into the concrete pathway.

"Yes…The wonders of GPS. Thanks for the offer. I'll take you up on that."

Bill shook hands with Tony as the large man departed. The crowd of mourners was also slowly breaking up. Bill turned back to look at the tall man and the familiar woman, but they had both disappeared. Looking around, Bill sought them out, but in vain. He frowned, and then made his way back to the car.

✦

"I see you found the place alright."

Tony had walked over to Bill's car, which was squeezed onto the drive behind the big man's 4 x 4. Cars were parked along the length of the road, and a small flurry of black-clad folk shuffled past the back of Bill's car, which was jutting onto the pavement.

Tony had been smoking outside his front door, and appeared to have been waiting for Bill to arrive. Or perhaps he had simply wanted a last puff of nicotine smoke before going to the wake. Bill didn't care either way. He wasn't looking forward to meeting Lyn's husband, Alan. But he needed to ask him some questions in person. It was no good over the telephone. Not only was it all a bit difficult to explain, but there was also the issue of security to consider.

Lyn had never discussed anything important with him over the phone; their chats had always been friendly and platonic. If he had ever steered the conversation towards the subject of the documents she sometimes sent him in the post, she had quickly changed the subject, and covered herself with a harmless riposte. She had clearly worked in the intelligence services for many years.

"It was kind of you to wait for me, Tony," confessed Bill with a weak smile. "It's not easy to attend a gathering like this when you don't know anybody. But I really do want to pay my respects."

"I just want to see the look on their faces when they find out you're a journalist from London, mate," laughed Tony. It struck Bill that Tony was not exactly overcome by grief at Lyn's death. But then, he was only a neighbour. Bill locked his car up and accompanied Tony along the road. It was a quiet suburban street, full of semi-detached houses with small, well-managed gardens.

In the distance were the Cotswold Hills. It was a prettier, more relaxed version of where Bill lived in southwest London. He briefly imagined retiring to the West Country with his wife Helen. She would probably like it out here, too, he decided.

In the drive of Lyn and Alan's house were two cars, the second sporting the old system of number plates, and battered on the driver's side.

"That's Christine's little run-around," offered Tony. "I've helped her sort it out more than once. The clutch is a bit knackered, but it still runs. That boyfriend of hers, Colin: he's a bright bloke, but wouldn't know one end of a spark plug from another. I don't know what they teach them in these schools nowadays. He's up at Oxford. He started this term. Like I said, he's a bright lad."

Bill stopped behind the little car. "Why's she got that sticker on the bumper, Tony?"

The sticker showed a red disc. To either side of it was a long bolt of blue lightning extending right and left. In the centre of the red disk was written "2012" in bold black print.

"Don't you know, Bill? "The End is Nigh", mate," he intoned sarcastically. "We've only got three months to go before we all cash in our chips."

"So Christine's into all that mystic stuff about 2012, is she?"

"More Colin, I'd have said. But, yeah, she's mentioned it once or twice. She's got a few books on the Aztecs…"

"Mayans," Bill corrected him, perhaps a little too quickly.

"Yeah, well, if you ask me it's all a load of old nonsense. If these Mayans had been that sharp they'd still be about, wouldn't they? Anyhow, let's go in: I'm parched."

✦

Standing in the hallway, Bill looked into the lounge. It was packed with people, almost all of them standing up, chatting to each other over paper plates loaded with buffet food. Many were trying to negotiate the art of eating from a flimsy plate which was precariously balanced in one hand, using their other hand, which was effectively disabled by a glass of drink, whilst simultaneously being jostled on all sides. Bill didn't fancy the carpet's chances much.

Bill and Tony worked their way through the room to the buffet table, and organised themselves with food and a glass of wine. Tony bumped into someone he knew, and began a conversation. So Bill took the opportunity to stand at the edge of the room with plate and glass in hand, performing his own culinary balancing act.

It quickly struck him how ordinary everyone was. Many of the gathering were probably colleagues who worked for the Government Communications Headquarters. Anyone present who was would have signed the Official Secrets Act, and have been privy to documents and secrets far beyond the reach of ordinary members of the public. They were almost all effectively in the spying business. But there were certainly no James Bond-types in the room.

Bill smiled to himself. If he was running the intelligence services, he'd want to recruit unremarkable people whose lives were ordinary, who didn't get themselves into situations where they might be blackmailed, or taken advantage of in some way. He figured that their ordinariness made them ideal workers at

GCHQ. And, to some degree, Lyn fitted into the same category - intelligent, dependable, and sensible.

Except that she was also the conduit of all those remarkable government leaks…

Bill noticed that Lyn's bereaved husband, Alan, was stood in the conservatory, accepting the condolences of several of his guests. He had recognised Alan's face from carefully placed photos of the couple dotted around the room. Bill took a last gulp of supermarket white wine, and walked over to join the group.

A tall elderly lady was speaking in a dry, toneless voice, "…of course, I was so shocked when I first heard the news. I said to Vera, I said 'She can't be more than fifty…'"

"Forty-six," remarked Alan.

"…and she wasn't a smoker, or anything like that. I know she liked the odd glass of sherry, but that's hardly likely to give you cancer is it? And Vera said…"

"Excuse me, I'm sorry to interrupt, but are you Alan?" asked Bill.

Alan smiled the wan smile of a man saved.

"That's right. Are you one of Lyn's colleagues from work?"

"My name's Bill. Sort of…Look, I'm terribly sorry about your loss…" Alan waved the opening sentence of his speech aside. He had clearly heard many of them that afternoon. Bill continued, "I need to have a chat with you if I may," he glanced at Alan's elderly protagonist, "in private?"

"Of course! I've taken up far too much of your time, dear," she said to Alan, and, giving Bill a long look, she worked her way back into the living room. The other assembled guests also ebbed away politely, to rejoin the gathered throng in the living room.

Alan raised an eyebrow. Bill corrected his previous judgement about the house's occupants: If anyone in the house could have carried off playing James Bond, it was Alan. At least, the Roger Moore version of Bond, anyway. Which was ironic, really, because Bill knew for a fact that Alan did not work for GCHQ. He was a social worker.

"Look, could we speak in the garden?" asked Bill, realising that he was breaching whole layers of funeral etiquette. This was, after all, the wake of Alan's late wife. But his host seemed pleased to get away from the formality for a while, and led the way through the patio door.

The garden was fairly long, and beautifully presented. A tree at the bottom of the garden was just taking on some autumn colour, and the flower beds were full of the summer's bedding plants, creating colourful, thoughtfully presented displays. The two men walked across the patio, and stood next to the shed. Bill half expected to see Tony out there smoking, but he was nowhere in sight. Alan took out a packet of cigarettes, and offered one to Bill, who declined.

"I've often considered it ironic that it wasn't me who went first," said Alan. "I'm a twenty-a-day man. Just can't kick the habit. Damn things. Lyn never smoked, and she's the one who got cancer. There's no bloody justice, is there?" He paused, and looked at Bill expectantly.

"I knew Lyn back at Keele Uni," explained Bill. "We met up again through the 'Friends United' website a couple of years ago, and we've emailed each other every so often since then." Alan nodded, and kept on smoking, all the time eyes fixed on Bill. They had narrowed somewhat. Bill couldn't really see any easy way of saying what he wanted to say, and Alan was probably already getting the wrong idea. He pulled out the NASA memo from his jacket pocket and handed it to Alan.

"What's this?"

"I'm not exactly sure myself, but your wife sent it to me. You see, I don't know whether you know this or not, Alan, but every so often she would send me stuff that the government wanted leaked to the press. Usually it was material they wanted in the papers before the real story broke, to get the public used to the bad news. Sort of damage-control."

"Are you a journalist?"

"Yes, I'm a correspondent for one of the tabloids. I wouldn't break the story myself; just pass it along to the appropriate hack. It's all part of the game, although it's quite unusual to have someone at GCHQ as the source. Usually it's Whitehall. I should stress that she wasn't intending to be disloyal to her country, or anything like that. The whole business of government leaks is just part of the process of government spin and control of the news in the media."

Bill was relieved that Alan wasn't shocked by what he had just been told. At least, he wasn't conveying surprise. Perhaps he already knew that Lyn was involved in this kind of covert practice. They were married, after all.

"So what's this all about?" Alan asked, pointing at the NASA document in his hand.

"Lyn sent it to me about 5 weeks ago. I didn't have a clue what it was. It didn't relate to any of the current news stories. There was no context at all. It's just a list of 12 names with the NASA letterhead. You can see that Lyn wrote one line under it."

"Yes, I can see that this is her handwriting, but she's written a line of nonsense. What is this, some kind of code?"

"Actually, yes, she used to send me material in a coded format. I guess she had plenty of training in that department." Bill offered a half-smile, but Alan wasn't in the mood for light-hearted quips. "We had developed a cipher, a kind of code. It wasn't exactly top-drawer security, but it would prevent a lay person reading something sensitive if a document fell into the wrong hands. My decoded version is below it."

"Doesn't that risk someone reading it, then?"

"I suppose, but, to be honest, the whole thing makes so little sense, I didn't think it would make any difference. What she wrote was, 'Ezekiel One.

12/21/2012.' Look, the point of all this is that I don't think this particular document was an official government leak. I think this was something Lyn herself wanted me to see. I think she leaked it without authorization."

"And this happened five weeks ago? Lyn was only diagnosed with the cancer a month ago. A glioblastoma, the doctors called it. It was a very aggressive tumour." Alan paused, as if digging deep inside for strength. He took a puff on his cigarette. "It had metastasized before she even got to see a surgeon."

"That's the thing that's been playing on my mind. It's the reason I came here today to see you. I think her sudden illness and her involvement in this document's appearance may be connected. I'm just not sure what to do about it."

"Look, Bill. That's your name, right? Are you trying to imply that her illness had something to do with this?" Alan fanned the document around in front of Bill irritably. "Because if you are, I'm really not in the mood for this. I just buried my wife today, for God's sake."

Bill tried to look sympathetic, but resolute. Alan continued, "Lyn didn't speak much about her work. You know that she signed the Official Secrets Act? Why would she jeopardise her career over a list of names and a line of numbers? What could possibly have been that important?"

Bill felt things slipping away from him. Alan's body language was becoming increasingly uncomfortable. He had dropped his cigarette to the ground and had stepped on it. Bill quickly tried to explain the little he knew, "Ezekiel One is a verse from the Bible. 12/21/2012 is a date, in the American fashion: month, date, year. It's the 21st December this year: the Mayan End of the Age."

Alan looked incredulous. "And the list of names?"

"All of them are young religious zealots: Jesuit priests, Evangelicals. Fervent, committed Christians to a man. All twelve of them are men. I've researched each and every one of them in depth, trying to discover what your wife might have known. There's no other connection that I can find, and no obvious connection to NASA. I've hit a dead-end, but my concern is that there might be some kind of cover-up at work. Your wife might have been trying to expose it, and that might have put her life in jeopardy."

Alan handed Bill the memo. "It all sounds very unlikely, to be honest. I'm sorry, Bill, but I've heard enough. I'm not sure what this is about, but I can't help you. Even if you're right, and Lyn did leak this to you, I don't know anything about it. I really don't think her illness can possibly have anything to do with this nonsense. Perhaps you've been making up stories for your tabloid newspaper just a little too long, and you're starting to see things that simply aren't there."

Alan turned and walked back to the house.

Bill looked down at the NASA memorandum miserably. He knew that this had been a long-shot. It could have been worse, he thought, attempting to console himself: Alan might have hit him. He knew a few politicians who weren't beyond a violent physical reaction if cornered by a journalist with a bad news story. It was lucky for him that Alan was a social worker, whose temperament had likely been smoothed by years of dealing with difficult clients.

He decided to make a quick exit, before Alan got the chance to share the meeting with anyone who might take greater exception to Bill's unusual imposition. He followed Alan back into the house, and quickly worked his way through the assembled crowd, heading for the front door. Breathing a sigh of relief, Bill stepped out the front door and briskly walked down the street.

As he approached Tony's house, however, his face fell. Bill's car was blocked in by a BMW.

"Bugger," he muttered.

There was no way he was going to be able to manoeuvre his car out of the drive. He either had to go back to the wake and ask around for the identity of the car's owner, or sit in the car until they came out at some point later in the afternoon. At least, he thought, this wasn't an Irish wake. He might still be there by morning!

As he considered his options, a young woman ran up to him from the direction in which he had come. The girl appeared to be about seventeen years old, with mousy brown hair cut into a long bob hanging just above her shoulders. She reminded him of how Lyn used to look when they were at university together. He grimaced. This was clearly Christine; had she come to berate him for upsetting her father? If she had, he was well and truly cornered now.

She stopped in front of him, slightly breathless. As she spoke he got the scent of something from her breath, something he had not smelled for over 20 years. She'd been smoking weed! On the day of her own mother's funeral!

"Were you the man who was just talking to my Dad?"

"Yes, look, I'm sorry about all that..."

"You don't understand. I want to help!"

"Sorry?"

"I want to help! I want to find out who murdered my Mum!"

"Look, I'm not saying anyone murdered her. It's just that, well, she might have got into some trouble with the authorities." Bill realised he was sounding a little patronising.

"But what about all that stuff you said to my Dad? All that stuff about the end of the Mayan Age? Maybe she found out how the world is going to end! Someone might have killed her for that. I need to know!" Christine started to break down and cry. It was a pitiful sight. Feeling somewhat uncomfortable, Bill extended his arms and gave her a hug. She was weeping uncontrollably. This is great, he thought, all I need now is for her boyfriend to come around the corner and see this.

There was an uncoordinated rush of footsteps heading in their direction from Lyn and Alan's house. Bill looked up and met the eyes of a young man, whose formal black attire was looking distinctly dishevelled, even dirty in places.

He was perhaps nineteen, and wore his hair quite long, which partially hid a strong, handsome face. His physique was lean, like a long-distance runner. Sure enough, it was Colin. Bill realised that they must have both been smoking pot in the shed. Quite apt really: pot in the shed. They must have overheard every word of his conversation with Alan.

So much for a high security gathering!

Bill gently disentangled himself from the still-wailing Christine. She fell into Colin's arms, distraught. Colin's face was hard to read, thought Bill. He didn't seem angry, or upset, or in any way emotional at all. He was just studying Bill with a sharpness that belied his evident drug intoxication.

"I know quite a bit about the Mayan Age. I know Lyn was interested in the subject, too, because we used to talk about it over a cup of coffee now and then. She got me reading all about it. We both want to help, Mr…?" Colin was fishing for Bill's name. As paranoid as Bill had become lately, he didn't see any problem in telling this young man his name. He thought it might instil an element of trust between them.

"Bill Bainbridge. Look maybe you can help, I don't know. You both probably know more about this Mayan business than me, given that sticker on your car, and the books you say you've read. I'd never even heard of it until I got this document sent through to me. And…if Lyn sent me this on her own volition, she may have held back some more information for me that she was unable to send because of the sudden progress of her illness."

"You want us to go through my Mum's things?" spluttered Christine.

"No, no, nothing like that. Look, if you just happen to come across anything, here's my email address at the Daily Standard. You can write to me and I'll come back out here to meet with you. Just don't write any of it down over the Internet, or talk about it over the phone." Bill took a pen out of the glove compartment of his car and wrote his email address onto the back of a till receipt.

"What *is* Ezekiel One?" asked Colin.

"From what I can gather, it's about the weirdest verse in the Bible ever written. It describes a vision of a prophet in the Old Testament named Ezekiel. The event took place in Mesopotamia hundreds of years before the birth of Jesus. The verse seems to describe a UFO encounter, or something similar."

"What's that got to do with NASA, and these twelve priests?" Colin looked suitably confused.

"To be honest, I haven't the faintest clue, but I intend to find out. But the most pressing issue for me right now is how to move my car. You wouldn't happen to know who the owner is of this BMW, would you?"

Colin looked at the car, nodded, and ran back towards the house. Christine was calmer by now, and stayed with the stranded journalist.

"I'm very sorry about your Mum, Christine."

"It's okay, I just need a little time. I want to find out what she knew."

"So do I, believe me. She was a dear friend of mine many years ago, before you were born. If something happened to her, I want to find out and make sure that justice is done. But, really, I hope this just turns out to have been a coincidence."

"I hope so, Mr Bainbridge, but I'll see if I can find anything out. Either way, none of this is going to bring my Mum back. But it might help me to come to terms with what's happened, if I can understand a bit more about this secret life of hers. Dad doesn't want to know, but I do. She might have been a national hero, for all we know!"

Bill smiled, reassuringly. A few moments later, Bill's car was unblocked, and he was driving back towards London, quite uncertain of what lay ahead.

CHAPTER TWO

On the fifth day of the month in the fifth year of the exile of King Jehoiachin, the word of the Lord came to Ezekiel son of Buzi the priest, in Chaldaea, by the river Kebar, and there the hand of the Lord came upon him.

Bill looked down at his watch and frowned.

The police officer in front of him was going through a security questionnaire. A second officer to his right was holding a sub-machine gun in his arms, pointed towards the floor. "Not holding you up, are we sir?"

Bill tried to smile in a relaxed manner. Given that he was scheduled to meet with the Chair of the Intelligence and Security Committee he could quite see why the officers were being particularly scrupulous. Or at least, they were giving the *impression* of being scrupulous. But did they actually have to make him late for the meeting? Bill realised that he was probably coming across as being stressed. He hadn't slept properly for days, and it was starting to show.

The police officer looked up from his clipboard and said, "So, Mr. Bainbridge, you're a political journalist with the Daily Standard, but you've never actually been inside the Houses of Parliament before? That's the bit I don't understand, sir."

"I'm a junior member of the team," mumbled Bill.

"Sorry, sir? I didn't quite catch that." The policeman was clearly starting to enjoy himself.

Bill spoke up, a trace of exasperation in his voice, "I'm not a lobby journalist. I'm a relatively new member of the political team at the Standard. I was told by my editor yesterday that Anne Potter-Smith MP wanted to do an interview, and that she had specifically asked for me to be the journalist whom she spoke with. And she wanted to meet me in her office. So my editor arranged all the security passes to get me into the Commons. That's why all the security clearances are last minute."

The two police officers exchanged glances, and then stood apart, allowing Bill to walk through the security cordon. "Do you know where her office is, sir?"

"I'm sure I can find it," muttered Bill darkly, as he adjusted his identification badge.

"We'll see you later, then, sir."

"Much later..." chimed in the police officer sporting the sub-machine gun.

The officers both suppressed a laugh. They were right, Bill thought. There was no way he was going to find her office in the notorious maze of corridors beyond St. Stephen's entrance. For security reasons, there were no maps or floor-plans available to consult, and no formal reception area in this most archaic of institutions.

The problem was, like most men, Bill hated to ask for directions.

After passing through St. Stephen's Hall, Bill stepped into Central Lobby. He looked up at the four mosaics of the Patron Saints of Britain and Ireland, one each hanging above the four entrances to the lobby. Ahead of him was St. Andrew, guarding the entrance to the more social parts of the Palace of Westminster, including the bars and the terraced restaurant. The House of Lords was to his right, the Commons to his left. Given that Mrs. Potter-Smith was a Member of Parliament, he thought his best bet lay with the Commons. He passed under the Welsh Patron Saint and headed through to the Members' Lobby.

It was bustling with people, mostly middle-aged men in well-tailored suits. Some of the faces were immediately familiar. One or two of them belonged to politicians Bill remembered recently interviewing. Bill even recognised some lobby journalists from various newspapers and broadcasters, mingling amongst the MPs. Facing him were two large bronze statues, Winston Churchill to the left of the entrance before him, and David Lloyd George to its right. Strangely, the darkened statues had been rubbed along the top of their feet, creating shiny, uniform patches which glinted in the artificial light of the lobby.

Bill realised that he was looking directly at the entrance to the Commons Chamber. To the side of the statues were small kiosks in the lobby. These were adorned with pigeonholes, some of which were lit by small lights. There were short queues of politicians leading up to the kiosks, where post and papers were being exchanged. Bill wondered if he might be able to ask directions to Mrs Potter-Smith's office. While he considered his options, he felt a hand touch his arm.

"Bill, old son, what are you doing here?"

Bill turned and felt relieved to see an old friend. The well-presented television journalist who stood before him was a personality well-known to most of the British public. His face looked older here, in the House of Commons, than on television - perhaps lacking the magic of the make-up artists at the studio. His luck was in. "Hello, John. Am I glad to see you! I've got a meeting with one of the Members, and I'm running late."

"What are you doing interviewing MPs, Bill? That's not quite your bag, is it?"

"It's a long story. There have been a few changes since you jumped ship for the BBC."

"Well, I'll make you a deal. You explain it all to me and I'll find you your politician."

Bill happily agreed, and divulged the name of his interviewee. John thought deeply for a moment, and smiled. "C'mon, this way!" and they were off.

Bill said goodbye to his old friend, and stood before a darkly varnished door. Taking a deep breath, he rapped on the door loudly.

"Enter!" came the response, and he pushed open the door. He stood in a comparatively small office, made all the more compact by the dark oak panelling on the walls. The dimming light of a late autumn afternoon flooded through the windows, and beyond lay the River Thames, with its south bank facing him in the distance. In the maze of corridors Bill had walked through with John, he had become disorientated. It was a relief to get his bearings again.

Seated at the desk was the Right Honourable Anne Potter-Smith MP. She was immaculately presented in a pale blue suit. Mrs Potter-Smith was in her early fifties. Her hair was dark and cut fairly short, with the grey subtly coloured out. She was an exception to the old saying that politics was Hollywood for ugly people, thought Bill. Her power-dressing presented an imposing, yet feminine figure. She was the woman Bill had recognised at Lyn's funeral.

"Come on in, Mr. Bainbridge, and shut the door behind you. It's Bill isn't it?"

"Sorry I'm late. The security here is a bit of a nightmare, if you don't mind me saying."

"We are a nation at war, Bill."

Bill took the leather upholstered seat offered to him. Once sat down, he noticed for the first time a flat-screen television built into the bookcase to the MP's left. The volume was turned down, but the screen showed the Commons Chamber live.

"I'm keeping an eye on things in the House," she explained. "There'll be a vote later, and woe betide me if I'm late for that!"

"Which brings us to the matter at hand, Mrs. Potter-Smith. The security amendment to the new Terrorism Act..." Bill pulled out his notepad and pen. His mobile phone, electronic notepad and recording equipment had already been confiscated by the House of Commons police. Bill suspected that they were going to be thoroughly examined during his stay in the Palace of Westminster.

"Call me Anne," she said simply. "I think we have a little matter to discuss before we move onto His Majesty's Government's Act." Bill hadn't yet got used to the idea that the government belonged to *His* Majesty. After such a long reign, it was difficult to accept the loss of Queen Elizabeth II. Her oldest son, Charles, was soon to have his Coronation. Rumours of exactly what the ceremony would involve filled the gossip columns of the newspapers. But one thing was already clear; he would not be crowned King Charles III. The new sovereign would be known as King George VII.

Anne Potter-Smith poured a glass of red wine from a bottle whose green label was adorned with the portcullis emblem of the House of Commons. She then offered it to Bill.

"I like to think of this as the House Red," she quipped dryly. He smiled in feigned appreciation, and readied himself for the first sip. It was as bad as he had always imagined. How many bars did they have in the Palace of Westminster? The building still resembled a Gentleman's Club, despite numerous reforms. All of the bars and restaurants served this ghastly table plonk. It was amazing any work ever got done at all! Lost in thought, Bill failed to notice his companion's judicious look at his reaction to the wine.

Dame Potter-Smith stepped over to the window and looked out across the Thames towards the MI6 building at Vauxhall Cross, an organisation whose activities she personally had the responsibility to scrutinise.

"You don't care much for the House Red, I see."

"Well, I suppose it's not the worst thing I've ever tasted."

"You've been a journalist for how long now, Bill?"

"About twenty years, altogether."

She walked over to her desk and picked up a file, opened it and started to leaf through the documents within. "Nineteen and three-quarters of which were spent as the Standard's restaurant critic. Then, inexplicably, you were moved into the political section of the paper during the summer. So, let's see. Halfway through the 2012 Olympics, when the world is focused on the cultural spectacle that London has to offer, the city's main paper takes their highly experienced restaurant critic away from his routine copy, and shoves him into politics. Tell me, Bill, why would your newspaper do that? You've got no knowledge of politics at all. You might know a fair bit about wine, but you've hardly got a nose for politics."

Bill tried not to visibly squirm in his seat, but he had a cold sweat running down his back. He reminded himself that he was supposed to be interrogating the Minister about the amendment to the Terrorism Bill, not to be on the receiving end of her pointed questioning. But he had feared something like this might happen.

He had been digging into the backgrounds of the 12 men whose names had appeared on that NASA list. They were all unavailable for interview, or seemingly for anything else, for that matter. Various excuses had been given by the contacts he had made: religious retreats, seminaries, sabbaticals. All of the reasons for absence were vague in character, and impossible to follow up. These twelve men were simply nowhere to be found.

He was also on the verge of giving up, despite the prods from his new editor, Doug, during their infrequent meetings. Doug wanted results. It was clear that the management at the Daily Standard were treating the story as a priority, despite its distinctly odd overtones.

The Chair of the Intelligence and Security Committee, like all politicians, was fond of the sound of her own voice, and continued her monologue.

"Since the summer you've had just three major articles published, each one of them about the autumn Party Conferences. As far as I can discern, the most interesting aspect of all three articles seems to have been about the catering.

Which, I'll admit, *was* very funny, and has needed saying for *years*. But you're clearly still interested in food and drink. So, tell me, Bill. Why did they make you a political correspondent?"

Bill drank some of the House Red, which was starting to become more appealing by the minute.

He had a good idea what Anne Potter-Smith was driving at. When he had received the Ezekiel One document from Lyn he had immediately taken it to the newspaper's chief editor. It was evidently a hot news item, if only someone could figure out what it was actually about. After consulting with the newspapers' owner, the editor decided that there was a need to keep the story under wraps.

He wanted to minimise the number of journalists who came into contact with the story. As such, instead of passing the leak onto another journalist, as he had in the past, Bill had found himself transferred into politics, along with the document. The reasoning was that because all the previous leaks he had received had been political in nature, this one probably was too. The editor had hoped that Bill would be better placed to investigate the document if given access to the newspaper's regular political sources.

But, things were not going well, at all. It was becoming apparent that the document was not some kind of weirdly coded allusion to some spicy scandal, as they had initially suspected. Instead, they were beginning to suspect that document should be taken at face value. It might actually be something to do with NASA, after all. Bill had begun to speculate that it might have something to do with the secret discovery of alien life.

But this personal intervention by the security committee Chair was now making him wonder whether Ezekiel One was a juicy political scandal, as they had first suspected. Twelve priests, all now in hiding...Just how big *was* this story? Was this some kind of scandal, which went to the heart of the religious establishment?

Anne had been staring at him for several seconds waiting for his reply, which never came. She raised her eyebrows in a matronly way, and walked over to her television. Abruptly, she adjusted the volume sharply upwards.

"Just a minute, Mr. Bainbridge, I need to hear this," she said loudly, providing an explanation that Bill had not sought.

The television showed the chamber of the House of Commons - mostly empty. An opposition MP was getting into the swing of his speech, with the odd appreciative, but unintelligible mutter from the backbenchers behind him. The Minister raised the television volume to an unexpectedly loud level.

She then closed the file she was holding and placed it down onto her desk, right in front of Bill. He couldn't make out any of the words on the cover, but he assumed it was all about him.

"We know all about your arrangement with your source at GCHQ, Bill." He was unable to prevent momentary shock appearing on his face. "There's no point trying to deny it. But, don't worry. I'm not about to hang you out to dry.

You see, we were the ones who supplied Lyn with the documents in the first place." She paused meaningfully, and then added, "Most of them, anyway."

"I saw you at her funeral, Mrs. Potter-Smith." Bill decided to play his Ace. He had recognised Anne Potter-Smith at the time, but he was not sure who her tall male companion had been. He had wondered whether she had stood by the pyramidal tombstone on purpose, perhaps projecting a symbol of her political power. Did the Freemasons let women in these days?

"Yes, I had met her once or twice, and I was quite fond of her really." Anne was serene. "She came over to SIS headquarters several times a year for debriefing. We are inclined to think that it was during one of her excursions to HQ in London that she got wind of the document you now have in your possession. It's possible that she was in contact with some of our American friends. To be honest, we're not sure where she got it from. Perhaps you might have some idea?"

Bill was stunned. Why was she telling him all of this? Was he being recruited as a spy?

His head was starting to spin…the House Red? He decided to try to play it cool. He shrugged nonchalantly. Now it was his turn to do some fishing. "We've no idea either. We thought it was some kind of sex scandal, something very unpleasant perhaps."

Anne's look was that of a teacher at a boys' school who had caught her teenage pupils with a top-shelf magazine. Perhaps not then, thought Bill.

"Bill, I need to warn you that there are elements within the intelligence services that would like to ensure that your investigation goes no further. Politics can be a dirty business, and you are meddling with matters of national security. You are in a vulnerable position."

"Do you mean that I might suddenly get cancer too?" Bill's interjection was genuinely hostile.

The Member of Parliament looked downriver, and watched the London Eye slowly turning.

"I hope not. But you need to tread very carefully. If I can protect you, I will. But I cannot be seen to support your investigation. If you move before the time is right, before you have collected enough *evidence*, then I will not be able to save you from the inevitable consequences."

She turned towards him and lowered her voice still further. She was barely audible above the droning of the televised opposition MP. "It is clear to us that your current lines of enquiry have arrived at dead-ends. We would suggest that you visit Dr. James Clarke in Oxford. His particular field of research may spur you in the right direction. He has some…unusual ideas."

With that, she sat at her desk, and used her remote control to lower the television volume. She was not looking at Bill anymore, but seemed to be staring into space. "Sorry about that, Bill, I really did want to catch that speech. What with the vote, and all that. So, where were we….that's right, the Terrorism Act. His Majesty's Government is fully aware of the objections raised by Liberty and other organisations regarding our new amendment, but we consider it vital in the interests of National Security to pursue the 90-day maximum detention without charge for terrorist suspects."

She turned to look out over the river at the Secret Intelligence Service's bizarre-looking headquarters, and then continued to pour out standard government rhetoric.

Still in a mild state of shock, Bill began jotting onto his notepad in shorthand, starting with the name "James Clarke..."

CHAPTER THREE

I saw a storm wind coming from the north, a vast cloud with flashes of fire and brilliant light about it: and within was a radiance like brass, glowing in the heart of the flames.

"Bill, will you *please* come away from that bloody window!"

Bill took one last look at the men working in the street below. The road was amply lit by yellow sodium streetlights. Two white vans were parked up onto the pavement outside his house, badly. They had been there all evening. Four men were labouring away around an opened utility hatch on the pavement, doing God knows what. Bill closed the edge of the curtain he had been peering through and returned to the dining table, to join his wife Helen. Her face was a mixture of irritation and concern.

His wife of fifteen years was seven years his junior, and was still as pretty as the day he had married her. She was wearing a white top and pale blue jeans. Her long auburn hair adorned pale shoulders. Bill and Helen had never had children, and both of them had thrown themselves into their careers.

Helen was a schoolteacher at the local comprehensive school. She was used to miscreant teenage boys, and sometimes she brought home her managerial tactics for the undoubted benefit of her husband.

"Well, I don't know what on earth they're doing out there!" said Bill defensively, as if by explanation.

"Whatever it is, I'm sure it's not a plot by MI5, Bill." Helen's tone was more placating now. "This meeting tomorrow has really got you on edge, hasn't it? I do hope we're not going to have another episode of your insomnia tonight. I'm taking 9S tomorrow, and you know what they're like! I'll need my wits about me in the morning."

"I'm sorry, love, but the government Minister pretty much spelt out how much danger I was in at the moment. She was totally paranoid, turning the volume up on the telly to drown out her discussion. I think I've got the *right* to be a bit edgy, don't you?"

"She's not a Minister, Bill. She's just an MP who serves on the Security and Intelligence Committee as Chairperson. She answers to the cabinet office, and her remit is oversight of the activities of the security services. She doesn't actually control what they do." Helen had been doing a bit of homework of her own.

"Whatever, her paranoia was real enough."

The couple fell quiet momentarily, as each stared at the finished meal in front of them. The smell of vinegar hung over the table, reminding Bill's tastebuds of the takeaway fish and chips he had just eaten. Although it was one of his favourite meals, he had been too distracted to properly enjoy it. He picked up his opened tin of lager and poured the pale brew into his half-filled pint glass. Quickly, he knocked back the beer, washing down the last vestiges of his meal. Helen broke the silence.

"Do you want to talk about it?"

"If I'm in danger because of what I might know, then I don't want you getting dragged into it, too."

"But I'm your wife. If you can't discuss this with me, then who else can you discuss it with? You haven't been sworn to secrecy, and I might even be able to put a fresh perspective on things for you."

Bill looked uncertain.

"If I can handle 9S, I'm sure I can handle MI5." She smiled engagingly.

Bill laughed, and shifted position in his chair. He was pleased to have the opportunity to get some of this off his chest, if he was honest with himself. At this stage what he actually knew was very little, and it made even less sense.

"Okay, but you've got to keep this under your hat. This might be a big news story one day: The biggest thing that's ever happened to either of us."

"Big enough to take you off the restaurant circuit?" Helen's sardonic wit was misplaced, Bill felt. But he took a deep breath and launched into the madness that was Ezekiel One.

"I have a leaked NASA document in my possession, provided for me by a contact I used to have at GCHQ in Cheltenham." Helen looked puzzled, so Bill continued, "The Government Communication Headquarters. It's this huge spy base, which monitors phone calls, emails, broadcasts, you name it. They act on behalf of the British Government, in conjunction with similar agencies in the USA, Australia, Canada and New Zealand. This woman who worked for them, she used to send me stuff. I passed it on to other journalists at the paper, and these leaks would be made public."

"What's her name?"

"Her name was Lyn. She died recently, of a very aggressive cancer. A cancer she contracted shortly after I got this document from her."

"How did you get to know her?" Helen's questions put Bill onto the defensive.

"I knew her at college. Long before I met you. We used to hang out together - she was fun. We lost contact after graduating, until coming across each other over the Internet on one of those websites that helps you locate long lost school mates. Given what's happened since then, I suspect that online reunion might have been contrived by another agency: it was all a bit too neat really.

"She worked for GCHQ, and I worked for the Standard. The leaks were all clearly 'official' in nature. They generally bolstered the government position. That was until this one. This one was just plain weird.

"I still don't know what it's about, even after looking into it for the last four months. The leaking of this document led to my move into the political section of the paper. The newspaper owner, Mr. Provotkin, wanted the information handled by as few people as possible, so I got shifted along with it."

Helen looked uncomfortable. She was evidently unhappy about Bill's Internet liaison, even if it was related to his work. Bill decided to press on with the story. His reunion with Lyn had, after all, been innocent enough.

"The document is simply a list of twelve names. Each one is of a priest of one Christian discipline or another. They're all very learned. Some of them have special backgrounds in ancient religions, ancient languages, and cultures. Others have more scientific or technical backgrounds. All of them are really into God in a big way; very zealous. I've found all this out through my various investigations, but I've not been able to track a single one of them down. They're all seriously unavailable.

"The only other thing on the document is a handwritten note from Lyn. It says "Ezekiel One 12/21/2012". That's an important date. It's the last day of the Mayan Age. A lot of New Age people are expecting the end of the world to happen on that day. So it being tied in with Biblical prophecy through the Book of Ezekiel may be significant. But I can't work out the connection there.

"My new editor initially thought it might be some kind of saucy scandal involving all these priests. I guess that's what he hoped for anyhow, so we could do a big story in the Sunday paper. But all these guys are clean as a whistle, as far as I can determine anyhow."

Helen interrupted his thoughts. "I noticed you started reading up on Space after your meeting at Parliament. What made you change your mind on what to investigate?"

"Anne Potter-Smith told me to go and see this academic bloke in Oxford. She said that his area of expertise was connected with the 'Eze 1' document."

"That's what you call it?"

Bill laughed. "Yes, very American, I know! It is NASA, after all. So, anyway, I set up the meeting with him, and started reading everything he's written in the hope of figuring out the connection. Not that I can understand all that much of what he writes, to be honest. He's an astrophysicist."

"Bill, I don't understand. If Potter-Smith knows what 'Eze 1' is all about, then why this game of cat and mouse? Why not either stop you in your tracks, or come out with it?"

"I don't know the answer to that, love. It's clear we're being manipulated. I think we're being given enough clues to hopefully work out what's going on, so that we can be seen to break the story independently of the Government. Maybe they'll then deny it, whilst really being glad it's out in the open. You know how these things work. But…the British Government isn't really all that interested in space exploration. They don't fund very much research in that area. So why should they have any interest in this whole thing at all?"

"So what do you think it's about?"

"This academic in Oxford, Dr. James Clarke, is an expert on the outer solar system. He looks for comets, and minor planetary bodies beyond the big outer planets. It's all pretty dry stuff. But when you tie that in with a Biblical prophecy about the end of the world, then I've started wondering whether 'Eze One' might have something to do with a comet threatening the Earth. Sounds like a Hollywood movie, doesn't it?"

Helen wasn't laughing. In fact, she looked very worried indeed.

"That's a very scary thought, Bill. So what's the tie-in with the 12 priests?"

Bill shrugged. He had no idea at all. "That's what I'm hoping to find out tomorrow, when I meet Dr. Clarke. I've told him the Standard wants to do a feature about his research. Why we'd want to do that would be anyone's guess, but he seemed to believe me. They live in their own little bubbles, these academics."

Bill could sense Helen's continuing unease and shifted the topic to a lighter note. "He's very eccentric you know: A real Eco-Warrior. He wouldn't see me at all if I drove to Oxford. No cars, he said. He insisted I take the train. Apparently, he's going to meet me at the train station on his bike: I'm just hoping it's not a tandem!"

"I suppose if he's that into environmental concerns, he can't have secret knowledge of an impending disaster, can he? I mean, if you knew the world was about to end in a month or two, you wouldn't worry about carbon emissions. That's reassuring, at least."

Helen seemed to be trying to convince herself more than Bill. She stood up and walked over to the window, and carefully drew back the curtain slightly. Looking out, she half-whispered, "I wish they'd flaming well finish up out there and go home!"

Chapter Four

In the fire was the semblance of four living creatures in human form.

Bill hadn't been to Oxford for years, and had certainly never made the journey by train. For such an historic city, he had expected the train station to be a dishevelled shadow of some former Victorian glory. Instead, he found a modern, bustling terminus full of young, vibrant people. Feeling his age, he walked out to the car park and was very promptly greeted by a young man with a ragged beard, and blonde locks well beyond collar length. The man was in his late twenties, and wore scuffed jeans, and a tweed jacket with leather elbow patches.

"Mr. Bainbridge, I recognised your photo from your column in the paper. I'm a big fan you know, even though I don't eat out in London all that much anymore. I still like to keep up with the culture."

"Dr. Clarke, I presume?" Bill smiled warmly at his welcoming party of one. "Glad you liked the column. I was taken off restaurant reviews in the summer, I'm afraid. Much to my dismay, I assure you."

"Yes, I know. Your successor lacks your cutting wit, if you don't mind me saying." Dr. Clarke looked up at the sky briefly, "I think we'd better get moving; those clouds look a bit ominous. It's just a ten minute walk up into town."

He grabbed his bike, which had been untidily propped up against a lamppost, and started to lead the way to the main road. Bill strode after him.

"If you don't mind me asking, why have you come to do an interview with an astronomer, Mr Bainbridge? There isn't *really* a 'Restaurant at the End of the Universe' you know."

"Sorry?"

"Douglas Adams. 'The Hitchhiker's Guide to the Galaxy?'" James Clarke looked at Bill, whose face was blank. "You're not even a science fiction fan, are you?" He laughed, but his eyes remained quizzical. Bill realized that he might have to play some of the cards in his hand, but very, very carefully. Better here, walking along the pavement of a busy street, than somewhere more easily monitored.

"I need to ask you some questions related to your field of expertise, Dr. Clarke. It's difficult for me to explain exactly why, but basically we're working on an important story about NASA. We're hoping you might be able to supply us with some background information."

"Hmmm…I'm intrigued. But why don't you just ask one of the NASA guys? They're usually media-friendly."

"Let's just say that this story might not portray NASA in the best light." Bill had looked into Dr. Clarke's background and was aware that the young academic had once failed to join the space agency as a graduate. He hoped this early disappointment might still retain some leverage. He was right.

"They've had another balls-up with one of their probes, have they? Can't convert yards into metres, that sort of thing?"

"Yes, that sort of thing." The two men crossed the busy road precariously. "Dr. Clarke, have you ever come across the name 'Ezekiel'?"

"He was an Old Testament prophet. Wrote some garbled mumbo jumbo about weird creatures in a fiery machine." Dr. Clarke stopped in his tracks. The first drops of rain started to fall onto the road. "This isn't about UFOs, is it? Because if it is, I have to warn you that our interview will be very short indeed. I've got several funding proposals in the pipeline, and I don't need to be associated with those nutters."

"No, it's not about UFOs. We think it might be something to do with a body in the solar system: A comet, perhaps."

"You mean you don't actually know what it is you're investigating? Now I'm really intrigued, Mr. Bainbridge. Let's get moving. My college is just over the next road."

"If it's all the same to you, I'd rather go and get a coffee in town. Where's a popular spot for the locals?"

Bill wanted to discuss the subject in the open, where surveillance would be hampered by background noise. Dr. Clarke's office may already have been bugged. The younger man nodded, and led the way into the high street, eventually turning left down a service road between two of the shops. The streets were busy with people. Students were walking between the colleges and academic departments, and Oxford locals were out shopping. There were even some off-season tourists wandering about. Christmas decorations were already appearing in the shops, a couple of months too early in the opinion of everyone but the retailers themselves.

The rain was getting heavier, and Dr. Clarke fumbled with his lock as he chained his bike to some railings. He then showed Bill through an entrance into an indoor market. "It's not quite up to your culinary standards, Mr. Bainbridge, but at least it's dry." The indoor market contained neatly arranged, wooden-framed boutiques. They seemed to offer an idyll which had escaped the supermarket age, and the market was reassuringly busy with people of all ages. Along one interior wall of the expansive building was a series of small restaurants and tea-rooms.

The two men found a table in one of the cafés and sat down. Bill looked around him to see if they were being watched. The lack of evidence of surveillance did nothing to soothe his paranoia. On tables around him students and locals chatted away, between themselves or on mobile phones. One or two students were busily tapping away at laptops.

"I'm not aware of any astronomical body named after Ezekiel," said Dr. Clarke, after giving his order to a pretty, probably undergraduate, waitress. "That wouldn't be how things work anyway. New asteroids or minor planetary bodies are usually first given a complex numerical classification, and then given a name by the International Astronomical Union after a period of time.

"It's different for comets. New comets are usually named after their discoverer. Things have got more complicated in recent years, because it's more difficult to distinguish between the various types of bodies out there. But prophets from the Old Testament don't really feature at all. The politically correct way of naming new cosmic bodies is to rely upon various archaic mythical sources. The more obscure the mythos you choose your god or goddess from, the better. Mind you, I suppose Ezekiel isn't exactly mainstream... But even so, Judeao-Christian names are out of the question. Ezekiel isn't a comet, Mr. Bainbridge, I'm quite sure of that."

"It's reassuring to hear you say that. My wife will be very relieved anyway."

"Why?"

Bill realised that he had inadvertently given away another part of the jigsaw. The discovery of a new comet was not generally considered to be a bad thing. Helen's concern had only emerged as a result of the connection with the Mayan calendar date of 21st December 2012. Since he seemed to be getting nowhere with the name Ezekiel, he decided to reveal one further card.

"My information is that the name Ezekiel is linked with the date 21/12/2012."

A slightly pained expression drifted across Dr. Clarke's face. Bill continued, "Both of those pieces of information are linked to your work, Dr Clarke. I don't know how yet, but it's a matter of some importance. There appears to be some kind of secret at a governmental level, something to do with NASA and space. Can you think of anything that links your work with these pieces of information?"

"My work involves the detection of cosmic bodies beyond the orbit of Neptune. Some of those bodies are like asteroids, many of them are like the minor planet Pluto. Some of them are long-period comets. I'm interested in trying to figure out the dynamic relationships between the various bodies we discover, to better understand the solar system's origins.

"It's hard to see why that would have anything to do with Mayan calendars. The Mayans knew nothing about the outer solar system. Their main astronomical interest lay with the planet Venus."

Bill scratched his head. The conversation was not heading in the right direction at all, and Dr Clarke was his last lead. He corrected himself: Almost his last lead. He had not heard from Christine and Colin since travelling back from Cheltenham. He assumed they had not come across any further clues at Lyn's house. It was probable that Alan had intervened and talked them out of even looking. Bill decided to keep the conversation going a while longer, in case the young astronomer thought of an idea.

"When you applied to NASA, what kind of work were you interested in doing there?"

"Some post-graduate work. About three years ago, they were very keen on sending probes to the Kuiper Belt. That's the area of space beyond Neptune. It's a bit like a second asteroid belt. We've been finding lots of new minor planets in that area of space in the last decade. Some of them have very unusual properties."

"How so?"

"Well, many of them appear to have been the subject of catastrophic collisions. Which is odd in itself, because everything is very spread out in that part of space. The chances of one body striking another are, well, astronomical! So, that's quite a puzzle for us to provide an answer for.

"Then there are the actual orbits of these bodies. Some of them are very difficult to explain. They should be nice and regular. But many aren't.

"It's almost like they've been disturbed from their original trajectories at some point early in the history of the solar system. Perhaps by a passing star. Perhaps due to the migration of the known planets. Or, there may have been some kind of companion object out there at some point."

"Companion object?" Bill's attention was drawn to a man who took a seat at a table a short way from their own. He was evidently not a student. His smart clothes were not in keeping with the atmosphere of the rather downbeat café they were in. The man ordered a drink and started to read a newspaper. He was a handsome man, and had attracted the attention of some of the women in the café, although he appeared oblivious to their glances. Bill thought the tall man looked pale, though, like one would at the end of a long winter.

Perhaps he was from Scotland.

"Yes, like a brown dwarf, for instance," the astronomer's soft voice brought Bill's thoughts back to the matter at hand.

"What's a brown dwarf? Sounds like a P.C. version of Snow White." Bill joked, half concentrating on Dr. Clarke's discussion, half attentive to the café around him. Bill found himself eyeing the man cautiously. He seemed vaguely familiar. The man had blond hair, swept back across this head, and his symmetrical facial features betrayed no emotion.

"It's a failed star. It's a planet more massive than Jupiter, which is heavy enough to start burning nuclear fuels to create light. But it never gets enough of a chain-reaction going to become a proper star. These brown dwarfs shine brightly for a while, then die out and become dark.

"That makes them difficult to locate using telescopes. But, theory indicates that there should be as many brown dwarfs as there are stars. So statistically, there's a fifty: fifty chance that there's one between here and the nearest star. Some people even believe that there might be a brown dwarf orbiting the Sun."

"Sounds half-baked. Are any of those people actual astronomers?"

The young academic took a sip of hot coffee. "Oh, yes. You'd be surprised. A few decades ago this idea was very popular. The existence of such an object was thought to be connected with extinction events, like the demise of the dinosaurs.

"The people who suggested this idea believed that extinction events on the Earth were caused by comet showers periodically sent our way by a brown dwarf orbiting the Sun at a great distance. They called the object 'Nemesis'. But there are problems with the Nemesis theory."

"Like what?"

"Like… where is it?" Dr. Clarke laughed, breaking through Bill's tension momentarily. Bill was getting edgy, and suspicious. The tall man at the nearby table was now talking quietly into a mobile phone. It was just as well they'd changed the subject away from Ezekiel One, Bill thought. This nonsense about brown dwarfs was harmless enough if the smartly-dressed stranger was listening in.

"So, what's a brown dwarf got to do with what you study, Dr. Clarke? I must have missed that bit."

"Well, if one of these objects had been born alongside the other planets at the birth of the solar system, it might have moved around the Sun in a wide orbit. That's what we find sometimes in other star systems. These little companion dwarf stars can be very loosely connected to their parent star. If that was the case in our system, then the brown dwarf might have sent all these little outer solar system bodies into the weird orbits we observe today."

"But you say this object is no longer there. So what happened to it?"

"Any number of things, really. It might have drifted away into an even looser orbit around the Sun. Or it might have been lost to interstellar space, to become a cosmic wanderer. Quite a lot of brown dwarfs are loners, drifting through space. These wandering brown dwarfs may have been ejected from other star systems early in their development."

In a flash, Bill suddenly remembered where he had seen the man before. The man had been Anne Potter-Smith's companion at the funeral in Cheltenham! Seeing him here again in Oxford was too much of a coincidence. Particularly, given that the meeting with Dr. Clarke had been proposed by the M.P. in the first place. Was this a trap? A knot developed in the journalist's stomach, and he felt beads of cold sweat on his back.

Bill fumbled around in his pocket and pulled out his wallet and a pen. He took out a card, and scribbled his mobile phone number on the back. He handed it to Dr. Clarke.

"I'm very sorry, Dr. Clarke, but I'm going to have to call time on our interview. The return train to London leaves in about 20 minutes, so I'd better get going. Thanks for the chat, and you can always reach me on this number if you think of anything else that might be useful for the feature."

"Okay, well it was nice to meet you…" Dr. Clarke looked perplexed, and rose from his seat as Bill stood up. Bill put a ten pound note on the table, and left quickly.

As he briskly walked away he had a lucid moment of self-awareness, and realized that he was panicking. It seemed very clear that he was being followed by a government agent, a fact that confirmed his paranoia. But this was not the best way to deal with the situation. It's too late now, thought Bill.

As he left the confines of the café and walked into the indoor market, he briefly looked back. Dr. Clarke was calling over to the waitress, to pay for the two coffees. The stranger remained at his table, holding the newspaper in both hands, but was now looking over at Dr. Clarke.

Bill suddenly walked right into someone, sending him flying. Apologising, he stooped to help the man up, who also apologised in turn, in true British style. What was he apologizing for? Getting in the way? The man had been stood in a queue of people, waiting to be served milkshakes and smoothies at a window set into an internal plasterboard wall. The rest of the people in the queue looked on, bemused.

Bill apologized again, as the man rejoined the queue, muttering darkly. He was no James Bond, he thought to himself. He couldn't even feign an uneventful exit. He momentarily looked back at Dr. Clarke, who was flirting with the waitress, completely oblivious to the presence of the government agent sat at the next table.

The tall man had put down his paper and was now watching Bill. They briefly made eye contact, which Bill immediately attempted to avoid in an altogether too furtive manner. Disconcerted immensely by this encounter, Bill swiftly walked out into the street and hurried back towards the train station, fearing for his life.

The low autumn sun had come out from behind the clouds, casting long shadows across the pavement.

Night-time was fast approaching.

✦

James Clarke scratched his head. He had met comparatively few journalists during his career as an astronomer. If Bill Bainbridge was anything to go by, hacks were a weird lot. The London newspaperman had arranged their meeting, travelled all the way to Oxford, and then suddenly dashed off halfway through the interview. Somehow, James didn't think it was to get back to the office and put together a speedy article for tomorrow's paper.

He looked around, hoping to watch the cute waitress as she walked back to the cash register. His eyes met those of a pale man wearing a well tailored suit sat at the next table, who was staring at him. The stranger smiled warmly. He was holding a mobile phone, which he quickly pocketed.

"Excuse me. I couldn't help overhearing some of your conversation just then," said the man. His voice was American, possibly with a southern accent. James smiled, and raised an eyebrow slightly. There were a lot of odd people in Oxford. He wasn't in the mood to socialize with a 'nutter-on-the-bus' character.

Undaunted, the American continued. "I have a great interest in astronomy. I heard what you said about this Planet X idea. It's something I read about a while back. Have you got a moment? I'd sure like to ask you a few questions."

Momentarily, James looked back at his half-finished cup of coffee. The man seemed on the level. What harm could it do? He looked back. "Okay, that's fine with me. Take a seat."

Chapter Five

Each had four faces and each four wings; their legs were straight, and their hooves were like the hooves of a calf, glittering like a disc of bronze.

"So what do you think of this one? Do you like it?" Helen held up a long black dress by its hanger and swirled it casually in front of her, looking at her reflection in the long shop mirror.

"It's alright," replied Bill, in a non-committal sort of way. Helen's eyes lifted towards the ceiling.

"I think it might be a bit too formal. Nice, though."

Bill had passed through his clothes shop tolerance limit some time ago. It didn't help that it was a Saturday afternoon on busy Oxford Street, in central London, with just three weeks to go until Christmas. His idea of Christmas shopping was a quick zap around the shops on Christmas Eve afternoon. After all, many of the shops would already be discounting at that late hour, and bargains would be there to be had. Traipsing around Oxford Street on a busy Saturday afternoon was his idea of hell.

He sulked quietly at the periphery of his wife's personal space. The shop was busy, and noisy. A strong back-beat from the store's music system accompanied the slow dance of the female shoppers as they blissfully wove their way around the racks and stands. Steadfast male companions stood back, forlornly, clearly disaffected by the contrived ambiance of the shop, or by the goodies on offer.

"Maybe we should go and get something to eat," she suggested, knowing that a full stomach would improve his mood. She took his incomprehensible muttering as a positive acknowledgement, and led the way out of the shop, all the time surveying the lines of clothes and shoes.

Once into the street, Bill's eye was caught by a young man with scruffy hair handing out leaflets. Too late to avoid the young man, Bill accepted the leaflet begrudgingly. He looked down at it. At the top of the leaflet was a bright red circle with 2012 written onto it. To each side were the now familiar lightning symbols. This emblem was appearing everywhere, particularly in the form of graffiti. A swelling youth sub-culture was building around the notion of impending catastrophe.

Bill scanned down the leaflet. He put his hand out and touched his wife's arm, which brought her to a halt.

"There's a 2012 author doing a book-signing at that book shop over the road, Helen. He sounds interesting. Why don't I meet you in one of your shops in fifteen minutes time?"

"Okay Bill. I'll be in Dotty P's about four shops down the road. Don't get held up too much though; I'm getting hungry."

Bill nodded and looked for a gap in the traffic to cross the street. The traffic was mostly slow-moving taxis and London buses, and he quickly made his way into the bookstore. A sign by the door indicated that the book-signing was taking place upstairs, so he headed for the escalator and strode up the moving staircase to the first floor.

He spotted the author by the front window of the store, sat at a table piled high with books. The tall Georgian windows looked out over the grey street outside, giving the bookshop a feel of an old library. A small queue had formed in front of the table. The author, Marcus Everett, was chatting away with the woman at the front of the queue, who was holding a copy of his book, along with several bags of shopping.

Bill walked over to the table, joined the small queue, and picked up a paperback copy. The book was entitled "The Day After 2012". It was illustrated with a large spaceship orbiting the Earth. As he waited in line, Bill started leafing through the pages.

The first half of the book seemed to cover ground that had become very familiar to Bill over the last few months. There were illustrations of Mayan frescoes, and explanations of their complex calendar systems. A discussion of the potential meaning of the 2012 date took up several chapters.

Bill concluded that this was a very new book. Some theories, which had been noisily doing the rounds over the Internet, were now being discredited by Mr. Everett. In particular, Bill noticed that the arrival of "Planet X" was no longer being hailed as a potential harbinger of doom, as it had been in previous offerings of the conspiracy genre.

Planet X was a hypothetical planet residing in an eccentric orbit. It was thought to crash through the solar system every 3,600 years. This concept was based upon the maverick research of an author named Zecharia Sitchin. Some had believed until surprisingly recently, that this object was on its way and on a direct collision course with Earth. This idea seemed to have been the basis for the 2012 emblem that adorned so many walls and T-shirts. The red circle containing the 2012 number represented the returning planet. The lightning represented its alleged activity levels as it approached the Sun.

Bill suspected that Marcus Everett was, in this case, ignoring the graffiti writing on the wall. Planet X wasn't coming - at least not this year. It would have been visible to the general public by now, let alone the astronomers.

Similarly, the equally popular Near Earth Object collision theory was noticeable by its absence in Everett's book. With just a few weeks to go until the big day itself, a celestial collision of some kind seemed out of the question. This new book reflected that reality.

So what would take the place of catastrophe, Bill wondered?

Bill's recent conversation with the astronomer James Clarke had yielded little in the way of potential catastrophic scenarios from outer space. The young academic had seemed quite sure of his ground, and had no time for the 2012 question. The fact that their meeting had been subject to some kind of surveillance, in the form of the tall government man from the graveyard in Cheltenham, had given the event added poignancy. But the mysterious tall man had not continued to follow Bill, and, so far as he knew, nothing untoward had happened to Dr. Clarke either.

Bill had reached a dead-end with his investigation, and had mentally given up on the whole story. His editor, unfortunately, had not.

About halfway through Marcus Everett's book, Bill stopped turning the pages. His animated reaction to the chapter heading in front of him must have been fairly obvious, because Marcus Everett and the small gathering of fans all turned towards Bill questioningly.

Bill smiled in a manner which he hoped was reassuring. But his mind was reeling. The chapter heading was entitled "E.Z.1: A Cosmic Ark?"

Bill and his colleagues had been calling the investigation 'Easy One' for a while now. They enjoyed the sense of irony involved. After all, the search for any kind of lead at all had proven extremely difficult. Yet, here was a public reference to a "Cosmic Ark" named "E.Z.1." Not only that, but the reference was intimately connected with the Mayan prophecy for 2012. Assuming one used the American pronunciation for the letter 'z', it was obvious that there was a connection here to Ezekiel One, thought Bill.

How was it possible to have spent all that time trying to track down the truth about Ezekiel One, only to stumble upon it when out Christmas shopping, of all things? Had fate played a part?

Bill quickly skimmed through the opening pages of the 'E. Z. 1' chapter.

A number of doubts quickly crept into his mind as he read. If there was so much secrecy surrounding Ezekiel One, then it seemed very strange indeed that information about it was published, let alone by someone as obviously lacking in official credentials as Marcus Everett.

Bill looked over at the author, who was listening intently to a book idea suggested to him by one of his fans. Everett was in his mid-thirties, Bill estimated. He wore casual clothes. His haircut was a cheap one. He looked more like a geek than a professor of Mayan culture. Bill looked back to the first page of the book he held in his hands. The author's biography suggested conspiracy theory, rather than academic excellence.

Returning to the E.Z.1 chapter, Bill discovered that the Cosmic Ark idea related to a large unidentified object allegedly orbiting the Earth at a great distance. There were a number of fuzzy photographs of a misshapen object in the plates section of the book. It was hard to discern any detail. Several official NASA documents also appeared among the plates. Largely blacked out, there were scattered references in the remaining official text to E.Z.1. The context appeared to be rocket launches over an extended period of time, perhaps 18 months in total.

Was Ezekiel One some kind of clandestine space program?

"Would you like me to sign that for you?"

Marcus Everett's relaxed voice broke through Bill's internal debate. Bill looked up to see that he was at the front of the queue. He smiled, and handed the book to the young author.

"Yes, thank you. I was wondering...what does E.Z.1 stand for?" Bill carefully used the British pronunciation "zed" for the letter "z."

"I discuss that in the book, towards the end," replied the author. "Given the evidence I have managed to collect from various sources in NASA, I think it's likely that it stands for 'Extra-terrestrial Zone One.' You see, I strongly suspect that this is some kind of Ark being built in space to ensure the continuation of our species should the Earth be destroyed."

"You really think that could happen? There are only a couple of weeks to go until 21st December. There doesn't appear to be any real threat to our world that might surface in that time."

"I agree. Which is why I've written this book. I believe that the Mayan question is metaphysical in nature. I believe that the end point of their calendar marks the ushering in of a New Age. I *believe*...that our species is about to take a great stride forward in its evolution."

"So where does this Cosmic Ark fit into your ideas? If Humanity is about to blossom, then surely there is no need to escape our world?"

"Although many of us can see a brighter future ahead, those people of power who control our planet remain unenlightened. They fear for their loss of power and have turned to technology to safeguard their futures. They have built this great Ark in the sky to see themselves through to the other side. Then, they will return to our world and regain control, where they will pursue the same materialistic agenda that has held sway for the last 5,000 years." Marcus Everett paused, and opened the paperback up to the opening page. "Whom should I dedicate the book to?"

Bill's initial enthusiasm for this young man's research was fast dissipating. He appeared to be a crank. Yet, he had uncovered some fragments of truth, it seemed. He might hold the key to understanding the secret of Ezekiel One.

"Oh, 'Bill', that would be fine. Thanks. Can I ask you one more question?" The two other people in the queue behind Bill shuffled impatiently. Marcus Everett nodded engagingly.

"Do you know of any plans to take priests to this Ark?"

The author looked at Bill blankly, and then his face darkened. He shook his head dismissively and retorted, "I should have thought that celibate men would be the least likely candidates to fill an Ark, wouldn't you?" Marcus Everett turned to the next person in the queue, and offered to take the book held tightly in her hands.

Bill was now quite convinced that Mr. Everett held one or two pieces of the jigsaw puzzle, but that the young author had no real idea what the complete picture was that he was trying to build. Still, Bill now had a new lead, and one that he could actively pursue in the run-up to the Mayan End of the Age. If

Marcus Everett's book contained enough detailed information about this alleged Cosmic Ark, then Bill might be able to persuade Dr. Clarke to look for it with one of his telescopes. Even *academic* astronomers must still look at the sky, after all?

Buoyed up by this unexpected turn of events, Bill took the book towards the counter to pay for it. One of the customers on the downwards escalator caught his eye momentarily. It was the man from the graveyard in Prestbury again! The man was as pale as Bill had remembered him from his previous two encounters. This time, his smart suit was replaced by casual, but expensive clothes. A gold watch twinkled in the bright light of the shop. The man stared ahead of him, down the staircase, seemingly oblivious of Bill's gaze.

Bill caught his breath as the man's face sank below the first floor level. Over the last few weeks Bill had rehearsed his reaction to meeting the pale government agent again. This time, he would not panic and run. Instead, he was determined to confront the man. Feeling confident, Bill ran towards the escalator. He stopped at the top. The man stepped off the escalator onto the ground floor and walked towards the shop's front entrance.

Bill realised that he still needed to pay for the book. He couldn't just dump it and come back for it because it had been signed and dedicated. Cursing under his breath, Bill took the book to the till and paid for it with cash. Thankfully, there was no queue.

Bill hurried down the escalator, and stepped into the bustling commotion of Oxford Street.

The tall man was nowhere in sight along the pavement. He could have slipped into any of the shops lining the street, or into a taxi, or even onto a bus. A classic red London double-decker bus was slowly moving up the street though the traffic towards the shop obscuring the view across the road.

Bill looked into all the taxis moving slowly along the road, and ran up to the side of the bus, peering into the lower section. Faces stared back at him. The tall man was nowhere to be seen. Determined to confront the government agent, Bill worked his way through the crowd down Oxford Street, peering into the busy shops. Again, he had no luck. The pale spook had disappeared as quickly as he had appeared.

Bill came up to the clothes shop his wife was in, and went in to join her. At least he now knew that he was definitely being followed. Once may possibly have been coincidence, but twice was not. What puzzled him was why the mysterious government agent was being so open about it. It was almost like he wanted Bill to know he was shadowing him. Bill spotted his wife in the shoe section at the back of the shop, and he made his way over to her. She turned and lifted up a pair of black, high-heeled shoes, smiling as if to encourage a positive opinion from her husband.

There was a sudden flash of extremely bright light. Bill saw his wife's face turn into a visage of horror.

He tried to turn, but found himself lifting off the ground. He was flying through the air towards her. She, in turn, was also being flung through the air away from him into a rack of shoes. Then his ears resounded to a great crack.

Like thunder from an ominous sky, the noise amplified to a deafening level.

The shop shook, and groaned heavily. Bill heard sounds of shattering glass from the front of the shop. Screaming involuntarily, he crashed headlong into the same shoe rack as his wife had hit just a fraction of a moment before, and the two of them, along with all the shoes, scattered across the floor. Pain resonated throughout his body.

Bill instinctively held his arms up across his head for protection. Debris was flying across the shop. Broken glass shards span through the air, striking into walls, people and the rapidly disintegrating shop fittings.

Then the thunder stopped.

It was replaced almost immediately by screaming, and the sounds of creaking masonry. Then a chorus of fire alarms sprang to life in the street. Bill looked up. The darkened shop was full of dust, and screaming people. He moved towards his wife. His hand slid on a wet floor. He looked down to see that hisright arm was covered in blood. A shard of glass was sticking out of it, and he was bleeding profusely.

"Bill…?" Helen's familiar voice sounded distant, yet they were barely two feet apart. "Are you alright?"

"Yes, but my arm…" He clenched his teeth, and pulled the glass shard out of his arm. He let out a great yell and held onto the gaping wound in his arm with his free hand. Blood poured through his fingers. "I was hit by some glass. I think I'm okay."

Helen moved towards him. She seemed remarkably composed, Bill thought to himself. His breathing was heavy, and he tried to relax himself as he lay flat on the floor. The room was spinning. The combined screaming and noise of the fire alarms created a hellish din all around them.

Helen removed his jacket, ripped off the sleeve of his shirt and strapped his arm up. He yelled out in pain, and came close to passing out. He worked hard to control his breathing as his wife held his arm above his body.

"Thank God you're alright, Bill," exclaimed Helen. "What happened?"

Bill carefully sat up, and looked through the dust of the store's darkened interior. Outside was oddly dark as well. The distant sirens of emergency vehicles began to crescendo through the ever-present cacophony. Bill staggered to his feet, holding his arm. His wife helped him up. He felt light-headed.

"These people need help…" she intoned blankly, as if not knowing where to start. Other figures had begun moving about in the dust too. Others remained on the floor; either writhing about, or just lying very still.

"I need to find out what happened." Bill started to make his way unsteadily through the wreckage, towards Oxford Street.

"Bill…BILL!" Helen yelled at him. But he didn't turn back. He knew his wife was fine, and that she would begin to tend to the injured as the emergency services made their way to the scene. That was her nature.

Inside him was another urge…the urge of the journalist to get a story. It was what had kept him working on the Ezekiel One story for the last five months, despite every setback. It was what made him tick professionally.

The shop front was devastated. A great force from outside had ripped through the glass, metal and timber of the store front. Fallen masonry littered what had once been the border between the shop and the street. Several bodies lay beneath the grim wreckage.

Bill carefully worked his way onto the pavement outside. The whole street was a scene of carnage. Damaged cars with their windscreens blown in, pointed in the direction of the source of the blast. It was up the street, in the direction Bill had come from before he had entered the clothes store. All of the shop fronts in that direction were blown in. Fires had started in several of the shops, with billowing black smoke pouring out. The dim December light was blocked by the dust and smoke. Flashing blue lights began to emerge from the gloom.

Bill then saw the point that had been the source of the blast. The whole top section of the red double-decker bus he had just walked past was destroyed. Jagged metal remains of the side of the top deck of the bus twisted into the air in seeming agonizing torment. The roof of the bus was gone. Fragmented remains of the roof had crashed into some taxis further up the road.

People were moving around now, pulling bodies out of the wreckage. Some simply collapsed in the street, sobbing.

Aching to understand, Bill stumbled up the street towards the bus, his shoes cracking their way across a river of glass underfoot. He realised that the red London bus had stopped next to the bookshop he had just been in. Looking up, he saw that the first floor of the bookshop had taken the full force of the blast. The front of the shop was gone. There was considerable structural damage, with girders and masonry sticking out into the air redundantly. Smoke poured out of the wide-open first storey of the building. The ground floor seemed relatively unaffected, shielded from the main shock of the blast by the body of the bus.

The main impact of the explosion had been upwards and outwards from inside the top storey of the bus, Bill decided. It must have ripped through the upper floors of the adjacent shops, and caused lesser, but more diffuse damage to the shops further away.

Bill picked up some speed and ran into the entrance of the bookshop. Smoke wove dark patterns across the ceiling of the ground floor. He put his hand over his mouth and ascended the now stationary escalator. The heat of the fires raging within the first floor of the shop, and the acrid stench of smoke and burning bodies, prevented him from making it to the top. Bill grabbed hold of the warm rubber handrail with his wounded arm and steadied himself, grimacing in pain.

There was no way Marcus Everett could still be alive up there.

Bill made his way back down to the ground floor, choking. He heard a call for help in the gloom of the broken bookshop. Books and glass lay scattered over the ruins of cleaved shelving and prone bodies. The sprinkler system had already kicked into life and was washing the dust out of the room's atmosphere. The freezing cold water created muddy streams across the floor. Various piles of human and inorganic debris appeared as soggy islands in the dank gloom.

Moving towards the stricken cries, Bill quickly found a teenage girl lying across one of the piles of strewn books. She was soaked with water, diluting her own blood into a rosé-coloured pool around her.

Sobbing uncontrollably, she appealed to the stranger before her, "Help me, please! My leg's broken!"

Bill knelt down beside her. A girl of perhaps 13 years, her matted dark hair fell across her pale face. Her lips had a bluish tinge to them. Bill looked at her legs. Blood had soaked through her jeans above her left knee.

"We need to get you out of here," he said urgently.

The girl nodded and, straining with the pain, she tried to sit up. Her pale face whitened further. Bill caught her as she slumped backwards. Holding her unconscious body up, he kicked away several sodden books to clear some space around them. Then he put his undamaged arm under her legs and stood up with the girl cradled in his arms. She was heavier than she looked, and he fought to regain his balance. The pain from his injured arm was almost unbearable. He took a deep breath and steadied himself. He could feel his own blood pouring out of the wound to his arm.

Carrying the girl, Bill staggered to the front entrance, across the wet floor of broken glass and rubble. Suddenly, he heard a great creaking noise resound through the building above him. He felt a sudden rush of adrenaline and fear. His heart raced. His mind cleared of the hell around him, and his attention focused on just one thing: Survival. Suddenly energized by an inner strength he had never felt before, he ran towards the street, the girl held tightly in his aching arms.

Before he knew it, Bill was clambering out into Oxford Street, his unconscious load groaning heavily. He stumbled down the road, and safety. His stinging eyes were partly blinded by smoke and sweat. Ahead of him he thought he could see Helen. She was about thirty yards away. She was amongst a group of people being held back by two policemen. Some of the onlookers were taking photos with their mobile phones. Their camera flashes flooded the scene with pure white light.

Helen broke through the line and began running towards him, shouting above the din of alarms, sirens and a helicopter hovering overhead.

An almighty crash behind Bill sent him toppling forward. He fell to his knees, still holding the girl close to him. He gently let her down to the ground. The blood from her leg had covered the front of his shirt. His torn sleeve was saturated red.

He looked back. Part of the ground floor ceiling of the bookshop appeared to have collapsed. A cloud of dust billowed out of the front of the shop across the street, and masonry toppled out of the entrance to form fresh mountains of debris. The police were shouting warnings, and moved the crowd back further.

Helen reached him just ahead of two women in luminous green jackets. The two paramedics immediately set to work. They seemed oblivious to the destruction all around them. One assessed the girl's consciousness level and vital signs, while the other tended to her leg using a splint from her bag.

Bill was breathing fast and hard, his head swimming. His wife knelt down and clutched him tightly. She shouted at him through her tears.

"You fool! You damn fool!"

Chapter Six

Under the wings on each of the four sides were human hands; all four creatures had faces and wings, and their wings touched one another.

Normally, having to wait several hours in an Accident Unit for treatment would have been a slow and painful waste of time. But for Bill and Helen that evening, it proved an invaluable opportunity to wind down. It had been a horrific afternoon, caught as they had been in the middle of the worst bomb-blast in central London since the Second World War. It had already been condemned broadly as a despicable act of terrorism: A cowardly attack which had cost the lives of over 100 people, with hundreds more injured, many of them probably fatally.

After Bill had carried the girl out of the collapsing bookshop, he had almost collapsed himself. Helen had sat on the wet pavement, amongst the glass and debris, and cradled his head in her lap.

As the minutes ticked by, uniformed personnel of various descriptions appeared on the devastated scene. The timing of their arrival was exponential in character. After perhaps just five minutes, there were literally hundreds of police, paramedics and firemen. The police quickly sealed off the area, and pushed the growing crowds at the scene's periphery backwards. Other police closed nearby roads and directed the traffic, which had been blocking Oxford Street all afternoon, away from the bombed out area. Overhead, a police helicopter had hung in the air noisily, no doubt helping a central control headquarters to coordinate the Major Incident response.

In surprisingly little time, entry and exit routes had been established to the disaster scene, allowing paramedic crews to bring ambulances close to the perimeter of the police cordon. Similarly, fire and rescue vehicles arrived, and their crews and equipment were quickly deployed to cut victims of the bombing out of the wreckage of the taxis and buses in the street. Fires in the surrounding shops were extinguished efficiently, and people who had been caught in their interiors were evacuated out into the street.

The epicentre of the bomb-blast was cordoned off separately. Armed officers took control of the inner perimeter. Access to what was left of the double-decker bus was strictly managed, by a contingent of police officers. In time, a forensic team would arrive to begin the pains-taking process of sifting through the entire area for clues to the origin of the bomb. The cratered-out mass of red metal that had once been a London bus seemed an unlikely container for surviving human life, but incredibly, traumatized victims of the blast were cut out from its lower deck, including the driver.

There was precious little left of the top deck to even conduct a search. It must have been clear to the occupants of the police helicopter that no one could possibly be alive up there.

During this time, the paramedics had worked on the girl who had been carried out of the bookshop by Bill. Her leg was bound and splinted. An intravenous needle had been inserted into her arm, and a bag of clear fluid was dripping quickly through the line. Through the oxygen mask, Helen could see that her colour had improved significantly, and her breathing had settled to a more normal rate.

Amid the enveloping chaos, the paramedic crew skilfully transferred her onto a stretcher, and wheeled her away. Helen had not seen any relatives of the girl appear. There was no way of knowing who she had been with in the bookshop, or even whether they were still alive. She may have been orphaned by the terrorists.

After about ten minutes, Bill began to feel his life force returning to his injured and exhausted body. Someone had draped several blankets over him, and one over his wife's back. Her reassurances had allowed the attending crews to leave them be, instead moving on to other victims whose injuries were significantly worse. Stretchers containing tightly secured people were moving past the couple towards the waiting ambulances. The walking wounded were similarly being gently led from the scene, supported by each other in many cases. Many of the victims were distraught; beside themselves with disbelief, shock and, in many cases, visibly overcome by grief of personal loss.

Blankets had been laid over the dead at the scene. Some of the bodies were attended by grieving relatives. Many of these unfortunates were themselves clearly injured.

It had been a harrowing scene. The imprint of the day's events would be felt for many years to come.

Now, hours later, Bill and Helen sat in the relatively peaceful confines of the Surgical Outpatients Department of St. Thomas Hospital. The terror and horror of the day had been replaced by inaction on their part. They had become patient observers, waiting their turn for attention as the staff of the packed hospital rushed about frantically. Bill's mind went over the events he had experienced over and over again, like a broken film reel on a cinema projector.

They had been ferried in a taxi, commandeered by police officers at the scene, to the central London hospital from the scene of the explosion. No money had exchanged hands: the taxi driver simply dropped them off near to the entrance of the Accident Unit, and headed straight back to Oxford Street to offer his services once again. The Emergency Department of the hospital had clearly been overwhelmed. Ambulances had lined up down the street. Backdoors had been opened wide as senior nurses had moved between the vehicles, assessing the victims inside, alongside the paramedic crews. The more needy cases had been rushed straight into the Emergency Department, to be met by teams of doctors and nurses.

The scene in the emergency department was almost as harrowing as the bomb-site. Bodies lay on trolleys, some moving, some not. There were cries of pain and distress throughout. Staff rushed about purposefully, but their faces betrayed the signs of stress they were surely feeling as their normal daily routines were turned upside down.

Bill had listened to the conversations of the staff around him, rather like a passenger on an aeroplane watching for signs of stress in the cabin crew. The hospital seemed to be enacting a Major Incident policy in a well-rehearsed manner. Surgical theatres were being cleared of routine cases, beds were swiftly emptying throughout the hospital and extra staff were being drafted in from anywhere they could be found. But it was clear that the staff in the hospital felt overwhelmed.

During their brief sojourn in the packed Accident Unit waiting room, Bill and Helen had seen television pictures from the scene of the explosion. Initial speculation by security specialists, interviewed by the news anchorman, had laid the blame firmly at the door of al Qaida. The nation's capital had already been on a heightened state of alert in readiness for a suspected terrorist attack. The only thing that surprised anybody was the extent of the devastation caused by the atrocity.

Bill's injuries had been briefly assessed, and he had been sent through the Emergency Department to a quieter part of the hospital to wait for treatment. The Outpatients Department had been cleared of its routine clinics, and the staff there had taken on an emergency role instead, which had caused a certain amount of chaos. But Bill's fellow patients waited without complaint. They seemed only too pleased to have been removed from the horrors of the Emergency Department.

Unlike the Accident Unit, there was no television in the Outpatient Department, and the couple had waited patiently, without news, for Bill's turn to be seen. His arm needed stitching by a reasonably senior doctor, it had transpired. He had had an X-ray and a blood test in the course of the four hour wait. There had been concern that he had lost too much blood, but Helen hoped he was simply in shock from the bombing. The Capital's emergency blood supplies would surely be sequestered in no time, as the theatres filled with major trauma cases. If Bill needed a blood transfusion, he would need admitting overnight into the hospital as an in-patient.

His arm had been supported with a sling. Over time, blood had seeped through the bandaging and had very slowly spread across the sling as well. Then it had dried and matted to his arm.

Numb with shock, neither had felt like breaking the silence between them as they watched the urgent activity of the hospital staff around them. After they had been offered what must have been a fifth cup of tea by a hospital volunteer, Helen made what was, for her, an unusual observation.

"Did you notice how that woman over there just looked at us?"

"No." Bill was weary.

"She stared at us for a good twenty seconds, as if she recognized us, but couldn't make her mind up if she was right or not."

"Maybe she's one of the parents of the kids at your school."

"No, I've never seen her before. You know what my memory for faces is like."

Bill shrugged, and then clenched his teeth in pain. He resolved, yet again, to keep his arm as still as possible. The painkillers he had been given were nowhere near strong enough. But he wasn't about to make a fuss, given what was going on around him. He was grateful just to be alive.

"I saw somebody I recognised today," he mumbled.

"You mean that Marcus Evett person you risked your neck to save?" Helen's tone was sharp.

"Marcus *Everett*. No, not him. I'd only just met him for the first time today."

"So why, for the love of God, *did* you go into that building for him, Bill?"

"Because of what he had written about. Look, I'll show you what I mean. Can you pass my jacket over?"

Helen frowned, and passed the jacket to her husband. He had taken it off in the clothes shop when she had bandaged his arm up. He had left it there, and, as was her habitual habit, she had cleared up after him. She had picked it up, unthinkingly, and taken it out of the shop into the street with her.

She had put it to good use by draping it over him when he had collapsed. The inside of the jacket was now caked with her husband's dark, dried blood. That jacket needed binning, she thought to herself. But Bill would probably just get it cleaned and mended.

Bill laid the jacket onto his lap, and pulled the book out of its right-hand pocket. The book was still in the bookstore's colourful plastic bag. As he struggled along with his one useful arm, Helen helped him and pulled the book out of the bag. She looked at the front cover, then let out a low sigh, tainted with mild disapproval.

"Open the book to Chapter Nine," instructed Bill.

Helen thumbed through the book and came to the opening page of Chapter Nine. She read the title.

"Wow. Okay, I see what you mean, Bill."

"I haven't read much of it. I haven't had much chance yet."

Helen smiled. "So, did you get a chance to talk much with Mr. Everett?"

"Briefly, yes. I don't think he totally understood what E.Z.1 was about. I think he'd been given some information, and had deduced the rest. Rather like me, really, only I haven't written a whole book based on the little I know. I'm struggling to come up with a single article for the paper."

The couple's conversation went quiet for a moment, until Helen turned to her husband, her brow furrowed.

"If it wasn't Marcus Everett you recognised today, then who was it?"

Bill paused for a moment longer before replying. He had a good idea how this was going to sound to his wife. His own thoughts were dark and paranoid, borne out of the trauma of what he had experienced earlier that day. Part of him was struggling with the idea that everything was somehow connected. He looked Helen in the eye, "I saw the Tall Man again."

"Where?" Helen had already been briefed about Bill's two encounters with the tall government agent, after his trip to Oxford in the Autumn.

"In the bookshop, just moments after I'd finished talking with Everett. I was walking over to the till to pay for the book and I saw him going down the escalator. I wanted to chase after him, but I had to pay for the book before I left the shop. By the time I'd made it downstairs he'd gone. I went out into the street and looked around for a while, but there was no sign of him. That's when I came to find you."

Helen frowned, and looked back across the room. A nurse who had been walking through the department slowed down in front of them, stared at the couple for a couple of seconds, smiled as if in recognition, then continued on her way apace.

"Why does everyone keep staring at us?" Helen asked.

"You're almost as paranoid as I am."

"You've every right to feel paranoid at the moment, Bill." Helen's supportive comment surprised Bill, who was expecting castigation. She continued, "You've seen this man three times now. He pops up just at the moment that you're making some progress on the Ezekiel thing. It's almost like he wants you to be aware that you're being watched."

"I agree. But my worry is that the bombing is somehow connected with this too. I know that sounds mad, but think about it for a moment. That explosion affected the first floor of the bookshop. Marcus Everett had been seated right near the window. He would have taken the full force of the blast."

"Bill, that's bonkers. Why on earth would Marcus Everett be targeted by al Qaida?"

"We don't know for sure it was them, do we?"

Helen put her arm around his shoulders, carefully. "This is not a case of friendly fire, Bill. A suicide bomber blew himself up on a London bus. It's just coincidence! Look, the government have been warning about a terrorist attack for months. That's why they've been trying to get their Act through Parliament. You spoke with the security minister yourself."

"She seemed a lot more interested in Ezekiel One than terrorism. She warned me that my life was in danger. She said that if I moved too soon, then she might not be able to protect me."

"So, do you think the Tall Man is hanging around to protect you?"

"It makes sense. I've seen him with Mrs. Potter-Smith. Maybe he was a security detail, and she assigned him to my case."

"Maybe..."

"All I know is that if I hadn't followed him out of the shop, I would have been killed this afternoon."

"But how could he possibly have known that a bomb was about to go off? If he worked for the government, and knew of such a plot, he would have evacuated half of Oxford Street. It must just have been a coincidence, Bill. He's clearly following you. That's obvious. Maybe he is protecting you, I don't know. But to tie him into this whole horrible terrorism business is taking things too far."

Bill felt his shoulders sag. He was sure that his wife was right. But an even darker thought had occurred to him. It was a thought that refused to disperse entirely. He wondered whether the tall man had actually been the bomber. The tall man had had the time and opportunity to get onto the bus close to the bookshop. The traffic had been moving slowly, and he could have leapt onto the bus as it approached the shop. There would have been enough time to get up the stairs, and set the bomb off. This assumed, of course, that the tall man was a suicide bomber...

Bill decided that this particularly extreme line of reasoning was too paranoid to share with Helen. He realised he was probably suffering with post-traumatic stress. He resolved in his own mind to sleep on things for a few nights, and then see if the darkness of that idea was still shadowing him. He also wanted to see the news on the television to get some idea of how the investigation into the terrorist attack was going. It was possible that some terrorist cell in Britain would admit responsibility, or that CCTV footage would show the bomber getting onto the bus long before that fateful drive past the bookstore.

Bill's dark thoughts were interrupted by the approach of a short man of Indian descent wearing surgical scrubs. He was carrying a green and white printed document. "Hello, Mr. Bainbridge. I'm Dr. Patel. If you could come this way, I'd like to sort this wound of yours out."

Dr. Patel led Bill through a set of doors to a corridor containing a number of small rooms, presumably used for clinics. They went into the third room, where a nurse was busy setting up a dressing trolley. She looked tired and harassed.

Bill lay onto the static examination trolley. The window of the room looked out over the River Thames. It was dark and still outside, and the Houses of Parliament were illuminated beautifully, with the reflections of the lights sparkling across the river waters. Bill pondered on the fact that he had been in an office in Parliament just a couple of months or so ago, looking over the river at this very hospital. It was ironic. He wondered if Mrs. Potter-Smith was working in one of the offices, where the yellow lights twinkled in the windows of Westminster.

Bill took his sling off and exposed his arm to the doctor, who, now attired in apron and gloves, quickly set to work. He cleaned the gaping wound, which set it off bleeding again, and then injected local anaesthetic. After allowing some time for the anaesthetic effect to kick in, he sewed stitches into the deep wound. Bill clenched his teeth, and, looking away, concentrated on the light reflections playing on the river. In the distance he could see several helicopters flying over the capital, and beams of light prowling across the face of buildings.

The doctor's pager beeped loudly. He ignored it.

A blonde woman in a smart suit appeared in the doorway and caught the attention of the nurse, who walked over to her, gloved hands held carefully upright. They whispered to each other as the doctor continued his work. The nurse glanced at Bill. She nodded, and returned to her place by the dressing trolley. She smiled at Bill warmly. Bill smiled back, perhaps a little uneasily.

The woman in the smart suit had moved back into the corridor towards the waiting area.

After about five minutes, the doctor visibly relaxed and straightened himself up, placing a curved needle and thread into a dish on the trolley. He started removing his apron and gloves. "That should take care of it, Mr. Bainbridge. Are you allergic to anything?"

"Not that I'm aware of."

"Good. We'll supply you with some antibiotics. You'll need to finish the full course."

The doctor washed his hands, picked up the green and white admission notes from the desk and wrote in them. He then looked up from the notes.

"We've had your blood results back from the lab. You're a bit anaemic as a result of your injury, but not so bad that you need a blood transfusion. Just take it easy for a while. I'd avoid work for the next week. You can self-certify sick leave with your employer. I'd also go and see your GP later this week if I were you. You will probably find that you suffer flash-backs and bad dreams for a while. It's quite normal after experiencing extreme trauma like you have today. Your GP might be able to help arrange some counselling. You'll also need to go to your GP if your wound starts weeping at all, or if your arm swells up."

Dr. Patel looked at his pager, muttered darkly under his breath, and walked towards the door. "Thanks Doctor!" called Bill after him. Dr. Patel waved his hand without looking back, and was gone.

"Mr. Bainbridge, one of the hospital managers needs to speak with you when you leave," said the nurse, still smiling warmly. "She said she'd wait for you with your wife."

"Thank you. I can't think why she'd want to see me though. Have you any idea what it's about?"

The nurse started to dress his sewn-up wound, and set Bill up with a clean sling. "Apparently, there are a lot of reporters and TV cameras outside the main hospital entrance waiting for you, Mr. Bainbridge. Mrs. Campbell said she would explain everything."

Bill was puzzled. He was expecting that he would be called upon by his editor to create some copy about his first-hand account of the bombing. But the hospital policy had been to turn mobile phones off in clinical areas, so he had not been in contact with the office since the bombing itself. He hoped he wasn't about to get whisked off to Oxford Street for some kind of on-the-spot interview. He was feeling shattered, physically and mentally.

"Do you mind if I turn my mobile phone on for a moment? I need to see if I've had any messages."

"You carry on. I don't know why they have that policy anyway. The phones don't affect cardiac monitors or anything else in the hospital. The consultants are always on their phones. I don't see the harm in it, myself."

Bill turned on the phone as the nurse cleared the suture pack from the top of the trolley. He had 28 new messages. Bill scratched his head. That was 27 more than he had expected.

The nurse wrote in the admission notes, and fetched a box of antibiotics from a wall-mounted cupboard. She gave him some further advice about looking after his wound. The local anaesthetic had worn off now, and Bill was painfully aware of the damage to his right arm. Bill pocketed the antibiotics and walked out of the clinic room, thanking the nurse.

As he walked into the waiting area beyond, his wife and Mrs. Campbell stood up. Helen was beaming a huge smile. A scruffily dressed man in his twenties stood near the two women. Bill recognised him as one of the junior staff at the Standard. Bill smiled and nodded at him, and the young man reciprocated. Mrs. Campbell introduced herself, shaking the hand on Bill's good arm vigorously.

"My name is Mrs. Campbell. I'm in charge of media relations at St. Thomas's Hospital NHS Trust. How's your arm, Mr. Bainbridge?"

"I'll live. What's all this about?" Bill looked over at the junior reporter enquiringly.

Mrs. Campbell pulled out her mobile phone and started texting in a flash of digits. She handed the phone to Bill. The phone's video screen sprang to life, displaying a BBC newsflash about the Oxford Street bombing. Behind the news anchorwoman was a highly pixilated image of Bill on the screen. The text that accompanied the story was too small to read, but Bill didn't have to wait too long before the anchorwoman began to read from her autocue.

"Amidst the terror and tragedy of today's bomb attack have been stories of great heroism. A video taken at the scene by an onlooker just minutes after the blast has been uploaded onto the Internet, and has already received millions of hits. The video shows a man who had been injured running *into* the shop immediately adjacent to the site of the bomb blast. A minute later he is seen running back out of the shop, carrying a young girl in his arms...."

The video played, and Bill strained to make out the detail. He saw himself on the screen pelting out of the shop with the girl in his arms. Clouds of smoke plumed from the shop behind him as the camera shook.

"...just before the shop's ceiling collapsed. The girl would certainly have been killed were it not for the heroic intervention of this man. The girl has been identified as Jessica Turnbull by members of her family. She is currently being treated for her injuries at a central London hospital. A hospital spokesman has said that her condition is stable, and that her family is by her side. It is not yet known who her rescuer was, but he was clearly badly injured on his right arm, and is probably also currently receiving medical treatment at one of London's central hospitals..."

A very poor image of Bill appeared on the screen, showing his blood-stained arm bandaged up with his torn shirt-sleeve.

"...Jessica's uncle, who lives in Luton, has told the BBC that she is expected to make a full recovery from her injuries. He has praised the actions of her rescuer, and passes on the gratitude of her whole family."

Mrs. Campbell stopped the video and replaced the mobile phone into her pocket.

"I uploaded this video from the online BBC news channel about 2 hours ago. In the meantime, the identity of Jessica's rescuer has been discovered, and his whereabouts traced. Which is why there's a pack of reporters, TV crews and paparazzi outside the main doors of this hospital, Mr. Bainbridge. They're waiting for you."

Bill was too stunned to speak.

"How did they find us here?" Helen asked.

"Apparently, after this news item broke you were identified by other patients and their relatives inside the hospital. They contacted the news desks. I'm sure it wasn't any of our staff, Mrs. Bainbridge, but we'll investigate the matter in the course of time. At the moment, everyone here is working flat out just trying to keep on top of this Major Incident. In the cold light of day we can try to establish whether there have been any breaches of patient confidentiality."

"Don't worry, Mrs. Campbell," said Helen, reassuringly. "By the sounds of things, they would have tracked Bill down anyway."

"I've got twenty-eight messages on my phone," contributed Bill. "They can't all be from the boss. Well, probably not, anyhow."

"Talking of whom," interjected Mrs. Campbell, "Your proprietor has sent Mr. Atkins here to take you back to your office. My concern here is that we manage that process appropriately."

"Yes, that's right," broke in the young reporter, handing Bill a sheet of typed paper. "Doug has sent you this script to use as a press release. He's instructed me to tell you not to answer any questions, and to keep to what's written here. He's arranging for the Standard to bring in a publicity consultant to handle your exposure to the world's media. He wants you back at the office pronto. They want an exclusive for tomorrow's front page and time is..."

The young man's excited rhetoric was cut short by a withered look from Bill. "So much for the doctor's advice to rest for a week..." Bill muttered to his wife, and started reading through the document. At least they would be getting a lift home, thought Bill. The couple had travelled into central London by train and the "Tube" earlier in the day, and it would have been a long taxi ride back home. Public transport was massively disrupted in the wake of the terrorist attack.

"If I can rush you just a little bit, Mr. Bainbridge. We've got a cordon of our security team waiting outside, along with a few of our porters. We could do with getting them back to work in the hospital. As you can imagine, we need all the staff we can get right now."

Mrs. Campbell was all business. Her mood then lightened a little, "You did a great thing today, Mr. Bainbridge. It's given a lot of people hope during a dark chapter in the life of this city."

"How's Jessica?" Bill asked suddenly.

"She's at Guy's Hospital. She sustained a compound fracture to her femur, as well as some minor lacerations. She has been in theatre for the last hour or so. They'll keep her in for a few days I should think. Her family sends their best, and are looking forward to thanking you in person at some point. Now, I really think we should make a move. Mr. Atkins is going to bring his car around to the entrance."

The young man took the hint, nodded, and set off ahead of them. Mrs. Campbell led Bill and Helen Bainbridge along the main hospital corridors. As they reached the main entrance they could see a scrum of people outside, some of them bearing television cameras. Lighting rigs had been set up, brightly illuminating the front of the hospital entrance.

"When I get the signal, could you move through the entrance and stand to the left in front of one of the hospital's signs? If you read your statement there, Mr. Bainbridge, then one of our security personnel will see you safely to your car."

Bill was astonished by the intensity of his reception by the media. He had worked for the Daily Standard for many years, but had never worked under these sorts of conditions, and certainly not as their news-subject. He felt a great nervousness come over him, temporarily dispelling his underlying sense of exhaustion. But he also felt a sense of pride. His actions that afternoon had been natural, and to a great extent reflexive. He had not run into the bookshop to save a girl, but to find out what had become of Marcus Everett.

Perhaps if there was any meaning at all to what had happened in the last twelve hours, it was that he was supposed to have been at that place at that moment. Perhaps he was meant to save Jessica Turnbull, and that the succession of unlikely events that had preceded that dramatic moment had simply served to facilitate that happy outcome.

Perhaps, in this dark world, there was some hope after all.

Mrs Campbell turned to Bill, and smiled. Shaking his hand, and then that of his wife, she bade them farewell. Bill turned to face the crowd of his peers in the London press pack, and then looked at his clearly proud wife. Looking into her eyes, he suddenly felt like the Centurion stood at the back of Caesar's chariot. He whispered a few words of caution to Helen.

"These animals stick you up only to knock you straight down again, love. Come on, let's get this over with."

Chapter Seven

They did not turn as they moved; each creature went straight forward.

The offices of the London Daily Standard were located in Kensington, one of the boroughs in the more fashionable West End of the city. After Bill had faced the press and delivered the prepared statement, which simply lavished praise on the work of the doctors and nurses of St. Thomas's Hospital and promised more information about the day's events at a later time, he and his wife had been whisked away in the company car. They had been driven back across Westminster Bridge, past the Houses of Parliament and on through the fashionable boroughs of Westminster and Knightsbridge.

Life in the city appeared to be almost normal by this time, except for security cordons on the roads leading towards Buckingham Palace. There was a concentrated police presence around St. James' Park, which cleared as the car travelled further west through the city. But, apart from the heightened security, Londoners were going about their normal business in the darkness of a cold December evening.

Helen was asleep in the backseat of the car by the time they reached the Standard's office, her head nodding against Bill's good shoulder. Mr. Atkins pulled up outside the main entrance. The building was unusually full of light for a Saturday evening. There was going to be a large overtime bill at the end of the month.

Bill leaned Helen back gently, and gave Atkins his home address. He gently kissed his sleeping wife on the forehead, and carefully climbed out of the car. In seconds, she and the car had disappeared into the night.

Bill had long recognised that his role within the Standard's organisation was not a vital one. Doing restaurant reviews for the Sunday paper, and occasional related copy for the Daily was a cushy number, and he knew it. His expense account was accordingly generous, but his kudos amongst the hacks he worked alongside was not so good. In recent months, this had started to trouble him. Perhaps this was a sign of a mid-life crisis emerging? He wasn't sure. He had been happy doing his little stint for years, but recently he felt that he needed a bigger challenge. Suddenly, his inner wish had been granted. He was adjusting to the unexpected excitement this had brought relatively well, he thought. But he was not sure how he was going to adjust to the change in his professional profile that his seeming heroic exploits would undoubtedly bring.

He got an early hint of this when he was applauded by the reception staff and security team as he entered the Daily Standard's foyer. There was clearly no need to show his I.D. badge today - which was just as well, because it was on the hall table at home. Bill smiled as cheerfully as he could given the throbbing pain in his repaired arm, and made his way through the building to his office. The reception staff must have tipped his boss off because the chief political editor was already waiting for him, perched on the edge of his desk.

"Evening, Doug." Bill was casual.

"What have they been doing to you, Bill? Open heart surgery? You've been ages in there!" Doug was smiling, but the Sunday paper's deadlines were clearly playing on his mind, and on the creases of his brow. The editor was a barrel-chested man in his early sixties, whose love of the good life was balanced by a cynical disposition towards his fellow human beings. Despite his occasional mood swings, Bill liked him.

"I'm sorry to drag you back to the office after the day you've just had, but we'd have missed the print deadline if you went home and worked from there. We've been holding the front page for the last hour. We *have* to have your story. It'll look great in tomorrow's paper!" Doug looked at his wristwatch. "You've got thirty-eight minutes to turn out 1,500 words about what happened to you today. I want emotion, Bill. Blood and guts. Got it?"

Bill nodded, took the sling off his arm and took a seat behind his desk. His computer was already switched on and his account logged in for him. He had long ago realised that Doug had very little interest in secret passwords and data security. The editor made it his business to keep a close eye on the work in progress of his staff. Doug's sizeable posterior that had been decorating the edge of Bill's desk, was replaced by a steaming cup of cardboard coffee.

Bill set to work, his fingers tapping speedily across the keyboard. He had spent the car-ride to the office orchestrating his tale. His main difficulty was explaining to the nation why he had so heroically run into that burning bookshop in the first place. He would have to mention that he had just been in there and had met the now presumably deceased Marcus Everett. But that by itself would not explain why Bill had left his wife's side and hurtled back to the bookshop, injured, to save his new acquaintance. To attempt to explain the sense of urgency he felt about the Ezekiel One investigation would be unwise on a number of levels.

Bill felt it would be best to mention having been in the bookshop to buy "The Day After 2012" just before the bombing. It would at least create context, and even provide a sense of irony. After all, the creator of that hope-filled book title was now dead at the hands of a presumed suicide bomber.

It occurred to Bill as he wrote that Jessica was doing a perfectly normal Saturday afternoon activity for a teenager. She was in town, probably with a small gang of her mates. Her parents were alive, and at her bedside in the hospital. So, they had clearly not been present at the bombing. Bill wrote in his account that he had seen a group of teenagers milling around the bookshelves when he left the bookstore. As his wife had bound his injured arm, the thought had occurred to him that these children were without their parents, and may have been hurt badly by the bomb blast. Feeling a sudden rush of paternal anxiety, he had dashed back to the bookshop to help.

Bill looked back over the paragraph that he had just written. He did not feel proud of himself for having created this bald lie, but what other option was there? If he tried to explain Ezekiel One, he would be branded a lunatic. Without the evidence he needed to break the whole story, he might even be placing himself in further danger at the hands of…whom? The Tall Man? Or, some other (perhaps foreign?) intelligence agency?

Shaking his head, Bill ploughed back into the text. Haunted by the scene of horror he had witnessed that afternoon, he concentrated on a graphic description of the hellish world he had plunged into, as he had returned to the bookshop. He railed against the insanity of the terrorist act; the cold-blooded, calculating murder. He then described the dangers of the collapsing bookshop, and the discovery of the girl, lying broken on a soaking wet floor strewn with shattered glass. Her rescue was a reflex that anyone would have attempted in the same situation, he argued. Then he described his relief and exhaustion upon getting safely back out into the street.

Finally, he tied the whole thing up with a warm tribute to the professionalism of the emergency services, the hospital staff and the stoic qualities of his fellow Londoners caught up in the travesty of the Oxford Street bombing.

He sat back and breathed out deeply. His word count showed 1,830 words. There were 10 minutes left to proof-read the text. He had purposely over-shot because he knew that Doug would edit the piece down substantially. He always did.

Finally finished with five minutes to go, Bill e-mailed the document to his boss, and then sat back and drank the now cold cup of coffee. He realised, as he knocked back the foul brew, that he hadn't eaten anything since breakfast.

✦

An hour later, Bill stood in Doug's office. His boss had just sent off his copy to be slotted into page one and two of the paper. He had left the piece unaltered.

"Shut the door, Bill. We need to talk."

Bill looked out into the open-plan office beyond. There was still a great deal of activity going on, even at this late hour. He closed the door, and sat down opposite his boss. He had already taken the opportunity to grab some junk food out of a vending machine to stave off his sudden bout of intense hunger. He had also done some begging around the office for some strong painkillers. It never ceased to amaze him the assortment of prescription drugs that could be found in a woman's handbag.

Doug opened a drawer in his desk and pulled out an already opened envelope. He pulled out the contents: A letter and a second, sealed envelope. He read the letter to Bill.

"Dear Sir,
I'm hoping you may be able to pass this letter on to Mr. Bill Bainbridge, who I believe is a member of your staff. My mother used to send Bill various sensitive documents when she was alive, but I am concerned that his post is now being monitored and intercepted. Please wish him well with his continuing investigation."

Doug passed the sealed letter to Bill, along with the handwritten letter and envelope. "I've had this letter in my desk for a couple of days, Bill. I've been hoping to arrange a meeting with you this week. It seems circumstances have brought that meeting forward."

The envelope was postmarked from Cheltenham, and had been posted mid-November. It was simply addressed to "The Political Editor, The Daily Standard, London." The unsigned letter was handwritten in a female hand.

Bill opened the envelope. He was surprised it was still sealed. Doug may have steamed it open and resealed it, he imagined. He opened up the photocopied document inside. It was a densely written medical report of unknown provenance, about one of the men whose name had appeared on the Ezekiel One list. The middle paragraph stood out particularly. It summarised a psychological report. The report assessed the subject's ability to endure a very long space flight.

At the bottom of the document was a handwritten line in pencil. It was in Lyn's handwriting, and had been created using their shared code.

"What does it say?" asked Doug, unconvincingly.

"Do you remember the Muppet show?"

"Yeah. Why?"

"They had a sketch on that show called 'Pigs in Space.' This looks like the sequel. Ever heard of 'Priests in Space?'" Bill handed the document over to Doug. His boss scanned the document briefly, and put it down onto his desk.

"You know, Bill, I think someone's taking the piss."

"Maybe…" Bill was wondering the same thing.

"And the code?" Doug pointed at the bottom of the document. Bill picked it up again and looked at it. He shrugged. "I'll have to dig out my cipher and figure it out. One bit of it looks like another date, though. The cipher's in my office. It won't take long to figure out. We weren't operating the 'Enigma Code,' or anything complicated like that."

"Okay, let's go and take a look."

Bill and Doug took the letter and headed through the open-plan office. Several of the staff looked up, and called out to Bill, congratulating him on his act of bravery that afternoon. He smiled warmly.

"I don't suppose you've had a lot of chance to soak all this adoration in, have you Bill? You know, this all looks very good for the paper," said Doug. "We've got a publicity specialist drafted in to take care of arranging interviews for you over the next couple of days. Anything you write is exclusively ours, of course, but we figure that some TV exposure wouldn't go amiss. Those images of you coming out of the burning bookshop carrying that girl have struck a chord with the nation at large.

"It also helps that you're a media man yourself. I think people would have expected a journalist to just stand there and take photos, and not do what you did. So it makes the whole profession look good. That guarantees the story wider exposure within the industry."

"I see..." was all Bill could manage. Doug was even more cynical than he had given him credit for.

"And they'll probably end up giving you a bloody medal." The two men walked into Bill's office, and Doug shut the door. "You're in the public eye in a big way, Bill. If we can crack this little mystery of our 'Priests in Space,' we could use this exposure to make Ezekiel Onc very big news indeed."

"First I think you'd better start paying me danger money," Bill half-joked as he started looking through one of his files for the cipher. The prescription painkillers he had scrounged were starting to kick in, and he was feeling a little high. "There's more to what happened this afternoon than I reported in the article."

"Go on."

"The reason I ran back to the bookshop was because I needed to find out what had happened to Marcus Everett."

"He's the author you mentioned?"

"Yes." Bill picked up his jacket, which was draped across the back of his office chair, and dug out the book from its side-pocket. Thumbing through the pages, hc arrived at Chapter 9, and he passed the book to Doug with that page opened. For a while the two men sat on opposite sides of Bill's desk, reading through their respective documents. Bill finished first, and leaned back in his chair.

"Lyn's written 'Final Launch date set for 30/11/12'"

"That was yesterday..." intoned Doug.

"The Muppet Pigs are already in flight, mate. We're too late. This story's already happened."

"Why's it a 'final launch date?' That either implies other launches have taken place already, or that the date kept getting changed." Doug was flicking through pages of Marcus Everett's book. His face became a picture of disbelief. "This Everett bloke seems to think that the Yanks have been building some kind of mini-city in orbit around the Earth. He says here that the construction of this thing has been going on steadily for years, and is more or less an open secret at NASA."

"I don't know how much of what he's written there is true, Doug. It could be a lot of conjecture built upon some scraps of evidence. A bit like what we're doing right now ourselves, to be honest. I asked Everett about 'Eee Zed One' and he didn't correct me to the American pronunciation. He also didn't make any kind of connection with Ezekiel. Ezekiel does not appear in his index at all. Instead, he seemed to think that 'Eee Zed' stood for 'Extra-terrestrial Zone.' Like the whole thing is some kind of Space Ark, in preparation for the changes to come."

"You mean the end of the Mayan Age? I seem to remember we carried an article about that a couple of weeks ago. All the kids are crazy about it right now."

"That's right. Marcus Everett was an independent researcher who looked into the Mayan culture and, in particular, their complicated system of dating. He believed that the authorities are aware of specific threats to planet Earth, and that they are collecting what they think they might need to safeguard the continuation of human existence. He alleges that they are building this Ark in space like a latter-day Noah."

"Sounds mad, but I suppose it makes some kind of sense if the threat is real enough. Just look what happened today! Maybe that's the shape of things to come over the next few weeks."

"But, then why send up a dozen celibate monks? That's hardly an efficient way of propagating the species, is it? That aspect of this story makes absolutely no sense to me at all. And, think about it - if you wanted to save humanity, you'd put everyone you wanted to save into an underground bunker. Why go to all the expense of building this huge space station? Apart from anything else, it could attract a lot of attention if word got out...which it seems to have. Building a bunker is a lot easier to cover up. Literally."

Bill picked up the medical report from the desk. "And look at this psychological report. It talks about a very long space flight. Is that the same as placing an astronaut in a space station which is parked in orbit for months at a time? It seems to imply to me that the astronaut is supposed to be actually going somewhere."

"But where?"

"I don't know. Mars, perhaps. They've been talking about that for a long time. Maybe they've just decided to build the rocket without telling the general public. Maybe that was the only way they could get the money. Or maybe they intend to set up a colony on the Moon."

"And the priests?"

"You've got me there, Doug. That side of things doesn't make sense from any angle at all."

"In which case, we still don't have a story. Even with this new document. There's still a distinct possibility that this is all a hoax, and that someone's trying to make the Standard look stupid. I've been thinking that all those leaks might have put us in the government hit file. Perhaps this has all been fabricated by the intelligence services to discredit us publicly when we break the story."

Doug folded his arms across his chest. "We need proof. Proof that isn't in the form of leaked photocopies, or the wild speculations of some crackpot author. We need independent, verifiable proof."

Bill had already come to the same conclusion. "I'm planning on going back to Oxford to meet with Dr. Clarke again. I'm hoping I can persuade him to try and locate this Ark with one of their telescopes. That's if the thing's up there at all. He might also have some contacts at NASA. He tried to get a job there once. We might be able to establish whether there was indeed a rocket launch yesterday, even if it was supposed to have been a satellite launch, or something. It would be hard to hide a rocket launch, I would have thought."

"Well, you'd better pencil all that in for later in the week. You're going to be having a busy few days doing interviews and TV programmes. If the rocket's already gone up, then I guess there's no rush, Bill. Elvis has already left the building!" Doug started to stand up.

"There's something else I need to tell you about." The big man sat back down. Bill continued, "I'm definitely being followed. There's this tall bloke I've seen three times. The first time was in Cheltenham, the second in Oxford, and the third in the bookshop on Oxford Street this afternoon."

Doug looked sceptical, "Are you sure?"

"Absolutely. When I first saw him he was with Anne Potter-Smith, at the funeral of my GCHQ contact. She seemed to be trying to keep a low profile. When she noticed me, she seemed to get him to eyeball me. Then they both disappeared. Then in Oxford, he turned up again. I was in this student café with the astronomer when he sat down at a nearby table. I don't know if he was listening in, but it was definitely him."

"And this afternoon?"

"I saw him in the bookshop again. I'd just finished my discussion with Marcus Everett. The man was going down the escalator. I followed him out of the store, but, again, he disappeared. You know what happened next."

"That doesn't mean this is all for real. If we are being set up by MI5, or the secret intelligence services, or whoever, then he might be openly stalking you to create the impression that you're onto something. It's all a bit obvious, isn't it? If he was a professional spy, you wouldn't even know he was around. In fact, they'd have a team of different individuals trailing you, to prevent you from making the connection. I wouldn't worry about it."

"That's alright for you to say, Doug. You're not the one being followed. You're not the one who almost got his arse blown up in central London today!" Bill's temper was fraying. He needed some sleep.

Doug was unfazed by his reporter's loss of cool. He thought about it for a while.

"Maybe we can set up a photo opportunity with Potter-Smith. The government might like that, anyhow, and we're holding all the cards on this story. We could insist you have the photo taken with her because of the interview you did with her a while back. That would give you the chance to ask her who this bloke is."

"Like she's going to tell me…"

"It's worth a shot. She might give you a few more pointers on the direction to take."

"I don't know, Doug. Look, if Ezekiel One is as important as we think it might be, then it's possible that people are getting killed to keep this story out of the papers. My contact in GCHQ suddenly gets a killer cancer. Marcus Everett gets blown to bits at a book-signing. Perhaps I'm next. Or even you!"

It was Doug's turn to show a little emotion, "Did you bang your head when that bomb went off? That explosion was the work of terrorists, Bill. No government agency, no matter how deranged, would bomb its own people like that. If they had wanted to take Everett out they would have knocked him off quietly. In fact, I doubt his book would ever have seen the light of day."

"That's not how disinformation works, and you know it. They give you a nugget of truth, but wrap it up in a load of crap. So the truth then appears to be fiction, or the fiction truth. Marcus Everett might have been deliberately misled.

"His book might have been serving some purpose to the intelligence community. The problem then emerged when I chanced across him. It was like having different parts of the jigsaw suddenly join up to create a better picture of what's really going on. The two of us seen talking together might have set off a chain of deadly events."

Bill could see he was getting through to Doug. His own now profound sense of paranoia was infectious. Doug put his hand up to his face and rubbed his right eye. He deliberated for a moment.

"Okay, let's assume that your line of reasoning is correct. You're the only person now holding all of the pieces of the jigsaw together. If you're right, and I hope to God you aren't, then you'll be targeted next. Or me."

Doug let out a slightly deranged laugh. He looked quizzical, even humorous, "Would they really kill a national hero? If they do intend to stop this story, then killing you would be counter-productive. You've got too high a profile right now. The fact that you're investigating government leaks would inevitably come out of any inquest into your death. The conspiracy theorists would have a field day."

"So my heroic antics this afternoon may actually have saved my life?" Bill had not considered this possible twist.

"Hey, I'm assuming this mad idea of yours has some kind of validity. Frankly, I think you're just high on your painkillers!" Doug was enjoying himself. He enjoyed nothing better than sarcastically drubbing his reporters to their faces, preferably in public. It kept them sharp, he calculated.

"That bomb was al Qaida, Bill. It would take days to plan a bombing in central London on the scale we saw this afternoon. They couldn't organise that in just a couple of minutes! If the bomb plot was known to the British authorities, they would have acted upon it. They would have closed down half of London if they had to. They've done that before."

Bill could see the sense in what his boss was saying. It was reassuring too. Perhaps it was natural to imagine that a random event that traumatised you might actually have been directed at you. Perhaps Dr. Patel was right; that he did need some counselling. Maybe he had suffered some mild concussion. Bill momentarily considered whether this would be a good time to self-certify for a week's sick leave.

"I'm sorry. You're right. I'm not used to all of this political stuff."

"I'm sorry too, Bill. You've been through hell and back today. You don't need me getting heavy with you." Bill smiled at Doug's intended quip. Doug often joked disparagingly about his own weight. "I'll get reception to order you a taxi home. We'll pay for it. In fact, I think we'd better see if we can get you a pay rise as well. It's not exactly danger money, like you hoped for, but you are raising our profile during a national crisis, and we should recognise that. Besides, that copy you just wrote was almost decent journalism. That makes a nice change around here."

Doug stood up, and put Marcus Everett's book onto the desk. "I'll see you tomorrow Bill. We'll send the publicity guy, Cliff Maxwell, around to your place about 10am. He'll be able to go through a few pointers on how to present this story on camera, and we'll probably have an itinerary worked out for you by then. You might even have some paparazzi outside your front door! In the meantime, have a think about whether you'll do that photo-shoot with Potter-Smith. It might prove very useful indeed."

So much for a week off sick, thought Bill. He nodded despondently, and stood as his boss left the office. He then collected up all the documents on the table and put them in a plain card file. Sitting down again to wait for the call from reception about his taxi, he picked up "The Day After 2012" and opened it up to the dedication page. He looked at the inscription and signature scrawled illegibly across the bottom of the page. It was dated 1st December 2012.

Analysing the erratic scribble, Bill wondered if Marcus Everett had unknowingly just signed his own death sentence. He shuddered at the thought, and then turned the pages to begin reading Chapter One.

The taxi was held up in heavy traffic on the outskirts of the London borough of Hammersmith. Bill sat in the back of a black London cab. The glass screen dividing the vehicle was half shut, and the driver was now humming along to the radio. He had explained that there must be a gig on that evening at "The Odeon," the old name of the main concert venue in Hammersmith.

The illumination from the street lights was too dim to read any more of the book. Bill was finding it heavy going anyhow. He had been thinking about how he was going to persuade Dr. Clarke to search for Everett's space ark EZ1. It seemed unlikely that the academic would be persuaded by the fairly fantastic descriptions given in the main body of the text. However, having looked through some of the photographic plates in the book, Bill had seen some supporting documents of purported sightings of the object made by amateur astronomers. Some very grainy images, allegedly taken using telescopes, were printed alongside the documents. The images could really have been of any point of light in the sky. There was no way of discerning any features on the supposed object.

Even so, Bill hoped that the technical information supplied by the amateur astronomers might be enough for Dr. Clarke to figure out where this orbiting spacecraft was, and perhaps use his telescope to get a better quality image. It seemed reasonable to Bill to assume that a professional astronomer would be able to do a lot better than the amateurs cited in Everett's book.

Bill pulled his mobile phone out of his inside jacket pocket and turned it on. He still hadn't looked through his messages. They now numbered well over 50. He knew that it would be the same with his answering machine at home. There would be calls from family, friends, colleagues, newspapers, television stations, etc. The next couple of days would be frantic. There would be little opportunity to contact Dr. Clarke. He just hoped that the astronomer had his mobile phone switched on. Calling up the number from his phone's address book, Bill made the call.

He was in luck. "Hello," came the relaxed sound of Dr. Clarke's voice.

"Sorry to interrupt your evening, Dr. Clarke. This is Bill Bainbridge."

"Really? Goodness, what are you doing phoning me? I mean, didn't you just survive a bomb blast or something? I saw you on the television earlier this afternoon."

"Yes, I've had quite a day all in all. I suspect the next few days will be a bit mad, although hopefully not quite as dangerous! The reason I called you is that we've had some more information on our investigation. I could do with some help if you have the time available this week."

There was a pause. "I'm not sure how much help I can be to you, Mr. Bainbridge. This story is clearly very important to your newspaper. But I suspect that my technical expertise will be somewhat surplus to requirements."

"I'm sure that the paper will be able to reimburse you some expenses for your time. My editor is particularly keen to make some progress here."

"Oh, I'm not interested in your money, Mr. Bainbridge. Look, I tell you what. I'll give you some time later this week to look into your new lead. But, in return, I would like to ask of you a little favour."

Here we go, thought Bill, raising his eyes to the roof of the cab.

Chapter Eight

Their faces were like this: all four had the face of a man and the face of a lion on the right, on the left the face of an ox and the face of an eagle.

The applause was warm and prolonged. Bill stood at the bottom of the lecture theatre, looking up at the clearly appreciative audience. He decided that it was good to be a national hero.

The Lindemann lecture theatre at Oxford's Martin Wood Complex was packed. The complex was used by the University's physics department during the day. The evening's lecture was open to all, and had been organised by Dr. James Clarke on behalf of his college's debating society. Although the lecture had been hastily arranged, word had got around based upon Bill's unexpected, and probably short-lived, celebrity. Students were sat on the stairs, and stood up alongside the walls of the auditorium and in the doorways at the back. The packed auditorium would surely have been an unusual sight for regular attendees of physics lectures. After all, the science departments in almost all English universities were in sharp decline.

Dr. Clarke strode across the floor towards Bill, applauding magnanimously. Remarkably, the young academic was even scruffier that evening than the first day Bill had met him. His hair had grown longer, and his pair of jeans exhibited a large tear at one of the knees. The room gradually quietened down, and Dr. Clarke turned to address the audience.

"I'd like to express my thanks to Bill Bainbridge for taking the time to come up to Oxford this evening to provide us with such a detailed account of this week's tragic events in London. The bombing itself was clearly traumatic and devastating to everyone who was caught up in it, and I am sure we all extend our deepest condolences to all those affected by the loss of loved ones in this horrible tragedy.

"I personally found Bill's first hand account deeply moving, and I know it touched many of the other members of this audience deeply. But I think his account went further than the evident complex emotional impact of such a travesty. He has also placed the event in a useful political context, both nationally and internationally, as one might expect of a political journalist of Mr. Bainbridge's experience."

Bill slightly raised his eyebrow at this comment. Giving an impromptu evening lecture at Oxford University was an honour, certainly, but it was also a stressful occasion, at the end of what had already been an extremely stressful week. But, the guest lecture was Bill's "payment" for the help of the astrophysicist, and he was trying his best to put the young academic firmly in his debt. Dr. Clarke was looking up at the lecture hall clock.

"I think we have time for a couple of questions. Yes, you in the middle wearing the blue shirt. Your question?"

"Mr. Bainbridge," began the tousle-haired youth, "have you had a chance to see Jessica since the blast?"

"Yes, her parents asked me to come and see her at Guy's Hospital on Tuesday. She's doing fine. She couldn't remember anything that had happened, which I suppose is quite normal in these circumstances. So she didn't remember me at all. So, at least she won't have that adding to her post-traumatic shock." There was a ripple of amusement through the audience.

"The meeting was probably more useful to me, really, because it allowed me to meet again the person I had helped out of that building. I was able to focus on the person, not the event. I'd been doing so many interviews with the press and the TV news people that my memory of the event was becoming like a television clip as well. Seeing Jessica again brought the reality of the whole thing home. Particularly, the frailty of our condition as human beings. It's sobering to reflect on how a single act of madness can suddenly destroy so much potential. I guess the victims of the 9/11 outrage must have felt the same at the time."

Dr. Clarke pointed at another upraised arm.

"Can I ask…what made you run into that burning building?"

"That's a difficult one to rationalise in front of you all, in the quiet, reflective environment of a lecture hall. I suppose when we're affected by an event as disorientating as a bomb blast, we tend to fall back on our instincts. I knew my wife was fine. She had just patched my arm up as best she could. I remember that I had to get out into the street, to see what had happened. Perhaps that was the basic reflex of a man who had spent his life in journalism.

"But, I must admit to you that I am not a courageous man particularly. Once I was out in the street and could see the destruction all around me, my mind focussed on where I had just been. The bookshop. I remembered the people inside; the author I had just met, my fellow book buyers in the queue, and the children downstairs. Something just took a hold of me, and in I went."

"Did you see the author?"

"No, the first floor of the building was engulfed in flame. It seemed hopeless. So, I concentrated on trying to find survivors downstairs. That's when I came across Jessica."

"Did your copy of Mr. Everett's book survive?" This was the third question from the same person. There was a palpable groundswell of discomfort in the room, as if the questioner had stepped over an invisible social barrier. People started to shuffle uncomfortably, and there was some muttering at the back. The man was hogging the proceedings, and this question seemed irrelevant. Or, perhaps there was something more that was irritating this particular group of people, thought Bill.

He took a closer look at his inquisitor. The lanky youth wore a baggy grey shirt, and his tousled hair fell across his bespectacled face. It was Colin,

Christine's boyfriend from Cheltenham! Bill wondered why he hadn't recognised him before during the lecture. He had a good memory for faces, normally. Bill showed no outward expression of recognition.

"Yes, it survived. I left it in my jacket pocket, which I had taken off when my arm got cut." Why did Bill suddenly feel like he was answering questioning at a police station? "Happily, my wife left the scene with my jacket in her hand. She's used to tidying up after me."

There was ripple of polite amusement in the lecture hall. Dr. Clarke pointed to another raised hand, but before the next question could be asked, Colin came up with a fourth question. It was asked far more urgently, his tone that of an excitable psychotic, "Mr. Bainbridge, did you read the book?"

This time, the perseverance of the questioner crossed way over the line of academic etiquette, and a pulse of angry muttering was emitted by the attendees. Bill clearly heard one of the students behind Colin say, "Just shut up, Haddock. What's that got to do with anything?"

Dr. Clarke raised his hands, saying, "A different question, I think." He pointed again at the upraised hand, which had remained aloft throughout the outburst.

"Mr. Bainbridge, who do you think carried out the bombing?"

"It seems likely that it was al Qaida, or some kind of active al Qaida-affiliated cell operating in Britain. But, as you know, there has been no claim by any group for the bombing. CCTV footage taken in the city along the bus route has also failed to pick up any suspicious activity, as far as I'm aware. It's a bit of a mystery, isn't it? Usually, a suicide bomber will make a video before setting off on his attack. Or, there'll be a group that has prepared a suicide bomber.

"But, none of the bodies recovered from the wreckage of the bus has fitted any known intelligence profile for a potential attacker. But despite all this, it remains highly likely that al Qaida were behind this atrocity. It fits with previous attacks earlier this century."

"Are you aware that some commentators have speculated that the bomb might have been placed onto the roof of the bus, or on the side close to the top? They've suggested that it was some kind of mine attached to the bus. What do you think about that possibility?"

"From what I could see at the scene, the top of the bus looked like it was blown apart by something exploding inside the upper deck. But, I'm not an explosives expert. The blast certainly impacted heavily against the first floor of the surrounding shops. When I think that I had stood in front of that first floor window just minutes before the explosion…well, it doesn't bear thinking about, to be honest."

Bill suddenly felt worn out. He had spent the last four days touring around TV studios, appearing on various news and current affairs programmes. He didn't feel much like a hero, despite the excitable buzz he felt amongst people he met coming into contact with him. In fact, he felt slightly fraudulent under the intense gaze of the public. But the country needed a hero to help it through the trouble, and from a media point of view the whole thing made a lot of sense. Given his job, he couldn't turn his back on the role that had been thrust upon him.

Agreeing to do this impromptu lecture for the debating society at Dr. Clarke's college in Oxford was light relief, in comparison to the other media events he had attended. Except that he had not counted on the appearance of a rather intense Colin Haddock.

The young student stood up, as if to leave the auditorium. Many of his fellow students turned to look at him.

"Can't you all see? That bomb blast was targeting the author Marcus Everett! He was assassinated to stop the truth from getting out! We've all got two weeks left to live, and here we are debating a non-existent suicide bomber."

With that Colin worked his way out of his row of seats, dislodging other students. There was stunned silence. Before reaching the exit at the back of the auditorium, he turned to face Bill.

"You're the only person who can sort this out in time," he shouted. "You've got the proof about the U.S. Government's preparations for the End-times. What on earth are you doing parading around the country like this? The clock is ticking away, Mr. Bainbridge!"

The now red-faced young man turned on his heels and stormed out of the auditorium. The door clattered shut behind him, resonating around the silent room. The silence was broken by a visibly embarrassed Dr. James Clarke.

"Well, I'm terribly sorry about that, Mr. Bainbridge. It seems like young Haddock has spent too long in the college bar this evening. Which college is he in, anyway? Anybody know?"

"Jesus," someone yelled from the back.

"Right, I shall have a word or two with one of the fellows there. We can't have that kind of behaviour from our under-graduates, and certainly not in front of an invited guest speaker. I think it's probably about time we called an end to this meeting. I would again like to thank our guest, Mr. Bill Bainbridge, on delivering an emotional and thought-provoking lecture for us this evening. On behalf of everyone, I would like to wish him a safe trip back to London, and all the best for the future."

Dr. Clarke's words were met by warm applause, and the audience began to shuffle out of the auditorium. Dr. Clarke turned to Bill.

"I'm so sorry about that outburst. I'm not sure what it was about, to be honest."

"Unfortunately, James, I think I do. I've met Colin briefly before, under unhappy circumstances. It's quite a coincidence that he's a student here in Oxford, to be honest. I met him in Cheltenham. His girlfriend is the daughter of an old friend of mine."

"All the more reason for him not to behave the way he did. What was he going on about, anyway? All this talk of the end of the world! I've been hearing that a lot around the colleges lately. I've even had questions about it in some of my lectures. There seems to be some kind of unrealistic expectation that my knowledge of astronomy might in same way provide the key to the understanding of the Mayan prophecies. Quite ridiculous, I can assure you."

Bill did not reply immediately, but looked pensive. He folded up his lecture notes and returned them to his jacket pocket. With a grim look on his face, he caught the astronomer's eye. "Have you looked into the Mayan calendar system, Dr. Clarke?"

"Yes, well, I will admit it's absolutely fascinating. To a certain extent, I can see why there's all this fuss about the end of the Mayan cycle. Their Long Count was 1,872,000 days, I seem to recall, which is quite a staggering concept for a civilisation living in the jungles of the Yucatan peninsula. It's not every day that such a count of days comes to an end. The last marker for this cycle was in 3,114 BC. The current fuss is about the next marker, on the 21st or 22nd December, depending upon who you listen to."

"That's a truly huge number…it's the sort of period of time you'd use for a returning comet, or something like that." Bill tested the waters carefully. "Is it possible that the Mayans were marking such an event, something their ancestors had seen in the sky thousands of years before?"

"Even if that was so, how could they have established the periodicity of the comet?"

"I'm sorry… the what?"

"The duration of the comet's path around the Sun. They would either have to have been extremely sophisticated astronomers, to work out the comet's complete orbital path from its short visible passage through the heavens at perihelion, or else they would have to have maintained records of the observation of this special comet from the time of its last visible passage over 5,100 years before. That seems extremely unlikely, Mr. Bainbridge. That's so far back into the Stone Age that it defies belief."

Bill shrugged slightly, unconvinced by Dr. Clarke's scepticism. The Lindemann Lecture Theatre was now empty, except for the two men. Dr. Clarke began to tidy his things from the desk at the bottom of the lecture theatre, and then went around tidying the room after the students. Bill helped him to clear up the assorted drink containers and snack bar wrappers. Dr. Clarke grumbled about the lack of environmental awareness shown by the litter-bugs.

"Once we're finished in here, Bill, we'll head over to my office at the Physics Department. It's up in Keble Road. If you've got some astronomy questions you want answering, that will be the best place to start."

"Don't you work in an observatory?"

Astonished, Dr. Clarke looked up at Bill questioningly, and then laughed. "I think you'll find professional astronomy has rather moved on from simply looking through telescopes. Oxford University does have a telescope: The PWT. But we don't actually use it much for academic study. It's more for sight-seeing really."

"I don't understand?" Bill's confusion was tinged with a certain amount of disappointment. He had been looking forward to getting a chance to track down EZ1 in the heavens.

"Professional astronomy requires the use of some very specialized instrumentation, like the Hubble Space Telescope, or radio telescopes. Or, we use very powerful telescopes perched on the top of mountains, where the sky is clear and free of pollution."

"How do you do that when you're teaching in Oxford?"

"We buy time on them using money from research grants. Sometimes, we go to the location of the telescope to work, during the University holidays, or sometimes we gain the information we need directly from the people working there, operating the instruments.

"My own work involves scanning certain parts of the sky over a period of time, and recording changes in the star patterns in the hope of discovering new asteroids or comets. You see, the heavens are in a constant state of flux. Some things move quite quickly, like asteroids, and the planets near to the Sun; Mercury and Venus. Other things move extremely slowly, and are effectively stationary. Distant stars and galaxies fall into this category.

"As a general rule of thumb, the further an object is away from you, the slower its apparent motion. So if you find something moving across a star field, the chances are it's relatively close to you. If you spot the object several times over a long period, you can establish how far away it is and work out its orbital path.

"This would be very difficult work to do using a classical style telescope, making photographic plates of the night sky every night, and looking over them meticulously. Pluto was discovered that way, but it took years of work by the astronomer Clyde Tombaugh. Nowadays we prefer to cut a few corners, so we use computers. Technology has come a long way in the last 80 years!"

"Let me get this straight. You're looking for new objects in the solar system by comparing pictures of the sky over long periods of time. Sort of like a child's 'spot the difference' puzzle?"

Dr. Clarke laughed warmly. "It's a bit more complicated than that, because you have to take into account the movement of the Earth around the Sun, but you've got the general idea."

The two men had shut up the lecture theatre, deposited the rubbish they had collected into bins, and were leaving the conference complex to begin the ten minute walk into the centre of Oxford. The astronomer clearly enjoyed the open air of the December's night sky, despite the cold. He began to point out various stars and winter constellations that managed to break through the yellowish orange glow of light pollution hanging over the city.

Bill was getting used to his companion's ideological stance on the use of cars. But at that moment he wished he was in a car with the heater on. As the two men strode briskly through the streets of Oxford, Bill decided it would be imprudent to point out the air-miles involved in jetting off to foreign observatories set atop far-flung mountains. Dr. Clarke would have to walk an awful long way to off-set that!

CHAPTER NINE

Their wings were spread; each living creature had one pair touching its neighbours', while one pair covered its body.

James Clarke's office, in the Department of Physics, was surprisingly tidy. Bill had expected piles of papers, and books cluttering up untidy shelves. Instead, the office was relatively airy, with the single desk dominated by computer equipment. There were family photos, and framed diplomas mounted neatly onto the wall, and a coffee machine with a set of large mugs sat invitingly on top of a waist high book shelf that ran the length of the office. The bookshelf was laden with neatly arranged books, journals and miscellaneous files.

The two men drew seats up around the computer screen, and sipped at coffee that had been quickly prepared by the astronomer. Bill pulled his box of antibiotics from his jacket pocket and took his night-time dose. He wished that he had brought along some painkillers as well. His arm was aching. It was a constant reminder of the close shave he had had with death only five days previously.

As Dr. Clarke logged into his computer, Bill marvelled at the tidiness of the office. The academic term at Oxford University had already come to an end for many of its undergraduates, and Dr. Clarke had said that he was going to throw himself into his research over the next few weeks. Bill suspected that the meticulously tidy office had something to do with that. It was amazing how the procrastinating mind could busy itself with house keeping.

Perhaps Bill's quest for answers to the Ezekiel One riddle was welcomed as a similar distraction by the academic.

"So, you want me to search for a hidden spaceship in orbit around the Earth, that may be acting as a repository for survivors of a disaster set to befall this planet in two weeks time?" Dr. Clarke intoned dryly. He was clearly up to speed.

Bill thumbed through his now battered copy of Marcus Everett's book and located a table of numbers in Appendix Four. He handed it to Dr Clarke. "Yes, I know this sounds mad. But certain aspects of this story fit with some intelligence that has leaked out from the British government. There may be something to it."

"There's no way anyone could have kept something like this secret."

"They haven't. That's why we've got the leaked documents. Someone high up in the British government wants this made public. The important thing for us is to get some proof of the existence of this spaceship, so we can substantiate the story when we publish. Otherwise, everyone will just fall about laughing."

James turned the book over in his hands and examined the front cover, his fingers keeping the page opened.

"The author is the same man who died in the Oxford Street bombing: The same man that Haddock was yelling at you about."

"Yes, there is a link. Colin Haddock has a girlfriend in Cheltenham. Her mother was the conduit for the government leak that alerted us to the Ezekiel One story. She worked for GCHQ, and used to regularly send us sensitive information."

"You said 'worked?' Did they find out and sack her?"

"Sadly, she died a couple of months ago of a brain tumour."

"A brain tumour, you say? They can cause confusion, of course. Perhaps in her illness, she was influenced by Mr. Haddock? The tumour may have muddled her judgement. Maybe he's the source of the leak, not the Government."

"I knew my source for many years, and she seemed to keep her wits about her right up to the end. But, I agree, that's a possibility. That's why I need to find out the truth before publishing anything at all about this story. If it's a hoax, then you should be able to debunk it. All we have to do is pinpoint this spacecraft."

"It will be my pleasure, Mr. Bainbridge," said Dr. Clarke through a smug smile. "Even if it's just the size of a regular satellite, your mystery spaceship should be easy to find, if it's out there." He looked back at the book's appendix, and began to open up a program on his computer. The table in the book contained the times and coordinates for various sightings of the alleged object in the heavens. All of the sightings had been catalogued by amateur astronomers, and were referenced back to their sources.

Dr. Clarke entered the data into his computer program. He worked away for about half an hour, without comment. At the end of that time, he sat back and rolled his chair away from the desk. He picked up his now cold cup of coffee and finished it off.

"I've found a recognisable pattern to the data, or at least most of it. A couple of the points are off, but most of it tallies with a possible object in a high orbit around the Earth, approximately 900 km above the surface of the Earth."

"So it exists?"

"Don't get too excited, Mr. Bainbridge. It just creates a theoretical possibility, and shows that there is some consistency to the data presented in the book. It also provides us with a trajectory, so we can establish where this object is in the sky at any point in its orbit. That should give us the potential to find it. First of all, I want to establish whether this is simply a known object which has been misidentified as an 'unknown.' I'm not sure whether you're aware of this, but there are literally thousands of objects floating around the Earth. Satellites, space debris, spanners dropped by astronauts during spacewalks, you name it. There are some monitoring stations that keep an eye on all of it - mostly military people, actually. NORAD at Space Command in the States is the main centre for the continuous monitoring of everything moving around in space. Here in Britain, similar work is carried out by RAF Fylingdales in Yorkshire."

"That information is in the public domain?"

"For the most part, it's available on the Internet. We astronomers need to have some kind of idea of what's moving around up there. So let's just say we have privileged access to some of the unofficial data, in addition to what you can pull up off the Internet. It may not be exhaustive, but it should be fairly comprehensive."

Dr. Clarke returned to his keyboard and began to pull up other programs and files. He tapped away for a while, and brought up pages of data, arranged in tables, onto his screen. Scanning through the data, he stopped and pointed at one line.

"That's it."

"Wow, just like that? So, what is it?"

Dr. Clarke copied and pasted the reference and carried out a series of specialised searches. Eventually, a short description appeared on the screen. "It's some kind of Department of Defence satellite," the astronomer explained. "Its function is classified. It's probably some kind of spy satellite. It was launched just over two years ago."

"Are there any images of what it looks like?"

"No, not in the official blurb, anyhow. Let me hunt about on the general Internet for a while. You'd be amazed at what's out there. A lot of amateurs monitor this sort of stuff, and put their research onto the Internet."

His computer mouse whisked back and forth, clicking away. "The object has an official designation of 2010-032A. It doesn't appear on the NORAD main site, but is available through other more obscure resources. Surveillance satellite…blah, blah, blah. Ooh, look at this. We have an image."

A photo of part of the night sky appeared, full of points of light. A single streak of light cut a path across the image. Dr. Clarke looked at it for a while, and brought up the technical information about the image. He frowned.

"That's a bit odd. Look at the density of the stars in the image, Bill." He referred to the journalist by his first name for the first time that evening. "Look at the white line across the image. That's the reflection of the satellite as it traverses the sky. The streak indicates its relative motion across the sky during the time it took for the camera shutter to make the exposure. Look just above the white line."

Bill couldn't see anything, and said as much. "Exactly. Look at the distribution of stars. They stop above the light reflection. That's very odd. It's almost like the light from them has been blocked out by something attached to the satellite."

"A lot of the satellites I've seen in photos have large arrays of solar panels attached to them. Could that be what's blocking out the light?"

"No, solar panel arrays would reflect light too. The light reflected from the tiny satellite and its solar array together should be making that white streak. This is something else - something that does not reflect light."

Dr. Clarke saved the image, and did some further searches for images of 2010-032A, using its official designation. He saved several images, and arranged them in chronological order. He brought them up onto the screen one at a time. Bill could see that the dark bands on either side of the white line were growing larger with each successive image. "It's getting bigger over time."

"Yes, I agree. I've never seen anything like it." Dr. Clarke was staring at the computer screen. His forehead appeared deeply furrowed in the reflected blue light of the screen. After a few moments, he spoke again.

"Not only that, but there are recorded attempts to photograph this satellite that contain no reflection of light at all. It's almost like the satellite is not where it should be. Instead, there's an amorphous streak of darkness across the star field background."

"How could that be?"

"Perhaps because whatever's sat on the satellite has completely blocked the light from its reflective surface. The satellite has been imaged in different parts of the sky, and with different angles to the Sun below the horizon. Whatever this thing is, it's big enough to completely block out the Sun's rays from hitting the satellite. At least, that's the case on *some* of these images. This seems to be a phenomenon that becomes more frequent as we move towards the present day."

The astronomer sat back, and swung around in his chair to face Bill. "You know, this is so weird. Someone else out there must have spotted this anomaly."

"But the satellite doesn't appear on the official NORAD website, so how would anyone know how to track it?"

"I'm talking about astronomers like me, who build up our own map of the sky independently of NORAD and other official agencies. There are colleagues out there who make a bit of a hobby of watching the super-secret satellites up there. In case one of them, say, disappears, or falls out of its usual orbit."

"Does that happen?"

"Oh, yes," Dr. Clarke laughed gently. "Now I'm the one who sounds like a conspiracy nut! Look, the Yanks have put up all sorts of hardware into space. So have the Russians, and the Europeans, and even the Chinese. There are spy platforms. Recently, there has been the emergence of a new class of satellites, what you might term killer satellites. They're capable of moving around using their own propulsion systems.

"Every so often, they go on a hunt. For instance, let's say a foreign power puts up a satellite that hangs over a sensitive military establishment in the United States. The Americans might then take it upon themselves to dislodge it from its normally stable orbit into a decaying one. All they have to do is give it a little nudge with one of their killer satellites, either by direct collision or through the use of a particle beam.

"It's likely that the other space powers do the same: Tit for Tat. It's like the old Cold War, only no one knows about it. It's beyond most people's frame of reference, unless a civilian satellite gets accidentally taken out. Or, one of these decaying satellites makes it through the atmosphere and crashes to Earth.

"When that happens the authorities blame a bad solar storm, or say that the satellite has decayed naturally into an unstable orbit and is going to fall to Earth. What very few people realise is that the satellite has actually been attacked by a foreign power."

"I had no idea."

"Well, officially it doesn't happen, of course. America controls the waves up there. They are very interested in building up space-based anti-ballistic missile defences as a shield against nuclear attack. They're not about to publicise their work. It might compromise their eventual goal of a shielded American continent.

"The Chinese and the Russians have been working on the same idea. If one of your own satellites gets hit you aren't going to tell the world that it was taken out by the other side, are you? It might expose your own activities up there, which are generally in contravention of various UN treaties."

"Listening to you, it's almost as if there's a war going on up there!" Bill was astonished.

"Well, I wouldn't want to over-dramatize it. It's more like the defence of territory, or creating protective borders in space above the Earth. There are satellites whizzing around all over the place. But if you stick a spy satellite in a geo-stationary orbit about sensitive military sites, it's going to provoke a response, isn't it?"

"Does EZ 1 fall into that category?" Bill pronounced the American version of the letter Z.

"EZ 1?"

"It's what Marcus Everett called 2010-032A. He obtained that information from someone inside NASA. He didn't have the official designation you've come up with. Or, at least, he didn't publish it."

"Well, whatever it's called, it's certainly an odd little beast. It's just a pity we can't see what it looks like. Let's see..." Dr. Clarke started tapping away at his keyboard again, "If I cross-reference the orbit of your 'EZ 1' with my sky searches...then we might be able to...see if it moves across our more detailed deep sky images taken in Hawaii last summer..."

"Hawaii? Nice work if you can get it."

Dr. Clarke grinned, "Yes, beautiful place generally, but I spent most of the time on top of a bloody volcano. You might want to go and make us a couple more coffees, Bill. We're in for a long night."

✦

It was 1:30 in the morning. Bill had already planned on staying in Oxford overnight, but not necessarily in the office of an astrophysicist. He had phoned his wife for a chat. All day, her pupils at school had been coming up to her with various newspaper clippings, showing her the photos taken of her and Bill. She was in a good mood, "Even 9S behaved themselves today!" And, she didn't seem to mind too much that her husband was away. In fact, when he had done the restaurant reviews, his absence from the marital home had been a fairly regular event as he travelled to cities up and down the country. It was only relatively recently that he had been confined to London.

Bill was awakened from drowsy half-sleep by Dr. Clarke. He was still sat on the same plastic chair, half-slumped against the wall. His injured arm was aching, and his right leg had gone to sleep. He looked at Dr. Clarke through tired, bleary eyes. Thankfully, the artificial light from the room's energy-efficient bulbs was soothingly dim.

The astronomer seemed uncharacteristically excited.

"Look at this, Bill."

On the screen was a large amorphous-shaped black hole in the surrounding star-field. Unlike the other images, this one was not a streak.

"This image was taken in August. You can see here that the starlight is being blocked by a large, dark object. It's a bit like a silhouette. I've calculated the size of this thing based on its distance from the Earth, which is around 900km." He paused, perhaps for effect. "You won't believe it."

Bill scratched his head. "Try me."

"This satellite is almost a kilometre across!"

"What?" Bill found himself suddenly alert. He knew next to nothing about satellites, but when he had heard about them on the television news they had usually been compared in size to a washing machine or a small car. If a normal satellite was the size of a car, then Ezekiel One must be the cosmic equivalent of a traffic jam!

"The object is about nine hundred metres at its longest point. It's absolutely incredible. I've checked and re-checked my figures. This thing is absolutely enormous!

"The shape is very hard to make out, but it's at least 600 metres wide in places. I'm beginning to think that your friend Mr. Everett might have been onto something. This thing is big enough to house hundreds of people." Dr. Clarke grinned at Bill, "Maybe a few species of large mammals as well."

"Two by two…"

"I just can't believe this thing hasn't been spotted. Something that big just orbiting around the Earth for months, perhaps a year or two, and no one's even aware of it. They've clearly been building this space station over a reasonable period of time, at least since the launch of the initial satellite in 2010. How has it possibly remained a secret?"

The astronomer was genuinely amazed.

"Well, I suspect that the security surrounding this project is incredibly tight. In fact, I've experienced it first hand already. This is something we're going to need to discuss, Dr. Clarke, given how much you now know about this 'Ezekiel One' object. There is a precedent for this kind of level of secrecy. During the Second World War, there were thousands of personnel working on the Manhattan Project, and yet it was kept a well-guarded secret right up until the dropping of the atomic bomb on Hiroshima."

"That was during a world war. This is entirely different. Surely a significant proportion of the personnel working on such a colossal project would be civilian? It seems unlikely to me that the authorities could keep a lid on such an immense operation."

Bill found himself in the position of having to provide answers for questions that had been wracking his mind for some time, particularly about the ability to maintain secrecy over an extended period of time. But he had not been aware, until this moment, of the size of the Ezekiel One project. This revelation made the level of secrecy necessary to contain such an operation mind-boggling.

His experience of the death of two people connected with the exposure of Ezekiel One had made him very uneasy about this aspect of things. If other people before them had come close to bringing the story into the open, then perhaps they had suffered a similar fate.

In his darkest moments, Bill had pondered on the possibility that there was a hit squad operating under the aegis of one of the military intelligence agencies. The repercussion of that possibility was that Western governments, most likely the USA, would be prepared to countenance the assassination of their own citizens to hide the truth. It was a dark thought indeed, but Bill felt that it was a possibility that he should not entirely dismiss. It would be better to be mentally alert, and vigilant about an attempt on his life, even if it meant allowing obvious paranoia to get the best of his usually balanced judgement. He was not in a mood to sound reassuring to Dr. Clarke.

"I think you should be aware that people connected with the exposure of this secret have died. Their deaths appear, on the surface at least, to be unconnected. But, personally, I would not rule out the possibility of foul play. If other people connected with this project have come close to whistle-blowing, then they might have befallen a similar fate before the secret was exposed. There's no way of knowing."

Dr. Clarke's mood swung back to scepticism. "That's preposterous. Western governments don't act like that! I think you're seeing things that aren't there, Mr. Bainbridge."

"I'll grant you that my own personal experiences recently have coloured my judgement on the matter." Bill briefly reflected on the fact that it was now 2a.m., which didn't help. The mind could play funny tricks on you in the middle of the night. "But, it's clear to me that a secret of this magnitude calls for a remarkable level of security."

"Which, by itself, would have cost an absolute fortune. How did they raise the money for this? It must be a trillion dollar project...." The astronomer's voice trailed off, and he looked back at the dark object on his computer screen. "It's just impossible."

"I agree. It looks on paper like utter madness, and that was our initial reaction to this story, too. But, here we are, and here *it* is." Bill pointed at the amorphous dark blob, outlining its shape with his index finger.

"I've read all about so-called 'black projects' hidden in defence budgets. The Department of Defence, or the Army, hide expenditures by recording massive overspends in their accounts for simple supplies. For instance, in their financial records they might be seen to buy dollar-packs of nails for $100 each, that kind of thing. Then they shovel the unaccounted-for money into their pet project. I seem to remember that that was how the Americans developed Stealth technology. It looks like they've used that same 'Stealth shielding' here, on a spacecraft."

"You don't raise enough funds to build something like this by saving a few bucks on nails, Mr. Bainbridge. This stealth space station, if that's what it is, would have sucked up half of America's defence budget."

Bill shrugged. "I don't have all the answers, Dr. Clarke. There are aspects to this story that defy belief, I agree. But if they did it with the A-bomb, then there's a precedent for American Government's ability to maintain absolute secrecy, at all costs. Maybe they've been diverting money from the war in Iraq, or siphoning off cash from Iraq's oil trade. I don't know."

Dr. Clarke went quiet for a moment, lost in his own thoughts. His right hand flicked the computer mouse about, playing with the dark shape on the screen.

"What did you say they call this thing again?"

"The documents that we have in our possession use the moniker 'Ezekiel One.' The NASA source that Marcus Everett quotes calls it 'Eee Zee 1.'"

"And he thinks it's an Ark? Does any of your leaked information support that idea?"

"No, we've got a list of people who may actually be on it, but that's about it."

"You think it's manned at the moment?" Dr. Clarke exclaimed, clearly shocked.

"My source at GCHQ indicated that the 'Final Launch' would take place on 30th November. I imagine that it's already fully operational, and ready. It's currently just sitting up there, spinning around the globe, just waiting. The question is, for what?"

"So, who are these astronauts that have been sent up to our Cosmic Ark?"

"I'm afraid I'm going to have to keep that to myself for the moment, Dr. Clarke. I think that information is just so dangerous that I don't want you to be even more exposed than you already are. Rest assured that the names and background of the men involved do *nothing* to shed any light on the mystery. In fact, they deepen the confusion surrounding this project considerably."

"Are they world leaders, or perhaps leading lights in their field of expertise?"

"I know what you're thinking. The answer is no, but I don't want to get into a game of 20 Questions about this. Trust me, no good can come of you knowing this information. If it becomes useful to share what I know about them, then I will."

Dr. Clarke shrugged, and folded his arms across his chest. "I assume you're now going to publish your story?"

"I'm not sure that we've got enough to go ahead with it yet. I think that we need a better image of this object, rather than just a silhouette across the night sky. Otherwise, it will just read like a UFO story. It might make for an interesting side item in the paper, but it won't exactly be making the front page. Is there any way we could get a better image of this thing?"

Dr. Clarke looked thoughtful for a moment. "Well, I can give you a disk containing all of the data and images that I've collated so far. I can also carry on searching through my data library to see if there are more of these 'sightings.' If we collect a series of pictures, we might be able to do some kind statistical analysis of the edges of the craft and come up with a sharper outline."

Dr. Clarke smiled to himself. "It might be a good project to give to my graduate students. But, I don't want any of us appearing in your newspaper article, Mr. Bainbridge. I'm happy to help you with your investigation, because there is clearly public interest at stake. There is also a scientific side to this. I'm sure a great many of us in the scientific community would like to know how they pulled this off, and what kind of technology they're using. I could also ask some of my colleagues to look into this. They might have contacts at NASA, or they might be able to get some better images from their own data sets. We might be able to shed a bit more light on this mystery by bringing more people into the loop, so to speak. But, it will take some time. Many of my colleagues work for other universities, which don't break up for Christmas as early as Oxford does, so they might not have the spare time I'm currently enjoying. I wouldn't expect anything too quickly."

"I'd be grateful for any further information you can come up with, Dr. Clarke. I really appreciate your time."

"Another possibility is to bring in some of the amateur astronomers." Dr. Clarke could see Bill looked sceptical. "Don't look like that. You'd be surprised. Some of the enthusiasts out there have some amazing observation equipment. They'd get onto this in a jiffy, and they might come up with some good photos."

"Whatever works, Dr. Clarke. My editor will no doubt worry that by opening this up, we run the risk of the story falling into the hands of some of our rivals. But, to be honest, there is no story here without the documents in our possession. Time is also running short. We really need to publish something before the 21st December."

"It's also getting late." Dr. Clarke started saving files onto a compact disk. "Where are you staying tonight?"

"At a hotel not too far from here. But I think I'll take a taxi tonight if it's all the same to you. Do you have a copy of the Yellow Pages here?"

The two men wound up their extended meeting, and Bill called a taxi. Dr. Clarke gave him the CD containing the data he had put together that evening, and locked the office up. They then set off down a stairwell towards the front entrance to wait for the taxi to arrive.

"Dr. Clarke, I really should warn you to be on your guard. I've got very good reason to believe that at least one security agency is involved in maintaining secrecy around this project. When we met last month, I was followed. I've also had an encounter with the same agent since then."

Bill thought it best not to elaborate on that. But Dr. Clarke seemed unfazed. He was lost in his own thoughts. They walked out of the front entrance into the bracing cold of a cloud-free December night. Frost had developed on the windscreens of the cars in the road. The city streets were quiet at that time of night. Bill looked up and down the street to see if anybody was about. He had not spotted the Tall Man during his excursion to Oxford, or, indeed, since the day of the bombing in London. But Bill had remained on his guard. Given the fact that the Tall Man knew of Dr. Clarke's involvement already, it seemed quite likely to Bill that the academic's office was already bugged, and that the content of their conversation that evening was already downloaded on Intelligence Agency computers somewhere, awaiting analysis, and possible action.

"I'm just an academic physicist, Mr. Bainbridge. Somehow, I don't think I'm important enough for that kind of attention. The data and images I've put together for you this evening are already largely in the public domain. It's just a case of knowing where to look.

"There are many other astronomers and physicists who could have accessed this information for you. Many of them have access to images taken by much better equipment than ours. So, it seems to me that I don't pose a significant risk to anyone."

"Even so, I think that if you have some good information for me it would be best to send it through the post, or to set up a face-to-face meeting again. I don't mind travelling out here to see you. Communicating over the Internet and by phone is not going to be secure."

"You're very paranoid, Mr. Bainbridge, if you don't mind me saying."

"Well, you know the old saying: 'Just because you're paranoid, it doesn't mean they're not out to get you!'" Bill attempted a wry smile. "I have good reason to be careful in my dealings with this case. I've had a crystal clear warning from a senior political figure in this country that this investigation is potentially hazardous. The government has expressed knowledge and interest in my investigation of 'Ezekiel One.' That's one of the reasons that I've been taking it so seriously, despite the very eccentric nature of the case. And bear in mind that I've also had something of a close shave with a terrorist act this week, which has brought home our mortality in a big way. I just think we need to be cautious."

"Fine! I'll do what you think is best, and phone you to arrange a meeting if I come up with anything particularly significant." At that moment, the taxi pulled up outside the Department of Physics. The men shook hands.

"Will you be heading back to London in the morning?"

"Yes, but I have someone else to catch up with first. Thanks again for all your help, Dr. Clarke. You've provided us with the evidence we need to take this story seriously, wherever it eventually leads us. Rest assured that we'll keep your name out of this. We take the confidentiality of our sources very seriously. I'll see you again soon, no doubt." Bill opened the door to the taxi and started getting in. The luminous clock on the car's dashboard showed that it was 2:30 a.m.

"Cheerio, Mr. Bainbridge. I'll see what I can come up with in the next couple of days. I'll be in touch." With that, Dr. Clarke shut the car door, and walked back into the Department of Physics building.

Astronomers were used to late nights, after all, Bill thought.

"Where to, mate?" the slightly countrified accent of the taxi driver broke the short silence. His radio control speaker crackled.

"Good question…" mused Bill quietly to himself.

CHAPTER TEN

They moved straight forward in whatever direction the spirit would go; they never swerved in their course.

Turl Street was resplendently golden in the morning sunshine. The low light of the bright morning sun reflected back and forth across the close, high walls of the street, setting off the warm colours of the Cotswold stone beautifully. Bill dodged several cyclists as he wandered up the street, past Tudor-style buildings, containing quaint shops set into their ground floors. It was a rustic scene, barely seconds away from the hustle and bustle of the Oxford commercial centre.

To his right loomed the exterior wall of Jesus College, the foot of which was decorated with bicycles. A towered structure dominated the centre of the tall wall, below which could be found the main entrance to the college. Several students were coming and going through the entrance, often in pairs, holding bags and books and chatting nonchalantly. He approached the small entrance to this grand old college, and then stopped to read the sign posted by the front gate.

It forbade casual visitors.

Walking into the small entrance hall, Bill admired the winter light streaming in from the inner Quad beyond, and the slightly mediaeval architecture of the old buildings which were set around the carefully manicured square. What a fabulous place to study in, he thought. The sense of history was pervasive.

The moment was broken abruptly by a polite but insistent 'Ahem!' from his immediate right.

Bill turned to see a grey-haired college porter looking directly at him in a questioning manner. "Do you have business at Jesus College, sir?"

"Yes, I'm trying to locate one of the undergraduates here. A young man called Colin Haddock."

"Are you a relative of his?"

"No, I'm a family friend." This was technically correct, Bill supposed, although the young man's mood towards him the previous evening had been anything but friendly. "I'm in Oxford for the day and was hoping to stop in and see him."

"And you know that his living quarters are in this building, sir?"

"This is Jesus College, isn't it?"

"Yes, but there are other accommodation blocks located elsewhere in the city, and the College owns other property which it provides for its students here and there too. What makes you think he's housed in the main college?"

Bill was starting to sense that the porter was a "Jobsworth" sort of character, despite his well-spoken manner. Any attempt to sidestep the Rules would likely be met by that interminable phrase "That's more than my job's worth!"

"I'm not sure which accommodation block he lives in, to be honest, but I do need to see him. Look, my name's Bill Bainbridge and I gave a lecture at the University last night. I was a guest of Dr. Clarke in the Physics Department. Colin came along to the lecture, and I wanted to catch up with him before I head back to London. Is there any way that you could contact him and tell him I'm here to see him?"

"Not really, sir. This isn't a hotel you know. We can't just let any members of the public wander in and out of here. We have the safety and security of our students to consider."

Bill tried not to let his irritation show. "I understand that. Is there any way I can get a message to him?"

"I'm the only porter on duty at the moment. Much of the university has broken up for the holidays, so we're a bit thin on the ground. Otherwise, I would have had a wander up to his room myself." The porter shrugged and smiled.

"So he *is* here, at the College?"

The porter gave him a quixotic smile. "Whoops," he exclaimed mildly. "Maybe I should see some identification, eh?"

Bill rummaged around in his jacket pocket and pulled out his National Union of Journalists press pass, complete with the tangled cord he used to occasionally hang it around his neck. He showed it to the porter.

"You seem familiar, sir. Do you work in television?"

Bill raised an eyebrow. "Not exactly, but I was on the news several days ago. I was caught up in that bombing in London."

The porter stepped back slightly and eyed him up and down. "You were that bloke who saved that girl, weren't you? Blimey, that was really incredible. I saw the pictures on the telly. It was like something out of a war movie."

"It's not something I'd like to go through again, I can assure you." Bill hoped that his current status as a national hero would provide him some leverage with the porter. He was to be disappointed.

"Well, as much as I admire what you did, I still can't let you just wander into the college looking for young Haddock. If you take a seat over there, by the pigeonholes, I'll keep an eye out for one of his mates. They might be able to go and get him for you."

Bill sighed and looked at his watch. He had two hours before his train left for London. He'd already lost several hours sleep that night, and had gotten up early to arrive at the College in time to meet up with Colin before embarking upon the journey home. He had not anticipated this antiquated system of intra-college communication. Resigned to a long wait, Bill took a seat as instructed. After about ten minutes a group of young lads wandered through the porter's lodge from the Quad. The porter called them over, and they chatted momentarily, looking over at Bill. Then one of them came over. He wore a long colourful scarf, and was growing a very unsuccessful beard.

"You're Mr. Bainbridge, yeah?"

"That's right. Are you one of Colin's friends?"

"Sort of. Look, if you want I can take you over to see him. But you'll have to be quick. I've got a lecture in ten minutes."

Bill stood up, and followed the lad back to the porter's reception desk, where he was provided with a visitor's pass, which took the form of a plain white sticker slapped untidily onto the lapel of his jacket. The group of mostly male students gathered around him made admiring comments about his recent London exploits in a blokey manner. Bill thanked them graciously, before following his guide out into, and then across, the inner quadrant.

"Do you know Colin well?" asked Bill as they strolled through the College grounds.

"Not really. I'm reading engineering, and he's a Classics student, or something like that. He hangs out with some really weird characters, to be honest. I've always found him easy to get on with, but I don't like the company he keeps. He's having breakfast with some of them in the Hall at the moment. I'm not even sure why they're all still at college: The 'Mickey Mouse Subjects' broke up last week. Right, here we are."

Their short tour of Jesus College came to a sudden end. They walked into the Hall, which was a large, oak panel-lined refectory dividing the two open Quads set within the tall walls of the college. Bright light was streaming diagonally through the large, airy room. Large, heavily framed portrait paintings hung from the oak panels, and the yellow, plastered walls above. One painting was of Queen Elizabeth I, which complimented the historic feel of the ancient hall. Long tables and benches were set out in an orderly fashion across the floor. They were sparsely populated by small groups of students, noisily chatting over breakfast.

Bill's guide pointed over to the other end of the hall, and promptly departed back into the First Quad.

Bill had never eaten at a college at Oxford before, and wondered what the food was like. It smelled pretty good. He smiled as he realised that old habits died hard. He couldn't eat out without sub-consciously reviewing the restaurant. He walked directly over towards Colin.

Colin sat with two other lads and a girl, all of whom looked to be in their late teens. They were immersed in deep conversation, and didn't notice his approach.

"Can I join you?"

Colin almost fell off his seat. "Mr. Bainbridge..." he stammered, "What are you doing here?"

"I've come to see you and have a chat, Colin."

"If it's about last night...Look, I'm sorry about that. I had a couple of drinks before going to your lecture, and I was bang out of order walking out like that."

Colin's friends looked bemused.

"Do you mind?" Bill gestured to the girl, who was sitting at the end of the bench, and she moved up to give him some room. He sat down next to her, and thanked her cordially. Bill sensed a slight atmosphere amongst the group. He had interrupted something, he surmised: They had appeared as thick as thieves as he had walked up.

"I'm not bothered about that, to be honest, Colin. What I'm interested in is why you think that the world is about to come to an end."

Colin looked around the small group, exchanging cagey glances with them.

"Who is this chap, Colin?" asked one of the lads. The questioner had a crisp, Home-Counties accent, and ruffled curly hair.

"This is Bill Bainbridge. He's the reporter from London I was telling you about, the one who was on the scene when Marcus was taken out. You know - the guy in the papers. Bill, I should introduce you to my friends."

Colin indicated the lad who had just spoken, "This is Ben, and this is Claire…" The girl sitting next to him smiled shrewdly. She had dark make-up and the clothes she wore were all black, "…and this is Julian." Julian's hair was short, his appearance casual. He looked at Bill with a furrowed brow.

The four students were all in their late teens. The three male students wore a subdued mixture of dark T-shirts and baggy jumpers, with blue jeans which had seen better days. Their haircuts were cheap, and unadventurous. More effort had gone into Claire's appearance, as was evident by her carefully-maintained Gothic look. Bill decided that, despite her heavy black make-up, she was quite pretty. Bill sensed that the group was evaluating him, perhaps weighing up whether he was trustworthy or not. He suspected that their social clique was unusually exclusive, even for college students. He decided it best to dive straight in with his questions.

"Last night, you seemed very certain that we face some kind of disaster in a couple of weeks. What makes you think that, Colin?"

"I knew it!" Colin was angry, but he contained his rage better in his own college than he had at the lecture the previous evening. "You haven't read that book at all, have you?"

"I've not had a lot of time in the last couple of days. But I've read some of it, and I've been following up some interesting leads. In some respects, Everett appears to have been correct." Bill decided to bring some bargaining chips to the table.

"Oh yes?" asked Claire, excitedly, "What have you found out?"

Bill was surprised that Colin's friends were even aware of what they were talking about. He hadn't remembered seeing them at the lecture the previous evening, and he thought it likely he would have remembered this Gothic looking student. But their interest in the conversation was bordering on intense. He was addressing the group, it seemed.

"There may be some truth to the idea that the Americans have been building some kind of secret platform in space. That's all I know. I don't know what it's for, or even if it's significant. I wanted to see if you had some kind of idea what the meaning of the Mayan date was. Marcus Everett seemed to link these two things together. Do you have any idea why?"

"Because of the Earth-changes, Bill. They've already started. The whole world is approaching meltdown!"

Colin spoke quickly, and passionately. The pitch and volume of his speech were steadily rising. The Hall became noticeably quieter as other students looked across. Many of them sniggered amongst themselves, sharing inside-jokes with their friends. After a few moments they resumed their meals, and conversations.

Colin's face was reddened, either with anger or embarrassment. He continued in an urgently whispered tone, "Look, everything's going pear-shaped. The environment is trashed, and a self-reinforcing cycle of destruction has begun. Our tampering with the balance of nature has triggered a global catastrophe."

"Why do you think it's going to take place in the next couple of weeks?"

"Because the people who have engineered the destruction of the world's resources have been collecting their profits for the last couple of years, and are all clearing off," said Julian, joining the fray. "This space project is just one of many. There are underground bases and an armada of ships, all set to whisk away the rich and powerful when the Earth-changes start."

"What do you think is going to happen?"

"A new Ice Age, that's what." Claire spoke, her tone that of someone absolutely committed to her belief. "Ice Ages happen suddenly. They don't just build up over decades or centuries, but cover the globe catastrophically. The climate change associated with pole-shifts occurs so fast that the world is overcome. There are floods, high winds, and destruction on a massive scale. Whole species are wiped off the face of the Earth. These events were described by the Maya people. And we're living during the End Times!"

"So you think that the Earth's poles are going to reverse in a couple of weeks' time. I see." Bill was disappointed that the theory wasn't a tad more original. The group picked up on his scepticism, and shifted in their seats defensively.

"If something like that isn't about to happen, then how do *you* explain EZ 1?" demanded Colin, maintaining the inappropriately-used English pronunciation of the acronym.

"I don't have all the answers, Colin. I'm still trying to make sense of it all. You all seem to have your minds pretty much made up. But where's the evidence to support your claims? The world seems to be ticking along pretty normally, from what I can see. I haven't seen any evidence of a mass exodus of the ruling classes. Chance would be a fine thing."

"Well, they're keeping things under wraps, to stop a panic. That's why they murdered Marcus!" Colin was quite agitated now.

"You don't have any proof of that, Colin. We don't even know who blew that bus up. And if *they* had wanted to kill Everett, they could have simply shot him. There was no need to kill all those innocent bystanders as well. What purpose would that have served?"

"The intelligence services don't work that way. They have to cover their tracks, make their assassinations look like they occurred naturally, or accidentally."

"Colin, if the intelligence services were that worried about the imminent end of the world, why would they be bothered to maintain such an elaborate smoke-screen?"

That infallible logic seemed to stop Colin in his tracks.

"Are you still writing for the Standard?" The sudden interjection came from Ben.

Bill nodded. His inquisitor continued, calmly. "What do you know about the '2012 Movement'?"

"I've never heard of it."

"But you've seen our stickers around, haven't you?"

Bill recalled the fiery globe with the lightning symbols that he had seen on Christine's car, as well as on the T-shirts of the people handing out flyers close to Marcus Everett's book-signing. He hadn't realised that the symbol belonged to an actual organisation: An organisation that this group appeared to be a caucus of.

"Yes, I've seen them about. Your girlfriend's got one on her car, Colin," Bill said. He then noticed that Ben looked across at Claire in a peculiar way, perhaps expecting a reaction to that observation, but the girl remained impassive. "I'm not sure that I've heard of the '2012 Movement,' though. Sounds like an orchestral piece of music."

None of the group laughed at Bill's light-hearted quip. They obviously took this whole thing very seriously indeed. Was he amongst the members of some kind of cult? Intense teenagers like these sometimes got sucked into ideological cults, Bill thought. Universities were often breeding grounds for fanatics. But usually these fanatical cults were religious in nature. The 2012 question was more of an alternative theme. Followers of a cult interested in Mayan prophecy would surely lack the complete certainty that comes with deep religious conviction.

"The '2012 Movement' is a growing organisation of researchers and truth-seekers around the world." Julian took up the story, "It holds conferences and publishes books delving into the Mayan mystery."

"Sounds nice. Keeps you kids off the streets anyhow," Bill had decided to be deliberately provocative in the hope that the group would let down their guard in their desire to promulgate their views. But Julian chose to ignore him.

"In the last year, as the day of The Return has approached, the atmosphere in the organisation has become more…radical."

"Sorry, but what do you mean by "The Return"? The return of what, exactly?"

Colin interrupted moodily "You really should have read that book before coming in here with all of your questions. You're playing with only half a deck of cards at the moment, Mr. Bainbridge. Unless you're holding an ace up your sleeve, perhaps?"

Bill was genuinely mystified as to what the group was talking about. His blank look must have seemed innocent enough, and Julian continued, triumphantly.

"The Return of Nibiru, Mr. Bainbridge. The solar system's missing planet."

The term "Nibiru" rang a distant bell in the journalist's mind. During his researches into the 2012 question, he had come across a great deal of speculation about a planetary body called Planet X. This object was unknown to present day astronomers, but was apparently spoken of in the ancient texts of Mesopotamian civilisations thousands of years ago.

Claire began to explain the 'Return of Nibiru' to Bill, while the three male students watched his reactions carefully. "Nibiru was a word from a very ancient language called Sumerian. It meant 'The Crossing' or 'The Ferry', and was supposedly the returning planet of the gods. Its appearance in the skies occurred just once every 3,600 years. No one seemed able to definitively say when the last date was that Nibiru had appeared."

It occurred to Bill, as the young woman spoke, that the story was ripe for filling in gaps in other mysteries, like the Mayan Long Count.

Bill was sure that most writers who had addressed the possible solutions to the meaning of the Mayan mystery had by now discounted the return of Nibiru. It had been shown, to most people's satisfaction anyway, that relatively straightforward observations of the heavens would have pinpointed the approaching planet years before its actual alleged arrival date. As the end of 2012 had approached, the chances of Nibiru turning up had evaporated. At this very late stage, it was now simply out of the question.

So why were these four presumably intelligent and well-educated students still advocating such an unlikely point of view? Bill interrupted Claire, sensing that her lecture would go on half the morning.

"Look, I just spent half of last night in the office of an astronomer who's an expert on the solar system. If your missing planet was on its way then don't you think he would have told me?"

"The '2012 Movement' doesn't think that Nibiru is about to appear amongst the planets, Mr. Bainbridge," answered Ben. "Our understanding of the history of Nibiru is that its interaction with the Sun causes a pole shift across the entire solar system. It will affect the Sun, and every planet orbiting the Sun, including the Earth. The Mayans were simply warning us that this event is now upon us."

"So, I suppose you think that the authorities know about the existence of Nibiru, and have covered it up? Perhaps you think that this explains why they have built their escape pod in space, where pole-shifts will be safely avoided?"

Claire took up the story once again, "When the Sun shifts, the change in its magnetic field will be an incredibly powerful event. It will bombard the inner planets with a massive dose of radiation. That's why they've built such a large space station. It's designed to counteract the effect of the cosmic rays."

Claire's description of the End of Everything was almost smug.

"Surely to have that kind of effect, the planet Nibiru would have to be absolutely colossal: Like another star, or something. A star in our backyard would have been spotted during the time of Galileo, for goodness sake!"

The group exchanged tired glances.

"You really should read the rest of Marcus' book, Mr. Bainbridge. You'll find the answers in there." Colin's insistence was becoming mantra-like. "Look, as enjoyable as this is, I'm going to have to head off before long: I've got to get back to Cheltenham this afternoon.

"You've asked us a lot of questions this morning, Mr. Bainbridge. I've got one question for you. Do you remember the second NASA document that Lyn had in her possession, the one that we sent you a few weeks ago?"

Bill nodded. Colin leaned forward, speaking in a hushed tone, "What did Lyn write at the bottom?"

"She wrote 'Final Launch: 30/11/2012.'"

Colin sat bolt upright, his face a mask of intense emotion. He spoke dramatically: "So, they've already gone up there? That means that all the preparations are now in place. There's no stopping the Exodus now..."

"My God! We're too late," exclaimed Ben.

"Too late for what?" Bill was tiring of the students' unwavering commitment to their paradigm.

"To stop it, of course!" Ben was unequivocal, "The '2012 Movement' is planning a series of demos up and down the country next weekend. We want to expose the government's complicity in this. We want to show how they're controlling the information about The Return. We want the world to realise how the Western governments are controlling the masses, and preventing them from taking the necessary steps to prepare themselves for what is to come."

Colin took up the verbal baton. "You want to be the hero the TV says you are? Then stick this story in your paper, Mr. Bainbridge. You might yet give people the chance to save themselves!"

Bill sat silently for a moment and looked around at the four students sitting with him. This interview had not gone the way he anticipated. He had been expecting to talk with Colin Haddock and hear a selection of New Age theories about a change of global consciousness, or something. Instead, he was coming face to face with a concentrated dose of student radicalism. If Ben was correct, this crucible of anti-establishment rhetoric could be multiplied many times across university campuses up and down the country. Bill wondered whether that really would prove to be the case. Was this 2012 Movement an organisation which reflected the real mood amongst the youth of Britain, or was its support critically undermined by that greatest of politics' foes - apathy?

Right now, he couldn't really imagine thousands of yelling demonstrators marching along the freezing winter streets of the nation's cities, in support of a *conspiracy theory*.

But that cynical view was tinged with a great doubt. Bill had evidence that at least part of that conspiracy theory was true. The American space agency had indeed been constructing a massive space station in high orbit, in complete secrecy. It was evidently the biggest and most expensive space programme ever undertaken, and its purpose was far from clear. That it was somehow tied in with the end of the Mayan cycle seemed highly probable to him, though. But, "Ezekiel One" also appeared to be linked in with astronaut training specifically geared up to withstand long periods of time in space. And yet, he couldn't believe that the purpose of this exercise was to allow a select few to escape the Earth as destruction loomed.

As he deliberated, Bill looked at the sunlight streaming through the windows of the ancient hall. The world was surely not about to end.

"I think our newspaper would be interested to feature your demo, when it takes place. That's assuming you manage to mobilise a significant number of people. But I don't think we'll be screaming "The End is Nigh!" from the rooftops. For that kind of statement, we will need to present an awful lot of watertight evidence. We're not in the business of panicking people."

The students peered at the journalist with a mixture of looks, expressing mild disgust, disbelief and contempt. Colin spoke for the group. "But you have the evidence already. You just told us that you know about the Space Ark's existence, and that rockets have been launched taking astronauts up to it. You've seen first hand the way Marcus Everett was killed as he spread the word about what's been going on. What more evidence do you need?"

Bill found himself playing the part of the Devil's Advocate. "It's still not enough. Both of those events could have more rational explanations. The Space Ark, as you call it, could simply be a NASA space station, which has been constructed with an entirely different mission in mind. It could be part of a Manned Mars programme, for instance."

"So why the secrecy?" Colin was in an irritable mood now.

"I don't know, but you know as well as I do that the funding needed for that sort of project must be phenomenal. Maybe it's the only way NASA could do the work; using money siphoned from other government departments. After all, it's been an election year in the States. Maybe the whole thing is too much of a political hot potato."

"That's rubbish. A president seeking re-election would have held up such a project as a positive act by his Administration. Anyway, he got re-elected, so why the secrecy now? Why not let the world know?"

"Maybe that's what's going on here. The leaks we've received. Perhaps that's the way the truth is supposed to come out. It may have nothing to do with your Mayan cycle at all. We may just be pawns in a larger game. I can think of other possible reasons, too. Dr. Clarke was telling me last night that there is some kind of Cold War going on in space at the moment. Each of the space powers is fighting a secret war with each other to keep their spy satellites and orbiting military hardware functioning up there."

"Seriously?" said Claire, who seemed quite intrigued.

"That's what he said. Apparently, the U.S. has deployed some killer satellites to remove some of the satellites of the other powers that they consider a threat. I've been wondering whether this 'Eee Zee One' is actually some kind of military platform used to deploy its killer satellites. It could be the next step in an escalation of this secret war."

This idea seemed to strike a chord with the group, and the animosity he had just experienced receded a little. Perhaps that was the right antidote to a conspiracy theory, thought Bill: another conspiracy theory. The group had picked up on the name "Eee Zee One" as well, and were exchanging banter about it.

Bill interrupted, sensing victory. "Well, that's why I need to be cautious. The government leaks we were in receipt of may have repercussions I haven't even considered yet. If our newspaper publishes information about this space station then that information could spark a major diplomatic incident, and might compromise American security. So I need to know exactly what we're dealing with here. Otherwise this story will explode in our faces."

"Well, the Yanks shouldn't be sticking that sort of hardware up there in the first place, should they? That's their lookout. If you have a big story like this, you should publish it. The public has the right to know what's going on above their heads!"

Colin was adamant, his appeal containing the conviction of youth. But Bill recognised the truth in what he said. The story needed to be exposed, come Hell or High Water - a possibility that the 2012 Movement appeared to think was imminent. But that didn't mean wrapping the story up in some kind of New Age conspiracy. Bill still didn't know how to pitch this story.

"I agree with you. But I need more time to establish what's really going on."

"But people also need to know that something big is going to happen in a couple of weeks. They need to have the chance to prepare. Even if it's just making sure they've got plenty of food and water, and to strengthen their homes against the wind and ice."

"People are easily panicked. If you put out a panic story like that, a lot of people could get hurt. It could turn out to be for nothing. Then you've got blood on your hands." Bill tried to appeal to the students' common sense.

"I work for a responsible newspaper. We need to think through what we put in print, and the repercussions for the wider public good. There needs to be a balance struck here between disclosure in the name of public interest, and the safety of that self-same public. That is not an easy job, believe me."

Ben said "Whatever!" rather brusquely. He stood up to leave, and Claire and Julian followed his lead.

Bill turned to Colin as his friends departed. The young man bade farewell to his friends as they left in the direction of the First Quad. The Hall was now almost empty of students. Suddenly alone, Colin seemed more relaxed.

"Where did you find that document, Colin?" asked Bill softly.

"It wasn't difficult to find, actually. Lyn had stuck it in with a bunch of other work-related documents in a sideboard. Christine went through the lot one day when her Dad was out. He'd have gone mad if he knew. He's struggling at the moment, to be honest."

"Was there anything else?"

"No, that was the lot. The other documents were payslips and security questionnaires. There wasn't anything else internal. No GCHQ stuff."

"Colin, I hope you don't mind me asking, but how did you get in with this crowd?"

"They're just friends. They're a lot more tuned into what's going on than the other students here. The other lot are all just here to get their degrees and get some big jobs working in the City. Most of them are asleep to what's really going on in the world."

"Look, be careful, alright? If what your group is claiming has even a single shred of truth to it, then you could all be putting yourselves in great danger. Try to keep out of harm's way."

Colin nodded and stood up. "I've got to go and get my stuff together. I stuck around to catch your lecture last night. But Christine's expecting to see me this afternoon. Look, I'm sorry about last night. I'm glad you dropped by this morning, and that we've had a chance to talk all this through."

The two shook hands. "I'm sure we'll bump into each other again. Send Christine my best, and take care of her. Things can't be easy right now."

Colin walked through the door to the second quad, and Bill headed back to the porter's lodge to sign out. He had some time left before returning to the train station. A walk around the town centre might help to clear his head, he thought. He was feeling the weight of the world on his shoulders, and desperately needed a good night's sleep. But time appeared to be running out. Sleep would have to wait.

CHAPTER ELEVEN

The appearance of the creatures was as if fire from burning coals or torches were darting to and fro among them; the fire was radiant, and out of the fire came lightning.

Bill looked up from his keyboard, and across the street from his first floor window. It wasn't the best view from the office, but at least it wasn't just a brick wall on the other side of the glass.

The streets were wet with recent rain, and a cold wind pressed up against the windowpane every so often. It was Tuesday afternoon, and London was as busy as usual. The streets were already lit, and colourful with Christmas lights. Christmas was just two weeks away, and there was the inevitable succession of shopping, office parties and family plans to attend to. He and Helen had spent the weekend catching up after an insanely busy week. Following his return from Oxford, Bill had taken a couple of days off work, to rest his arm.

The pressure of Helen's teaching job had prevented the two of them from discussing all that had gone on. It was perhaps a good thing for Helen to throw herself into her job, Bill thought. But he was beginning to feel more and more drained as the week had gone on. He needed to stop, take stock and rest.

Doug had shown considerable understanding about the need for some sick leave, which surprised Bill. But then, he had gone along with the editor's plans, and had made the required tour of TV studios in those first few days after the bomb blast. Memories faded fast, however, and the interest in his heroic actions had soon waned.

Bill did not have a substantive story to submit yet. He had presented the material he had gathered about Ezekiel One to Doug the afternoon of his return from Oxford. They both agreed that more evidence was required before the paper could move towards publishing the story. Bill hoped that Dr. Clarke might come up with something. Failing that, the student rallies planned for the following weekend might bring forth a good opportunity to air some of the evidence for the first time. That was if the demos came to anything at all, which Bill sincerely doubted.

Doug had also set up a photo-shoot for Bill with Anne Potter-Smith the week after, as insurance against other complete dead-ends in the investigation. But that left just days before 21st December. After that crucial date, the story would be a non-starter, rather like the Y2K Prophecy of Doom after Millennium night had passed. Ideally, the story needed to be published around 19th December, when interest in the completion of the Mayan Long Count was at its greatest amongst the general population.

Lacking words and direction in his writing, Bill's eyes wandered out of his window. In the street below his office he saw a traffic warden slowly trundle along the pavement. She checked the parking tickets and permits displayed inside the windscreens of the tightly parked cars along the street. She stopped in front of a black BMW and began to talk with the person who was sitting in the passenger seat. Bill couldn't see the passenger, but could just make out the driver.

The occupants of the car were in an ideal spot to view the main entrance of the newspaper offices.

The traffic warden appeared to have been presented with a card, or permit of some description by the passenger, and held it up to study it more carefully. Bill could tell from her reaction that it was a form of identification that she was unfamiliar with. She checked it over with a great deal of scrutiny.

At that moment, the telephone on Bill's desk rang.

"Hello, this is the Daily Standard, Bill Bainbridge speaking, can I help?"

As Bill issued his customary telephone greeting, he saw the driver in the car put his hand up to his left ear, and gesticulated to his passenger to be quiet with his right. The traffic warden and the passenger now seemed to be having quite an argument, and the driver shifted in his seat in an agitated manner.

"Mr. Bainbridge, this is James Clarke." The astronomer's voice was thin and crackly, and the sound of the reception on the line indicated that he was using a mobile phone. "Look, I can't speak for long. I'm at a conference at Imperial College. I have some material you will definitely find interesting. Is there any chance we can meet up this lunchtime?"

"Sounds good to me, James. Imperial College is just down the road from my office. I can hop on a bus and meet you outside the main entrance if you like."

"Tell you what, how about meeting me outside the front of the Albert Hall, facing Hyde Park? At 1pm?"

"Okay. I'll see you then."

"Good! Cheerio, Bill. I think you'll like what I've come up with." The academic sounded chirpy. He then hung up the phone.

Bill watched the driver as he took his hand down from his left ear, and then started to write something down on a small pad of paper.

The passenger was, by this time out of the car, standing on the pavement, remonstrating with the traffic warden who had begun to write out a ticket. Despite the verbal barrage, she calmly completed the parking ticket and ceremoniously handed it to the red-faced man.

Bill looked at the man carefully, soaking in the detail of his appearance, and that of his still seated colleague. He had a strong suspicion that he would see the two of them again later that day. The car's engine sprang into life. The red-faced man took the ticket, and, swearing loudly, got back into the car, which promptly pulled out into the dense traffic. Several horns sounded in irritation, and the car screeched off.

So much for subtle surveillance techniques, thought Bill. At least this time he would be better prepared.

+

A cold wind swept across Hyde Park. Bill looked across the oasis of greenery, and watched as several Londoners jogged along, walked their dogs or hurried about their business. Every so often, a squally series of showers caught on the breeze. Dodging puddles, Bill walked briskly towards the entrance to the Albert Hall. He could already see a lone figure by the main doors, taking shelter below a black umbrella in front of the grand Victorian edifice.

Bill had been reading up on surveillance techniques recently. He was now armed with an all-new panorama of paranoia. Either of them could be secretly bugged already. If not, even a whispered conversation could be eavesdropped upon by correctly-focussed scanning equipment in the hands of professional spooks. Their words could be lip-read, their expressions photographed, their non-verbal communication imaged and analysed.

Where he had once created a (probably useless) cipher for use in coded transmissions between himself and his GCHQ contact, Dr. Clarke was blissfully unaware of the potential danger he was in. Even if he was made aware, he would probably remain nonchalant about the whole situation. The idealistic mind tended to gloss over the more basic human instincts that drove military men.

Sure enough, as Dr. Clarke recognised the approaching journalist, he waved and loudly hailed Bill by name. Bill did not reply, but instead pulled out several white cards from his pocket. As he reached Dr. Clarke, he presented the first one. The astronomer looked at him quizzically, but seeing the firm expression on the hack's face, read the card quickly.

"Don't look around! I am being followed. There are two men in a black BMW who are watching my movements. They know about this meeting."

Dr. Clarke raised his eyes to the sky and began to speak. Bill cut him off with a sharp gesture, and presented him with a second card.

"Please follow my instructions. I have arranged a meeting place that will prevent us from being overheard. They will not be able to see us there, either, so you can pass over any disks or photos at that point. Please follow me."

The astronomer looked Bill in the eye. After a moment, he nodded, and indicated that Bill should lead the way. Bill led Dr Clarke along the wet streets, past Imperial College, and towards the Science Museum. He had not seen the black BMW, or its irritable occupants, but he was working on the assumption that they could see, and hear, him.

The two men walked briskly into the entrance of the Science Museum. Dr. Clarke let down his umbrella and shook it vigorously. While he did so, Bill walked up to the nearest admissions desk.

The government had decided to allow the museums in London to charge admission fees in 2012, which was a departure from their previous policy of free admissions. They had anticipated a large number of tourists in the summer, as part of the Olympics celebrations in the city. But that was back in the summer, when the capital's tourist attractions had been heaving with people. Now it was mid-December. There was no queue, and the admissions cashier looked dully at him.

"Hi. A colleague of mine pre-ordered some tickets this morning using her credit card. I'd like to pick them up please."

"Have you got the card with you, sir?"

"No, but I have the numbers of the card and the other particulars with me." Bill handed another white card over, this time to the cashier. After several seconds of activity with his computer touch-screen display, the cashier printed off four tickets and handed them over with a receipt.

During this time, Bill's eye had been roving around the entrance hall. Through the entrance appeared the BMW passenger. He made no eye contact with Bill, who quickly averted his gaze. Hopefully, not too quickly, thought Bill. The man sidetracked towards the stairs leading up to the toilets.

Bill thanked the cashier and indicated to Dr. Clarke to follow him into the museum. Their admission tickets were duly collected by another bored member of staff. The two men made their way to a long escalator that ascended into a large, beautifully lit display of the Cosmos.

"I've not been in here before," admitted Dr. Clarke somewhat sheepishly. "It's rather good, isn't it?"

"You must have come here when you were a kid, surely?" Bill was astonished. His companion was, after all, a science PhD.

The astronomer shook his head. "No, my parents would have preferred me to have become a doctor. But I always had a fascination for the stars."

As the escalator ascended, Bill looked out at the massive planets displayed in mid-air around them. He wondered where that damn rocket was actually supposed to be going. That was one of several remaining mysteries left unresolved by his discussions about Ezekiel One. The passenger cargo of the space station, which the astronomer next to him had confirmed as a reality, was trained to withstand a very long distance flight. But to where?

None of the planets was a natural contender for a space colony. Not even Mars, the surface of which would make Siberia in the depths of winter seem hospitable. The Moon was too close, Venus too hot. Bill stared at the regal sight of massive Jupiter. A couple of its major moons were like frozen billiard balls. Below their surfaces were thought to be great oceans, perhaps containing a myriad of life-forms. But would such a water-world on a Galilean Moon make a good environment for a human colony? Bill doubted it.

Beyond Jupiter, things just got colder and colder. Saturn's moon Titan at least had an atmosphere. Which would be fine, if you wanted to live on the cosmic equivalent of a garage forecourt. The freezing-cold atmosphere on Titan consisted of a mixture of hydrocarbons more reminiscent of petroleum than Earth's breathable air.

It seemed as though frigid Mars was the only possible contender. Maybe NASA planned to somehow convert the planet's environment to one more suitable for human life. After all, if they could put something like Ezekiel One together, then perhaps space technology was much further advanced than generally given credit for. Humans had succeeded in converting the Earth's biosphere during the few hundred years since the Industrial Revolution: A process which was accelerating, if advocates of Global Warming were to be believed. Perhaps humans, in their wisdom, were about to export those same environment-altering skills to Mars. Global warming would do that frozen, barren rock no harm at all!

The escalator brought the two men to the top, and they made their way through the upper floor of the science museum. Surreptitiously, Bill kept watch for the BMW occupants. He looked down at his watch, and guided the astronomer through the halls of science swiftly.

Dr. Clarke had thankfully avoided discussing the matter of their meeting, but felt freer to expand the journalist's knowledge of the many exhibits they passed. He had fallen into what must have been a familiar lecturing mode of thought; his audience of one a captive in this science heartland. Bill let the many insights wash over him. He focussed only on his wrist-watch, and on their movements in and out of the various halls. Timing their arrival to perfection, Bill led Dr. Clarke up to a large booth. The desk in the booth backed onto a large television display, showing a grainy image of an astronaut vaulting around the lunar surface.

Bill presented his two remaining tickets to one of the attendants on duty. "Thank you, sir. The show is about to start. You'll need these glasses. Please come this way."

She presented two pairs of dark glasses, and led the men through a set of doors into a small lift foyer. They took the lift and ascended to another atrium. Dr. Clarke gave Bill a puzzled look, but said nothing.

The attendant showed the men into a large, darkened theatre. The seats were arranged like a lecture theatre, and reclined back. The walls and ceiling overhead gave the impression of a planetarium. The room was far from full; scattered groups of people were settling down to watch the show. Bill led Dr. Clarke through rows of seats to an uninhabited spot far from the entrance. They took their seats.

Music began to issue loudly from surround speakers, ushering in the "Age of Spaceflight."

"We can talk more freely now," said Bill.

"You're mad." The astronomer was phlegmatic.

"Maybe I am, Professor. But I *am* being followed, I can assure you of that! We may not have a lot of time. What do you have for me?"

The 3-D cinema experience began, brightly and loudly. Neither Bill nor Dr. Clarke donned their glasses, which created a disorientating experience when they looked up at the screen. Dr. Clarke pulled out a computer disk and gave it to Bill. He spoke quickly and excitedly, in the fashion of a young student who had cracked a difficult conundrum.

"I've discussed our little discovery with several colleagues at universities in Britain and abroad. Between us we've come up with some fairly good images of EZ 1. I can confirm that it is very sizable indeed. Our mean values for its length are approaching a kilometre. One end of the craft seems bulkier than the other. The whole thing is huge. It has more the shape of a whale than a traditional rocket. Strangely, there don't appear to be any solar arrays attached to the craft. So we're not sure what its internal power source is, but we expect it's powered by nuclear energy."

"You mean it has a nuclear reactor on board?" Bill was shocked.

"It's only speculation, but to power a craft that size would require a great deal of energy. Nuclear power would be the obvious answer. That would contravene several major conventions on the use of outer space."

"Hmmm, maybe that's one of the reasons they're keeping a lid on this thing."

There was a sudden disturbance at the entrance to the theatre. Light streamed through the now opened door, and loud voices could be heard emanating from the atrium beyond. Two men strode into the almost pitch-black theatre. Their silhouettes froze in place momentarily in the doorway, before an attendant came up behind them and shut the door. The theatre returned to its darkened state.

"That's them, I'm afraid. Have you got anything else, Dr. Clarke?" Bill whispered hurriedly in the academic's ear, at a pitch just loud enough for him to hear over the noise of the music, and commentary of the 3-D movie.

House-sized astronauts were cavorting across the curved walls of the planetarium.

"One of my American colleagues is involved in a satellite project which monitors the Sun's activity. The satellite is in orbit around the Earth and takes photos of the Sun, watching its corona, that sort of thing. She and I did some calculations, based on the orbits of EZ 1 and her satellite, and worked out the point where your space station occulted the Sun."

"What do mean by occulted the Sun?"

"Rather like your friends stood in that doorway just then. Their shapes were silhouetted by the light coming in from behind them, into the dark room. If EZ 1 happened to cross the line between the monitoring satellite and the Sun, then its silhouette would show up on an image taken at that moment."

"I see. Did you have any luck?"

"Indeed we did, Mr. Bainbridge. In fact, we were lucky not once, but twice." Dr. Clarke pulled out some printed cards from his coat pocket. In the glaring white light of the Moon Landing movie, Bill carefully scrutinised the cards. They depicted circular images, with a central dark circle. Bill pointed at it.

"What's that?"

"That's the camera's automatic blotting of the bright light coming from the centre of the Sun. Look to the top right corner." Bill saw another dark blot against the bright, ultrasound-like background. The outline of the shape was clear and distinctive. It was the elongated, smooth shape of a spaceship.

"Wow," Bill mumbled under his breath. He looked at the second image, which showed the same craft from a different angle.

"We've been able to take the two shapes and use a computer model to work out what this object looks like at various angles: To build up an overall picture of its shape in three dimensions, as it were."

Bill turned to the third card, which showed single line diagrammatic representations of the spacecraft at different angles. It was a beautiful design; sleek and naturally proportioned throughout. A section on the back appeared to be an array of thrusters, like a traditional rocket. The craft was evidently designed to go somewhere. Its elegant design almost seemed to have been created to impress, and was distinctly different to the sort of rambling space station traditionally placed in orbit by NASA or the Russians.

"It's amazing, like something out of a science fiction film," offered Bill, slightly in awe of what they had discovered.

"Yes. We're of the opinion that this spacecraft is not only designed to travel somewhere, but is possibly made in such a way that it could enter the atmosphere of a planet and actually land."

"Seriously?"

"Well, this aerodynamic form is not required in the vacuum of space, because there's no air resistance. But it would be very useful indeed if re-entering an atmosphere. However, the size of this craft is *so* enormous that it couldn't possibly get off the ground again! NASA has built this structure in orbit for a reason, Bill. It is simply too large to blast off from the surface of the Earth. The thrust required to allow it to escape the gravitational pull of the Earth's gravity would require a remarkable quantity of fuel. Of course, it's *possible* that this spaceship is carrying such a payload, but I don't think it's very likely. If the spaceship landed on a small planetoid or moon, then it might be able to get off it again, but not a planet the size of, say, Mars. If EZ 1 landed on Mars, I think it would be a one-way trip."

"So this really is an Ark, then?"

"I don't know. It could be what a science fiction buff might call a 'mother ship.' It might contain a smaller spaceship that would explore a planet and return to it as it sits in orbit above the planet. Or it might make a landing itself, and become a permanent colony on the surface of the planet. The size and design of the thing suggest that the options are being left open. Almost like the designers aren't quite sure what the astronauts will discover when they arrive at their destination. It's certainly an odd way to proceed, anyway. And this flexibility of purpose, which has been built into the design, would have made the whole project exceedingly expensive."

"How many of your colleagues know about this, James?"

"About a dozen, but I wouldn't be at all surprised if rumours start to spread quickly throughout the astronomical community. It's quite an interesting little mystery. Whether any of them go to the press, I'm not sure, but if they do, it's likely to be to some of the more specialist magazines in the field. I'm not sure that my colleagues would want to be publicly associated with the discovery of this object. It's too much like a UFO, to be honest."

"So the story's already out. Well, I suppose it was inevitable. We'd better make our move soon."

"Oh, Mr. Bainbridge, I do hope you're not including me personally when you say that! I'm afraid I'd rather not have my name associated with this spacecraft, either. There are too many questions still unanswered, and I have a professional reputation to maintain. I'd like answers, of course, but only for my own sense of curiosity."

"I understand. Actually, I was thinking more about the newspaper, but I take your point. Tell me, where do you think this object might be heading?"

"That's what I wanted to ask you, Bill!" The astronomer laughed gently, "You seem to have more information about that aspect of things than you're letting on. Perhaps you might find this a useful juncture to reveal the identity of the spacecraft's passengers? It might help to shed light on that particular question."

"You won't believe me if I told you."

"We've gotten this far. I think you'll find I'm more open-minded than you give me credit for."

Bill deliberated or a moment. He was acutely aware that somewhere in the room were agents who were attempting to eavesdrop on their conversation. The movie had perhaps another ten minutes to run, and it seemed likely to Bill that he would not get another chance as good as this to have a frank discussion with Dr. Clarke without them being overheard.

He mulled things over in his head. On the plus side, he was now much further along as a result of the astronomer's involvement. On the negative side, that involvement had allowed news of the existence of Ezekiel One to spread among various scientists.

If the Daily Standard was going to publish, now was surely the time.

"Okay. There appears to be some kind of religious connection here. EZ 1 stands for Ezekiel One, a verse in the Old Testament. I think we've already talked about that, haven't we?" The astronomer nodded.

"Well, our information about some of the astronauts follows a similar theme. Twelve of them are drawn from the priesthoods of several Christian organisations. Some are Catholics, some Evangelicals, some more moderately protestant. These twelve men have disappeared from view over the last year or so. They've been sent off to private seminaries, that kind of thing. They are all highly educated men. Each of them is under thirty years of age. Documents we have in our possession prove that NASA has been preparing them for a long distance voyage in space. The question in our minds is, 'Why?'"

The astronomer mused over these revelations for about twenty seconds before responding. Bill watched the befuddled screen, his own thoughts racing.

"I hate to say this, but I have absolutely no idea what the connection might be, either. Unless this Space Ark is starting up some kind of religious colony...There's enough room on this spaceship to carry a lot more than twelve people, after all. Perhaps the President of the United States wants our species to make a new start somewhere else, under some kind of orthodox religious guidance? The twelve priests might just be the religious contingent of a much larger group, sourced from many walks of life..."

The astronomer's voice trailed off. He looked Bill in the eye, briefly, and then continued on with his train of thought. "That would make Mars a realistic destination I suppose. If they landed this vehicle on the planet's surface, it would provide a ready-made bio-sphere. No need to construct domes, or anything like that. But, I have to say, this is totally out of keeping with the normal direction NASA takes. It is, fundamentally, a scientific organisation. Such a move towards religious orthodoxy in the space program would be anathema to those running the organisation."

Bill smiled to himself. Dr. Clarke's academic verbosity was a world away from the tabloid depiction of this story that was crystallizing in his own mind. The Americans had a religious dimension to their public life that was absent in the UK and indeed, much of Western Europe. The founding fathers of the early American colonies had been devoted religious men, many of whose families had escaped religious persecution and bigotry in Europe. Was this some kind of 21st Century equivalent, where new colonies were established on Mars and dedicated to righteous living and proper Christian observance? The founders of these new colonies would be leaving behind the corruption of modern life, after all.

It did not seem an unrealistic ideal from the point of view of, say, a right wing American evangelical, particularly if the establishment of Martian colonies was in response to a perceived threat to life on Earth, or some kind of religious-minded apocalypse, like the "Rapture".

But such a venture would surely never pass the scrutiny of the secular public institutions. The objections of the scientific community, including NASA, would pale into insignificance when seen in the context of general public opinion. Such a radical expedition would need a veil of secrecy for it to succeed, for certain, which was exactly what EZ 1 had, in spades.

To Bill's mind, this story was becoming increasingly explosive. This was no longer just about a secret government project to build a fabulously expensive space station. It was now a story which potentially raised questions about the religious disposition of the politicians at the top of government, and how their religious vision shaped the future of Humanity's survival.

Moreover, the story might, just *might*, presage the Apocalypse!

The movie about the Apollo astronauts was coming to an end, in a blaze of stirring music and patriotic imagery. The sparsely populated theatre began to stir as the film-goers collected their belongings together.

"Thank you very much for your thoughts, Dr. Clarke, and for these images. I think we're likely to publish an article in the next couple of days based on this evidence. We'll keep our sources confidential, of course."

"I do hope so. If you want to keep this as an exclusive, it might be best to move quickly. A number of the people I spoke with are now aware that you're working on a story to do with this."

In the continuing darkness of the auditorium, Dr. Clarke could not see the look of disdain that passed across the journalist's face. But he must have realised that this would not be greeted as good news. "It was only fair that I put my colleagues in the picture as to why I was seeking information on this subject. After all, their reputations are at stake as well."

"Okay, well, I suppose that was inevitable. Look, we had better stop our discussion about this now, before the music finishes. I don't know who these blokes are who are following me, but they're in here somewhere. I'll walk you back up to the college."

The two men rose, and left the theatre, following the orderly, shuffling crowd. Bill quickly spotted the agents, who had, fortunately, been sitting in a different section of the auditorium. Bill's efforts to retain secrecy might mean nothing at all though, because if the agency who was spying on him was also monitoring Dr. Clarke, then the cat was well and truly out of the bag anyway.

The journalist reassured himself that these men had not behaved aggressively, or even threateningly, despite that possibility. They would also not necessarily be aware that Bill was now in possession of the evidence he had sought. The images that he carried in his pocket were dynamite. If he was in danger, then the trigger point for action against him would surely be the disclosure of those images.

In fact, all hell could break loose.

Dr. Clarke was clearly not a superstitious man, and had seemed quite unaware of what the true implication of this story might be. To Bill, it appeared as though the Americans were preparing for the imminent end of the world. Bill felt a cold chill run down his spine. His pace quickened as they emerged from the auditorium, and strode into the artificial light of the museum of science.

It was time to see Doug, and get the show on the road. If the Apocalypse was coming, there were over six billion people to warn.

CHAPTER TWELVE

As I looked at the living creatures, I saw wheels on the ground, one beside each of the four.

A low-flying helicopter swept across the sky above the tumultuous crowd. The placards and banners were raised into the air in a common salute of rebellion. Hyde Park was teeming with thousands upon thousands of demonstrators, the multitudes assembling together on a damp Saturday afternoon. Dark clouds hung low in the sky, providing a gothic backdrop. The procession converged upon a hastily erected stand in the centre of the park, where loud music was letting rip across the normally placid waters of the Serpentine.

Bill followed the stragglers to the periphery of the chanting throng. It was his second occasion to visit Hyde Park that week. Just a couple of days ago, he had been scurrying through the park to meet with Dr. Clarke. Since that first visit, his disclosure of the existence of Ezekiel One had reaped a media whirlwind.

A man with a bull-horn was working the crowd: "The Truth! The Truth!! TELL US THE TRUTH!!!"

Angry fists were punching the air all around, as the people joined together in a chorus of anger. Quite a few of the placards bore posters showing the face of Marcus Everett, with the word "Murdered" scrawled below the photos in red paint. Banners printed with the now familiar disk and lightning logo appeared alongside more specific warnings of doom. Some of the placards read "One Week 'Til We All Die". Others echoed apocalyptic strains from the Bible.

Towards the south-east corner of Hyde Park, Bill could see a long line of police assembling on horseback, in full riot gear. The low midwinter sun broke through the clouds, shedding golden light through the heavy clouds. Like an old landscape in oils, the light was ominous, and atmospheric. There was the potential for ugliness, certainly, and some of the activists seemed hell-bent on stirring it up.

When Bill had first heard about the plans for mass student demonstrations, he had imagined a bedraggled crew of New Age hippies mixed in with the usual anti-social suspects. That this event was gaining such remarkable momentum was in no small part down to his hard-hitting articles.

He looked across the muddy battlefield-to-be with concern. He did not wish to have the casualties of this showdown between the students and the police on his conscience. But, the matter was well beyond his control. His presence was as an observer, not participant. He wasn't even recognised by the members of the mob around him, which was probably an advantage. The beauty of writing for a newspaper was that your face was not broadcast. In fact, his name had not become associated with the story either.

The revelations that had become public during the middle part of that week were associated squarely with the newspaper itself. Then, like summer lightning spreading across humid skies, the revelation of the existence of Ezekiel One had become a global phenomenon. His major contribution to the breaking of the story had taken place in the relative media shadows of a newspaper feature, which suited Bill.

He thought it ironic, though. After all, two weeks before, he had been feted by the media and public for his actions at the Oxford Street bombing. The implications of this story were far more significant, and Bill should have once again been projected into the public eye. However, more prominent media celebrities had grabbed the story and had run with it, stealing the inevitable limelight through the medium of television.

Perhaps this was for the best.

Bill thought back to his crucial meeting with Dr. Clarke. The astronomer's balanced and careful analysis of the nature of the Ezekiel One object could now be seen in stark relief, compared with the shrill cries of the youthful mob. Bill was not naïve. He had recognised the danger of popular sentiment overwhelming reasoned debate about the existence of this secret spacecraft. But the cover-up had been massive, and the fear of an Apocalyptic end to the year 2012 was growing, daily, in the public mind.

Who could possibly deny that these two situations might be intertwined?

As the crowds coalesced around him, Bill thought back to his meeting with Doug that week, and the rapidly arranged meeting with the senior staff of the newspaper. As he had anticipated, the chief editor of the Daily Standard had decided to publish the story quickly. The images of the massive spacecraft, complete with a confirmable orbital trajectory, had proved sufficient grounds to place the story into print, despite the conspiracy theory undertones.

The Standard revealed that it had obtained leaked NASA documents, but held back on their precise content. It had published the images, but kept their provenance secret, by censoring out the data on the images that would pinpoint their sources. Using Dr. Clarke's anonymous analysis of the shape of the craft, the front-page article had revealed that NASA planned for Ezekiel One to leave Earth's orbit, and travel a great distance through outer space. The newspaper speculated that the Ezekiel One rocket would set up a human colony on another planet, ensuring the survival of the human race if disaster was to befall the Earth.

The only aspect of the story which had been left out was the list of astronauts, and the religious connotations involved with their disclosure. The editor had decided that this aspect of the story was simply too bizarre to include in the initial copy, and would diminish its impact. Instead, the Standard would hold this particular ace up its sleeve in case the paper itself was subject to a backlash from the Authorities.

Within twenty-four hours, amateur astronomers had confirmed that EZ 1 existed, and was indeed a big dark spot, but no one had yet been able to produce contemporary images as good as the ones taken when Ezekiel One had occulted the Sun. This lack of direct evidence had bolstered NASA's position. Its stance, in the face of a bombardment of media scrutiny, was total denial. It maintained that EZ 1 was simply a surveillance satellite, and that the images had been doctored to make it appear to be something it wasn't.

NASA, echoed later by the American President, proclaimed the whole story a ridiculous hoax. Official images of EZ 1 were widely circulated, and the sceptics went to work. They demanded that the scientists who had provided the Ezekiel One data reveal themselves. They demanded that the Daily Standard provide information about its sources.

The newspaper, naturally, refused to do so.

The hope on NASA's part, that its claim of fraud would stick, proved elusive. The story had captured the public imagination on both sides of the Atlantic. With the Mayan long count coming to an end in just one week's time, the idea of a kilometre-long escape pod - financed by the world elite - made sense to many. The story had raised the spectre of looming planetary disaster in the public mind, and talk of prophecy and doom had taken on the character of an epidemic. Conspiracy theory was now rife throughout the Western world.

This volatile mixture of secrecy, and End-of-the-Age angst, had brought forth a small army of debunkers. Technically-inclined sceptics had taken to the airwaves picking holes in the scientific evidence supplied by the Daily Standard. But there was a far more ferocious contingent of armchair commentators who simply opted to ridicule the entire story.

Despite the publication of the solar satellite images of Ezekiel One, and despite the on-going reports of amateur astronomers pin-pointing the dark mass of the spacecraft in orbit, the negativists simply proclaimed the whole story a fabricated monstrosity. Without public scrutiny of the scientists who had come up with the data, they argued, there was no way the story could be taken at face value.

The polarisation of the debate surrounding Ezekiel One was about to be made much worse, as Bill was experiencing firsthand. This particular demonstration had been planned well in advance, as he had discovered when he had spoken with the students he had met in Oxford. He had even managed to get an article into the Standard about it after their meeting. But where the event had been destined to be something of a flop, based as it was on the eccentric ideas of a clique of doomsday authors, the revelations about NASA's secret construction of a Space Ark had propelled the intended march into the public limelight. It had quickly become a focus for anti-government sentiment.

Bill worked his way around the back of the amassing crowd in Hyde Park. He had initially walked over to the site of the demonstration with several photographers. They had since disappeared off to various parts of the park to capture exclusive images. Bill spotted photographers from other newspapers circling the crowd, as well as several television crews.

One TV reporter was interviewing a selection of random demonstrators, many of them wearing the distinctive 2012 T-shirts, worn over fleeces and jumpers. As media attention focussed on segments of the crowd, the excitement grew.

Bill felt a hand lightly touch his arm.

"We meet again, Mr. Bainbridge."

Bill looked around and found himself facing Claire, one of the 2012 students whom he had met at Jesus College, Oxford. She was immediately recognisable by her black hair and gothic eye make-up. Her ears and nose were pierced several times, and her clothes were a dishevelled series of thin layers, mostly black in colour. Claire wore a stout pair of army boots, with purple laces. There was no sign of her friends. She smiled at him, warmly.

"Oh, hello. It's Claire, isn't it?" He offered his hand, perhaps a bit too formally given the circumstances of their meeting. But she smiled again, and instead gave him a light hug.

"Yes, that's right. I wasn't expecting to meet you here, at our little gathering. I guess you're covering it for your paper?"

Bill nodded, and then found himself having to shout his reply over a blast of vitriol emanating from a loudspeaker close by. "I can't help but feel a little responsible for all this, Claire! There are a lot of very angry people here."

"Of course there are. It's a demo!"

"Yes, but aren't all you 2012 people supposed to be into free love, and stuff like that? The mood here is downright ugly."

"The mood's angry because there's good reason to be angry. The world's in a mess. We've used up all the resources, we're poisoning the land and sea, and now, when it's too late to put things right, the people at the top are all going to piss off and leave us to face the consequences."

"You still think that there's going to be some kind of ecological disaster next week?"

"Absolutely. How else can you explain this spaceship of yours, Mr. Bainbridge? It's an escape pod. A life-raft. They've been preparing for decades. They've been collecting seeds and DNA specimens, and storing them underground in Norway for years. NASA has been secretly building this huge spacecraft using untold billions of dollars in black budgets. On the Eve of Destruction the rich elite will get into their rockets and take to the skies. Then the world will be hit by a pole shift and a great flood. Billions will die, and then, if there's anything left to come back to, our masters will return to regain control. If not, they'll go somewhere else and start all over again. So, of course we're angry. We've been betrayed!"

"You've got a very bleak outlook, Claire, if you don't mind me saying."

She smiled in response, with the certainty of profound belief. She could see in Bill's face that he was toying with the same beliefs. Her look was a knowing one.

Their conversation was interrupted by an incredibly loud speech from the main stage, made by a prominent, dissident politician from the Government's own backbenches. He was applauded and cheered on as he called for NASA to reveal all they were hiding about Ezekiel One. He castigated government politicians for sitting on their hands, instead of ordering an immediate and urgent inquiry into the matter.

Bill scribbled the main points of the speech down into his notepad, in shorthand. As the speech wound up to tumultuous cheers, Bill turned to Claire.

"I read the rest of that book. The one by Marcus Everett. It got very strange towards the end."

"Well, it makes a lot of sense to me."

"Even the stuff about… what was it called again…the brown dwarf? Surely they must have detected something like that by now?"

"They have, Mr. Bainbridge. That's why they've built Ezekiel One."

"I don't follow you."

Claire fixed Bill with a cool stare, and spoke quickly with a half-smile on her darkened lips. "The ancient texts describe a mythical companion to the Sun that crashed through the solar system during its infancy. After causing havoc among the planets, including ours, this fiery world continued to orbit around the Sun at a great distance. It cooled down, and went dark, as tiny brown dwarfs do."

"But what evidence is this idea based on? A distant unseen planet which is capable of disrupting the cycles of the Sun: It seems so far-fetched!"

"You read the book, Mr. Bainbridge. The evidence is in there."

"Yes, I read what was presented as the evidence, and a lot of it seems solid. But, Marcus Everett still didn't answer the central point: Where is this brown dwarf?"

"I don't know any more than Marcus did. But he had his sources, and he stood by them. He published his story just like you published yours. Maybe he didn't have all the answers when he wrote the book. Maybe you didn't have it all correct either, when you wrote your article."

Claire smiled at him again, perhaps a little facetiously this time. He got the impression that she enjoyed niggling him. Perhaps she was flirting with him a little bit, too. "But whether you got it right or not, you got the world's attention, which is a lot more important. And now here we are…"

"Yes, here we are. Indeed."

The caucus of demo organisers on the main stage appeared to be having an impromptu committee meeting, to the tune of some extremely loud house music. The crowd, whose ranks were still swelling, began to dance rhythmically up and down in time to the music. The politician was visibly agitated, and appeared to be appealing to the younger organisers. The exchange grew heated, but was drowned out by the music. Bill thought he recognised Ben amongst the organisers.

"Isn't that your mate Ben up there?"

"Yes, that's right. He's one of the main organisers," Claire shouted back. She was dancing up and down, visibly excited.

The Member of Parliament seemed to be losing the argument he was having with his younger colleagues, and stormed off, red-faced. One of Ben's friends walked to the front of the makeshift stage. He took hold of a microphone, and shouted forcefully over the thumping backbeat.

"Let's take this demo to Downing Street!"

There was a moment of stillness. The authorised and contained demo was now about to test the full force of British Law by attempting to march into central London, through some of the most sensitive security areas in the country.

In their way lay a blue wall of mounted, armoured police.

"Bloody hell! Claire, get out of here!" shouted Bill.

He looked at his young companion as he turned, preparing to escape. She met his face, defiantly. A slightly twisted smile edged up from the corner of her mouth. She winked at him. At that exact moment, a cacophony erupted all around them.

Sods of muddy winter grass of Hyde Park were gouged out of the ground, as the crowd surged towards Hyde Park Corner. Bill and Claire were swept along in the human torrent, their feet barely able to keep their balance. Bill lost his footing several times, and almost felt himself fall under the stampede.

Banners and placards were hoisted high above the heads of the crowd, and then lowered down like pikes in front of an advancing mediaeval army. Missiles began flying through the air in miscellaneous directions. Ahead, the mounted police stood their ground. The police helicopter reappeared overhead, and a bull-horn from above urged the crowd to stop and disperse.

Beyond the mounted police officers, Bill could see a second cordon, this time of armoured police vans, riot police and water cannon. Golden sunlight glinted off the metal. He battled to free himself from the streaming torrent of youth, but his efforts were in vain.

The mounted police charged towards the advancing ranks of demonstrators, and the melee began. Large swathes of the disorganised rabble were soon on their heels, chaotically retreating back into the dank, midwinter parkland. Behind the panicked human herd, the war-cries of the more hardened radicals and trouble-makers were interspersed with great shouts of pain and distress as baton repeatedly struck bone.

Disorientated and breathless, Bill criss-crossed through the park, avoiding the worst of the trouble.

He could see police officers on horseback wheeling their steeds about, as they brought their long truncheons to bear. Here and there, escaping combatants could be seen, bloodied and bruised. Police officers on foot entered the park en masse and began forcibly removing demonstrators, marching the wet, muddy and blood-stained youth towards waiting police vans.

Eventually, Bill was clear, running away from the battle, back towards the stage. His heart was thumping wildly in his chest. He passed a television crew bravely heading in the opposite direction.

Bill looked towards the stage. The demo's generals could no longer be seen there, and the area around that central focal point was quickly clearing. People were running in all directions, mostly towards the main roads, which bordered Hyde Park. The police helicopter, buzzing the remnants of the crowd as it fled the scene, seemed to be searching for the ringleaders.

Bill was no longer with Claire. They had separated in the melee. As he ran towards the south bank of the Serpentine, he looked back to see if he could see her. There were trampled bodies all around, but she didn't appear to be amongst them. The surrounding streets were filled with the sounds of sirens, and accelerating emergency vehicles, but Bill was in no mood to repeat his heroics from two weeks before. She, perhaps more than he, was well capable of taking care of herself.

He made his way briskly westward, quite prepared, if necessary, to make it all the way back to his office in Kensington on foot. Once again, he had found himself at the heart of unexpected violence in Britain's capital city, and, once again, his job was the foremost thing on his mind. He realised that there were more important things to attend to than creating journalistic copy. As he jogged along, he pulled his mobile phone from his jacket pocket to contact his wife.

✦

There was frenzied activity in the newsroom of the Daily Standard. A wall-mounted screen showed a 24-hour news channel, depicting scenes from the riot in Hyde Park, and a running written commentary scrolling horizontally below it. If the volume of the television was up or not, Bill had no way of knowing. The shambolic open-plan office was a noisy arena of activity. Amid the mountains of papers and office equipment towering above their desks, journalists busied themselves with typing up articles, and shouting at each other across the room. The photographers had returned from Hyde Park, and were disseminating their images through their own computer stations.

The duty editor was pooling the resources, and focusing individual journalists on which aspects of the day's events to cover. He looked up as Bill strode, bedraggled, into the office. Bill acknowledged his look and quickly attempted to take cover by heading for his office. "We're in the shit now, Bill," the duty editor called across the room, irritably. "You'd better get to work. We've going to have some explaining to do!"

Bill let the comment pass, and made for his office. Once in the sanctuary of his own space, he sat down and put his head and arms onto the table. Breathing deeply, he paused for thought.

His newspaper had backed his article on the basis that the man on the street should know what's going on. It was simple spin: The government is hiding something, and we want to know what's going on, especially since we finance the government through our taxes. But things were changing fast. Whatever the truth of the matter, the repercussions of his story were plain to see. Political extremists and radical activists were using the revelations about Ezekiel One to attack the monolithic structure of government.

It didn't matter what the individual chip was on each of the radical's shoulders. They might be anti-globalisation, or anti-war, or extreme left-wing activists. It scarcely mattered. From their point of view, the story about Ezekiel One had simply been an opportunity to ride a popular ground-swell of anti-government feeling, and fear. The 2012 Demo had been co-opted by extremists.

From the editorial point-of-view of the Daily Standard, such activity was to be vigorously opposed at all costs. A breakdown of law and order was a higher priority than the search for truth. Bill found himself batting on a sticky wicket.

He needed to come up with an article which strongly criticised the extremists who had turned the demonstration into a riot. A condemnation of violence was needed, even if that meant conceding that his article published earlier that week was partly to blame for the whole sorry episode. He would have to defend the right to freedom of speech, and of a free press, whilst castigating the hotheads who had roused the mob to its violent heights. At least he could describe the melee from a first-hand point of view. The mud on his shoes, and his soaking wet clothes were a constant reminder of the afternoon's events.

He turned his computer on, and set to work. Tomorrow, he could save the world. Today, he had to save his own skin.

✦

Bill's first-hand account of the riot in Hyde Park had been sent through to Doug for editing. In turn, Bill was now editing the work of other, more junior, journalists on his team. To his relief, word had come through to the office that the newspaper's proprietor had made a public statement saying that he stood by the editorial integrity of the Daily Standard. That, in turn, had given the editorial team the room to put a "don't shoot the messenger" spin on the story.

Bill's article had been too defensive in tone, and this was being re-shaped by Doug. Bill had been asked to put more weight into his description of the human impact of the story: the violence and emotion he had witnessed. He had been explicit in his descriptions of the violence, on both sides. The paper would support the police entirely, but also indicate to its readership that the feelings of the crowd were strong for a good reason. The public needed answers if further disquiet was to be avoided. Bill was relieved by this editorial stance, and happily touched up the article he was editing to abide by the party line.

While he worked away at his computer, his eye caught a glimpse of an airmail letter lying under a pile of correspondence in his in-tray. He had received a lot of mail that week, particularly e-mail. Much of it expressed concern about what the existence of Ezekiel One might mean. Some of it was scathing of his journalism. Some of it was written by the green-ink brigade. He had little time to reply to any of it, but he had worked his way through the mountain of correspondence in case new leads emerged.

Pausing from his work, he picked out the airmail letter. It was marked "Par Avion," and was postmarked in Paris. Bill knew several restaurant owners and critics in Paris, but the handwriting was unfamiliar. There was no return address on the envelope.

Bill opened the envelope and read the letter, which was handwritten in faltering English, in loose and wispy calligraphy.

"*Cher M. Bainbridge,*
My name is Dr. Eugene Sacher. I read your recent article with interest. I am currently employed as a research engineer at the University of Paris, but I have spent many years as a consultant for both ESA and NASA. My field of expertise is plasma physics.
During my time at NASA I came across information which is relevant to your investigation. It is clear to me that everything is about to come out into the open, and I would like to share with you my own, not inconsiderable, role in the creation of Ezekiel One. Now is the time for the people to know why it was built, and where it is destined to go.
In light of the sensitive nature of our discourse on this matter, I would urge caution regarding the security of our meeting. I do not want the details of our meeting aired over the phone, or across the Internet. My identity must be maintained with the strictest confidence, at least for the time being. I would ask you to meet me in the Exhibition of Mesopotamian Antiquities in the Museé de Louvre in Paris at 2 p.m. on Tuesday 18th December 2012.
You must not attempt to confirm our meeting directly. However, if you do wish to confirm that I am who I say, then ask an associate, who speaks French, to phone my office on Monday morning. You can reach me through the university switchboard. When asked how my aunt is at the moment, I shall reply that she has been suffering with a lot of headaches recently. Then you will know that I am who I say I am.

Please make sure that you are not followed.

Yours,
Dr. E. Sacher"

Bill read the letter through twice, and then considered its contents carefully.

His attitude towards his own security had relaxed in the last few days. Although he had clearly been followed the day he had met with Dr. Clarke, nothing untoward had come of it. He had returned to his office on the bus, and had written the story up. After several editorial meetings, the article was given prominence in the newspaper the next morning. There had been no attempt to sabotage the release of the story at all. This had surprised Bill, whose paranoia was acute at that point. Since the release of the article, he had not detected any surveillance directed at him. He had assumed that he was no longer a threat to whatever agency had been watching him. The story was out, and that was the end of his part in the matter.

However, the letter from Dr. Sacher re-ignited some of his fears. It seemed to imply that there was more to the story of Ezekiel One than he knew about. Bill now wondered whether the lack of reprisals against him might reflect the possibility that he had been wrong somewhere along the line. The danger in all of this might lurk in a truth that had not yet revealed itself. This French academic was offering to spill the beans about NASA, and was going to considerable lengths to hide his tracks. Bill needed to be cautious once again.

Bill picked up the phone and, within moments, was connected. "Doug, Bill here. Can we talk?"

✦

The two newspapermen sat in a huddle at one of the newsroom desks, amid the chaos and noise of the open-plan office. Doug finished reading the airmail letter.

"Sounds like an opportunity we can't afford to miss. But we need to plan this carefully. We need to do a bit of background research on this Sacher chap, Bill. But if we're going to avoid this coming to the attention of your spooks, we'll need to cover our tracks well."

"What do you suggest?"

"My son is home from college for Christmas. I'll get him to go around to one of his mate's houses and do some searches over the Internet about this guy. I don't think we should make any electronic reference to Dr. Sacher at all from this office, or from your house. I think we'll need to assume that we're being monitored. Hmmm...French Letters don't normally cause this much bother."

Bill smiled. "Who's going to make the phone call on Monday, Doug?"

"Leave that with me. I'm at the Rotary Club this evening, and one of my longstanding friends there is an engineer. I'll persuade him to make the call on our behalf. Then all we need to do is organise how you get over there. If you fly out of Gatwick..."

"I'm not flying anywhere, Doug. I don't do flying."

Doug raised his eyes to the ceiling. "That's just great! Well, you need to get there and back in the same day. You've got that photo-call with Potter-Smith on Wednesday - unless she cancels, of course - and I want you here on Monday to wrap up some more pieces about the fallout from this riot. You know as well as me that we're going to take a hit over this. They're going to accuse us of irresponsible reporting, and they'll wheel out the big guns this time. Thank God the boss is behind us..."

Doug handed the letter back to Bill. "So it'll have to be the Eurostar then. That's one aspect of this we can't keep under wraps. We can't exactly create you a new identity for going through passport control, can we?"

"But if I'm being followed, then they'll easily pick up the trail once I get into Paris. They'll have a couple of day's notice of my travel arrangements. That's going to be a problem."

Doug thought about it for a while, and looked down at the floor between them.

"Look at the state of you, Bill. You've covered in mud! What have you been up to?!"

The two men laughed. Doug tapped a pen against the remaining surface of the mess-strewn desk and looked at Bill.

"You've been to Paris a few times, right?" Bill nodded in reply. "What's your knowledge of the Metro like?"

"Not bad, I suppose."

"Good. I think you'll have to lead the spooks a merry little dance, mate, to get them off your back before you get to the Louvre. After all you've been through recently, that should be relatively straightforward."

CHAPTER THIRTEEN

The wheels sparkled like topaz, and they were all alike: in form and working they were like a wheel within a wheel, and when they moved in any of the four directions they never swerved in their course.

Even on a cold winter's morning, the light that shone through the great glass ceiling of St. Pancras station was splendid. The arching metal and glass structure was expansive enough to cover a series of platforms, some of which played host to the long Eurostar trains.

Bill looked up at the scintillating glass. The sun was slowly rising between the London buildings surrounding the station, banishing the darkness that had characterised Bill's journey across the city thus far. He was wary, even at that time in the morning.

His sense of paranoia had emerged once again, and he had half expected to evoke a reaction at the check-in, particularly given his minor celebrity status. But he had come through that, and passport control, without the slightest glimmer of recognition from the staff present. It was, perhaps, just as well. The riot in Hyde Park had been a disturbing incident, and other flare-ups had taken place across the Western world. Part of him still felt responsible for the troubles.

Finally, as he had emerged from the security check, with its X-Ray machine searches, Bill had allowed himself to relax a little. At least any potential stalker could have no weapon on them by now. He hoped.

The mandatory hour-long wait for the train had also been uneventful, and there was no sign of any spooks tailing him. Then the long-awaited call for the train had been made, and Bill had taken a deep intake of breath. If there was going to be trouble for him personally, it would be in Paris. He had been promised answers about Ezekiel One, and the implications might be staggering. That made this trip potentially very dangerous.

The escalator transported him up from the ground floor waiting area to the train platform, which was built into the relatively new, and massive, first floor structure, which dominated the extensively modernised station.

St. Pancras was the jewel in the crown of Britain's normally troubled train network. It felt a bit like an invasion of sorts, like a foreign power had installed a fabulous gateway to the Continent in the heart of old, dirty London Town. The sleek Eurostar trains played the part of European Trojan Horses, stealthily stealing in the ranks of their fellow citizens of the European Union. But, like the Greek classic itself, you couldn't help but admire the beauty and sheer audacity of the gift.

Bill was travelling very light indeed. He simply carried a small laptop computer in a carrying case. The train maintained a wireless network and he intended to use his time on the train to work. Hopefully, he would have a great deal more to write on the return journey.

He looked up and down the platform at the people around him. It was not possible to scrutinize everyone, but he was on his guard to watch for the men who had followed him the week before. He also wondered whether the Tall Man might be around, somewhere, although it had been a while since they had last encountered each other. The other travellers around him presented a mixture of business men and women, tourists, and people travelling back home to the Continent for the holidays. Christmas was just a week away — an uncomfortable fact that had been buried in the back of Bill's mind. He still had not bought a present for Helen, or for anyone else for that matter. If the opportunity arose, he would seek out some of her favourite labels in Paris. But, somehow, he doubted he would have the time.

Bill approached Carriage Seven and was met by a stewardess who addressed him politely in French.

"Bonjour, Monsieur."

"Bonjour, Madame."

"Can I see your boarding pass, please?" The stewardess had switched immediately to English. Bill realised his French was lousy, but he persevered nonetheless.

"D'accord. Voila."

"Merci beaucoup, Monsieur," she looked at his automated boarding card carefully. "You're in seat number eight, sir. Bon voyage."

"Merci, Madame."

Bill stepped onto the train. He was in one of the first class cabins; a bonus borne out of the necessity to book with only a couple of days advance notice. The cheaper seats had all been booked up some time ago, and the newspaper was paying anyway. It was a rare perk. The meals and drinks that were part of the package would save him time and effort in Paris.

Bill found his seat and made himself comfortable for the journey ahead. He watched his fellow passengers embark, and tried to memorize their faces as they passed by his seat. It seemed entirely possible that an agent might have picked up his trail as early as this, and would be shadowing him between London and Paris.

As a hopeful decoy, Bill had arranged an interview with an English restaurant owner, whose business was located in the centre of Paris. The interview had been set up by e-mail, an insecure means of communicating. Bill hoped that this interview would act as cover for his real meeting at the Louvre.

To bolster this plan further, Bill intended to write up the bare bones of a fictitious article about the Parisian restaurant concerned on the way to the French capital. His related internet searches might amplify his false intentions for the trip amongst eavesdropping snoops.

It was worth a try, anyway.

An immaculately presented businesswoman sat in the seat opposite Bill, smiled briefly at him, and took out a folder of papers. Spreading the papers across her half of the table between them, she quickly immersed herself in work. Bill watched through the window as the Eurostar began to effortlessly glide out of St. Pancras station on its way to France.

After a while, the train began to duck up and down through a sporadic series of underground tunnels. His ears felt painful with the internal pressure of sudden acclimatisation to the depths of the tunnels, as they sped along under the streets of London. He winced occasionally, as his ears became painful and looked around him. No one else seemed remotely bothered by it.

Still, he thought to himself, this was a lot better than getting onto a plane. He pulled his laptop out of its case, and booted the computer up. It was time to pretend he was back in the restaurant review game.

+

Bill strode along the platform alongside the Eurostar. The partial yellow livery of the train's exterior painted a bright, cheerful line through the grey and brown interior of the Gare du Nord train station in Paris. Two large skylights broke the darkness of the high station roof, and the side walls of the building were punctuated regularly by arch-shaped windows. But the late morning light emanating through these windows did nothing to lift Bill's spirits.

He stared at the bustling station before him. It seemed squalid in comparison to St. Pancras, and a sense of foreboding gripped the reporter.

There was no passport control or customs to endure this side of the English Channel. Before he knew it, Bill was walking through the main reception area of the station. Armed soldiers wandered around, checking for suspicious baggage, and suspicious-looking travellers. Their guns were an unnerving sight for an Englishman at the best of times.

Bill's natural inclination was to go outside the station and hail a taxi. But his task was to get himself well and truly lost in the Paris Metro system. Swiftly, he made his way through the threads of pedestrians, and descended the stairwell into the underground system. He pulled out his Metro pass, which had been purchased alongside his Eurostar ticket, and approached the jostling queues of Parisians at the automatic barriers ahead.

He was not even confident this trick was going to work. If the authorities in Paris were connected with whatever agency had been following him in Britain, then they would be able to watch his movements through the city's underground system without even needing to tail him. The whole area would be monitored by closed-circuit television cameras, after all. Likewise, when he eventually arrived at the Museé du Louvre, he and Dr. Sacher would both be filmed as they moved through the building. There would be security cameras everywhere there, too.

But that, in a way, was Dr. Sacher's problem. For some reason, he had chosen one of the most highly monitored areas in Paris to conduct this supposedly secret meeting. Presumably, the physicist knew his enemy better than Bill did. Or else, he had read a lot of pulp fiction.

Bill considered this for a moment: Would he find himself tracked down by a cowled, albino monk? Was the location of their meeting some kind of joke, aimed at highlighting the fictitious nature of his findings? Or, was there actually something on display at the Louvre that offered a clue to the whole story of Ezekiel One?

Bill reached the front of one of the lines, and inserted his ticket into the Metro automated barrier machines. It popped up again about a foot along the top of the machine, and he picked it out of the machine. He pushed through the barrier and quickly made his way through the Metro station's expansive interior. It was full of people, mostly younger than thirty, moving in all directions. There were boutiques here and there, amid the myriad escalators and staircases. The corridors of the Metro were noisy, and perhaps a little edgy. It had a different atmosphere to the more familiar London Underground system, where the more reserved denizens of that city went about their business in a quiet, resigned fashion. Here in Paris, the atmosphere of the place was more excitable, the graffiti more lurid and bold.

Bill headed towards the entrance for the blue, number 2 line. He had to go through another set of barriers, but some of them weren't working properly, and frustrated young Parisians were climbing onto the automated barrier machines, and jumping over the malfunctioning barriers themselves. Fortunately, Bill's ticket worked, and he was through the barrier without difficulty. But the chaos around him increased his inner tension.

He headed for the line that went in the direction of Porte Dauphine. He planned to ride the underground train to the Charles-de-Gaulle / Étoile station and then make his way down the Champs Elysées, moving in and out of the myriad shops and arcades that lined this most famous of Parisian streets. Then he would descend back into the underground system at the Franklin D. Roosevelt Metro station, and would pick up the cadmium red number 1 line towards Château Vincennes.

That would take him past the Louvre.

If he was confident that he had not been followed, he would get off at the museum. But, if he spotted someone following him, then he would still have some time available to continue through to the busy hub of Châtelet. From there he would improvise, hopping on and off Metro trains in an effort to leave his pursuer behind. The whole plan hinged on his ability to spot someone shadowing him. Bill hoped that his paranoid fears, shared also by his boss, were unfounded.

Hurrying down a flight of steps, he began his escapade.

The Champs Elysées was not how he had remembered it from his younger days. It was probably busier than ever, but the corporate sector had moved in and taken over the entire street, it seemed. Cinemas showing American movies sat alongside airline outlets and, incredibly, car showrooms.

The latter displayed weird and wonderful prototypes, each store offering cars with the promise of low fuel consumption and high performance. Bill was staggered that the French had allowed the romantic heart of this historic avenue to be ripped out of it.

He had been steadily working his way down the street, weaving in and out of shops, through the Christmas decoration-laden arcades which lead through to the parallel roads behind, and snaking back through shops further down the long boulevard. He had even managed to stop at Sephora, and had bought his wife some perfume at one of the counters. The store was packed with shoppers readying themselves for Christmas. The lights and bustle of the shop offered a good distraction, he reasoned with himself.

After about half an hour of frantic jostling and backtracking, Bill reckoned that he should have lost any tail he might have picked up at the Gare du Nord.

He made his way through the festive throng of shoppers towards the Metropolitain sign, which marked the entrance to the subway system at Franklin D. Roosevelt. As ever, he cast his eyes about, wondering whether he would catch a familiar face, or item of clothing, or some other tell-tale sign of recognition.

Bill clambered down several flights of steps, and walked through more automated ticket barriers, this time ever more crowded with thin Parisians, armed with bulging plastic carrier bags. Waiting for the east-bound subway train, Bill looked along the platform. The overhead electronic display indicated two numbers, the first one 00 and the second 02.

Once again, he scrutinized the waiting collectives of business people, shoppers and tourists. It was like a game of Pelmonism, but with faces rather than playing cards. He recognised no faces from his previous searches. The train screeched into the station and ground to a halt. The carriages were jam-packed full of people. The doors opened and people started to emerge from the train, pushing past those standing on the platform waiting to get on. After a few moments of orderly pushing and shoving, the waiting masses thronged onto the train, moving into the newly provided spaces swiftly.

Bill squeezed onto the train, but could go no further than the doorway to the train. He found the train acutely claustrophobic. He clung onto his laptop case, struggling to gain the slightest modicum of personal space.

The next train was coming in just two minutes, he thought to himself. He made a quick decision, disengaged from the ruck of people all around him, and stepped back, out of the train and onto the platform. As he did so, the buzzer sounded its familiar warning that the doors were about to shut. He was off that terrible train, just in time.

As he breathed a sigh of relief, a flash of movement caught his eye. From an adjacent set of doors, another man stepped out of the train. The man, dressed in a heavy winter coat and a black, soft cap, walked away from the train towards the exit, his back to Bill.

Bill watched him go, as the train pulled away and started to accelerate into the tunnel.

Was the man just late getting off the train, or was he following the journalist? He was of a stocky build, and walked with a heavy gait. He left the platform, climbing up a staircase, without looking back. In a moment, he was gone.

The platform began to quickly fill with more passengers, who spread out to wait the minute or so that was remaining before the next train was due to arrive. The man did not reappear on the platform. The next train duly pulled in, and Bill joined the unseemly scramble to embark. As far he was able, he tried to monitor the platform for signs of the stocky man, but the cavernous metro station was pandemonium. Bill found himself squeezed into the centre of the snaking metro train, as it quickly accelerated into the dark tunnel. He looked at his watch: He had about an hour to go before the meeting. He was now less certain that he had evaded any surveillance, and decided to take a detour.

After coming off the train at Châtelet, Bill moved up escalators to a dismal, concrete-walled shopping centre. The complex filled three stories of underground space between the metro lines and the Parisian street level. It had clearly seen better days. He moved through shops, up and down escalators, and even out into a terraced, open-air level set below the main streets. Gangs of young men were hanging around in the arena-like open area outside, smoking, their presence ominous and anti-social. All the time, Bill looked out for the stocky man.

After about ten minutes in the multi-level shopping centre, he again descended into the underground system and took a train south, disembarking at St. Michel. From here, he ascended to the street into the Left Bank district of Paris. The area was full of young students and bustling shoppers.

Walking up to the river quay on the south side of the Seine, he followed the street west, perusing the cluttered tourist shops and cafes as he proceeded. The street was in the shade of the sun, and was very cold indeed.

Eventually, he drew alongside the bridge over the river that would take him to the Louvre. Crossing the street, through the insane traffic, he walked across the Port du Carrousel. He stopped halfway across and leaned against the stone wall of the bridge. He looked back across the river. This vantage point provided excellent views along the banks of the Seine, and he was able to see clearly the pedestrians strolling along the streets from whence he had come.

There was no sign of the stocky man.

Reassured, Bill turned and continued across the bridge towards the Louvre museum. It was an incredibly beautiful building, stretching several blocks along the riverside. As he meandered along, a young woman walked towards him and bent over to pick something up from the pavement. He caught a glint of yellow metal on the floor, and she picked up her prize, holding it up before her.

The young woman appeared delighted with her find, and looked towards Bill, smiling. She was holding a man's wedding ring between her fingers.

"Quelle chance! C'est très belle, n'est ce pas?"

Bill smiled at her, but continued to walk past. Unexpectedly, she manoeuvred herself to stand right in front of him, blocking his way. She spoke directly to him.

"Vous êtes anglais?"

How did she know? Bill thought to himself. He hadn't even opened his mouth.

He nodded, irritated by this unwanted incursion into his mission. It suddenly occurred to him that she might present something of a diversion, an aide to make him drop his guard. He looked around the bridge warily, as she spoke to him in broken English. There was no one close to them.

"Monsieur, is no good for me. Look, is very big. Is a ring for a husband. You have it. It is gift from me."

She held the golden ring up before him, and tried to show him how it would look on his hand by gently grabbing hold of his left hand. Bill looked at the ring. It was certainly a handsome piece of jewellery. She seemed very keen to give it to him. *What was going on here?* Bill thought.

As she attempted to manoeuvre the ring onto one of the fingers of his right hand, Bill noticed that the woman had a tattoo on her lower arm. He looked at her clothes. She was clearly not a rich woman, but her clothes suggested that she was closer to poverty than to wealth. The French tended to dress to impress. She needs this ring more than me, thought Bill.

He began to pull his hand away from her, "Non, Mademoiselle, c'est pour vous."

But the woman persevered, and Bill wondered again whether this was some kind of distraction to entrap him. His eyes swept around the rest of the wide expanse of bridge. Cars were driving across it from the direction of the Louvre, and several other pedestrians could be seen walking across, mostly in a very leisurely manner. None of them appeared to be remotely connected with this odd woman.

Bill strained a forced smile at her, and passed by, assertively, moving further down the pavement towards the museum.

A road led from the open series of gardens that linked the grounds of the Louvre with the Tuileries, and a pulse of traffic was slowly making its way through the impressive opening in the side of the museum building. After walking for about fifty metres, Bill turned and watched as the woman crossed over the bridge and stood on the other side, looking across the Seine. She was no longer interested in walking in the direction he had first seen her heading in, it seemed. She was evidently a scam artist of some description, although it wasn't clear to Bill how she had intended to extort money out of him.

The bizarre encounter appeared to be unconnected with his reason for visiting the Louvre, he reasoned. If anything, the event had simply portrayed him as a harmless tourist, which would no doubt have helped his cover. He smiled to himself. At least she hadn't been an albino monk!

He proceeded through the grand gated archways set into the splendid Renaissance-style south wall of the Louvre, and turned left into the Cour Napoléon atrium beyond. The glass pyramids beckoned him towards the visitor's entrance, which was thankfully uncluttered by tourists. He swiftly made his way into the underground main reception hall set below the main glass pyramid.

He had barely ten minutes left to make the rendezvous.

CHAPTER FOURTEEN

All four had hubs and each hub had a projection which had the power of sight, and the rims of the wheels were full of eyes all round.

The bulk of the Louvre's Mesopotamian collection was housed in the ground floor of the Richelieu Wing. Bill had visited the museum many years before but, as with so many tourist excursions into the massive complex, had concentrated solely on the Italian paintings of the Renaissance. On that occasion, he and Helen had travelled to Paris during the summer, and had inevitably ended up queuing for ages to even get into the building. Their pilgrimage down the finely decorated halls of the Italian Renaissance to see the "Mona Lisa" had been more akin to attending a Premier League football match than an art gallery. The sheer weight of people had been staggering.

That visit had coloured Bill's perception of the Museum. He had anticipated a meeting held amid gaggles of Korean tourists snapping away, with camera flashes ablaze. On the plus side, the anticipated noise and bustle would create excellent cover for the meeting, in case he and the French physicist were to be overheard by agencies unknown.

However, the Mesopotamian Exhibit in December was practically deserted. There were very few museum staff visible, and those that were, outnumbered the visitors in many of the rooms.

Dr. Sacher had not stipulated the exact meeting place, within the section containing the oriental antiquities. Bill reasoned that the evidently paranoid academic was wishing to keep his options open, as to the where and the when. He felt confident that he had not been followed. If he had, then the security checks at the museum entrance would prevent a spy from bringing surveillance equipment or, worse, weaponry, into the building.

Bill mused as he wandered through the grand halls of the Richelieu Wing, when he suddenly found himself confronted by two enormous winged bulls with human heads, decorated in the ancient style of the Levant. The Shedu were each set to the side of a massive arched entranceway in the middle of the great hall. Bill walked between the massive stone statuary, marvelling at the grandeur of the pieces. He wondered how on earth the French had managed to transport these wonderful works of art across continents.

"They are supposed to offer us protection, Mr. Bainbridge."

A heavily accented voice wafted softly from the hall Bill had just stepped through. Dr. Sacher appeared before the Shedu, his face serious and focused. Bill smiled and offered his hand in greeting, which the Frenchman took.

"I'm glad you are happy to speak with me in English, Dr. Sacher. My French is very rusty, I'm afraid."

Dr. Sacher looked at Bill over a small pair of glasses, perched towards the end of his nose. The French engineer was shorter than Bill, and slightly portly. He appeared to be in his early sixties, and the hair on his head, although still retaining some dark, Gallic colour had thinned considerably with the years. He wore a dark brown leather coat and scarf, and smart leather shoes. He regarded the Englishman with interest, one eyebrow slightly raised.

"My English too is rusty, Monsieur, and more American than British. I worked in Florida during several years back in the Nineties." The academic paused momentarily, and lowered his voice, "I hope you were not followed."

Bill smiled confidently, "On this occasion, no. Although, I *was* accosted by a woman on the bridge outside the museum, about twenty minutes ago."

The physicist raised his eyebrow still further, and looked unsettled. Bill decided to elaborate on his encounter. He was still uncertain as to what had actually taken place.

"A young woman picked up a ring off the floor, as I walked towards her on the bridge. She claimed that she had found it. She then offered it to me as a gift."

The Frenchman looked at Bill's hands, "Did you accept it?"

"No, I suspected that she was trying to scam me."

"Pardon?"

"Oh, I think she was playing a trick on me, to get some money from me. I'm not sure how she intended to get money from me, by giving me something, though."

Dr. Sacher laughed, and patted Bill on the arm in a friendly gesture. "She would ask you for some money once you accept the ring. It is a common trick that the Romany people play on tourists in Paris. The ring was worthless — just brass."

Bill nodded. "Or a listening device, perhaps?" He teased his companion carefully, not wishing to alienate a man who seemed to think he was placing himself in considerable danger by arranging the covert meeting. Dr. Sacher ruefully acknowledged the possibility with an uneasy smile. He gestured that Bill should follow him, and they slowly walked through the empty halls, speaking quietly as they did so.

"The world is a very strange place, Mr. Bainbridge. And our place in it is perhaps the strangest thing of all. Are you Christian?"

"Yes, although I am not a big believer these days. My wife is more tuned into the Church than me."

"Well, my faith as a young man was very strong, for a Frenchman. One of the reasons I wanted to work in America was because I found the lack of spirituality in our society here, well, how do you say, distasteful. I believed in God, and in the power of Jesus Christ. The Americans are a remarkable people. They know the potential that is offered to us by science, particularly in technology. But they also keep the traditions of their forefathers. They are proud of their religion, so they can at the same time push back the frontiers of science and reject the significance of their discoveries on their beliefs."

Bill nodded without reply. He wasn't sure where this discussion was going. He hoped that Dr. Sacher wasn't a member of the green ink brigade. It would have been a long and expensive trip to waste on a series of demented ravings, if the academic's mild eccentricity turned out to be complete madness.

The Frenchman continued to talk methodically, as if providing the journalist with a well-prepared lecture.

"You see, when we search for truth, we expect to find the answers to be what we already believed before. We don't expect to have the beliefs we have had from our childhood challenged by what we find. When that happens, we try hard to hold on to our belief systems. Take these exhibits, for example. These Near Eastern antiquities were found in the nineteenth century, along with much ancient writing produced many thousands of years ago. Look at this Stele, for example."

Dr. Sacher indicated a basalt stele, prominently placed in the hall that the two men were wandering through. The elegant work of sculpture was set in two parts; a symbolic scene of a king and subject was fashioned into the top segment, below which ran long passages set in cuneiform script.

"This is the Law Code of Hammurabi, one of the ancient kings of Babylon. The Stele sets our law, and some history. The law came before the Bible by many hundreds of years. You see, when the historians started to understand some of this writing, they discovered a rich history of a pre-Biblical civilisation, which was more advanced than they imagined. They discovered that many of the early parts of the Bible had come from these ancient peoples. It caused a great upset at the time."

"Why?"

"Because some of the important, even sacred, accounts in the Bible had emerged from a non-Jewish source. The stories of the Garden of Eden, and the Flood, for example. These stories are older than the history of the Jewish people. They challenged the belief that the History of Mankind, in the Bible, was received directly from God."

Bill considered this for a moment. He wondered whether this lecture might have something to do with the priests on the NASA list. The connection, if there was one, was not at all obvious.

The Frenchman, lost in his own thoughts for a moment, continued the tour through the department of Near Eastern Antiquities. "Yet, despite this, most Christians in the world, and Jews I'm sure, hold their Biblical histories to be just that: the word of God. The *fact* that the history belongs to a completely different civilisation means nothing. The fact is ignored, even after more than 100 years of established archaeological evidence. Religious belief is a hard thing to challenge, no matter what the evidence to the contrary. We, as a species, do not like things which upset our understanding of our place in the world."

Dr. Sacher paused, and cast his eyes around the hall, before continuing. "While I worked at NASA, I was allowed to discover a secret which was very challenging indeed: One that shook my belief system to the core."

Now we're getting somewhere, thought Bill. He looked the physicist in the eye. "Was it anything to do with Ezekiel One?"

The Frenchman laughed softly. "Not exactly. You are right, though. I was one of the many hundreds of engineers working on that project. The planning and preparation for Ezekiel One has been going on for almost thirty years, you know."

"Are you serious?" Bill stopped walking, and stared at Dr. Sacher.

"Of course. The project began in the early Eighties, and was paid for with many tax dollars in the decades since. A discovery was made which unsettled many great scientists. It was decided that the discovery should be secret for an indefinite time. Even today, I do not know the exact details of the secret."

Bill must have looked crestfallen, because Dr. Sacher quickly added, "Don't worry, Mr. Bainbridge, I know enough. I think the secrecy may be coming to an end. At least, there is a chance for the truth to come out. Come… Let me show you something."

Bill followed Dr. Sacher towards one of the exits from the Richelieu Wing. Before reaching the *sortie*, the physicist stopped, and turned to his left. He indicated to Bill a coarsely hewn stele, exhibited in the corner of the last hall.

It showed a sculpture of a tall conical mountain, with a parade of soldiers climbing towards the top. At the front of the military line was a larger figure wearing a helmet adorned with horns. Before him, a ramshackle band of men lay slain, or begging for mercy.

"What is it?"

"It's the Victory Stele of one of the Akkadian Kings, Niram-Sin. He ruled in Mesopotamia over 4,000 years ago. The stele shows his victory over a tribal people called the Lullibi, who lived in the Zagros Mountains."

"Who's the giant?"

The physicist laughed his soft laugh. He was clearly used to receiving silly questions from his students. "The figure is thought to be the King, Niram-Sin. But he is wearing a helmet with horns, which is often associated with the Mesopotamian Gods. The identity of the main figure is not as important as what can be seen above the mountain."

Above the conical mountain were two radiant discs, of equal size. They looked like simplistic symbols of the Sun. Dr. Sacher described them, a trace of pride in his voice. "You are looking at the Akkadian image of two solar discs. Two suns which are shining on the victory of a king — a king who has been made a God by the sculptor."

"Why two suns?"

"No one knows. At least, not in the world of archaeology, Mr. Bainbridge. If the experts of the Near Eastern Antiquities have to comment about it at all, they simply say that they are two solar discs. There is no rational explanation. It is a mystery."

"But you think it is significant?"

"Yes. In fact, I know it is significant, because I am one of the few people on this planet who recognise the second sun for what it really is."

"And what's that, exactly?"

"A second Sun, Mr. Bainbridge. It *is* a second sun, right here in the solar system." His jovial eyes lit up with his smile, as he watched the journalist for his incredulous reaction.

But Bill was much less startled by this than the Frenchman had anticipated. "You mean a brown dwarf?"

The Gallic eyebrow shot up again. "Hmmm, I was right. Now really is the time."

He paused, and looked around. The two men were the only occupants of the room. He continued. "In the early 1980's an infra-red telescope was launched into space. It scanned most of the sky. Not all, but most of it. It found several warm objects. They were unusual, and many of them were explained away. But one of them continued to puzzle the scientists, who were working on the data from the orbiting telescope. There was even a public argument amongst the scientists on each side of the Atlantic. The American contingent wanted to ignore the discovery. The European scientists involved on the project criticised this decision. They thought that the heat source might belong to a massive planet orbiting the Sun at a great distance. However, their desire to investigate it was ignored, and nothing more was heard of it. In reality, this was an incredible discovery. The telescope, known as IRAS, had discovered a massive planet lying at the edge of the constellation Sagittarius. But before the scientists involved could do anything, a government agency visited them. They were persuaded, with a mixture of incentives and threats, to deny the discovery, and to discourage any claims that it might be significant."

"So you're telling me that a discovery made 30 years ago had been covered up all this time?"

"Oui."

"I find that hard to believe. We have a free press, and hundreds of scientists and engineers know about this. It must have leaked into the media during that time."

"It has. People have come forward at various times, but the idea is too fantastic. It sounds like the idea of a madman. This is because we have an established idea of what a star is like, and how it should appear. The fact that this is a Dark Star, and is very far away, makes it extremely difficult to find. Its exact location is secret."

"Do you know where it is, Dr. Sacher?"

"Not exactly, no. The information I have received is compartmentalised. I know that it lies about 1,500 times the distance between the Earth and the Sun away. I know that it takes about 60,000 years to orbit the Sun. During that time, it *sweeps out* an enormous volume of the solar system." The academic emphasised this with a broad sweeping motion of his arm.

"Sweeps out?"

"Yes, like a cosmic broom. Its movement beyond the planets has cleared out comets, and other cosmic bodies, beyond the outer band of asteroids we call the Kuiper Belt. The gap between this belt and the comet clouds beyond is one of the solar system's great mysteries. This Dark Star is the reason for the gap."

"That's what you call it: The 'Dark Star?'"

"Some scientists call it 'Sol B.' I prefer the 'Dark Star.'"

"And how does this Dark Star fit in with Ezekiel One?"

"It's obvious, isn't it?"

"Not to me."

The Frenchman scratched the back of his head, his face bemused.

"It's the destination for the spacecraft."

Bill couldn't believe his ears. He stood rigidly still, dumbfounded. The physicist sounded sane, but this idea was utter madness! In a moment of perplexed silence, Bill considered the last four months. There had been espionage, death, destruction, and riots.

For this?

The Frenchman eyed the correspondent carefully, assessing the Englishman's inner turmoil. He continued to present his case. "During the last thirty years, the Americans have been telling the public that manned spaceflight is almost impossible. After triumphantly setting their men onto the surface of the Moon nearly fifty years ago, using computer technology more like an abacus than a PC, they have since renounced their public dream of conquering space. They have not returned to the Moon, despite the technological improvements of fifty years. They last went there in a tin-can, and now they can barely get their people into orbit. That is their story, at least.

"But this has been false. You see, the problem with travelling to another planet is not arriving there, but returning. If you land on the surface of another world, how do you get off it again? You have to transport a rocket with you that is powerful enough to escape the planet's gravity, as well as the resistance of the planet's atmosphere. With the Moon, that it not too difficult. Its atmosphere is minimal. Its gravity is light. Mars would be much more difficult to escape from."

"I don't follow you, Dr. Sacher."

"The difficulty is the return journey. You have to have a massive rocket thrust to escape the world you are exploring. Carrying that rocket with you is impractical, especially when you have to maintain the life of the astronauts over a long distance, too."

Bill still looked blank.

"Mr. Bainbridge, the difference here is that Ezekiel One is not coming back."

"But, that means these men are heading towards a certain death!"

"Aren't we all? This spacecraft has been designed to be the home for these astronauts for decades. It recycles water and waste, grows food, and is powered by a massive nuclear reactor. After an initial rocket boost to get it away from Earth orbit, it will be propelled forward by a massive nuclear-powered engine. Because the solar system is mostly vacuum, it will continue to accelerate for over half its journey time. There is no resistance to its thrust. For ninety months it will accelerate greatly through space at high speeds. Then it will spin around, until it faces backwards, and spend another ninety months slowing down, using its nuclear fusion engine to slow down. Altogether, it will take over fifteen years to arrive at the Dark Star."

"But, why not just send an unmanned probe?"

"Because, at these great distances you cannot control the spacecraft effectively. Communications travel at light-speed, and that creates a very significant time gap. Even artificial intelligence would be incapable of dealing with the many unknowns involved. About 25 years ago, NASA covertly sent a probe in the direction of the Dark Star. The probe has a powerful telescope on it. In that time, it has covered only five percent of the distance. Yet, that mission has enabled the scientists to take extraordinary images of the Dark Star. It has planets of its own; a mini solar system of rocky worlds and asteroids. Some of the bigger worlds appear to have atmospheres, and perhaps even water. The planets that orbit the Dark Star are warmed by it, both by its heat and radiation, and by its gravitational force. It is an amazing discovery, it really is."

"So why the secrecy? Why not let the world know all about it?"

Dr. Sacher looked uncomfortable, and for a moment seemed to be immersed in his own internal debate. He beckoned Bill to follow him, and walked back through the halls of the Richelieu Wing, in silence. He led Bill to various stone monuments showing giant Mesopotamian gods, and gestured towards the ancient sculptures.

"Because of them."

"I don't understand."

"You have read the passage in the Bible that this spacecraft is named after, I presume?"

"Ezekiel, verse one?"

"Yes. It describes a visit made by the sky gods in a fabulous vehicle. The prophet Ezekiel was using visionary words to describe an actual event. The Americans have suspected for many, many years that our solar system contains *others*. They are not unlike us. Indeed, for a long time, they were here on Earth. They were revered as gods. They meddled with our species genetically, they taught us civilisation, they conquered our planet, and ruled the Earth during hundreds of thousands of years. Their presence is described in great detail in the ancient Mesopotamian texts."

"These gods — these *aliens* — they came from this Dark Star?"

"That is what is feared, yes."

"*Feared*?"

"Yes, Mr. Bainbridge. Feared! Their intentions towards us are unknown. They have not communicated with us for thousands of years. Although it is believed that they still watch us, they play no part in our continuing evolution. But, our governments do not want to risk their return, without knowing more about them. Ezekiel One is a manned reconnaissance mission. It is also a diplomatic mission. The men on board are to discover the intentions of these gods."

"That still does not explain why there is this veil of secrecy."

"But it does! For two reasons: First, the knowledge of the existence of these gods would destroy the wisdom of our major religions. It would break the rock that is the foundation of our civilisation."

"I don't think I agree, Dr. Sacher. There has been a cultural shift in our society towards the acceptance of the existence of other life in the Cosmos. There have been so many movies about aliens, and UFOs. I don't think people would find it that hard to accept."

"Ah, but you see, that is not the problem. It is the fact that these aliens are like us, that they were part of our history. Their existence has profound implications about how we understand the ancient texts. It would create doubt in the minds of people about what religion is really all about, or, at least, what it was all about in ancient times. This would be a dangerous change in understanding. Society needs stability to succeed. If the people lost their faith, then other belief systems could take hold. This would then start great social change."

"As a journalist, I don't accept that the risk of such a change is worth holding back the truth for billions of people. We have a right to know what is real, even if the facts are difficult for many people to accept."

"I think you underestimate the conservative nature of the people who really run this world, Mr. Bainbridge. They not only need to maintain civil order, but they also would prefer to maintain their own power within society. A change in commitment to another religious or political system of thought would jeopardise that."

It was clear to Bill that Dr. Sacher had thought things through. This cynical assessment of the political ramifications of the discovery of intelligent alien life elsewhere in the solar system must have been one of the factors which had elicited such caution in the physicist-turned-whistleblower.

Bill himself was already acutely aware of the interest shown in the story by powers unknown. The paranoia shown by the physicist was either based on his own reckoning of the political environment he was moving in, or else it was based upon darker influences in this man's life. Bill hoped to find out more as this fascinating interview progressed, but he was careful not to overstep the mark at this stage.

"You mentioned a second reason for the secrecy."

"Well, the second reason is even more important. There is one group of people who really must not know that the Dark Star has been discovered."

"Really? Who are they?"

"Why, the aliens themselves! The governments of this world do not want to warn these ancient gods that we know about them. They certainly don't want the aliens warned that we are sending an expedition to their tiny planetary system. To do so would risk the total security of all the mission, and might bring the ancient gods back to Earth. They might wish to control our world. That could lead to war. It might be a war we could not win. After all, our technology is likely to be many years behind theirs."

"In which case, why are you telling me all this?"

"I believe that these gods are no longer interested in what happens on Earth. According to the Book of Genesis, they tried to wipe us out, and failed. At that stage, they decided to withdraw from the Earth.

"I think that they are best left alone. I think sending Ezekiel One to the Dark Star is a very dangerous act, and by bringing the matter to the attention of the public, I am hoping that the mission will be cancelled. Ezekiel One could yet be used for other missions. It could go to Mars, for instance, and set up a colony there. But by attracting the attention of these ancient gods, we are meddling with things that are best left alone."

"How would the gods know that we know about them, if you see what I mean?"

"Our planet is buzzing with radio waves. The television pictures, that race around our world, also leak into Space. The gods may have been monitoring us that way for a long time. Or, they might have continued to watch us closer to home — perhaps from Mars, or the Moon. Or, even by retaining a presence here on Earth. Presumably, our official discovery of their existence would be a turning point for them."

"So secrecy is imperative, Dr. Sacher. Yes, I can see why the governments might have acted the way they have."

"But sending this craft towards their world is an act of folly. It could be seen as an aggressive act. There are many of us who have helped to create this wonderful spacecraft, who now doubt whether we have done the right thing. Like Oppenheimer before us, we dread the consequences of our actions, however noble the initial intentions. We feel it must be stopped."

"You're not acting alone, then?"

"No, there is a sizeable group of us. But the fate of the mission is not in the hands of the scientists. Instead, it is controlled by the U.S. Government.

"They do not want to listen. They have a different agenda to us. The mission is set to go ahead. Everything is ready. And, time is running out."

"It sounds to me like it's already too late, Dr. Sacher. The world now knows of the existence of Ezekiel One, but it has not brought forth the kind of reaction perhaps you would have liked. Most people believe the whole story is a hoax. Worse still, the story has become the *cause celebre* for a vocal and militant group of New Age radicals. Their actions last weekend in London have further alienated the general public in England. And, as you know, things have been heating up here as well, in Paris. I'm afraid to say, making your version of things public would probably make things worse."

Dr. Sacher frowned, "So, you're not going to print the story?"

"That would not be my decision, Dr. Sacher. But, it would help a great deal if you could actually provide some evidence for your claims. At the moment, you have just presented an argument. Besides these amazing exhibits in these halls, I am not sure what else we can present to Joe Public to back up your story."

For the first time that afternoon, Dr. Sacher looked downbeat. He had almost seemed joyful to be discussing this story, and perhaps with good reason. He had been carrying around this secret, and the burden that went with it, for years. Talking about it openly was cathartic, or at least a relief to finally lift the weight from his shoulders. Now, when it came to the crux of the matter, he was not so relieved to speak freely.

"I don't have any physical evidence to give you, Monsieur."

Now, it was the journalist's turn to look exasperated. "Come on, Dr. Sacher. You've been working on this project for years. You must have accumulated enough evidence for us to be able to independently corroborate your story."

"It is not so simple."

The physicist walked over to a nearby bench, and sat down. Bill took a seat next to him. They looked straight ahead at a presentation case, full of pottery and stone sculpture from Mesopotamia.

"I worked on the engineering side of this project. We built the engine; the nuclear-powered fusion engine. It is an extraordinary machine, Mr. Bainbridge. You might call it a work of art. You see, I see it as my life's greatest work. If I had developed this machine in an ordinary aerospace company, I would be receiving industrial honours and international recognition. The engine will revolutionise space travel. But, because of the nature of this project, my work is hidden for all time."

"They paid you well, though, I'm sure."

"Of course, of course... But money is not everything in life. I feel like an artist, who has produced a great work of art, but it will never be hung on any wall, nor seen by anyone. It is a difficult thing to live with. If the world knew about this spacecraft — what it is capable of — they would realise that we could leave this planet. We could make a fresh start on Mars, or on the Moon, or on one of the moons of Jupiter. It would revolutionise our understanding of our own potential as a species."

The physicist seemed genuinely mournful for the loss of control over his creation. This was evidently the real reason for his disclosure. But, the appreciation of his motivation could not be a replacement for hard evidence.

"I understand how important this must be to you, Dr. Sacher. But we must be able to *prove* what you have said. The public is very sceptical. They don't believe governments, but they also don't believe conspiracy theories, either. We have already broken the story of Ezekiel One. Independent astronomers have made sightings of the craft and placed their own photos of its silhouetted outline onto the internet. Yet, there is still a widespread belief that this is all simply a hoax. The government denies the existence of Ezekiel One, and that's good enough for most people. You've provided us with an even more perplexing theory, based upon your own experience of working in a secret government programme. You can easily be discredited by the government. Your career could be dragged through the mud. They will likely claim that you never worked for NASA at all. At the very least, we need to have documents proving that you worked on these programmes. But that probably won't be enough either. To persuade the public that you are right, we need to be able to get another professional astronomer to verify the existence of this Dark Star."

The physicist looked unsettled. He fidgeted on the bench for a while. Bill had already caught the faint hint of cigarette smoke on his clothes, and suspected that the scientist was probably urgently craving a smoke.

At last, Dr. Sacher cleared his throat. "Speaking personally, I don't know exactly where this Dark Star is. I know a couple of scientists who might know. I could try to persuade them to tell me. But this could be very dangerous. They are sworn to secrecy, and they might bring the whole matter to the attention of the authorities."

"Can you provide me with proof that you worked at NASA?"

"Yes, I can put some documents together and send them to you in London. That will take a couple of days at most. Finding out the location of the Dark Star might take a bit longer."

"Dr. Sacher, I'm not sure that we've got much more time left. You need to know something. We also have some documents in our possession about this spaceflight."

The physicist looked up quickly, apparently astonished by this revelation. He grabbed Bill's arm, his face suddenly urgent and focussed. "What documents? How did you get them?"

All of a sudden, it struck Bill that he might be talking with a government agent. After all, he had received nothing from the physicist except a very strange story. Could the whole thing be a set-up in order to extract information from him?

Bill looked the physicist in the eye. He imagined the man to be the manager of a fine restaurant. He imagined that the reviewer's identity had been exposed. This had happened on several occasions when Bill had been recognised whilst in the middle of a meal at a restaurant. It had always been interesting to watch as the service and quality of the meals had been suddenly elevated. That notwithstanding, it had always been the look on the face of the manager that was most telling.

Was Dr. Sacher's reaction one of genuine surprise, or had he known that Bill had the NASA documents all along?

Bill went with *genuine surprise*.

"We were provided with two documents from a British security source. We believe the documents to be authentic. Indeed, it was these two documents that led us to investigate Ezekiel One in the first place. The documents provided us with the name, which ties in with your story, Dr. Sacher. All this talk of flesh-and-blood gods makes sense, when put in the context of that chapter in the Bible."

"Yes, yes…but what else did the documents say?" The Frenchman was polite, but impatient.

"The first one listed twelve names, and the date 21st December 2012. The second provided us with the medical fitness of one of the men, with a long spaceflight in mind."

"And who were these men?"

"They were religious men. Priests. All of them young, and committed to their faith, and to their Church."

"The cargo…" Dr. Sacher looked pensive.

"I'm sorry?"

"These men are the diplomats. They are all experts in the language and culture of ancient Mesopotamia. Their purpose is to communicate with the aliens who live in the Dark Star system, and to find out about them."

"Hmmm, I'm not so sure about that Dr. Sacher. I've spent months looking into the backgrounds of these men, and I can assure you they are not all scholars in ancient language and culture. One or two of them, perhaps. But certainly not all."

"The date you mentioned. What does it mean?"

"We don't know. The second document mentioned a final launch date on 30th November."

Dr. Sacher nodded slowly. "Then the 21st December date is the day that the spacecraft will depart for the Dark Star."

"I guess that makes sense. It is also the last day of the current Mayan Age." Bill was fishing, but the physicist simply looked troubled, and faced forward again, lost in his own thoughts.

Eventually, he stood up, and extended his hand towards the journalist, who took it. "I will talk with my old colleagues and see if I can obtain the co-ordinates of the Dark Star, Mr. Bainbridge. If I get you the information, you will need to present it to an astronomer who has access to data from a very powerful telescope. Your amateurs will not be able to help this time."

The Frenchman sighed, and looked down the hallway towards the exit. "In fact, no one will be able to see the Dark Star at the moment anyway. You will have to work from previous images."

"Why's that?"

"Because the Sun is lying in the constellation of Sagittarius during December. So, the Dark Star planet is lying behind the Sun. The solar glare will prevent it from being seen from Earth at this time of the year. So you will need to refer to a professional astronomer who can look back through a large data base of sky searches."

"Don't worry, I have someone in mind. We will also need copies of your work documents at NASA. We must be able to prove you worked with the organisation."

"Yes, I will do that. But I plan to get away from the public eye when this story gets out, I must warn you. There will be some very upset people at NASA, and in the US government. It will be best if I am not easy to find." Dr. Sacher looked bleak. "In fact, it would be best if we do not leave this museum together."

The two men completed their handshake, and exchanged final pleasantries. Dr. Sacher indicated that Bill should leave first, and stepped back towards the exhibition hall.

Within minutes, Bill was riding the elevator up, through the glass pyramid of the Louvre's entrance hall, leaving the Frenchman to reflect further on the deep significance of the ancient works of Mesopotamian art, and how their fates were now entwined.

CHAPTER FIFTEEN

When the living creatures moved, the wheels moved beside them; when the creatures rose from the ground, the wheels rose; they moved in whatever direction the spirit would go; and the wheels rose together with them, for the spirit of the living creatures was in the wheels.

Bill looked at his watch as he stepped out of the entrance to the Musée du Louvre. The midwinter sun was hanging low in the sky south of the Eiffel tower, sending long shadows across the ground from the surrounding buildings of the Louvre. A cold westerly wind blasted through the open-ended gardens. As he walked away from the glass pyramid, Bill faced into the wind and looked out towards Paris.

Immediately in front of him was a great Napoleonic archway. As Bill looked ahead, beyond it, he could see the Arc de Triomphe in the far distance. The two arches appeared to be aligned. Along the route between the two grand arches were the Tuileries, the Place de Concorde and the Champs Élysées. A great line was drawn physically between the two Parisian archways, as if by an ancient astronomer keen to pinpoint a mark on the distant horizon.

The ancient Pharoahs of Egypt would have been proud of modern Paris, thought Bill. In the centre of this bustling European capital, the French had raised three glass pyramids at the focal point of a great line running between two grand arches. Those pyramids were built into the grounds containing many of the treasures of the ancient Egyptian civilisation. It seemed carefully designed to provide answers to questions unasked.

For a moment, Bill tried to imagine the scene before him as an analogy for what Dr. Sacher had been talking about. The two arches were the two suns of the solar system. The nearest, here in the gardens of the Louvre, was the Sun. In the far distance, at the end of the Champs Elysees, was the second arch: the second Sun. This sun was the tiny dark star.

Beyond it was the west of Paris: the buildings there represented the stars of the constellation of Sagittarius. In the glare of the Sun of the Louvre, the tiny brown dwarf, which lay symbolically at the far end of the Champs Élysées, would indeed be impossible to see.

That alignment was a big problem. For the general public, seeing was believing. If it was currently impossible for astronomers to view this tiny dark star, then the people would not accept the truth of its existence as being self-evident. It would scarcely matter how knowledgeable Dr. Sacher was about the existence of this planet. His testimony would be dismissed by various critics and debunkers. Bill wasn't even confident he was going to get this story past his editor. The plot was thickening beyond the scope of the general readers of their newspaper.

What had been a relatively straightforward story about a secret spaceship was becoming something far more complex. The spaceship "Ezekiel One" had been designed to explore a newly discovered, but top secret planetary system lurking at the edge of the solar system itself. If that was not mad enough, the fact that the planetary system was inhabited by god-like aliens was straining credulity.

Musing about the difficulties he faced back in London, Bill walked briskly away from the museum, towards the nearest subway station.

✦

Before long, Bill was standing on a crowded platform. He was waiting for a metro train heading east, towards the Châtelet hub. The claustrophobic nature of the subway was contrasted strongly with the open skies and landscaped design of the environment Bill had just enjoyed above. It snapped him back into the real world, and reminded him of the imagined dangers he had been so carefully avoiding just an hour before.

As the train approached, screeching its brakes, Bill looked up the platform at the other subway travellers. Warily, he gazed at the indifferent commuters.

The train stopped abruptly. Its doors opened to allow those choosing to leave the train to swell the ranks of those waiting to get onto it. As Bill coped with the intermingling of commuters, he saw a familiar head and coat. The stocky man who had got off the train with Bill an hour or so before was once again on the same platform as him. In fact, he was about to board the same carriage!

Bill felt his heart gallop uncontrollably. His mouth was dry within moments; its comforting moisture appeared to have drained down into the cold sweat now running down his back. Bill was suddenly gripped by the desire to run.

But, it was too late to back out of the station. He was packed into a tight group of commuters, and he felt himself swept forward onto the train. There was no chance of making a quick exit this time. The doors swished shut, locking Bill in with his nemesis. Thankfully, scores of Parisians stood between them, oblivious to their intertwined fate. Within seconds, Bill was feeling the sudden acceleration of the train. He grabbed hold of a nearby seat, only just preventing himself from being catapulted across the carriage. Looking up, he saw the stocky man just ten feet away from him.

The stocky man was looking directly at him. Bill had seen the man's face for only a short moment when he had encountered him before, on his way to the Louvre. But it was unmistakeably the same man. His rugged jawline, and off-set nose, matched Bill's fleeting memory perfectly, and the irregular stature of the man was quirky to say the least. His heavy coat provided the final, damning clue.

As the two men's gazes met, the stocky man stared at him momentarily. His eyes narrowed slightly. Then the man averted his eyes. Another shiver went down Bill's spine. He looked along the train, in the opposite direction. Unlike many of the subway trains where the carriages were separated from one another by a door, this train was open plan. As it jumbled its way along the tunnel, Bill could see right down the train's length. The carriages swung to and fro with the curves of the tunnel.

In the second carriage along from Bill's, a two piece band struck up a traditional French tune. The Parisian commuters in the carriage feigned indifference. Much as Bill hated accordion music, the sudden interjection of music gave him the excuse he needed to move away from the stocky man. He carefully worked his way through the busy train, towards the music. Looking back, he could still see the stocky man. He had not moved. But he was now watching Bill intently. As were several other commuters, Bill realised: He was not exhibiting normal behaviour on a subway train.

As he reached the carriage with the band on it, the music ceased, and one of the band members began to more around the captive audience with a plastic cup, touting for spare change. He reached Bill, and presented his cup to the Englishman. Bill dug his hand into his trouser pocket and pulled out some spare change. It was, naturally, British currency, and the musician scowled slightly as he watched the small, heptagonal twenty pence pieces drop into his cup. Bill shrugged and smiled, apologetically. He then scuttled towards the train door, feeling the train decelerating rapidly. The phosphorescent lights of Châtelet subway station beckoned.

Disembarking with a small flood of commuters, Bill looked back down the train to see the stocky man already heading up the platform towards him. Amid the swirling masses, Bill headed towards the *sortie*, his heart racing.

A flight of steps was quickly overcome, and he was into the grey and dismal interior of the main station concourse. Bill kept moving, his eyes seeking out the colour code of the line indicating Gare du Nord. For a frantic moment, in the centre of the bustling station, he couldn't locate the correct route. Bill looked over his shoulder, and saw the stocky man moving around in the jostling crowd behind him, as if circling. He looked around once again, his eyes locking onto signs for the blue and green lines. Either of them would do.

Suddenly, he caught a glimpse of green on a sign overhead. Bill set off apace. He ran out of the concourse, and continued to run along the moving pedestrian walkways.

Apologising in French, he bumbled past commuters, picking his way along the busy pedestrian route. Every so often, he stole a glance back the way he had come. Sure enough, the stocky man was in hot pursuit, maintaining a reasonable distance between them.

At the end of the long walkways, Bill took a flight of stairs at speed and sprinted towards the entrance to the green line. He quickly determined the northern destination of Orry-la-Ville, and made his way down to the subway station. The metro platform was busy, with the next train was expected in two minutes. Bill moved his way through the crowd, attempting to put some distance between himself and the stocky man. But his pursuer was keeping up.

Bill moved as far down the packed platform as he could, and made his way to the front of the platform, gasping for breath. Looking to his side, he could no longer see the stocky man. His mind was racing as fast as his heart.

It was a straight run up to the Gare du Nord from here, on a double-decker RER train. Once at the train station, he would be able to run to the international reception for the Eurostar train. Bill thought about the armed soldiers patrolling the Gare du Nord. It was the first time in his life he had felt reassured by the promised presence of armed police.

The RER train could be heard in the tunnel beyond, the piercing sound of its screeching brakes echoing through the subway station. Bill looked around once again, in the hope of spotting his pursuer.

His eyes locked onto a sudden blur of movement behind him. The stocky man was running at him, headlong, from the back of the platform.

In a sudden reflex, Bill stepped back. His brain instantly registered that he was moving away from one danger, towards another. He was now precariously close to the edge of the platform. The stocky man stared at him as he accelerated forward, a ferocious and determined look on his face. His hands were in front of him now.

He was going to push Bill into the path of the incoming train!

Bill's feet were frozen to the spot. His hands came up instinctively to fend off the imminent blow. A great screech of brakes came from the tunnel, and a massive gust of wind blew into the station, foreshadowing the arrival of the huge RER. A moment later, and Bill would be under the wheels of the train.

Suddenly, unexpectedly, the stocky man was on the ground at Bill's feet. The train thundered into the station.

Unbelievably, Bill remained standing. He was still alive!

In his fright, it took a moment for Bill to register what had happened. One of the commuters, who had been standing close to Bill, had tackled the stocky man to the ground! This commuter was currently holding the stocky man down, with some force. His face was turned away from Bill as the man held the struggling assailant down. One of his hands held the stocky man's head to the platform's concrete floor.

The train finished decelerating through the station. It ground to a halt, and its doors opened.

All around the three men, Parisians reacted in horror at the violent struggle in their midst, and moved back, as if they were sheep confronted by a wolf.

"Mon Dieu! Il voulait de se suicider!" shouted the man who had saved Bill's life. He was yelling at no one in particular. Then, maintaining his grip on his captive, he half-turned towards Bill.

It was the Tall Man! Bill's jaw must have dropped in amazement, because the Tall Man frowned at him impatiently. Bill could feel the weight of the train passengers offloading from the RER behind him. They jostled past him. Some physically tried to push him to one side, swearing loud, Gallic taunts. Bill remained unmoved. He was utterly confounded by what had just taken place.

"Get outta here!" yelled the Tall Man at him. The man's accent was American, possibly with a southern accent. The platform commuters began to get onto the train, through the door that Bill was stubbornly blocking.

"Go!!" The Tall Man's shout was firm. The stocky man suddenly lunged forward. He broke free. Partially. The pale-skinned government agent grabbed him anew. They wrestled, like stags with horns locked, seeming quite oblivious to the chaos around them. Parisians scattered around them, shouting and screaming.

Finally, Bill's feet obtained a connection with his brain.

He turned, and stepped onto the RER train. Its interior was bedecked with ugly graffiti, and glaring commuters. The doors closed automatically behind him. Breathing heavily, he looked back out onto the platform at the government agent, who was continuing to physically grapple with his intended assassin. The Tall Man's attention was locked onto his opponent, and the train pulled away, its acceleration almost tipping the journalist off his feet.

✦

The train came to its abrupt halt. Bill had begun to acclimatise to the sudden jolt. He had marvelled at how the regular commuters had been able to remain standing perfectly still, when holding onto nothing for support. The trick was in the feet, he had realised. As the RER stopped, he grabbed hold of the door handle with his sweaty hands and activated the door control. Perspiration felt cold on his back in the December chill.

The door swung open methodically, and he bounded out onto the station platform at Gare du Nord.

Had the stocky man managed to release himself from his unexpected captor? If he had, Bill knew the man would be arriving shortly on the next train. Looking up at the LED-lit display above the platform he saw that there would be another three minutes before the next train arrived. That was not much of a head-start.

The concrete floor echoed to the sounds of his heavy footfalls as he wove a course through the Parisian herd. He ran up flights of stairs, along corridors, through ticket barriers, through the concourse and up more steps. Within minutes, he was on the ground floor level of the Gare du Nord train station.

His breathing was very laboured by this time. Perhaps he just looked like a man chasing a departing train. In fact, he was running for his life.

Bill allowed himself a few moments respite.

He chose to stand near to several beret-clad French soldiers who were meandering around, semi-automatic weapons held pointed to the ground. Immediately, he felt safe once more. If an intelligence agency was out to kill him, then it was surely a covert operation. These soldiers would be no part of it. Unwittingly, they offered him protection from agencies unknown, possibly even working in conjunction with their own national government.

Once he had re-gained his breath, Bill walked across the station's concourse, and up the steps towards the Eurostar first floor departure lounge. To his right, he could see the Eurostar trains occupying the final two berths of the multi-platform station – steel chariots to return him to the relative safety of London. But was he really safe in London?

He had definitely been tailed by two operatives the week before. It seemed reasonable to assume that the stocky man worked for the same organisation as those two irritable operatives. Yet they had made no move to harm him. Bill could only assume that the stakes had been raised by his encounter with Dr. Sacher. Despite his best efforts, the security of his meeting had been compromised.

Another dark thought occurred to the journalist. Had Dr. Sacher been pushed under a train, on in front of a bus, or off a Parisian bridge?

Bill groaned through a short series of chilling visions. He wiped the perspiration from the palms of his hands onto his coat. He tried to settle his shattered nerves and proceeded towards Eurostar ticket office.

There was no queue at this particular terminal. The chaos of the Paris subway was making way to the more peaceful ambiance of the International Departure Lounge. Fumbling in his jacket pocket, Bill pulled out his automated ticket and swiped it through the machine. Laid-back attendants watched him with due regard, and he made his way through to the passport control, to be met by a British official sat within a small grey booth.

"Good afternoon, sir."

The English accent of the official was comforting.

"Good afternoon. How are you? Alright?" Bill realised he was mumbling, almost panicked. He tried once again to steady himself. The last thing he wanted was to be stopped, and questioned.

"Fine, sir, thank you."

His passport was duly scanned. The electronic details of his identity began their lightning-fast journey through the various banks of technological officialdom. The passport controller looked through the book, and at Bill. For a moment, the journalist wondered whether his identity would be flagged up as a black-listed subversive deserving of immediate arrest and detention by anti-terrorism intelligence officers.

How far did this conspiracy of enforced silence go?

"Here you go, sir. Have a good journey."

"Er, thanks…"

Bill accepted his passport, attempting to mask his nervous relief, and strode through the customs area to the departure lounge. His train was due to leave in just over an hour.

He deliberated about where to sit. The window seats offered a wonderful view of the complete interior of the train station. He would easily be able to see his homicidal pursuer come up from the metro station. But, conversely, he would also be highly visible himself.

Luckily, the lounge was quiet. The passengers for the current train had already embarked, and the tannoy was announcing its imminent departure. Bill wished he had been able to get onto that train for a swift escape, but it was too late. He would have to sweat it out.

He walked up and down for a while, and eventually found a seat which was partially camouflaged by concrete supports. From there he could watch the busy ground-floor level of the train station, whilst providing some cover for himself. Once settled, he dug into his coat pocket for his mobile phone and turned it on. It was a habitual practice of his to keep the thing stubbornly turned off, despite the irritation it caused to all and sundry.

He quickly dialled in a long number and waited. Within seconds, his boss at the Daily Standard answered.

"Hi, Bill. Where are you?"

"Still in Paris. I've encountered a bit of a problem."

"Not shacked up with some French floosie, are you Bill?"

Bill smiled. "I wish. No, I'm afraid it's worse than that." Bill took a quick intake of breath. "Someone just tried to kill me."

His boss paused for a moment. "Seriously? Are you alright?"

"Yes, I'm fine. Just shaken up, that's all." Bill looked around at his fellow passengers-to-be. He kept his voice low.

"Ever since I got into Paris, I've been followed by this bloke. I thought I'd lost him, but he popped up again when I finished my meeting with the physicist. He chased me through one of the subway stations, and then he tried to push me in front of a train."

"God Almighty! This is getting serious." Doug paused for a moment. He seemed to be weighing up a course of action. "How did you manage to get away?"

"He was tackled to the ground by …well, this bit you won't believe!"

"The French President?"

"Doug, I know this is going to sound crazy, but it was that Tall Man again. You know, the one from the book shop in Oxford Street. It's the fourth time I've seen him now."

"And he just happened to be in the Paris underground system?"

"Well, that's how it looked. He must have been standing just by me when this other guy made his move. It all happened in a flash."

"What happened then?"

"He held the other man to the floor. The Tall Man told all the other subway passengers that he must have been trying to kill himself. He told them this in French, mind you. It's surreal, Doug! Then he yelled at me to get on the train and get away. This he said in English. Which I did. I wasn't going to hang about, I can tell you. Then I got up here to the Eurostar terminal just as quick as I could. I've only just got here. I'm watching the station to see if either of them turn up."

"And have they?"

"No, I don't think so. There are armed police and soldiers all over the place here."

"Have you got any idea who this man is?"

Bill was barely listening. His eyes were scanning the platform areas below him. "Oh, I forgot to mention: this bloke had an American accent."

"The one who tried to kill you?"

"No, the tall bloke who saved my life. That's the second time he's stepped in to stop me getting killed. It's almost like he's some kind of guardian angel."

"Working for the government?" Doug laughed. "I don't think so, Bill."

"I just can't figure out how he ends up being in the right place at the right time like that."

"I don't know either, Bill, but your luck isn't going to hold out forever. At some point, one of these lunatics is going to have another go. We need to get you some protection until we get this story into the open." Doug paused again, and added, uncertainly, "You did get us a story, didn't you, Bill?"

"Yes, but we're going to need to talk about it. It's totally mad stuff."

The editor let out a long sigh. He muttered, "…as if we're not in trouble enough already. Okay, look, I'll come up with a plan and meet you at St. Pancras. Your train's on time, right?"

"Yes. Thanks, Doug. I wasn't exactly trained for this James Bond stuff, you know. After this is all over I'm going back to bloody restaurant reviews."

Bill could hear his editor laughing on the other end of the line. "Yeah, right. Okay mate, I'll see you at St. Pancras this evening. Oh, and Bill…"

"Yes?"

"Keep that bloody phone of yours switched on, will you?"

The newspaper editor hung up.

Bill replaced the phone in his pocket, and continued with his nervous vigil.

CHAPTER SIXTEEN

When the one moved, the other moved; when the one halted, the other halted; when the creatures rose from the ground, the wheels rose together with them, for the spirit of the creatures was in the wheels.

Helen ran up to her husband and flung her arms around him. "Thank God you're alright! I've been so worried!"

Bill held his wife in his arms in a warm embrace. "I'm fine, really. Not a scratch on me." Bill tried to look more confident than he felt.

"But Doug told me someone tried to kill you in Paris." Helen protested, "What's going on, Bill?"

Bill broke off his eye contact with his wife, and looked across the concourse of the International Rail Terminal at St. Pancras Station. He saw his portly boss striding towards him, accompanied by an equally portly gentleman dressed in a smart, but cheap, suit. The second gentleman's hair was cropped closely to his head, and he was carrying a mobile phone in his hand. He was looking around warily.

This was Doug's idea of security, Bill thought to himself.

"Subtlety has never been one of Doug's strong suits, has it?"

"Of course not, dear, he runs a tabloid newspaper. What do you expect?" The couple enjoyed a warm laugh, and then the man at the centre of the joke was with them. He grasped Bill's hand and shook it vigorously.

"Good to have you back in the land of the living, Bill."

"Glad to be back, believe me."

Doug turned around slightly, and introduced his companion, "This is Kevin Lord. He'll be keeping an eye out for you for a while."

"Nice to meet you Kevin."

"And you, sir." The security guard's handshake was vice-like. Bill maintained a steady look and smile, despite the feeling that his fingers were losing their blood supply. Bill assumed that Kevin was an ex-policeman, or perhaps a nightclub bouncer. He certainly lacked the Tall Man's panache, his south London accent contrasting sharply with the American's cosmopolitan drawl.

Doug motioned to the security guard, who drifted away by about ten feet. The four of them headed towards the main exit, Kevin maintaining a steady, diplomatic distance; his eyes alert and flitting from side to side as he assessed the people milling to and fro in the group's immediate environment.

The station's interior was brightly lit in white light, intermittently coloured by Christmas decorations in the shops and coffee bars. The great glass ceiling of this cathedral of public transport shone in reflected white light; rendering the darkness outside completely impenetrable.

"I've made some discrete enquiries with the Paris Gendarmerie," said Doug, his voice barely above a whisper. "I asked a contact I have there whether there had been any reports of a disturbance in the metro system today. After she checked around a bit, she came back to me and said that there were no reports of anything at all. Not even a pickpocket, or a drunk. Nothing. Certainly not an attempted murder!"

Bill shook his head. "Believe me, Doug, I was almost pushed in front of that train."

Doug touched Bill's arm in a gesture of reassurance and empathy. "Oh, don't get me wrong, old son. I have no doubt at all that what you say happened really *did* happen. It's just strange that there was no report of a disturbance. None of us like getting involved when we see a brawl in public, but you would have thought that someone on that subway platform would have contacted the police. Look, what I'm getting at is this: Do you want the police to investigate what happened today?"

Helen looked at Bill. Her face was easy to read. She wanted him to drop the covert investigation and approach the police. But Bill was not so sure. It was an argument he had been grappling with internally all the way back from France. If he did approach the police, what possible evidence could he provide to back up his claims? He was not hurt. There were no other independent witnesses.

Not only that, but how could he be sure that the danger he faced would not manifest itself down through the ranks of the police force itself? Even now, he had no idea what agency was following him, or attempting to kill him. The whole affair was nebulous and murky, and it was difficult to know who to trust.

But, on the other hand, someone *had* tried to kill him!

Bill attempted to reassure his wife with a sympathetic smile. He knew that he needed to talk with her about it all before coming to a decision. His one-eyed insistence on pursuing this bizarre story had excluded her influence, a rare event within their normally well-balanced marriage.

"I need a bit more time to think, Doug. I think we've got as much info about Ezekiel One as we're going to get. So, I'm not sure there's a whole lot more to investigate at this stage. I'm focused on getting this story into print right now. Once it's out there, there's no reason for me to be seen as a threat, is there? They'll back off, I'm sure. Whoever '*they*' are…"

"I agree, Bill. It seems to me that they're trying to silence you, or at least intimidate you into silence. We need to move quickly. Look, I don't think it's safe for you to go back home tonight. I've arranged for alternative accommodation. You'll like it."

Doug beamed at the couple. "Let's just say that not all our journalists get the chance to stay at the place I've got in mind. It's not normally reserved for the rank and file."

The group left St. Pancras Station and walked over to a waiting black taxi. Rain had been falling steadily, and a brisk wind blustered about. Kevin climbed into the front of the car, leaving plenty of space in the back of the traditional Hackney Carriage for the three remaining passengers.

Behind the glass window which separated the front and back compartments, Bill could make out instructions given by Kevin to the driver, and the taxi pulled out onto the Euston Road. The driver manoeuvred quickly, but illegally, across the road in front of Camden Town Hall. There was a loud chorus of complaining car horns. The taxi headed past the British Library towards the south west of the capital city.

"I think you should go to the police, love," implored Bill's wife, taking his hand in hers.

Bill could see Doug frown slightly. He could sense that the two of them had discussed this point at length, prior to his arrival.

"And tell them what, exactly? That an unknown assassin tried to throw me under a train, in front of about 100 witnesses, but was foiled by some kind of American James Bond character who just so happens to be following me around? It's not remotely believable, is it? I don't even know what happened to the two of them. The American yelled at me to get on the train, and I wasn't in the mood to hang around. The last I saw, the American had the other bloke in some kind of wrestling hold on the station platform, and everyone else was giving the two of them plenty of space."

"I can see what you mean, but even so; you were nearly killed!"

"I know, sweetheart, I know. But at least I'm back here now in one piece. It's over."

"Is it?" Helen was clearly emotional about the situation. "How do you know that they won't try again? At least if you went to the police they might be able to offer you some kind of protection."

"I doubt it."

From the look on Helen's face, she did too. Bill wondered whether her argument was a bargaining tool to extract greater security resources out of Doug. She's not daft, Bill thought to himself proudly. As if on cue, Doug chirped in.

"I think we've got the security side covered. Kevin here comes well recommended. But that's not all I have in mind. I'm taking you to Mr. Provotkin's apartment in Pimlico. He's away in New York at the moment, on business. You know how paranoid he is; his place is totally wired. No one can get in or out without his security team knowing about. You'll be much safer there than under police protection, which you probably won't get anyhow."

Bill had never actually met Mr. Provotkin, not even at one of London's more exclusive restaurants. The billionaire Russian had owned the Daily Standard since 2010, a takeover which had proven highly controversial at the time. But eventually, the fuss his buyout of the capital's newspaper had provoked had died out in the corridors of Westminster, and the national media had moved on to other stories.

After all, Mr Provotkin was now a British citizen, and had lived in London for a decade. More importantly, he was bitterly disliked by the Kremlin on account of his own pro-democracy attitude towards politics in the Motherland. Given the fate of many of his ex-pat comrades, he was constantly on his guard, and maintained a permanent contingent of private security officers at his various residences. One or two of them were rumoured to have once worked for the British Special Forces in Iraq.

Doug's idea of security was proving better than expected, and this was greatly reassuring to Bill. He nodded his approval to Doug, who then added, sarcastically, "This story of yours better be worth all this fuss, that's all I can say."

Bill squirmed on the back seat of the cab. "I need to discuss that with you, Doug."

"I'm sure. But not here. Let's wait until we're safely barricaded up in Provotkin's palace. I don't think we're going to have time to get this into tomorrow's paper anyhow. But we can get started tonight, and I can get some of the team to work on some complimentary articles tomorrow. I'm aiming to make the Thursday edition with a big splash."

"Hmmm. You haven't heard the actual story yet, Doug."

"Now you're really scaring me." A sardonic smile curled the edges of the editor's face. Bill knew that the tabloid paper was not going to want to cross every "t" and dot every "i".

Perhaps the sensational nature of the story would play in his favour, and ensure that the story made it into print before the 21st December. As it was, they only had a day in hand. The Mayan Age ended on Friday, and Ezekiel One would once again make the headlines, on Thursday. They were cutting things a bit fine.

Unaware of the urgency of time ticking past, the cab beat a slow and faltering path through central London's Tuesday evening rush-hour.

✦

"Coffee?" Helen's voice from the kitchen sounded decidedly upbeat. Her attitude had relaxed significantly since entering the apartment block. She had inspected the security staff on the building's reception floor. The security men were clearly a cut above the norm, with intelligent questions, and sharp wit.

Their sizeable office was dominated by CCTV screens and I.T. stations. Better still, they all looked as hard as nails. Kevin had immediately taken himself into a room by the apartment's front door and was to be seen no more. His constant presence in the flat was discrete, and reassuring. He seemed to have a good working relationship with the other men on duty.

Helen's real delight began when she crossed the threshold into Mr. Provotkin's actual apartment. The flat was undeniably tasteful and luxurious. No expense had been spared on the décor, with colour schemes built around gold and white. Antique furniture was offset by cutting edge television and sound systems. The grandeur of the apartment was splendid, trumped only by the comfort of the furniture chosen to dress the rooms. In one corner of the main reception room, an elegant chess set was laid out on a beautifully ornate coffee table, mid-game. Some Russian habits died hard, thought Bill.

By the door to the lounge was one of the Bainbridges' old suitcases, suddenly looking distinctly down-market.

Bill was taking a sneak peek behind the curtains. He looked across the river Thames at the city lights running along the south bank. The newly redeveloped Battersea power station was well lit, and offered a stunning spectacle at night. This was certainly a beautiful place to live, paid for by the Russian's sharp business acumen during the privatisation of Russia's energy monopolies.

Pulling back from the curtains, Bill thanked his wife for the offer of coffee, and took a seat next to Doug at the dining table. The older man was setting up his laptop computer. A few minutes later, Helen was seated with them, and they sipped on coffee and ate luxury chocolate biscuits from Mr. Provotkins' "secret" kitchen stash.

"Does Mr. Provotkin know we're staying here tonight?," asked Bill. For some reason, Bill felt out of his depth. He was unsure how to explain this mad story, and still sound sane. Yet, it was clear that the newspaper's proprietor was attaching significant importance to it.

"Yes, and he's okay with it."

"Right."

Doug's laptop was booted up, and he was scrolling through his emails. He took a swig of hot coffee and turned to Bill. "Okay, let's have it then." The editor opened up a new, blank file.

"It turns out that Dr. Sacher worked for NASA on black projects. He helped on the design and construction of the engines and power system of Ezekiel One. He's very proud of his work, and feels that the advances he made to science during the course of his work have gone unrecognised."

"Because the project is under wraps?" asked Helen.

"Exactly. His motivation in coming forward now appears to be to promote his own role in the creation of the most remarkable spacecraft ever made. He said that the craft is powered by a powerful nuclear reactor, and uses some kind of nuclear propulsion system, as well a traditional chemical rocket to get it out of Earth's orbit."

"So it *is* going somewhere then?" asked Doug.

"So he says. But not to Mars, or anywhere you might have expected. This whole project is a lot more ambitious than that. Dr. Sacher claims that Ezekiel One has been built to take its astronauts to a planet which NASA secretly knows about, but is unknown to the rest of us."

"Like in another solar system, or another galaxy?"

"No, not quite as far away as that. This secret planet is actually orbiting the Sun. It's just a long way out there. Way beyond Pluto, apparently. Except, well, it's not exactly a planet."

Doug had started typing as Bill had spoken. But he now paused, and scratched his head. Helen looked thoroughly bemused. There was silence for a moment. Bill realised that he had the advantage of having read the book by Marcus Everett. "The Day After 2012" had discussed the possibility of a brown dwarf at the edge of the solar system. That concept had been new to him at the time. It still seemed bizarre now, but he was getting used to it. He needed to find the right words to explain this concept to his wife and his boss.

"This is a really big planet. It's like Jupiter, but much denser, and much more active."

Which one's Jupiter?," asked Doug. His plump fingers had resumed their speedy dance across the keyboard. Their conversation was echoed by a chorus of quiets clicking sounds.

"Which one's *Jupiter?"* Helen's eyebrows raised in disbelief, her voice strained, but touched with humour. Doug might have been at the back of her classroom, pulling the hair of the schoolgirl in front of him. For his part, Doug did not rise to the bait. He shrugged nonchalantly, and continued to type away.

"It's the big gas giant, Doug. The one with the red spot. It's hundreds of times bigger than the Earth," she explained, a slight measure of condescension in her voice. Unabashed, Doug indicated that Bill should continue.

"Well, apparently, when gas giants grow to a certain size as they form, they ignite. It's a bit like becoming a star, but not quite the same. The planet burns very brightly for a while, then the fuel is all used up and it fades into darkness. It's still pretty active, and warm, but essentially dark.

"I found out a bit about this when I read that book by Marcus Everett. He was really interested in the idea too. Because for a while, this planet behaved like a star. It's known by some as a 'dark star.' When one of these planets is in its youthful phase, and very active, emitting lots of light, it's called a 'light-emitting planet.' They're sort of two sides to the same coin."

Bill took his Paris metro card out of his trouser pocket, and opened it out. Inserted inside was his ticket, and written on this, in biro, were several numbers. Bill looked at the numbers he had written down, as he had walked back out of the Louvre.

"Dr. Sacher says that these things are very common, but very difficult to find. And one of them, a very old one, is orbiting around the Sun. It's known as a sub-brown dwarf. It's sort of in-between a gas giant and a brown dwarf star. He claims that it takes about 60,000 years to circle the Sun. He also said that it's about 1,500 times the distance from the Sun to the Earth. Which is a fair old whack…"

Helen whistled softly. "That's impossible, surely?"

"What is?"

"Well, the whole thing. How can a planet that size have been out there all along without any of us knowing about it? And, even if it is out there — like Dr. Sacher claims — it's so far away! We can hardly get men to the Moon, let alone all the way out to this thing."

"I'm only telling you what he told me. He says that the existence of this dark star is the most closely guarded secret in America. *He* doesn't even know *exactly* where it is, even though he was working on the project for years."

"That's convenient." Helen was sounding distinctly cynical.

Doug was impassive, watching the debate with seasoned interest, weighing up the relative merits of the story.

"Maybe it is. He seemed pretty genuine to me. He said he's going to contact some of his old associates to see if he can pin its location down." Bill looked back down at his metro ticket. "He says that this dark star is on the edge of the constellation Sagittarius. Apparently, it's currently obscured by the Sun, so even if we knew exactly where it is we wouldn't be able to see it right now, anyway."

"That's also very convenient."

Bill shrugged in response. "I asked him for some proof, because I was as sceptical as you. He said he couldn't provide anything concrete, because he had never managed to smuggle anything out of NASA. But he agreed to send us proof that he once worked there and, like he said, he was going to try to corroborate this story with other colleagues. He was of the opinion that this story was going to break anyway, with the news having come out about the existence of Ezekiel One."

"Did you ask him about the priests?" asked Doug suddenly.

Bill nodded slowly. "Yes, I did. He didn't know about them, but he reckoned that they were the ship's cargo."

Doug and Helen looked equally baffled. Bill shifted in his seat uneasily, and continued.

"This is the craziest part."

"You mean *more* crazy than what you've just told us?" Helen was clearly unconvinced.

"I'm afraid so."

Helen and Doug exchanged glances, and then looked back at Bill.

He plunged in. "The priests are emissaries."

"Sorry?" Helen intoned utter disbelief.

"They're being sent to the dark star because of their expertise in ancient languages and culture. Dr. Sacher claims that the dark star system is inhabited. He says that there are other planets orbiting the dark star which are warm enough for water and life to exist there.

"Apparently, NASA has already sent a space telescope towards the dark star and it has sent back some images to Earth showing these other worlds. The scientists at NASA have analysed the images, and other data sent back from this probe, and have established that there is life in the system."

"My God." Doug was in shock. He picked up his coffee mug and finished the drink rapidly. "We've got work to do." He started tapping away at his keyboard rapidly.

"Are you serious? No one's going to believe this! It's total science fiction," exclaimed Helen.

"Who cares? It's a great story." Doug spread his fingers out as if to show off a newspaper headline. "*NASA scientist reveals truth about E.T.* Or how about, *Aliens on our doorstep, NASA man claims?* We can have some fun with this. It doesn't matter if it's verifiable or not. Just reporting that this NASA scientist has blown the whistle is enough to get the story into the open."

The portly editor was already halfway through a fresh paragraph of newspaper copy. Bill smiled. Sometimes working for a tabloid newspaper had its advantages. Helen was thinking like a college-educated reader of the broadsheets. Doug was aiming his article at a less discerning audience.

Helen looked at Bill disapprovingly, but he knew she understood the game. It was clear that Doug would be writing this story himself, and thereby taking immediate credit for the exclusive. The editor would then feature Bill in the story as the heroic investigative journalist, who had evaded assassination attempts to bring the story to the public's attention. That would allow Bill to write up a personalised account of what had happened in Paris that day, to add to the feature's drama and sense of urgency.

It would be explosive stuff, whether there was a shred of truth to the story or not.

As Doug worked his alchemical arts, Helen quizzed her husband some more. "Even if there is life on this dark star, what's that got to do with ancient languages on Earth?"

"The life isn't on the dark star itself. The dark star is sort of a boiling hot gas giant. The life is on one of the habitable worlds orbiting the dark star. The habitable world is thought to be like Earth. The dark star warms it up with its gravity and its heat output. But it would be much darker than here on Earth."

"Okay, I can see how that would work in principle. But what's all that got to do with human culture here on Earth?"

"Dr. Sacher took me around the Mesopotamian exhibition at the Louvre. He claimed that the gods of Mesopotamia were real people. They came from this home-world orbiting the dark star. He thinks that they had something to do with human evolution, and the development of our civilisation. He didn't know why the passengers on Ezekiel One are all Christian priests, particularly, but he thinks that their learning puts them in a good position to be ambassadors for Earth."

"Do you have any idea how mad that sounds, Bill?"

"Of course I do. His main worry is that we are drawing attention to ourselves by visiting these ancient gods of Mesopotamia, and that they might, in return, come back and visit us. He's concerned that this would be a bad thing."

Helen mused over things for a moment. "What do you think, Bill? Is this for real?"

"I don't know. I'd prefer to see some proof — like those images from the unmanned probe, for instance. But, to be honest, those kinds of images can be faked really easily these days with the right computer packages. I'm hoping he comes up with some co-ordinates for this dark star that I can take to Dr. Clarke in Oxford. He might be able to go back through his library of space images to track down an image of this thing. His opinion would count for a lot, certainly in my mind."

"It doesn't sound like we've got enough time for all that," Helen nodded towards Doug, who was still feverishly typing away.

"I'm still listening, you know," he replied. "Look, I want to substantiate this story as much as you do, but I don't think the good French doctor is going to come up with the goods. If he worked on the project for years, under the deepest security clearance, and still never found out where this dark star is, then why do you think he's going to come up with the coordinates now?"

Bill agreed. "He didn't sound very optimistic, I must say."

"I think the very fact that someone's tried to silence you is enough to create a positive spin on the accuracy of this story," continued Doug. "We've used stories provided by intelligence whistleblowers before, and the public tends to give them greater credence than you would expect. People assume that the government is hiding something, and like to read about what it might be. If we get some proof further down the line, then all the better."

"Who do you think is trying to kill Bill?"

"I don't know. Maybe the CIA. Maybe one of our lot. Does it matter? The point is that there is a government plot to conceal the truth."

"It's not that simple, Doug," interjected Bill. "Remember that my life was saved today by an American agent. I've seen him before, several times. He's obviously affiliated with the British government official in charge of our national intelligence services. It seems to me that I was actively protected by the British government, through the actions of an American agent."

"I don't think our readers are going to make the distinction. The point is, several agents have been following you, and one of them tried to kill you on foreign soil. Even if there is a battle going on within the corridors of power about whether this story gets out or not, at least one part of the government here or in the US is trying to stop this story."

"Which is another point that's bothering me. Dr. Sacher explained to me why they were going to these lengths to keep the project secret."

"Oh, yeah, what did he say?" Doug barely slowed down typing as he listened.

"He said that if the story got onto the television, or the radio, then the news would essentially be broadcast into outer space. The aliens, if that's what they are, although it seems as though they're essentially humans themselves, would be able to pick up the news that a manned spacecraft is on its way. Assuming that they're monitoring the radio noise coming from Earth, that is. Sending a spacecraft to their world might be considered an act of war."

Doug stopped writing and sat back in his dining room chair. He looked at Bill quizzically. Helen, who had long since dismissed the whole story as nonsense, helped herself to another chocolate biscuit from the bone china plate on the table.

Bill continued. "Television and radio transmissions leak out into space at the speed of light. If an alien civilisation is monitoring our transmissions, then they'd see from the news that we know they're out there. Surprise appears to be a key element in the success of this mission, whatever it might be trying to achieve. Dr. Sacher seemed to think that the purpose of the Ezekiel One mission was to send back military intelligence about the alien presence around the dark star. They are considered to be a military threat."

"Why?"

"Because, based upon Biblical accounts and other ancient literature, the alien people are warlike. In fact, they're just like us. That's what worries the military top brass. To be honest, Doug, this is the thing I'm having real problems with. If we break this story, will it bring some kind of alien invasion down upon us?"

Doug turned and faced Bill, and engaged actively in the debate. Helen munched on her biscuit.

"If that was the case, then why is the government trying to protect you? Anne Potter-Smith, who you're still meeting tomorrow by the way, is trying to help you to break this story. She wouldn't be doing that if she thought that you were about to unleash Armageddon."

"Maybe she doesn't realise what she's dealing with."

"Look, Bill, if we stopped to think about every consequence of our actions, we'd never put anything into print. If the Yanks wanted to keep this dark star secret, then they shouldn't have built a bloody great spaceship to go flying off there on some kind of barking mad military reconnaissance mission. They're the ones who are taking the risks, not us. Besides which, we're putting this story into a newspaper, not onto satellite TV. The aliens would have to have some pretty good telescopes to read our paper from up there."

Helen snorted her humorous approval.

"That's not the point," argued Bill. "Once the story's out, it's out. The television companies will pick it up and run with it too. Then the story gets beamed up to the dark star aliens at the speed of light. Then they come down here and get us. You want a story about the End of the Mayan Age? That's it, right there…"

"Not necessarily, Bill. Frankly, the whole thing is bonkers. We have no evidence, no proof. Just the testimony of a lone French scientist who, for all we know, might currently be lying under the wheels of a Parisian bus. This is a great story, Bill, but no one's actually going to take it seriously. But, by God, it'll sell newspapers."

"And that's all that matters to you?" Bill was getting irritated.

"Don't shoot the messenger, Bill," smiled Doug extravagantly. He turned in his seat and continued to work at his article. Within minutes he had completed a draft, and turned the laptop around so Bill could read it. Helen also moved around the table to read the editorial copy. After a moment, they looked at each other to gauge each other's reactions.

"It's good, Doug, very good," said Helen, her admiration declared, despite her inherent scepticism.

"Of course it's good. It's great!" The editor beamed confidently. "It's just a pity it'll have to wait until Thursday's paper. But that gives us some time to fill it out with some features; some science about these dark stars, some neat graphics of the solar system, and some more of those silhouette images of Ezekiel One.

"I'll get the graphic nerds in the office to knock out some top quality work in the morning. And maybe, just maybe, Bill, you can extract a little more info from Mrs. Potter-Smith tomorrow, to put the cherry on the cake."

Bill was feeling very tired by now. He rubbed his eyes, and muttered darkly under his breath.

"Does Mr. Provotkin drink?" asked Helen, suddenly changing the subject.

"Well, he's Russian, so what do *you* think?" Doug was buoyant.

Helen laughed, and stood up, making for the kitchen. "He's got to have a half-decent bottle of plonk in this place, don't you think? I fancy celebrating your safe return, darling."

"Sounds good to me," replied Bill, who slowly stood up, and headed for the kitchen. He suddenly felt famished.

"Sounds like my cue to leave," muttered Doug, who started to shut down the computer. "I'll leave you two lovebirds to it. Bill, your meeting with Potter-Smith is at 10 a.m. on the lawn outside Westminster. The usual spot: I think you could practically walk it from here.

"Don't be late, though, because there should be some TV crews there too. Kevin will be going with you, don't forget. Then you'd better head back to the office to write this story up in a bit more detail for the inside pages."

"Do you want me to let on that we're publishing on Thursday?"

"Well, she seems to be on our side, so if you have to talk about it to get more info out of her, then go for it. See how you get on. You've coped this far." Doug's sardonic smile flashed briefly across his face, as he was wrapping his laptop up into its case.

The comforting sound of a wine bottle cork being pulled from its tenure emanated from the kitchen, and Bill drifted towards the promise of fine food and wine.

CHAPTER SEVENTEEN

Above the heads of the living creatures was, as it were, a vault glittering like a sheet of ice, awe-inspiring, stretched over their heads above them.

As Doug had said, the walk from Provotkin's apartment building to the Palace of Westminster was a manageable one. In the subdued grey light of the winter's morning, Bill looked across at the Vauxhall Bridge as he headed north towards the Houses of Parliament. In the gloom, he could make out the headquarters of MI6. He reflected on the last time he had looked at that building, on the occasion he had been in Anne Potter-Smith's office in the Houses of Parliament. It seemed a long time ago now.

Kevin, who was walking alongside him, was in a talkative mood, and they had been going over some basic security strategies. Kevin had then moved on to discuss the appearance and behaviour of the men who had followed, and eventually attacked Bill. He seemed curious about the incident in Paris, and had begun to pry a little more pointedly.

"So, explain this to me again, Mr. Bainbridge. The stocky bloke had managed to get himself behind you in the subway, and ran forward to push you onto the tracks."

"Yes, that's right. I turned to see where he was, and I saw him lunge forward with his arms held out. There was a line or two of commuters between us, but there had been a gap between them that had given him a clear line at me."

"And then this tall geezer stepped in…"

"Yes, he tackled him like a rugby player. It was all very fast. They landed just behind me, and the Tall Man had the stocky man in some kind of wrestling hold. There was a struggle between them, but the Tall Man seemed to be in complete control. He told the other passengers, who were panicking a bit, that the man he was holding had just tried to kill himself. His French was very good. Then he turned to me and told me, in English, to get away. Which I did, by getting onto the RER. That was the last I saw of either of them. Neither of them seemed to follow me to the Eurostar terminal, and believe me, I was watching out for them closely."

"Did you recognise the Tall Man before he made his move?"

"No, I hadn't spotted him at all."

"But you were practically standing next to him, and he's, well, tall, right?"

"Yes, he's about 6' 5", I would say. But, for whatever reason, his presence didn't register in my mind. I was fairly distracted at the time."

"Look, here's the thing, chief. You say that this tall guy is known to you from previous encounters. You ran into this subway station in Paris, worked your way through a crowd of pedestrians, and you were then attacked in what was essentially a random point on the platform. If the Tall Man character had followed you into the station as well, you would have noticed him. So, you must have pretty much just run up and stood right next to him as he was waiting. Then he made his move to save your life."

"I agree, it's weird."

"It's more than weird."

The two men crossed over at the traffic lights by Vauxhall Bridge and made their way up Millbank. Within moments the Houses of Parliament were in sight up ahead. The familiarity of the Palace of Westminster did not prevent Bill and Kevin from staring it it for an awed moment. Bill recalled how Nicholas I, the Tsar of Russia, had described the building as a 'dream in stone'. Even in the murky mid-winter light, the majestic architecture of the Houses of Parliament was spell-binding. But such a momentary vision could never last long in central London. The noise of traffic and the bustle of pedestrians all around the two men brought Bill back to earth.

Kevin continued to speak his mind. "It's almost like the guy's psychic or something. No, I have to say, I think you've been scammed."

"Sorry? What did you say?"

"You've been scammed, chief. These two were clearly working together. What I can't get my head around is how the tall bloke ended up in just the right spot like that."

Bill was incredulous, and a touch irritated by the suggestion that he had been played. "Why on earth do you think it was a scam?"

"Because there's no police report of any violent incident. If things had gone how you said, then there would have been a right skirmish in that subway station after the train pulled out. Think about it. After the tall bloke had subdued the assailant, what would he have done with him next? Knock him out? Drag him out by force? Let him go, and then face the man off in public? Whatever he did there would have been a struggle, and a very violent one at that. Someone would have got their mobile out and phoned the police."

"I see what you mean…Except that mobiles don't work in the subway, do they? I'm not great with phones, mind you."

"Well, someone could have used a public phone, or pressed an alarm, or *something*. The only way that a report wasn't phoned in was if the two men just stood up after the train pulled out, and then strolled out of the station like nothing had happened. Which means that they were working together."

Bill considered this for a moment, as the two men walked past the Tate Gallery. If Kevin was right, then all along, the men who had been following him had simply been giving the impression of presenting a threat. But to what purpose? Perhaps the intention had been to make him take seriously a story that was in fact a hoax. He had been pondering that possibility during the night. Doug had been way too keen to publish this outlandish story. Maybe it was a trap to discredit the newspaper?

It was obvious that the Ezekiel One spacecraft was real enough, and perhaps they had embarrassed NASA, or the government authorities, by revealing the truth. This Dark Star story of Dr. Sacher's might be a red herring, to shift the Ezekiel One revelation into the twilight zone, where most sane people would discount it from that point forth. The story would then become just another crazy conspiracy theory.

"But how would the Tall Man know where I would be standing?"

"It would have been obvious which line you were heading for, because they knew your final destination. He may have manoeuvred behind you as the other guy got ready to make his move. But, you've got that same problem to answer whether the Tall Man is friend or foe. How did he turn up just at the right time, and in the right place?"

"That's not the only time that's happened, either."

"How so?"

"When that bomb went off in Oxford Street, I had been in the book shop that got the full force of the blast just ten minutes beforehand. The Tall Man had appeared, and I wanted to catch up with him, to ask him who he was, so I left the building. Then the blast occurred. I swear; I would still have been in that damned shop had he not appeared. So, you see, he's saved my life twice now. And that's just what I'm aware of. I've seen him four times altogether. Maybe other things have happened that I don't even know about on the other two occasions."

"Okay, well some of this might appear to be like he's using magic, but there may be a rational explanation. You might have a tracking device on you, for instance."

"No chance!"

"Have you had any surgery recently, or anything like that?"

"No…Er, hold on, well, yes. After the bomb blast, I had to have my arm stitched up. It was done over there, actually." Bill pointed across the river at St. Thomas' Hospital, perched on the South Bank opposite Parliament.

"Maybe the doctor who stitched you up inserted something into your arm."

Bill laughed., "That's ridiculous."

"Is it? Do you remember the name of the doctor?"

"Er, yes, it was a Dr. Patel. He was a surgical registrar, and he stitched my arm up in their Outpatients clinic."

"Right, okay, after you've had your interview with Lady What's-her-name, let's take a wander over the bridge and check up on this Dr. Patel."

The men had now proceeded past Millbank Tower, and were about to cross the road by Lambeth Bridge. In front of them were the Victoria Tower Gardens, set in the grounds of the Palace of Westminster. A sizeable group of media representatives had collected in the gardens, and were interviewing a smartly-dressed woman, who Bill assumed was Anne Potter-Smith, Chair of the Intelligence and Security Committee.

He was now completely confused. Was she on his side, or was there some kind of elaborate game going on to make him simply believe she was on his side? If he gave her too much information, would she wreck the publication of this amazing story — a story which revealed government knowledge of the presence of extra-terrestrials in the solar system? On the other hand, if the story was bogus, then would she lead him towards the worst professional judgement of his career, with the intention of making him a laughing stock?

Or, was she really on his side after all, despite Kevin's suspicions? They were now in the Old Palace Yard, and it had started to rain a little heavier.

Deeply perplexed, Bill headed towards the security perimeter, to check in with the police officers on duty. Kevin waited on Abingdon Street, looking around at the media personalities present. Bill was befuddled. He had no idea what was going on anymore, and could only hope that his imminent encounter with the Member of Parliament, in front of the nation's media, would clarify matters. He was not optimistic that it would.

✦

The flashbulbs were blinding for eyes accustomed to London's mid-winter gloom. Bill was standing next to Anne Potter-Smith, shaking her hand, to the clatter of camera shutters. Behind them, in the distance, was the modern architecture of the MI6 Headquarters, creating an apt backdrop for the photographs and television images.

The M.P. was beaming, and permeated the photo-opportunity with a selection of media-friendly sound-bites. Bill's iconic status was being built up in a politically expedient manner. She praised his bravery during the terrorist atrocity in London, praised the staff of St. Thomas' hospital, and praised the people of London for their traditionally steadfast character in the face of adversity. She talked about Bill's account of the bomb blast, and then also touched upon his article about the riot in Hyde Park.

The media pack sensed blood at this point, and began firing in questions about his own role in the emotional volatility of that event. One of the rival tabloid hacks accused Bill of stirring up trouble about the imminent end of the Mayan Age. Professionally dominant, Mrs. Potter-Smith skilfully manoeuvred the interview away from that particular controversy, and back to the safety of positive anti-terrorism spin.

Throughout, Bill kept his mouth shut, expressing a simple smile, and gratitude. Eventually though, the point came when he had to make something of a speech. He was brief, and to the point, deliberately self-deprecating and yet gallant in an understated way. He praised the hospital staff as well, although inwardly he was now plagued by the thought that the hospital doctor was not who he had thought at all.

He expressed his delight that the girl he had saved had made a full recovery. Finally, he made politically correct comments about the fight against terrorism.

After the event came to an end (in what had been just ten minutes in reality, but had seemed much longer to Bill), he found himself alone in the company of the M.P. in the garden. The hacks, cameramen, soundmen and photographers cleared up their kit and drifted away.

The politician and the restaurant reviewer stood beneath her large, black umbrella.

"I see you've brought along some personal protection." Anne Potter-Smith nodded towards Kevin, who was stood on the pavement outside the gardens smoking a cigarette.

"Yes, well, things have been getting a little sticky lately."

"So I hear. I've done my bit to provide you with some protection, Mr. Bainbridge. So, tell me, has it been a worthwhile investment? Do you have your story?"

"I still have a lot of unanswered questions. The main one relates directly to my own personal safety. Exactly who are these goons who have been keeping tabs on me all this time?"

"It's complicated, Mr. Bainbridge. Like I explained to you last time we met, the distribution of political power is not quite how it seems. The men who have been following you work for a facet of the American Government that is beyond the democratic control of its people. This organisation answers to a different power. They have a considerable interest in keeping news of Ezekiel One's mission out of the media."

"Why?"

"To ensure that the mission runs smoothly."

"You and the Tall Man, you're moving in a different direction with this, I take it?"

"The Tall Man?"

"Come on, Mrs. Potter-Smith, you know who I mean. The man who apparently saved my life yesterday in Paris."

The politician's face broke into a soft smile. "*Apparently?*"

"Yes, *apparently*. I have no idea who the good guys are anymore. For all I know, you people are playing with my mind. I need some simple answers from you."

She smiled again. "There are never any simple answers, Mr. Bainbridge, not in the field of National Intelligence, anyway. The Tall Man, as you refer to him, is an associate of mine who works on a freelance basis. He has, let us say, some unusual attributes, which come in handy every so often. He has a vested interest in bringing this story to the attention of the world."

"Is he a government agent?"

"Not exactly."

She shifted uneasily, as if deliberating whether to go on. She looked up at Bill, and spoke quietly.

"The governments of the world are not the only source of power on this planet. Our Western governments, particularly, like to give the impression that they are the servants of the people, who democratically elect them. But in reality, we are nothing more than a tier of middle management. Parties to the left, or to the right, it matters not a jot anymore.

"However, there are other powers which none of us, even in this grand old building, really entirely understand. These powers are very, very ancient. They are embedded into our highest social stratas, growing and changing as our societies grow and change. The important thing to grasp here is that these powers do not always act in agreement with each other. When they disagree, our nations can sometimes become divided, and wars result. Occasionally, when there is one dominant governmental power in the world, like there is now, the hidden powers pull that government in several directions at once, which creates confusion."

Bill could feel a headache coming on,. "I'm not sure I'm following any of this."

Anne Potter-Smith sighed. "America is very dominant at the moment, despite the economic recession it has been recovering from recently. It is particularly dominant in some of the areas that are most important to the powers I am alluding to. Military. Space technology. Intelligence. Communications. These are crucial areas of interest, and America is the only real player in town in these areas. So, control of these resources is hotly contested by the adversarial powers behind the scenes. In contrast, during the Cold War it was straightforward for these powers to align themselves with the two different superpowers. They used their influence to manipulate each of the superpowers to make progress in these areas that interested them. Then the Soviet Union collapsed economically, so the struggle has shifted almost entirely over to the other side of the Atlantic, creating an internal rift in the American political system."

"So, who are these powers? Do you mean something like the Freemasons?"

The M.P. laughed freely and touched Bill's arm in reassurance. "I'm sorry. That was just so funny. No, not the Freemasons. My dear man, have you not already guessed?"

Bill shook his head. Over the last few months he had tried to acclimatise himself to all kinds of bizarre truths, and half-truths. His internal model of the world had been badly shaken, but he was not sure he was ready to consider the idea that the history of the world was controlled by a centuries-old cabal of powerful warring factions behind the scenes. It was true that there were some very powerful men and women in the world who were capable of shaping governments, and their policies, and particularly their executives. Money and power went together in Western democracies, and he could see how there might be powerful king-makers behind the scenes of the democratic parties. But, at the end of the day, governments were created by the voting intentions of the electorate. That was an element that was not in the hands of a hidden power, by definition.

He suspected that this confusing rhetoric presented by the politician was further obfuscation, designed to keep him on-side.

"Well, I'm not even sure that I accept the basis of your argument. How could democracies be controlled from within?"

"Quite easily, I assure you, particularly if those powers control the media. The media shapes public opinion, the public opinion then shapes government policy, and democracy is seen to be done. There are rare occasions when the electorate does something it's not supposed to do, but for the most part, it behaves itself and acts in a predictable, and controllable manner. Your organisation is one of many that are systematically used to control opinion, events, and political outcomes. The trappings of democracy are simply window-dressing."

"That's very cynical."

"I'm a politician, Bill. Of course I'm cynical! Look, it's not important to me whether you accept what I'm telling you. But it is important that you get this story out before Friday. Because by Saturday, it will be too late."

Bill scratched his head, and sighed. "No one's going to believe it, so I don't really see what you're going to achieve, frankly. My editor loves the sensational aspects of this story, and it's a great tabloid scoop, but there's no actual proof. The story's going to be picked to pieces in no time."

"What do you mean, no proof?"

"All we've got is the testimony of one scientist, and a few ambiguous leaked documents. It's not exactly earth-shattering, is it?"

Anne Potter-Smith's face had turned ashen. She looked crestfallen, even a touch panicky.

"Do you know where it is?" she asked him urgently.

"Where what is?"

"The Dark Star, Mr. Bainbridge. The Dark Star!" The volume of her voice had raised significantly. Anne Potter-Smith's caution had been outdone by sudden panic.

"All I know is what Dr. Sacher told me. He wasn't very specific."

"He didn't give you the co-ordinates?"

"He said he didn't know where it was. But he was going to try to find out."

"Oh my God!"

The End of the World seemed to have come three days early for the Chair of the Intelligence and Security Committee. Her sheen of political arrogance had dissipated. Either Anne Potter-Smith was an Academy Award winning actress, or she had just received some very bad news indeed.

"You don't look very well, Mrs. Potter-Smith. Do you need to sit down or something?"

"The flaming idiot! *Of course he knew where the bloody thing is.* He lost his nerve, right at the last! Now he's ruined everything!"

"If it's any consolation, he said that no one would be able to image it at the moment anyway. It's lying behind the Sun, apparently." Bill suddenly realised what Mrs. Potter-Smith had just said. A chill went down his spine. "Did you just say 'knew,' like, in the *past tense*?"

The M.P. looked at him directly, presently a cold visage in the December drizzle. "Yes, Mr. Bainbridge, '*knew*'. Dr Sacher's body was fished out of the River Seine this morning. *Apparently*, as you like to say, he took his own life."

It was Bill's turn to look shocked. He had been concerned that Dr. Sacher's life was also under threat, but he was still dumbfounded by the news. The shadow of death seemed to be creeping ever closer.

"Weren't you protecting him as well?"

"Yes, but our resources don't match those of our opponents. You were our priority. It took us six months to persuade Dr. Sacher to come forward. The worst part is that *they* probably now know that he kept the co-ordinates secret. I'm sure their methods of persuasion were sufficient to extract that data from him. They no longer have anything to fear now they know that you don't know."

"Well, why don't *you* let me have the co-ordinates?"

The politician was losing her temper. "What on Earth makes you think *I* know? If I knew that information, this whole situation wouldn't be coming down to the wire like it is now. We'd have moved on this long ago."

"I see. Well, maybe you're not giving enough credit to the people of this country. They may believe the story anyway."

"You don't really believe that, Mr. Bainbridge. There has not yet been a general acceptance of the existence of Ezekiel One, and its position has been confirmed by any number of independent observers. So how are they going to accept the existence of a distant, undiscovered planet on the say-so of a suicidal engineer?"

"Okay, I take your point. I have to say, though, I'm not quite sure why this is so important. I mean, what does it really matter if people learn of the existence of this dark star? It seems to me that Ezekiel One is going to set off towards it anyhow, whether people realise it or not."

Anne Potter-Smith seemed distracted, as if recalculating. She replied to Bill almost absently, "Because the *Watchers* will then know that we know about them. For them, it will be an expected evolution of human awareness, and they will have a plan about how to make contact with us without causing our civilisation too much panic."

Bill had no idea who *The Watchers* were, but he wanted Mrs. Potter-Smith to continue with her absent-minded explanation, so he kept quiet.

"A diplomatic contact will be well established in time, and both sides will have time to adjust to the new reality. But if that ship just turns up out of the blue, carrying God knows what on-board, the stakes will be raised considerably.

Their reaction will be much less predictable, which makes it very dangerous for us here on Earth, believe me!"

"Yes, Dr. Sacher said something about that, too. If that's the case, then why are the Americans sending this spaceship out there anyway? Surely they must realise they are playing with fire?"

"Like I tried to explain before, Mr. Bainbridge, it's not exactly the Americans doing this, not under their own volition anyway. They're providing the manpower and money to make the thing happen, but the directing force is working behind the scenes. The President of the United States thinks he knows what he's doing, but we think there is another agenda at work that he's not aware of."

"So what does he think he's trying to achieve?"

Anne Potter-Smith looked uncomfortable. "Bill, I will tell you this in the strictest of confidence. This is not to get into your paper, or even past your lips, or so help me God I'll track you down and kill you myself!"

"I think I've got enough on my plate already, Anne. What does the President think he's up to?"

She sighed heavily. "He knows about the Watchers. He knows that they moulded our civilisation, that they had a hand in our genetic development. But he's convinced that we have something that they don't."

"What's that?"

"Jesus Christ."

Bill laughed. But Anne Potter-Smith did not join in. She was entirely serious, "The gods of Egypt and Mesopotamia, as some of these Watchers became, were pre-Christian era. They are therefore all pagan by definition, and spiritually bound for Hell. That's what the President believes, anyway."

"That's bonkers."

"That particular assessment would not reflect official British Government policy, Bill," she replied dryly. "But, yes, it doesn't make much sense to me either. Neverthcless, that's how he thinks. He sees himself a bit like the Spanish Kings who sent missionaries to the Americas five centuries ago. He wants to offer the Watchers the knowledge of the coming of Christ, and therefore Salvation."

"And if they don't fancy being converted to Christianity?"

"Then, whoever's in his job in about fifteen years time will be picking up the pieces."

"But you said that this isn't the true agenda for the mission."

"No, that was just the line that was sold to the President to get him to sink ten percent of America's resources into the project."

"What's the real agenda?"

"To be honest with you, I have absolutely no idea. But whatever it is, it's not good. Think about the analogy I just drew with the European conquest of the Americas after Columbus. Missionaries went hand in hand with soldiers. In my mind, I like to compare this mission with the Conquistadors making their way towards Mexico City."

"My God."

"Yes, you've got the idea. It sort of brings us nicely 'round to the Mayan End of the Age, don't you think?"

Bill's headache was definitely getting worse. Where his perception of this whole adventure had unravelled over the last twenty-four hours, it was now quickly reorganising itself into a whole new convoluted mess. "But the President surely wasn't involved in the death of Dr. Sacher?"

"No, the President is being manoeuvred, just like we all are. The agency that is trying to keep the lid on this story is acting independently, and ruthlessly. It is not accountable to the American people. You should also understand that there are parts of the U.S. Administration that have a real problem with what's going on, like the State Department, and we are loosely affiliated with their interests. Like I said, there are factions fighting between themselves internally to control this situation, even here, within the British Government. My side appears to be losing."

"You represent the British Government's interests though, don't you?"

"No, not really. My job is oversight of the security services, which gives me considerable influence and some useful contacts. But my stance on this is rather like that of the State Department in the U.S. We have our opinion about whether this project should be properly exposed, but that opinion is not shared by the White House, or by the British Cabinet, insofar as they even understand what's really going on."

"That would explain why you were so careful with security at our last meeting."

"Exactly. I'm acutely aware that my office is bugged by the very people whose work I am overseeing! The surveillance that we are both under is also why I chose to hold this photo-opportunity out here in the gardens, despite the weather.

"Because, even though we're under the noses of this lot..." she pointed towards the towering structure of the Palace of Westminster before them, "...and them..." she indicated the MI6 HQ across the river, "...we're at least not being overheard. I hope."

The journalist and politician stood in silence for a moment, in the gardens of the Houses of Parliament.

"I'd better go, Mr. Bainbridge. I need to reassess this situation with some of my colleagues, and work out what, if anything, to try next."

"My publisher intends for the story to be published tomorrow. We're working on finishing touches to the feature this afternoon."

"Good. I just hope that it ends up making some kind of impact with the broadcasters. If the BBC picks it up, then we may yet have a chance of saving this situation." She offered her hand for Bill to shake, which he did, and the two of them walked back towards the police cordon and concrete defences set up on the pavement on Abingdon Street. As Anne Potter-Smith walked towards St.

Stephen's entrance, shaking her umbrella dry, Kevin came up to stand alongside Bill on the pavement outside the Palace of Westminster.

"Right then, so we're off to St. Thomas' Hospital, then?"

"To be honest, I really don't think that will be necessary."

"She sweet-talked you, eh? You won't be sure until you've checked out that doctor who treated you."

Bill looked at the burly man beside him, dressed in his crumpled suit smelling of cigarette smoke. Was Kevin working for the other side too, he wondered? His sense of paranoia was acute, and probably not to be trusted. What he needed was evidence, so he could form some kind of rational judgement. But maybe they were all trying to work with only part of the story - even the politicians.

"Okay, let's go. We'll pick up a taxi from the hospital back to the office afterwards."

Kevin smiled, and slapped Bill on the back in a friendly manner. "That's the spirit, chief. I bet you any money that no one's ever heard of this Dr. Patel." The two men began to walk along the puddle-strewn street towards Westminster Bridge.

✦

Bill stood next to Kevin in the Surgical Outpatients Reception. Bill felt this was a waste of time, but he needed some normal human contact, away from the Ezekiel One conspiracy, which was threatening to engulf his sanity. The queue gradually worked its way along and it was soon Bill's turn to speak with the receptionist.

"I've come for my appointment with Dr. Patel," asked Bill, who had been prompted by Kevin with how to approach the situation.

"We don't have a Dr. Patel at the moment. He finished here last summer. Do you have an appointment card? It must have been made for one of the current registrars."

"No, I'm afraid I forgot my card this morning. It's sitting at home on the mantelpiece, would you believe? No, I'm certain it was Dr. Patel. I saw him after that bombing in Oxford Street. He stitched me up, and gave me an appointment to come back and see him after a few weeks."

"There must be some mistake. Dr. Patel took up a new post in Birmingham in August. You must have seen one of the other doctors. What's your name? I'll see if I can find you on our records."

"Bill Bainbridge." The scar tissue on his arm suddenly felt itchy, and Bill involuntarily scratched his arm. He exchanged meaningful glances with his security guard. The receptionist asked for other personal details, and finally found him on the computer.

"Yes, I can see that you were here, but there is no record of who treated you. You also don't have an outpatient appointment booked with us."

"Would it say who treated me in my medical notes?"

"Yes, I'm sure it would, but they're in the medical records department. We don't have access to them at the moment. I'm sorry, but it seems to me that they intended for you to be followed up by your G.P. I'm sorry you've wasted your time coming here today."

"I'm sorry that I've wasted your time, too. I'll go and see my G.P. then. Thanks."

Kevin and Bill left through a set of sliding doors.

"Told you!" the security guard triumphantly announced. Bill did not reply. He was now more confused than ever.

CHAPTER EIGHTEEN

Under the vault their wings were spread straight out, touching one another, while one pair covered the body of each.

"Dr. Clarke? It's Bill Bainbridge. How are you?"

Bill was seated at his desk. His computer screen was brightly lit in front of him, adding a bluish, flickering tinge to the low lighting in his office. He was looking at Internet pages about brown dwarfs, the planet/star hybrids to which category Dr. Sacher's Dark Star belonged. The largest of the brown dwarfs were practically normal dwarf stars, while the smallest were more like Jupiter, only smaller, denser and darker in colour. It was the latter type that Bill was studying.

"Hi Bill," came the chirpy voice from the other end of the line. Bill winced quietly. He was not in the mood for chirpy. "Strange that you should phone," continued the astronomer. "I was going to give you a call later."

"Oh, yes? What did you want to tell me?" Bill was beginning to despair of maintaining security over the phone. He didn't know if he was being tracked, bugged, spied-upon or followed anymore, or by whom. Doug's article about the Dark Star had been prepared for publication, and was now entirely out of his hands.

Bill didn't see the point of continuing to live in fear. Given what had happened to Dr. Sacher, if whoever it was who had been following him did really want him dead, they would have killed him by now. One assassin's bullet was all it took, and they had had plenty of opportunity to take a shot at him.

Bill was now convinced that the incident in Paris had been staged to instil a sense of fear and urgency in him, and it had worked. He had told Anne Potter-Smith practically everything he knew, and in return had been treated to a litany of paranoid ranting, most of which was absolutely unprintable in a national newspaper. He despaired of the whole business.

Bill could hear Dr. Clarke take a short intake of breath, as if preparing to reveal dramatic news. The astronomer spoke steadily and clearly, "Ezekiel One: It's gone."

"WHAT?" Bill's cloud of despair abruptly dissipated, to be replaced by sudden rage.

"Steady on, old chap! Don't shoot the messenger. What I'm trying to tell you is that Ezekiel One is no longer where it should be. We made some overnight observations during its projected fly-over last night. They came back blank. It has either moved into a new orbit, or it's gone completely."

Bill's world was unravelling. He felt his chest tighten, his pulse race. "Have you been able to find it?"

"You're not really being serious, are you, Bill? This thing is pitch black and covered with some kind of stealth technology plating. We only knew it was there because it was blocking out the starlight. What makes you think anyone's going to be able to re-locate it? No one even saw it go."

"But it wasn't supposed to go anywhere until Friday."

"Christmas has obviously come early this year. Actually, I have to tell you, I'm relieved it's gone, personally. I've had so many emails about this thing. I've had the local paper phoning me up about it, and all my students keep asking about it in the lectures and seminars. It's become a bit of a pain, to be honest."

Bill felt himself calm down a bit. Dr. Clarke was a kindred spirit, and his apparent nonchalance was reassuring. "No kidding. I'm starting to feel the same way. I went to Paris yesterday to talk to an engineer from NASA who claimed to know where Ezekiel One was heading to. I ended up getting attacked on the Paris Underground. And I can't get hold of him this morning."

"What's his name?"

"Dr. Sacher."

"Oh, yes, I've heard of him. He works for the University of Paris these days, doesn't he? He's big on plasma physics. Bright bloke."

"Yes, well, he had a strange story to tell. We're leading with it in tomorrow's paper."

"I hope you don't mind me saying, Bill, but why are you telling me all this over the phone? I thought you were trying to keep this investigation of yours under wraps? The last time we met, you had me running through the science museum like we were being chased by the KGB, or someone like that."

Bill laughed a dry chuckle. "We *were* being chased, by someone in the Intelligence services. I'm still not sure who."

"So why the sudden openness?"

"Because we've got our story, and it's ready to go, so what's the point in trying to maintain a low profile? It's all over our computers here in the office, so anyone keeping an eye on us could readily access what we've written remotely. They already know everything we know, and they know that we know it."

"Okay, well, I think I just about followed that! So, presumably you wanted to ask me something about what Dr. Sacher had told you?"

Bill decided to be blunt. "Yes, he told me about the existence of a small brown dwarf in the solar system."

The astronomer's response was cheerful, and not in the least bit surprised. "I do seem to remember telling you all about that possibility when we first met, Mr. Bainbridge. For some reason, you suddenly dashed off when I was halfway explaining it all to you."

"I remember it well. Yes, I'm sorry about that. The reason I left halfway through that conversation was because I'd just seen a man who had been following me. He's cropped up here and there every so often."

"I *had* wondered. You still think you're in danger, then?"

"I know I am, James. This story is bigger than you think."

"Maybe it is, maybe it isn't. Without your secret spaceship there's not a lot of evidence supporting this whole story, is there? Anyway, what did Dr. Sacher tell you about brown dwarfs?"

"He said that there's one in Sagittarius, about 1,500 times the distance between the Sun and Earth away."

"We call those Astronomical Units, Bill. It makes it easier to describe such immense distances. 1,500 Astronomical units is about 140 billion miles away. That's much further out than any solar system object we've detected up until now."

"Is it possible that something that big might be out there?"

"Oh, yes. There are precedents for that sort of thing elsewhere in different star systems. When these brown dwarfs are still very young, they shine very brightly. So, we can see them orbiting other very young stars in stellar nurseries.

"We've been able to measure some of their orbits, and some of them are very wide indeed. So it's possible that such a situation might apply to our Sun too. The difference is that our brown dwarf would have stopped shining a long time ago, and because of its distance away, it would be difficult to spot with a telescope. But some of the movements of comets and other bodies in the outer solar system have hinted at something big lurking out there, so I'm not all that surprised if what Dr. Sacher says is true."

"He said that it would have an orbital period of about 60,000 years."

"That sounds about right, for the distance."

"He says that it is on the edge of the Sagittarius, but he didn't tell me exactly where."

"That's a pity, Mr. Bainbridge. Without some means to verify its exact location, it would be very difficult to find. The Milky Way passes through Sagittarius, and it has some very dense star-fields.

"We tend to avoid looking there when we're hunting for our outer solar system bodies. It's too densely packed with background stars, and other cosmic clutter. We tend to concentrate our efforts on the darker constellations, like Pisces."

"So you don't have loads of images to refer to?"

"Not in Sagittarius, no. Like I said, it's a bit of a difficult place to hunt for needles, if you get my drift."

"Dr. Sacher also said that no one would be able to see it now, because Sagittarius is behind the Sun at the moment."

"Also true. The Sun and this little brown dwarf are in alignment, then." Dr. Clarke laughed, "I should think that would give our New Age friends a real lift."

Bill was not in a humorous mood. "Yes, well, I haven't heard much from that lot recently. The bad publicity following their little riot here in London on Saturday seems to have taken the wind out of their sails, as well as the fact that the world seems to be stubbornly heading towards a reasonably normal existence next week," said Bill.

He had heard rumours in the newsroom that there was a plan for another gathering of the 2012 Movement at Stonehenge for dawn of Saturday morning, to mark the advent of the New Mayan Age, as well as the Winter Solstice. He had long since realised that the 2012 Movement had no better idea of what the Mayan cycles were about than anyone else. If there *was* significance to the date, then the true meaning behind it was lost on everyone he had come into contact with.

And now that Ezekiel One had quietly lifted its cosmic anchor, and departed from its orbital mooring ahead of schedule, he was even less inclined to believe that the exact date was significant, at least in NASA's eyes. But only time would tell, and there were still three days of the Old Age left to go.

"Tell me, Bill, did Dr. Sacher say why NASA built Ezekiel One?"

"Yes, he did, but he wasn't able to supply us with any evidence. And now it appears he may have been suicidal, although he didn't seem like that to me when I met him yesterday. So his testimony is in question, to be honest. But we're running the story tomorrow anyway. It's potentially too big to ignore, despite the problems we've got with verifying it."

"So, what is Ezekiel One for, then?"

Bill realised that he was drifting off the subject. "Oh, sorry, James. Everything's happening very fast at the moment. He said it's heading out to the brown dwarf."

There was complete silence on the other end of the phone line.

Then Dr. Clarke cleared his throat, "This is supposed to be a manned expedition?"

"That's right."

"Bill, seriously - do not publish this story! You'll be a total laughing stock!"

"Why?"

"It's just not possible, or, at the very least, not remotely practical. Look, there are probes currently moving away from the Sun after having visited the planets — the Voyager and Pioneer spacecraft. They have taken almost forty years to travel less than a tenth the distance to this brown dwarf. By that reckoning, it will take Ezekiel One several hundred years to get there."

"Dr. Sacher said that a secret unmanned probe was sent towards the brown dwarf in the late eighties, and was already ten percent of the way there. Apparently, it has been secretly sending back detailed images of what he called the Dark Star system. He also said that Ezekiel One had a new propulsion system. It has a powerful nuclear-powered engine, apparently, and he claims that the spacecraft can accelerate to an amazing speed, and then turn around to decelerate for the second half of the journey."

"Okay, so how long did he say it would take to get to this dark star?"

"Around fifteen years, he reckoned."

"Okay. Let's assume he's right, and I have to say it stretches credulity, but let's just say that he really has invented something extraordinary to get them there in that time. The fact remains that human beings are not built to withstand the difficulties of living in space for that sort of duration. Living in a zero gravity field is fraught with difficulties. Bones lose their strength, muscles waste away. We have no real idea what the potential long-term problems are, because no one has been in space for longer than about six months. Even after that period of time, astronauts are left weak and debilitated. When they return to Earth after long periods of time in orbit, they have to undergo intense physical rehabilitation.

"That's just the physical side. The psychological pressures such astronauts would be under would be intense. They would likely crack up. After all, by your reckoning it would be over thirty years before they returned to Earth."

Bill felt Ezekiel One slip away from his grasp. "Dr. Sacher claimed that they were on a one-way ticket."

"Oh, come on! That's mad! Who in their right mind would get on a spaceship on a one-way trip into the void, never to return?" The astronomer paused. "Are you seriously going to publish this story?"

"The story gets worse, James, believe me. We recognise the problems with this piece. Like I said, this is a tabloid newspaper. We tend to make up a fair bit of the news ourselves, anyhow!

"My boss is deliberately going for a sensationalist angle on this, because we know that no one's actually going to take it seriously. Not without proof anyway, and Dr. Sacher no longer appears to be available to provide that proof."

"Why's that?"

"Because, from what we've been told by a reliable source, he was found dead this morning, drowned in the Seine. He appears to have killed himself."

"Another of your contacts bites the dust, Mr. Bainbridge. If I didn't know better, I would be fearing for my own life!" Dr. Clarke sounded a sarcastic note.

"To be honest, we're not absolutely sure what's happened to Dr. Sacher, There's nothing on the newswire about his death. There's nothing at all, which is very odd, frankly, because he was a prominent scientist in Paris.

"We've tried to contact him at the university, and all we're told is that he hasn't come into work this morning, and that there's no answer at his home. He doesn't carry a mobile phone, apparently. So, he's a missing person. But, saying all that, he told me he was going to make himself scarce when this story broke, so he might just have taken himself off into the country somewhere to lie low."

"This source of yours, who told you he had died. How reliable is he?"

"He's a she. Hard to say, really. On the face of it, you would think she was very reliable. But, who knows? The whole landscape around this story is very murky. It's hard to know what, or who, to believe."

Bill corrected himself, "With the exception of you, James, of course! At the moment, I'm assuming that Dr. Sacher has gone to ground. But he may have been got at by these people."

"Let's hope not. I'm planning on living for a good length of time yet. You're a dangerous person to know, Bill."

Bill laughed, picking up on the astronomer's dry, dark sense of humour. He was more concerned for James Clarke's health than he was letting on.

"Try telling that to my wife. Look, I'd better get on with this article, James. I need to figure out a way of incorporating the news of the sudden loss of our only real piece of evidence. Thanks for your input, and feel free to give me a buzz back if you come up with anything else."

"Cheerio, old chap. Try staying out of trouble for five minutes, won't you?"

Bill replaced the receiver and returned to his computer. He buried his head in his hands.

Suddenly, the door to his office swung open. A young woman stood in the doorway. Bill looked up, slowly, and recognised her as one of the junior reporters in the newsroom. She seemed to be slightly out of breath.

"Doug's been trying to get hold of you, Bill. Your phone's been engaged for ages. He needs to see you straight away."

"What now?" Bill grumbled under his breath.

He acknowledged her interjection by nodding despondently. Bill quickly saved his work on his computer, stood up and walked out of his office. As he passed the reporter, she whispered, "I don't think he's a very happy bunny."

✦

Bill reached the door to his boss's office, and stood outside it for a moment. It was not too hard to make out the shouting and swearing going on inside. Bill looked around the open plan office to see a dozen faces looking directly at him.

He took a deep breath and walked straight in.

"Where the BLOODY HELL have you *been*, Bainbridge?"

"You wanted to see me, chief?" Kevin's favourite expression was proving addictive. Bill momentarily wondered whether he might need a security guard when facing Doug's wrath. Feeling like he was caging himself in with a ferocious predator, he shut the office door behind him.

"Damn right, I wanted to see you! Exactly what did you tell Her Right Honourable Highness this morning?"

"Why? What's happened?"

"The Government has only issued us with an F-ing court injunction. They've banned us from publishing anything else about Ezekiel One. They've slapped a D-Notice on the whole story."

"You mean a DA-Notice?" Bill was beyond caring.

"Don't you get bloody clever with me, Bainbridge." Bill had never seen Doug so worked up, although his boss's erratic and unpredictable temper was well known. Doug practically slapped a document in his hands, and marched across his office to stare resolutely out of his office window.

Bill made a cursory examination of the document. The lengthy legal jargon of the DA-Notice indicated that the Secretary of the Defence, Press and Broadcasting Advisory Committee had presented evidence to a high court judge, who had issued a notice preventing the Daily Standard from publishing any material connected with "the alleged existence of the 'Ezekiel One' spacecraft", or the publication of any alleged leaked NASA documents obtained from GCHQ.

The document cited DA-Notice 05, which specifically covered the work of intelligence gathering agencies. There was no right to appeal, but the decision to apply the DA Notice in this case could be reviewed at the next meeting of the Committee, in the Spring.

In the *Spring*!

"That's it then. We're totally stuffed…" rumbled Doug, like an extinct volcano emitting puffs of ominous smoke. He turned round and faced Bill, his face a red glow in the pale December light pouring through his office window. "You must have said something this morning, Bill. She's in charge of the oversight of government intelligence, and now we've been sent a D-Notice. That's not a coincidence, Bill. No way!"

Bill decided that attack was the best line of defence. "That's not all, Doug. Ezekiel One's gone."

"What do you mean, it's *gone*?"

"Flown off, shot down, beamed up. How should I know? Dr. Clarke phoned me just now to tell me that it's gone. Either that, or they've figured out a way for starlight to be seen straight through it."

Doug leaned on the edge of his desk, and took a long breath. "So, the horse has bolted. That's just great. And now we can't even report on that development! The next thing that will happen is that some smart little Johnny Hack from one of the other papers will write some crappy piece claiming that Ezekiel One was never up there in the first place. We won't even be able to comment on it, thanks to that" – Doug stabbed his finger at the DA-Notice –"and we'll look like we were duped all along by some kind of early April Fool's joke. Just bloody wonderful!"

"I guess that's what comes of taking on the big boys." Bill pulled out the visitor's chair from the front of Doug's desk and slumped down into it. He replaced the DA-Notice on the table, and drummed his fingers, irritated.

But the beast had not entirely let go of his prey. "You still haven't told me what you told Potter-Smith this morning."

"I just told her we were going to publish tomorrow. To be honest, she told me more about this than I told her. It seemed to me that she was trying to get the story out there. In fact, she seemed pretty desperate to see it published. She told me she reckoned she was on the losing side."

"What did she mean by that?" Doug was curt.

"She said that the U.S. and British governments are split into factions, fighting over control of this project. The factions that wanted Ezekiel One to launch are firmly in control, apparently. She's part of an opposing faction that is fighting to have the story made public. She's been fighting for disclosure."

"Look, Bill, I've been a political journalist for years, and I can tell you with absolute confidence that what she is saying is total crap. Political parties might fight for control, but governments are governments."

"She seemed to be under the impression that someone else was in charge."

"Right, so, let's get this straight. The Chairwoman of the Prime Minister's Intelligence and Security Committee is telling a tabloid journalist that the British Government is being covertly run by someone else?"

"That's what she said."

"Bill, she was winding you around her little finger. Trying to get you to spill the beans on what we know before the article was published. Then, once she had that Intelligence, she could decide on what action to take, which was THAT." Doug again pointed at the DA-Notice.

"That's not the impression I got."

"Was there anything she specifically asked for, in the way of information?"

"Well, she seemed shocked that Dr. Sacher hadn't told us the exact whereabouts of his dark star object. She reacted to that badly, like he had let the side down. She claimed that they had spent six months persuading him to come forward, and that he'd blown it by not having the guts to reveal the position of this thing. She was pessimistic that the Ezekiel One mission could be stopped."

"The only thing she's managed to stop is us."

"I'm not so sure it was her. Surely it takes longer than a few hours to put a DA-Notice together?"

Before Doug could respond, his phone rang. He gave Bill a look that implied unfinished business, and picked up the receiver.

"Yes?...When did they release it?...I see…They did find a note?...Right, well, thanks for letting me know."

Doug replaced the receiver and muttered further expletives under his breath. Bill remained motionless, deliberating on how to engineer a quick exit.

"You were right about Dr. Sacher. He's dead." Doug's temper seemed to have cooled considerably. "There's been an item on the Associated Press wire. The French police have ruled out foul play. Apparently, he left a note. According to sources close to his family, he had been taking anti-depressants for several years."

"He wasn't suicidal when I met him, Doug." Bill was absolutely sure of that. If his head was reeling from the comings and goings of this mad conspiracy, he was at least convinced that he could still read the people he interviewed. Anne Potter-Smith might have proven to be an exception to that rule.

"I'm sure you're right, Bill. You may have been the last person to see him alive. He was reported missing yesterday evening. I think we've been out-manoeuvred."

"People have been killed because of the secrecy surrounding this story, Doug. They've been murdered with complete impunity. How can we hope to get to grips with these people, when they're capable of cold-blooded murder?

"This could be the biggest story this century, but we've got nothing of it left. We don't know where Ezekiel One is, or when it left. We don't know where the dark star is, that the rocket is supposed to be blasting off towards. Our main witness is dead, and now we've been gagged by our own government. It's over."

Doug raised an eyebrow, "You don't seem too upset by that."

"Mrs. Potter-Smith told me some things this morning that have made me seriously doubt my own sanity. Her version of why this spaceship was constructed is so bizarre that...well, she's either totally paranoid herself, or a very good actress. Even if we had all the evidence in the world, which we don't, and published the story in full, free of government censorship, I doubt the general public would believe it. Maybe it is best left alone."

Doug folded his arms. He stood by his window, looking out at glimpses of the sunset behind the London buildings.

"I want to get them back. Somehow. There must be something we can put into the paper that will piss them off, without landing us up in the High Court."

"I'll go away and have a think about it, eh?" Bill offered hopefully.

Doug nodded despondently, and Bill wasted no time slipping out of his office.

When Bill got back to his desk, he noticed that he had a phone message. He played it back on his speaker phone.

"Oh, Bill, it's James Clarke again. I've had an idea about what you said. Look, I know this is going to be a bit intense for a phone message, but bear with me. This brown dwarf is supposed to be about 1,500 Astronomical Units away, yeah? I think you said it has an orbital period of about 60,000 years?

"Well, let's assume that its orbit is roughly circular. You said it was lying on the edge of the constellation Sagittarius. Well, Sagittarius is, as I'm sure you know, one of the constellations of the Zodiac. As you know, there are twelve constellations in the Zodiac. If this 'dark star' of Dr. Sacher's moves around the Sun in the same plane as the other planets, then it would spend roughly 5,000 years in each constellation. 60,000 divided by 12. Maybe it's coincidence, but 5,000 years is roughly the equivalent of the Mayan Long Count.

"So, I had this sudden thought. Perhaps each Mayan Age corresponds to the movement of the dark star through a single constellation of the zodiac. That would fit with it being on the edge of the constellation. Of course, my hypothesis would rest on the assumption that the ancient Mayans knew about the astronomical cycles of the dark star, which is a trifle unlikely, frankly, given that we seem to be having trouble spotting the thing, even with all the technology we have at our disposal. But, for what it's worth, it seems like quite a neat fit.

"Look, sorry to leave you a quick message like this, but I'm in a bit of a hurry. Got to go! You can print it if you like. It's just a bit of fun. Cheers!"

The phone message cut off.

Bill quickly picked up the receiver and dialled an extension number.

"Doug…Bill here. I think we've got a new angle on this story. One we can actually use without ending up in the dock."

Chapter Nineteen

I heard, too, the noise of their wings; when they moved it was like the noise of a great torrent or of a cloud-burst, like the noise of a crowd or of an armed camp; when they halted their wings dropped.

The sound of movement downstairs woke Bill up. He stirred and opened a bleary eye. The light was on in the landing, and Helen was already out of bed. The bedside clock read 6:48. Bill groaned, and clambered slowly out of the lovely warm bed.

The central heating had been on for half an hour, which was hardly sufficient to shift the mid-winter chill. He shivered and hurried out to the bathroom. The noise of a whistling kettle drifted upstairs, complimenting the smell of toast.

Within minutes, Bill was seated at the breakfast table in their spacious kitchen, sipping on a hot cup of tea. Helen, fully dressed, was pottering around near the sink, preparing breakfast. The radio was on quietly, but Bill could just about make out the weather forecast on BBC Radio 4. A huge pile of newspapers sat on the other end of the breakfast table, as if pretending to be a paper guest, intent on keeping the troubled journalist company.

"They're doing the Scottish weather forecast again," muttered Bill, in a hypoglycaemic gloom. "I'm sure they featured England in there somewhere, but it must have been quick."

"You've got about eight weather forecasts in that pile of papers, Bill. Why don't you take a look?"

His wife had already been busy this morning. She had been looking forward to reading articles about her hero husband in the papers that morning, after he had had his photograph taken outside the Houses of Parliament. She had nipped down to the corner paper shop to buy a copy of each national paper.

Bill was distinctly less enthusiastic. He reached over and found the Daily Standard in the middle of the pile, and pulled it out. He opened to page 3, and scanned through the article he had crafted the afternoon before.

The article started with the title, "The Mayan Ages Explained." It gave a description of a tiny brown dwarf orbiting the Sun, presented in a more or less hypothetical way. The only evidence provided to back up the idea was from an anonymous source at NASA whom Bill had described ambiguously. The article then went on to link the possible existence of the tiny brown dwarf, currently lying behind the Sun, with the end of the Mayan cycle. There were several complementary images of Mayan temples, and a simplified drawing of the outer solar system showing where this dark brown dwarf might reside. The article worked backwards from the Mayan cycle to predict the dark star's orbital period, distance, and position. Essentially, the article predicted the properties of the dark star's orbit from theory, rather than presenting the information as a NASA leak.

The final paragraph alluded to the conjunction of the Sun with the dark star during the winter solstice, marking the beginning of the Mayan New Age, as the dark star slowly progressed from one constellation to another.

On the whole, Bill was very happy with it. It seemed a harmless piece of speculative journalism. Most importantly, it didn't name anyone, or compromise their security. Then Bill flicked through the paper and came across his photo with Anne Potter-Smith, alongside an article paying tribute to his heroism. All in all, this was an edition of his own newspaper he would be proud to show his grandchildren.

He sipped his tea, and put the Daily Standard down. Helen joined him at the table, and placed a plate of toast between them. She gingerly nibbled at a lightly buttered piece of toast, her face suddenly pale.

"Right, here we go," he declared wearily, and reached across her to pick up one of the broadsheets at the top of the pile. He thumbed through it. It didn't take too long to find much the same photo. But the accompanying article was quite different. It described Bill's investigation of the end of the Mayan Age as an elaborate hoax. Without naming Ezekiel One directly, it quoted professional astronomers who delighted in declaring that his alleged spacecraft was entirely absent. A reassuring image of a normal star-field was shown, where Ezekiel One should have been. The Daily Standard had been asked to comment, the article stated, but had declined.

"It looks like the DA-Notice didn't cover the other papers, and their negative spin," observed Bill, despairingly. "They're painting me as some kind of fool, and dragging Anne Potter-Smith down with me, by the looks of things. I bet you it's the same in every paper but ours. The Ezekiel One story is dead."

"Just like poor Dr. Sacher."

"Yes. It's amazing the lengths they've gone to, in order to cover this story up."

"You don't know that for sure." Helen frowned, and began counting on her fingers in school teacher mode. "Lyn died of cancer. Dr. Sacher was a depressive who was under a lot of stress when he spoke to you. Marcus Everett was killed by a terrorist bomb. There's no evidence that any of them were targeted by the security forces."

"How about the bloke who tried to kill me on Tuesday?"

"You know, maybe that security guard was right. Maybe that was faked to put you under pressure. It makes sense to me. They could have been playing with your mind so that you revealed your hand early. Maybe your conversation with Anne Potter-Smith was recorded, and the tape taken to a high court judge to get the court injunction."

"I don't know anymore, love. Maybe that's exactly what happened. It certainly makes more sense than the motive behind all this being for real." Bill looked up from the paper, and smiled warmly at his wife. "Thanks for the toast, by the way."

He pulled some more of the papers across and began to go through them, as he munched on the toast. His wife did the same — although her own toast sat on her plate, cold and ignored — and they compared the articles that appeared in each one. To varying degrees of hyperbole, they all slammed the Daily Standard for reckless journalism. Some even blamed the rioting of the week before on the "Ezekiel One hoax." Some were more sympathetic towards Bill himself, extolling his virtues as a national hero. But, in contrast to that, one of the more aggressive tabloids wondered aloud whether he had incurred a head injury during the bomb blast, which had clouded his judgement in pursuing the story about Ezekiel One. It all made for depressing reading.

Helen broke the glum silence. "It's amazing how they all picked up the fact that Ezekiel One has disappeared."

"They must have been tipped off by the Government. The whole thing looks very well orchestrated. I guess it's just as well that I'm regarded well by the public, because otherwise they might have gone the whole hog and burned me at the stake."

"Hmmm…yes, it's a witch-hunt alright. I'm sorry, dear. You don't deserve this."

"Look on the bright side. I'll be back to doing restaurant reviews in the New Year, and we can put this whole sorry affair behind us."

"Glad to hear that. The school breaks up for the Christmas holidays today, Bill. Why don't you take tomorrow off, and we'll celebrate the End of the Age by doing something a bit different?" Helen's tone was mildly sarcastic. Bill smiled. He finished a piece of toast, thoughtfully.

"I've got one more thing to do before I'm finished with this story. Doug wants me to cover the winter solstice down at Stonehenge. Do you fancy coming?"

"What, go and stand in a muddy field with hundreds of hippies and druids in the dark and cold, waiting for the sun to come up?"

"That sort of thing."

"Yeah, alright. Let's do it."

With breakfast finished, Bill walked out of his front door, buttoning up his coat. The streetlights created a yellowish haze in the dark road, already alive with traffic. A man was seated in a car parked right outside the Bainbridges' house. He looked over to Bill, waved, and opened the passenger door.

It was Kevin. Bill walked up to the car, and climbed in.

"I thought we'd decided to dispense with all this?" remarked Bill.

"Doug phoned me early this morning and sent me over to pick you up. He didn't want you getting onto public transport today."

"He's expecting crowds of witch-hunters on the Tube?"

"Sorry?"

"Never mind. So what's brought about this sudden change of heart?"

"Your astronomy mate in Oxford. He got knocked off his bike last night.

He's on the critical list." Kevin was just as much a blunt instrument with bad news as he was with security.

"Jesus. I'd better tell Helen." Bill made a move to get back out of the car, but Kevin stopped him with a refraining hand on his arm.

"Better not, chief. She'll only worry, and we could do without that at the moment."

"Yes, I dare say you're right. It's her last day at school today, as well: She's got enough to concentrate on. Okay, well, I appreciate you picking me up. If I'm going to be under the gun, I might as well enjoy the perk of having a chauffeur."

Kevin smiled, and started the car's engine. Within moments they were heading for the main tributary towards central London. Bill looked in the side mirror nervously, paying attention to the cars behind. He felt his paranoia welling up within, causing nausea and panic. He also felt guilty. Terribly guilty. Was Dr. Clarke the latest victim of a conspiracy bent on destroying the evidence of Ezekiel One? If so, Bill's determination to see the story through might have caused the death of a talented young man.

✦

Bill walked straight into Doug's office without knocking. Doug was seated at his desk, and a smartly dressed man was sat facing him, his back to Bill.

"Oh, I'm sorry. I didn't realise you were in the middle of a meeting."

As the man turned in his seat, Doug replied, "Come in, Bill. I don't think you've met Mr. Provotkin before?"

The Russian billionaire stood up and shook hands with the journalist, who had closed the door behind him. Mr Provotkin was surprisingly young-looking for his years. A tousled mop of dark hair presented the only chaotic quirk in an otherwise immaculate appearance. His suit was beautifully tailored from a subtly pinstriped cloth. His handsome face was unusually tanned for the time of year, and conveyed a seriousness that was in keeping with his vast wealth. Bill's mind flipped back to his recent stay at the proprietor's luxurious Chelsea apartment, and the expensive bottle of wine he and his wife had polished off. He managed an uncomfortable smile.

"Good morning, sir. It's nice to meet you."

"Yes, likewise." Mr Provotkin's accent was strong, but his English was fluent nonetheless. "I've just got back from New York, so you'll have to excuse me if I appear tired. But I needed to speak to you both."

Apprehensively, Bill pulled up a chair, and the men sat back down. It was still dark outside, and the window acted as a mirror, recording the meeting in reverse image. Mr. Provotkin folded one leg over the other, cleared his throat, and spoke without interruption.

"You have done a good job: Both of you. You have worked hard to break the secrecy surrounding Ezekiel One. It is not your fault that your efforts have been stopped at the last minute. There is still a chance that we can release this story. However, it will not be here in Britain. It is also no longer important to release the story straight away. How do you English put it? There's no point shutting the gate when the horse has bolted? I like this expression. Well, our horse has bolted, gentlemen.

"I have some contacts in the British government. After all, through my network of intermediaries, I have proven to be a generous political donor. But even that was not enough to stop Whitehall from stepping in. I even managed to stall the court injunction for a while. They started legal proceedings just after we published the first story about Ezekiel One. I had hoped that we would be able to obtain the proof we needed to break the full story. But we are facing a formidable enemy, gentlemen."

Bill felt uneasy. Mr. Provotkin's political stance was proving similar to that of Anne Potter-Smith. It seemed that the higher up the ladder of power these people went, the more paranoid they got. Bill reflected on the fact that the Russian security forces were known to be watching Mr. Provotkin, and his associates. It was little wonder that *he* was paranoid.

The Russian caught Bill's eye. He seemed to be weighing his employee up. The Russian continued his monologue.

"We have lost this battle, but not necessarily the war. What I am about to tell you must not leave this room. I have been negotiating a deal to buy one of the New York newspaper titles. At the moment, I cannot not tell you which. I am working through a consortium. The Americans are sensitive about their media being placed under the control of foreign nationals. Even British Russians!" He laughed at his own joke, the humour of which was entirely lost on the two newspapermen.

"Once I have secured this newspaper, we will have a platform to tell the truth about Ezekiel One. Ideally, I would like to own a television station, because that would provide us with the best opportunity to break the story. But, even my pockets are not that deep. My point is this. I want you to continue to work on this story. I need you to discover the exact position of the dark star. Once that is known, then scientists will be able to confirm its existence. Then we can warn the people of the world to prepare."

"Prepare for what, Mr. Provotkin?"

"War, Mr. Bainbridge." The Russian looked tired. He uncrossed his legs, and stood up. The journalists stood up in response. "Whatever resources I can provide I will. This is your first priority above all else, even if it takes us years to achieve."

The Russian smiled at Bill and extended his hand in friendship, which Bill took. "Once you have saved the world, Mr. Bainbridge, you can go back to your restaurants. I promise."

With that, the billionaire walked out of the office. Bill sat back down. Dawn light was starting to appear outside, and his reflection in the window slowly faded.

"Is it just me, or did that seem like we were being recruited into some kind of underground resistance movement?" Bill was irritable.

"Don't ask me, Bill. I was expecting him to give us the third degree about dragging his newspaper through the mire. You should see the papers this morning."

"I have. Helen bought them all this morning, thinking she could fill a scrapbook. She got a bit of a shock."

"I'll say. At least Provotkin didn't have our scalps, anyhow."

"What happened to Dr. Clarke? And how did you find out?"

"How did we find out?" The big man looked incredulous. "We work for a newspaper, Bill! The story came through on Reuters overnight."

"Don't you ever sleep?"

Doug ignored that. "He was the victim of a hit and run incident yesterday evening. He was cycling home from his office when he was hit by a car. The hospital says he's critical, but stable. There's no sign of the car that hit him."

"Naturally. Well, at least he's still alive, I suppose, which makes a change. I should go and see him."

"I don't think that would be a good idea, Bill. If you keep turning up around all these people who suddenly die, or get run over, the police are going to start asking questions. I think you'd better just keep away from the poor man for a while, at least until he's recovered. I don't think the doctors and nurses will appreciate the angel of death turning up on their ward."

Bill smiled despondently. He changed the subject, "Doug, do you really take all this stuff about Ezekiel One seriously?"

"We already know it's for real."

"That's not what I'm getting at. I mean where it's supposed to be going to: The purpose of its mission." Bill could see that Doug was non-committal. "Anne Potter-Smith told me some very strange things yesterday. She compared Ezekiel One with the Spanish Conquistadors. Travelling to this dark star was like their journey to Mexico five centuries ago, she said. Their mission was to conquer and convert. She seemed to think that was Ezekiel One's mission too."

"How do they even know that there's anyone out there to battle with? It could all just be idle speculation."

"Put it this way. Let's say we discovered life on Mars, intelligent but a bit backward. What would we do? Would we send spaceships out there and start, I don't know, trading with them or something? Or would we send the army out there and take over?"

"Human nature being as it is, we'd go out there and take over."

"Right. I mean, we haven't really changed over the last 500 years, have we? The problem here is...what if they're more dangerous than we are? What's to stop these 'Watchers,' as Potter-Smith called them, from killing everyone on board Ezekiel One, and coming after us?"

"You think that's what Provotkin is talking about?"

"I'm certain it is."

"Then, he's right. We need to be ready."

"Sure, Doug, sure. I agree. But the thing I can't understand is this: Why go out there in the first place? We'd be better off keeping our heads down until we know exactly what we're dealing with, and until we're properly ready to cope with any aggressive move on their part."

"That's a good point, I guess."

"It's why I don't believe any of it, Doug. None of it! I just can't believe humanity would be that stupid."

Chapter Twenty

A sound was heard above the vault over their heads, as they halted with drooping wings.

The nurses were out of handover, and were beginning their morning routines. Linen trolleys were laid up, and drug trolleys unlocked. The light of the dawn sky outside began to compete with the stark white fluorescent light of the hospital ward. An unhealthy smell pervaded the ward. In the December morning chill, few patients wanted the windows opened. The stale smell was an unpleasant side-effect of keeping warm, and one that visitors to the ward quickly became accustomed to.

The ward sister — a plump, bespectacled woman in her fifties — walked out of her office to the sound of one of the patient buzzers. She walked past a tall doctor stood by the medical notes trolley, rifling through the orderly sets of notes. The doctor was over six feet four, and paler than one would expect, even for December. She paused, frowning, and edged up to him.

"Who have you come to see, Doctor?"

The man stopped his search, and turned his attention to the ward sister, whose height was easily a foot less than his own. "Good morning, Sister. I'm Dr. Keye. I don't believe we've met before. I'm a locum registrar standing in for Mr. Forrester. I've come to see James Clarke."

Dr. Keye's accent was heavy, and certainly American, although the ward sister couldn't place just where from.

"You're very keen. It's not even eight o'clock yet! But, to be honest, I'm glad you're here. The night staff have been very worried about him.

"They've had the on-cover doctor over to review him, but, well, all he prescribed was a single bag of gelofusine, and then he needed to go and see someone else on the ward next door. The fluids have just kept things ticking over. Mr. Clarke needs an ABG and some cultures. He's been pyrexial overnight, and his blood pressure keeps dipping. He's 36 hours post-op, so he's probably got some infection somewhere."

"Thanks, Sister. I'll go see what he's like first. Where do you keep your blood bottles? I'll need to take some regular U&Es, FBC, a cross-match and a clotting screen, in addition to the arterial blood gases and blood cultures. Perhaps we should consider a central line as well."

"He's already got one. The anaesthetist put one in during his surgery."

The sister quickly gathered together a dish full of syringes, needles and blood bottles, and a sharps container.

"Let me know when you've got the ABG, and I'll send someone over to ITU with it."

With that, she was gone, leaving the doctor to search the the ward's main dry-marker board for James Clarke's name. He quickly located the bed, and walked briskly through the chaotic ward. Dr. Keye found James Clarke in a bay full of trauma patients. The area was a dishevelled mess, with bedclothes hanging off the beds, and used urine bottles propped up precariously on chairs. Bedside lockers and tables were covered with various personal effects; drinks, tissues, cards and chocolate bars. An unpleasant smell was emanating from a bed near the curtained windows, where a metal cotside obscured the identity of the sleeping, soiled patient. Thankfully, that one was not Dr Clarke's bed.

The astronomer was fast asleep. He was connected to an intravenous drip, through a line inserted just below his neck, and his left arm was connected to a machine which was noisily taking his blood pressure. It failed to wake him up. His right arm was in a Plaster of Paris cast, and the top of his head still showed signs of a bloody laceration. He was pale, and his breathing was rapid and shallow.

The tall doctor pulled the curtains around and put the dish of medical paraphernalia down on the bedside cabinet. He fished his hand into the pocket of his white coat and pulled out a small piece of metallic equipment about four inches long. He turned it on, and some lights emanated from it in a colourful pattern. Sitting upon the edge of the bed, the pale-skinned physician pressed the device against Dr. Clarke's chest and activated it. A flurry of bright lights was emitted, which quickly resolved into regular, rapid patterns. This was followed by a high-pitched droning sound.

The physician swore quietly, and tried to cover the device with his hand in such a way as to mute the device's chirping sounds. Holding the device in place with his left hand, the doctor's right hand flitted across a series of small controls on its central surface. This seemed to agitate the display of lights still further. More high-frequency notes spilled out into the hospital bay.

The doctor reached into his pocket of his white coat once again, and pulled out a small sealed tray full of ampoules. He opened the tray, and took out two of them, replacing the rest in his pocket. He put the ampoules in the tray the sister had given him, and put on a pair of surgical gloves. Using needles and syringes from the tray, he drew up several syringes of lightly coloured liquid, and then proceeded to inject the medication into a free port on the central line hanging below Dr. Clarke's neck. The astronomer seemed oblivious to the activity around him.

After a few moments, he repeated his routine with the metallic device. The flurry of lights was less erratic this time. Dr. Clarke began to stir. His eyes opened, and he looked around without fully focussing.

The doctor quickly replaced the metallic device into the pocket of his white coat, along with the used ampoules.

"Good morning, Dr. Clarke," said the American doctor in an authoritative manner. "I'm going to take some blood samples now. You will feel a sharp scratch, but please try to keep your arm still."

The doctor worked swiftly with a tourniquet to prepare the astronomer's left arm, and took a series of blood samples. When he was finished he collected the blood bottles together, and removed the tourniquet. By this time, Dr. Clarke was wide awake.

"What happened to me, Doctor?"

"You were knocked off your bicycle by a hit and run driver. You're lucky to be alive. You sustained multiple injuries, and you've had some internal bleeding. You also seem to have picked up an infection, probably on your chest I would say."

A puzzled look fell across Dr. Clarke's face. "Don't I know you?" asked the astronomer in a subdued voice. "Your accent seems very familiar."

"Yes, we met in town last month, at that student café. You'd just had a meeting with the reporter from London: The one who appeared on the TV news, after that dreadful bomb blast."

"Bill Bainbridge."

"Yes, that's right. I overheard a bit of your conversation before Mr. Bainbridge left, and then I asked you about it once he'd gone. I've always been fascinated by the stars. I'm sure you remember. We talked about your work on the solar system, over a cup of coffee."

"Yes, I remember now. Your name was Nathan, wasn't it?"

"Yes. Nice to meet you again, Dr. Clarke." The Tall Man smiled broadly.

"Likewise. So, you're a physician?"

"Yes, you could say that. I trained a long, long time ago," the Tall Man smiled enigmatically, and gathered his equipment together. He then pressed a button on the blood pressure machine, and the cuff on Dr. Clarke's arm inflated again. The astronomer winced slightly.

"How long have I been here?"

"Since Wednesday. The orthopaedic surgeons patched you up that night, and you've been semi-conscious for most of the time since your surgery. It's now Friday morning."

Dr. Clarke laughed, a look of disbelief on his face. "Friday already? The end of the Mayan Age!"

"So I've been told."

"Nathan, why doesn't my arm hurt? It's been broken, hasn't it, but yet it feels completely normal. No pain at all."

Dr. Keye shrugged, "They've been giving you a lot of pain relief, I guess."

"But it really hurt when you took my blood pressure just then." The astronomer moved the fingers of his right hand about in the air, and then moved his arm up and down. He picked up a jug of water with his right hand, and lifted it high above his head.

"In fact, all of a sudden, I feel absolutely fine!" Dr. Clarke's voice was exuberant. He replaced the jug of water on his table, and scratched his head, a look of puzzlement ingrained upon his face, whose pallor was normalising rapidly.

The tall doctor looked at the result of the blood pressure measurement and stood up to leave.

"It sounds like my job here is done." He smiled magnanimously, and began to pull the curtains back. Behind them stood the ward sister, her arms crossed. All of the patients in the bay were staring at James Clarke.

"What's going on, Dr. Keye?" asked the ward sister suspiciously.

"Is there any chance of some breakfast, nurse?" asked Dr. Clarke, his face now pink with colour. "I'm starving."

The Tall Man collected his tray of blood samples together and addressed the ward sister. "I've not got enough time to label these, Sister: If you would be so kind." He handed the tray to her, and pointed to the blood pressure. "His systolic is above 130 now. I think your nurses did an excellent job overnight, Sister. Dr. Clarke seems to be well on his way to a full recovery. I think you can get rid of the central line, and his catheter too. He should be able to go home by the end of the afternoon, all being well."

"I thought I heard a strange noise in here, Dr. Keye. Did you hear it?"

"A strange noise? No, I don't believe so…" The Tall Man towered over the ward sister, his face gently mocking.

The sister frowned, but said nothing. She collected the tray and notes and disappeared in the direction of the nurses' station. The other patients continued to watch Dr. Keye in complete silence.

"I'd better get to my next patient, Dr. Clarke. I hope that our paths will cross again soon. I'd really like the opportunity to ask you a bit more about your research. Quite fascinating."

"Thanks. I really appreciate what you've done for me. What was your last name again?"

The physician relaxed into a broad smile, and spoke quietly. "Keye. Nathan Keye. Some of my really old friends used to shorten it to 'Enki', after the Sumerian god of wisdom. But I don't hear people call me that so much these days."

"Right, well, Enki, look me up at the University and we'll get together one evening. I'll get the first round!"

"Sounds good, my friend."

With a brief wave, the Tall Man left the patient bay, and made his way past the nurses' station. He was quickly intercepted by the ward sister. She was putting the blood bottles into bags which had cards attached to them, and lifted up an arm to bar his way. "I need you to sign these forms, Dr. Keye."

"Certainly." He stopped and pulled a golden pen from his pocket, and then swiftly filled in the blood bottle forms.

"What did you just do in there?" The ward sister was watching him very closely.

"What do you mean? I went to take his blood, that's all."

"Let's just put it this way. Before you went in there he was a candidate for the intensive care unit. When you'd finished, he had made a complete recovery. I've never seen anything like it."

The Tall Man put his pen back into his pocket and smiled broadly.

"Let's just say I've been doing this for a long time."

Chapter Twenty-one

Above the vault over their heads there appeared, as it were, a sapphire in the shape of a throne, and high above all, upon the throne, a form in human likeness.

Even during the early hours of the morning, the A303 trunk road was busy. Bill and Helen had passed the town of Andover. It was where a huge supermarket distribution centre had been built three years before, on the site of an old airfield.

The site had once been the home of the Royal Flying Corps. The new "Megashed," as locals had taken to calling it, was one of the largest buildings in Europe. The resulting traffic was a nightmare, with huge lorries coming and going every minute on average, all day and all night. The town of Andover had accepted this Faustian agreement readily, selling its rural soul for the promise of 900 new jobs.

Like the crowded flight path into London's Heathrow airport, the trunk road carried the supermarket juggernauts, spread in an almost regular pattern along its length. Bill had driven past countless numbers of the roaring metallic beasts, as his car had sped along the dual carriageway towards the ancient site of Stonehenge. But now, as they drew closer to the monument, the road had shrunk to a single lane. Predictably, the lorries were clogging the road, their presence intermittently spaced to prevent any real progress along the road.

Interspersed with the lorries were vehicles of a distinctly less corporate character. Old vans, and converted ambulances, were daubed with artwork, the colour of which dazzled in headlights. A convoy of hippies and pagans was making its way towards this New Age Mecca. It was a surreal mix along the A303, modern combined with ancient, corporate identity combined with non-conformists.

As Stonehenge approached, the traffic on the busy road slowed still further. Eventually, the line of cars and trucks came to a halt about 3 miles away from the ancient site.

Bill and Helen sat in the warmth of their car, faces lit by the red brake lights of the van in front. Vehicles continued to drip past on the opposite carriageway, the white glare of their headlights penetrating the darkness of the Salisbury Plain beyond. Bill looked at the clock on the dashboard. He estimated that they had about an hour and a quarter to go before sunrise. The minutes ticked by as the cars remained stubbornly stationary.

"I wasn't expecting this many people."

"Yes, it's odd," replied Helen. "They usually have a few hundred down here, from what I can remember. I read in the paper last year that the winter solstice involved mostly just druids. And a few journalists."

She smiled a bleary smile. A week of pre-Christmas activities at school had taken their toll on her energy levels, not helped by the ridiculously early start to their journey.

The traffic moved forward about 20 yards, and abruptly halted again. To the right, a country lane meandered away from the main road, ascending the slight hill into the darkness.

"Do you fancy a walk?"

"Are you being serious? It's the middle of the night!"

"If we sit in this traffic for another half hour we'll miss the sunrise. If we set off now we'll be able to get there in time."

"It'll clear, Bill. Let's give it a bit longer. I don't fancy traipsing across the countryside, if I can help it."

"I'm not so sure that this traffic will clear. There must have been an accident up ahead."

Five minutes passed. Bill tuned into the local radio station, which was playing cheerful music. The station's regular news bulletin included nothing about any snarl-up on the A303. During that time, their car managed to creep forward a further six yards. They were now directly opposite the turnoff.

"Come on, Helen, let's walk. It'll be fun."

"I'm just thinking about my nice warm bed at home," she muttered. Then she began to arrange her scarf and fasten her coat.

Bill smiled, and edged the car into the centre of the road, to look beyond the van immediately in front of him. A line of red lights snaked into the darkness along the trunk road. Traffic had stopped coming from the opposite direction. He drove the car into the country lane. In his headlights, Bill caught sight of a gate barring entry into a field. The short muddy track leading to the gate beckoned as an ideal parking place. Bill carefully manoeuvred the car onto the track, and turned the engine and lights off.

Bill and Helen got out of their car, locked up and walked back to the road. They began their long march towards Stonehenge, past the frozen line of vehicles. The streetlights of the village of Amesbury lit the sky to their left.

As they walked along the empty right-hand side of the road, they saw other pedestrians walking in the same direction. More and more of the colourful old vans and battered old cars were parked up on the verge, leaving irate lorry drivers, and early morning commuters, to pick their way slowly through the obstacle course - when slow progress could be made at all.

"It must be an accident up ahead," Bill offered again.

"I haven't heard any sirens," replied Helen.

Bill's eyes were growing accustomed to the darkness of the road. Looking up, he could see a stunning canopy of stars across the sky. As a city dweller, it was an unaccustomed sight for Bill. The rarity of the view made it all the more poignant. The couple walked on in silence. They were following a line of folk wandering towards Stonehenge, like an Alternative pilgrimage through the cold and dark of the English midwinter landscape. Some of the fellow walkers were kitted out with torches, and even the occasional lantern.

Across the fields, more ramblers could be seen, converging in waves towards the ancient monument.

Suddenly, blue lights cut through the darkness. A police car worked its way along the main road, avoiding the crowds of pedestrians, who had been systematically abandoning their vehicles. It made tortuous progress along the congested route. After a while, the police car disappeared up the road. In the distance, Bill could see the lights stop.

"The road's completely blocked up ahead."

"Bill, have you seen all those people over there?" Helen pointed across the field to their right. The torch lights were spreading across the field like a moving carpet of light. There were hundreds of lights, all moving in the direction of the monument.

"I've never seen anything like it."

The couple climbed a slight rise in the road, past a line of halted traffic. Most of the lorries and cars had long since turned off their engines and lights, and were queuing up in silence. As the couple approached the top of the rise, they looked down at the road in front of them. The country road was a scene of complete gridlock, with cars blocking both carriages, all facing west. The police car up ahead was making a difficult three-point turn, its blue lights still flashing helplessly.

Suddenly, Helen touched Bill's arm. "Look!" She said breathlessly.

Across the plain, a swarm of tiny lights engulfed the ancient stones, which now stood about one mile away. All of the surrounding fields were covered in people making their way from all directions, and congregating at the ancient site. A particularly strong band of white light snaked across the field to their right. People were walking from the road across the field to join the line.

"I didn't think they let people onto the site itself."

"Maybe they didn't have a choice, love. Look how many people there are. No one can get in or out by road. How are the police going to stop them?"

She was right. The cars which still had lights on were all stationary for as far as they could see.

"You know, it's ironic. When they built that megashed up at Andover there was this great fuss about how the lorries would blight the area around Stonehenge. Now the stones are having their revenge. The supermarkets will have empty shelves today."

"C'mon, let's join them." Helen grabbed Bill's hand, and led him towards the open entrance to the field to their right where intermittent groups of people were making their way, trading concrete for grass.

After a while it became clear that they were walking along some kind of ancient track, with a slightly raised bank marking it on either side. Looking across the Down, Bill was captivated by the myriad of white lights on the ground.

They seemed to mirror the splendorous beauty of the stars above. Earth and sky had become as one.

Bill could feel a sense of growing excitement amongst the strangely clad ramblers around them. Their pace had picked up, in keeping with the movement of the troupe.

"You never did explain to me what happened to your story, Bill," Helen remarked suddenly as they walked along.

"We got a big response from our readers. There were loads of emails about the End of the Mayan Age, and about the dark star. I think the Ezekiel One story had a bigger impact than the rest of the media gave credit for. I think Marcus Everett had become something of a martyr to these people."

"You mean *these* people." Helen swept here arm around, indicating the crowds of alternative pilgrims stomping along the muddy bridleway.

"Yes, I suppose I do. I think our feature had given them a voice in the mainstream media. I don't think that happens very often."

"But the rest of the papers took your story apart, Bill."

"Only because Ezekiel One disappeared. They still couldn't adequately explain what it had actually been in the first place. For a while, there was real proof. There was tangible evidence that something big had been going on behind the scenes. I think that struck a chord with many ordinary people."

"Was it worth it, though? So many people you came into contact with got hurt, or died. They paid a high price for the truth."

"My boss seems to think it was."

"Doug?"

"No, I mean Mr. Provotkin. I had a meeting with him and Doug on Thursday morning. He wanted us to continue looking into the story, despite the setbacks. He seemed very keen to discover the truth."

"God, does that mean Kevin's going to become a permanent feature in our lives?"

Bill laughed. "No, we agreed to relax with the security. When I heard that Dr. Clarke had made a complete recovery yesterday and was on his way home, I felt a lot more comfortable. If someone had really been trying to kill everyone connected with Ezekiel One, I think they would have done a better job of it. Kevin got me thinking that the doctor at St Thomas' hospital had been a government agent, who had implanted a tracking device into my arm. This Dr Patel seemed genuine enough when he was stitching me up, but when Kevin and I checked at the hospital they said Dr Patel had finished working there last summer. Well, that got me really paranoid for a while. But yesterday I contacted the lady manager we spoke with that night. She told me that Dr Patel had been drafted back from Birmingham to help deal with the emergency. So there were never any suspicious goings-on at all. Certainly no tracking device. The threat to me, if there ever was one, seems to have passed. So I think we can dispense with Kevin's services, for the time being at least."

"I think you're right. I don't think the reasons Lyn and Dr. Sacher died have anything to do with Ezekiel One. It's all been coincidence. Hopefully, we can put it all behind us and enjoy the Christmas holidays, Bill. I know how much this has meant to you, but I'm exhausted with worry."

"I know, love, and I'm sorry. I've noticed how you haven't been eating well recently, especially at breakfast time. The stress has been tough on both of us."

Helen made no reply. Her face, shrouded in darkness, was unreadable.

The couple walked on in silence for a while. Eventually, the Avenue met the dividing line that was the A344. It, too, was completely clogged with gridlocked traffic. The gathered masses crossed the road, cutting through the line of mostly abandoned cars, and climbed up the slight embankment on the other side. The wire fencing had been cut, creating an opening sizeable enough for two people at a time to make their illegal entrance into the English Heritage site. Beyond the torn fencing, the crowds fanned out past the Heel Stone and over the ancient Downs, creating a stream of sparkling white light.

The ancient megalithic stones looked hauntingly beautiful in the dim light. Their role as timeless custodians of the English landscape was brought into stark focus against the dark horizon. There was some singing and chanting here and there, but to the most part, the sizeable crowd was remarkably tranquil. The sheer number of people in attendance was incredible. There were thousands of people present.

The area immediately around the stones was occupied by cloaked and robed men and women. Ancient rites were being observed, overseen by the stones themselves. It was a unique moment in time: The temporal conjunction of the winter solstice and the beginning of the new Age of the Mayans. There was no handbook devised to mark such an event. The ceremony was improvised, almost clumsy. But the moment was being marked, nonetheless.

"Bill, I've got something to tell you."

"Oh, yeah, what's that?" Bill was half-listening. The sky to the south-east began to take on a rosy tinge. The excitement in the vast crowd was electric. The chanting increased, accompanied by rhythmic drumbeats. Bill looked at his wife's face as they faced south-east, waiting for the Sun to rise. She looked serious. She frowned slightly, and pursed her lips, as if conducting an inner dialogue.

All of a sudden, a gasp went up through the crowd. Arms pointed up at the sky, and all eyes were directed heavenward. Bill looked up. Just above the horizon, in the direction of the approaching dawn, a bright reddish light had appeared in the sky. It seemed to flicker, like a burning celestial torch.

"My God! What is it?" exclaimed Helen, almost breathless with excitement.

A long-haired man dressed in a long coat near to the couple shouted in a baritone voice, "Horus!" Another man nearby declared his belief that the light was a UFO.

Bill was suddenly overcome with the realisation that he knew exactly what the light was. He was staggered. Had this moment been deliberately engineered? Was it possible that NASA was putting on a clandestine show of its own? It could not possibly be a coincidence!

"It's Ezekiel One," he muttered. He turned to Helen, sudden excitement overtaking his normal cautious demeanour. "It's Ezekiel One!" Bill began to fumble around in his coat pocket, and pulled out his digital camera.

"Ezekiel One?" the long-haired man yelled towards him. "The spaceship?"

Bill turned towards the man, his voice almost jubilant. "It's leaving Earth orbit. Those are its rocket thrusters. It's on its way!" Bill began to take a video of the moving light in the sky.

The flickering red light began to slowly move towards the horizon, in the direction of the rising Sun. It was fading rapidly as it went. Word of what Bill had said seemed to be sweeping through the crowd, causing great excitement. There was shouting, singing and laughing. Many of the observers tried to take photographs with their mobile phones, or video footage with their digital cameras. Most just stood and stared at the unfolding spectacle.

Within moments, the first rays of the Sun ripped through the night sky, and the great globe of red light emerged, victorious above the horizon. The tiny glow of Ezekiel One's rockets was entirely lost in the dawn light. A great cheer went up as the winter solstice was marked, and the crowd broke into spontaneous song and dance, accompanied by sporadic bursts of drumming.

"Was that really Ezekiel One?" asked Helen, dumbfounded.

"It must have been. They must have shifted its position in orbit slightly this week to hide it. But it was still up there, all along, waiting for the right moment to leave. It couldn't have been a coincidence that they marked that moment with first dawn light here. There must be a meaning attached to it."

"The start of the New Age?"

"I guess so."

"Well, that's a bit of a coincidence for us, too, Bill."

"What do you mean?"

Helen looked up at the dawn sky. "I'm pregnant."

"Huh?"

Helen looked at her husband and smiled. "All this time, you've been so embroiled in this James Bond stuff. You never even noticed my morning sickness. I'm almost eight weeks gone already, you mad fool."

Bill stood dumbfounded as his wife had spoken. Suddenly, his face broke into a broad smile and he whooped and cheered, dancing around the muddy field as the dawn brightened above him.

Ezekiel One cast its last rays of burning light upon the Earth, and was gone.

Chapter Twenty-two

I saw what might have been brass glowing like fire in a furnace from the waist upwards; and from the waist downwards I saw what looked like fire with encircling radiance.

Kosinski's hair was buffeting wildly about her face. The wind (or perhaps better to call it a wind-stream) usually carried it in one direction only. This familiar direction normally blew her long, dark hair horizontally away from the back of her head. But like macro-weather systems, the direction of travel of the air current was subject to alteration occasionally.

It was usually when someone else was present. The additional activity complicated the dynamic of the on-board micro-weather system. Kosinski cut an agile figure in her grey one-piece flightsuit. The synthetic cloth of the suit clung to her curves tightly as she exercised. She had been blessed with good looks, as well as intelligence, and she was adamant that she would maintain her fine figure in the years to come. This precarious exercise routine was a means towards that end, and she was keen to master it.

She looked down at the floor and continued to concentrate on her exercising. She focussed her attention. One foot in front of the other. Maintain a rhythmic, constant pace. Face forward into the wind, which was thankfully swinging back to its usual unidirectional flow. Taking care not to run. Mustn't run. Whatever happens, don't run.

She had made that mistake once, and could still feel the bruising that had resulted from the impact to her shoulder. On that awful occasion, she had cascaded through the whirling air into one of her colleagues. Like flotsam pulled up into a tornado, she had mimicked a human missile. The only reason neither of them had been killed was that there was not enough space in here to get any real momentum going.

She felt guilty just thinking about it.

Focus. One foot in front of another. Maintain the rhythm.

To be fair, they had all done it. Well, almost all of them. For a moment, she dared to look to the side. The walls rotated past her at terrifying speed. She immediately looked face forward again, her eyes concentrating their attention solely on the deck in front of her.

One foot in front of another. Don't run. Keep at least one foot on the ground at all times.

"Kosinski! I'm right above you!"

The jubilant yell was immediately recognisable as Shaw. His nasal East Coast twang was unmistakable. How did he do that? He must have got in as the drum had started to roll. There was no way he had managed to get into it when it was running at full speed. She hadn't seen him, anyway. But then she barely did anything other than look straight at the floor when she started her turn on the Gerbil's Wheel. Otherwise, she would get the nausea back.

Maintain the rhythm. FOCUS!

"You're a goddamn lunatic, Shaw. You could get us both killed!" She found herself shouting above the sound of the whirling wind.

"Relax, Kosinski. I know exactly what I'm doing. It's just a case of getting the setting on the boots right, that's all."

The soles of the astronauts' boots contained surprisingly powerful electro-magnets. They could be adjusted using a hand-held remote control. When activated, they held the astronaut to the metallic deck of the drum. They could be used in other parts of the spaceship too, but this was where they proved most useful. As the drum rotated, faster and faster, the boots' magnetic grip could be loosened, and the centripetal forces of the drum's rotation would push the astronauts' feet against the deck. The cruising speed of the rotation was set to create the equivalent acceleration to 1G.

For a set period of time each day, the astronauts could experience normal Earth gravity, by undertaking this strange exercise routine. The drawback was that the air did not rotate precisely with the drum. So the whole contraption became a wind-tunnel, with the astronauts whizzing around, their hair and clothes aloft in the steady breeze.

From the almost zero-gravity vantage point of the Gerbil Wheel's control room, floating safely behind the reinforced Perspex screen, the other crew members could wait their turn and watch their colleagues try to walk.

In fact, there was a very slight gravitational effect throughout Ezekiel One. This was provided by the constant acceleration of the nuclear-powered rockets engines. As the incredibly fast-moving particles were flung from the reactor through the rocket exhaust at the back of the spaceship, Ezekiel One was propelled further forward. The physical quantity of expended fuel was comparatively small, but the particles were ejected at such high speed that the immense spaceship enjoyed constant, if limited acceleration. After all, there was no air resistance in space to slow the ship down.

This constant acceleration provided the same effect as gravity on the ship. But instead of mimicking the Earth's gravity, Ezekiel One's "artificial gravity" was equivalent to standing on a large asteroid. At rest, the astronauts soon found themselves on the "floor." But, only a slight movement would propel them back to floating in the air once again.

Even so, the merest hint of gravity established a meaningful sense of direction. On a psychological level this was vital. On a physical level, it was nowhere near enough to maintain a crew of healthy astronauts. That was why they all had to exercise regularly on the Gerbil's Wheel, which was far from easy, as they had all quickly discovered. There was a fine art to it. It felt like walking in the centre of a hurricane. Shaw had cracked it early on. Kosinski was still finding her feet. But she persevered. For all her nausea and trepidation, it felt good to walk, like she had on Earth. Even if the impression of gravity *was* artificial, it made her feel human again. She just had to make sure she didn't get carried away.

One foot in front of another. Don't run.

If she ran…

It had happened two days before. It all took place so fast. At the moment when both of her feet had simultaneously left the deck, she was afloat once again. But her friend Gemma wasn't. She had come hurtling around, and the two of them had collided. It was not a pretty sight. The observers in the Gerbil control room had immediately shut the drum down, and, luckily, there had been no lacerations. Blood in almost zero-G made a real mess, particularly on the flight-suits.

Since then, she was to walk the Gerbil's Wheel in solitude, until she had refined her technique. It was shaming, but not devastating.

As a medical doctor, Kosinski had fought an internal battle in her own mind as to whether the Gerbil's Wheel was really worth using at all. On the plus side, it allowed the astronauts to continue to experience the force of gravity, even if it was only for half an hour a day. But in that time, they could walk two miles, if they paced themselves properly. That was probably more than most Westernised people on Earth walked in one day.

As the crew's walking technique improved, it was hoped that they would be able to ride the Gerbil's Wheel together in larger numbers, extending the time they each spent on it per day, and further sustaining their physical strength in space. The Gerbil's Wheel maintained muscle strength and tone, and kept their bones strong. But the downside was the inherent risk of serious injury on a spaceship in the middle of, well, absolutely nowhere. As the medical officer on board Ezekiel One, that was her problem, and her dilemma.

In the end, her internal debate had boiled down to one fact. If their bones significantly weakened over the next fifteen years in space, then they would be even more at risk of sustaining fractures. It was one of the reasons why the Gym was one of the most important areas on Ezekiel One, and why the fitness program undertaken daily by all of the crew was regimental and strictly enforced.

But perhaps more important in the long run, the astronauts' bodies had to remember *how to walk*! When they eventually arrived at their destination, it was a basic skill they would surely need. Otherwise, the gravity of the Homeworld - which was thought to be only slightly less that of Earth's - would prove crippling.

"Kosinski?" came a shout through the torrid air current.

"Yes?"

Kosinski found Shaw's presence mildly irritating, and her voice betrayed those feelings. It was not just that he had mastered the electro-mag boots and the Gerbil's Wheel so quickly (which contrasted so sharply with her own slow progress on that front). It was also that she had caught his eye on too many occasions during crew meetings. He was either watching her, or was attracted to her. Neither possibility was one she found particularly appealing.

"Have you spent any time in Area Six?"

That was an odd question. Why would she have been down there? Area Six was dominated by an electrical generator, and sat alongside the main nuclear reactor. The entire zone was a maze of shafts, ducts and bulkheads. Definitely an area for the engineers. Which was a point...Shaw was security, not engineering. What was his game? Arranging a clandestine meeting? Yuck!

"Why would I go down there?"

Area Six was the section of the ship closest to the nuclear reactor and the exhaust rockets. Due to the constant acceleration provided by the engines, the "floor" of each level provided artificial gravity towards the bottom of the ship. Essentially, when standing on the "floor" their feet faced the engine and rocket. So the engine room was at the bottom of the ship. The flight deck was at the top.

"Has Pierce mentioned anything about it?"

"Not to me. Why? What's troubling you?" Kosinski was relieved that Shaw was not making a pass at her, in this maelstrom.

"It isn't what's troubling *me*. It's what's bugging one of the engineers. They're not happy about one of the sealed compartments down there."

"Shaw, why are you telling me this?"

"Because I'm on opposite shifts to Pierce, and the only time I get to talk with him, *they're* around."

Kosinski knew exactly who Shaw was referring to, and it wasn't the engineers. Ezekiel One was carrying a group of passengers whose interests often seemed divergent from those of the real flight crew. These 12 priests were certainly aloof; even secretive, it seemed to Kosinski. Their eventual role was evidently important for the success of the mission, or they wouldn't be on board the spaceship, but their presence was already creating division and suspicion among the rest of the crew. Kosinski worried about the long-term effect of this division, given the arduous voyage ahead.

"Try Sunday morning," she joked. Shaw laughed, and she suddenly realised that he was right behind her. He had made his way around the drum, and was about to walk alongside her. There was no problem with that, of course, because the drum was designed to take pairs of walkers. It just breached an unwritten etiquette that had quickly evolved among the walkers as they, literally, found their feet with the device. In effect, Shaw was invading her personal space. It was un-nerving.

One foot in front of another. Maintain the rhythm. Focus!

Now alongside her, he looked across. She could see him clearly in the corner of her eye: The advantage of a woman's peripheral sight. She didn't need to take her eye off the deck in front of her. Shaw's upper body was well-toned, and his hair short. His jawline was clean-shaven, a pleasing effect which many of the male members of the crew had already dispensed with. But the fact that he liked to take care of his appearance didn't make up for his annoying mannerisms, at least in Kosinski's opinion.

"I need you to talk to Pierce. In private," he hissed through the noise of the constant air current. "Preferably in here, in the Gerbil's Wheel, where no one else can overhear you."

"Go on." Kosinski was intrigued.

The crew were barely halfway towards the Venus fly-by and already plots were hatching, and cliques were being established. The anthropology involved was one of the reasons she had agreed to go on this crazy trip. That, and her interest in (near) zero-G obstetrics.

The ideal unit size for a human group was about 100, and the crew of Ezekiel One was under-par by twenty-two. She strongly suspected that after fifteen years in an enclosed space - with a crew of young, talented, and (with the exception of several of their VIP passengers), sexually active adults - that gap would steadily close. She planned on writing ground-breaking papers on the development of human foetuses and babies in space. But, that would pale in comparison with her study of the anthropology of Humanity's first space colony.

"The guys in the hold have been doing some standard seismic studies of the structural durability of the ship. Don't ask me the details, Kosinski, because I barely understand a word of what they're talking about. But, they've calculated that there is more mass in Area Six than they can account for from their blueprints of the ship."

"How did they figure that out? We're practically in zero-G."

"Don't ask me. The guy who spoke to me explained it, but I'm no engineer. He said it had something to do with the way the ship resonates, and measurement of the distribution of the mass of the craft. Anyhow, they've found several extra tons in Area Six."

"Extra *tons*?"

"Yep. Tons. So they did some more studies in Area Six to figure out how the load was distributed, and they isolated it to one compartment. On the blueprint, the compartment is supposed to contain emergency liquid oxygen. But the actual loading suggests something much more massive."

"Can't they just take a look?"

"It's sealed. In fact, it's not even clear how you'd get into the compartment. But…"

He paused, momentarily, and Kosinski looked across at him. Focusing on his face, rather than the illusion of the rotating wall behind him, she remained steady. She smiled inadvertently, pleased at her sudden success at maintaining the Walk.

Shaw beamed back. Her smile swiftly faded, and she looked back towards the deck.

"…that's not the weirdest thing," he continued, evidently unphased. "After finding this anomaly, the guys began to run all kinds of extra checks, and double-checks. They've calculated that the oxygen consumption is slightly higher than they expected."

"Get real, Shaw. That's within experimental error. You've got seventy-eight people aboard this craft. They're telling you that the oxygen consumption is for seventy-nine? I'm sorry, but that's not enough evidence to start talking about a stowaway aboard this ship!"

"I'm not making myself clear, Kosinski. They calculated it for Area 6. They were able to break the oxygen usage down in different areas when the areas are sealed, which is most of the time down there. With just 5 of them down there, they found oxygen consumption for 5.4 people. With *none* of them down there, and the area totally sealed off, they still calculated oxygen consumption for 0.3 people."

"So, we've got, what, a dog on board?"

"They don't know, but they think it's got something to do with that compartment."

"That's nuts. Maybe there's some kind of equipment failure, or a leak in this compartment holding the emergency oxygen. There could be any number of explanations. Look, Shaw, I think we need to go on more than this before we start worrying Pierce about it. He's got enough to deal with."

It was Shaw's turn to sound irritated. "Kosinski, with all due respect, you're not in charge of security on board this ship. I need answers, and I need Pierce involved in this. But I want this investigated quietly, okay? I don't want *them* to know that we know. Got it?"

Kosinski looked down at her remote, and flicked her thumb over the screen. The drum began to slow, and the two astronauts both adjusted the controls for their electro-mag boots, to compensate for the dissipating centripetal force. Within seconds, they were held to the deck by magnetism alone. Kosinski tapped her screen again, and the boots released. She pushed herself off the deck and began to float towards the Perspex screen, which was opening into the control room.

She heard an odd rhythmic clanking noise behind here. Turning, she saw Shaw walking along the metallic wall.

Walking! Along the wall!

"Whoa," she exclaimed, "when did you learn to do *that*?"

Shaw was skilfully using his boot controls in synch with his stride. Synchronising the boot's electromagnetism with his movements, he was walking while in freefall. Like a two-legged spider, he marched down the wall towards the "floor." His gait was awkward, almost robotic, but he was still walking in zero-G.

Kosinski felt the familiar soft landing of the floor coming slowly up to meet her.

"It's easy. It's like juggling at the same time as using clutch control on a stick-shift. I'll teach you!" he chirped arrogantly.

What a moron, she thought.

✦

Pierce was strapped into a flight chair, staring at a flat screen display. It was scrolling down slowly, showing sets of seemingly random numbers. He seemed absorbed. In his black flightsuit, Pierce's natural good looks were complimented by his rank. Kosinski enjoyed being around him, although she disapproved of his three-day growth of stubble. The bags under his eyes were worse than last week, too.

Kosinski floated across to him, and took hold of a small handrail to steady herself. She swung around slightly, her long hair wild like fire. Within moments, her feet were infirmly placed on the floor.

"Do you mind if I tag along on your Two O'clock session on the Gerbil's Wheel, Pierce?"

"Oh, hi, Kosinski!" The ship's Commander was cheerful. "They've let you pair up again?"

"Yeah, until I knock someone else out. I wondered if you wanted to volunteer as a guinea pig?"

"A guinea pig on the Gerbil's Wheel? Sounds like a date!" He smiled, still staring at the screen.

"What's that?"

"A new transmission from the Homeworld. It was picked up by the Hawk 2 probe yesterday."

The Hawks were the unmanned probes which had been sent in the direction of the dark star decades before. Within a couple of years, Ezekiel One would be passing them both. But at the present moment, they were NASA's best means of surveying the dark star system.

A couple of years before, Hawk 2's trajectory had brought it to a position between the dark star and the binary star system Sirius. It had been a stroke of pure luck, because the craft had come into the range of beamed transmissions between the two systems. The beamed transmissions were narrow enough to have avoided the entire planetary zone of the Solar system, although the dark star and Sirius were practically opposite each other in the Earth sky.

The wide angle that Hawk 2 had taken out of the solar system had brought it within range of the transmissions. It was the discovery of these transmissions that had finally provided the impetus to build Ezekiel One. It was also the reason why the whole project was shrouded in the strictest secrecy.

"Do you know what it says?" Kosinski already knew the answer to that question.

The best super-computers that the National Security Agency had at its disposal had not cracked the code. They remained just that, digital code. But intelligent digital code, transmitted alternately from the Homeworld and from Sirius B.

All anyone connected with Ezekiel One knew was that the transmission beam carefully avoided the Earth. As far as SETI, the civilian Search for Extra-Terrestrial Intelligence, was concerned, Sirius A and B were dormant of life. NASA and America's intelligence and military chiefs knew better. It was not news they were keen to share with the public, or even the public's democratic representatives.

"No. NASA forwarded it to me, and also to our colleagues in Area Three." Pierce's tone almost remained neutral. Area Three had been dubbed 'The Monastery' by some of the crew.

"Why them?"

"Search me. That's why I'm looking through the file, to see if something else is embedded. But it's just the usual, unintelligible alien code." Despite his pessimistic appraisal, he continued to carefully study the file.

"Okay, well, have fun, and I'll catch you at two."

"Sure, that's great. Look forward to it."

Pierce is nice, Kosinski thought, as she pushed herself away from the floor, and floated away towards the entrance to the main deck below the flight deck.

Maybe one day he'd find the time to help her with her human fertilisation studies, she mused.

✦

The drum rotated, like a washing machine on slow spin. As it sped up, Pierce and Kosinski reduced the power of the boots, and began their bizarre exercise, side by side.

Beyond the huge Perspex screen, two figures floated in the control room. The two men were among the twelve inhabitants of Area Three, and their turn on the Gerbil's Wheel was due at 14:30. For whatever reason, they had arrived half an hour early, and were chatting among themselves.

"It must be nice having so much time on their hands," remarked Kosinski, her tone acidic.

"Now, now!"

"Shaw wanted me to speak to you." Kosinski was straight to the point, keeping her voice low.

"Has he figured out how to dance in space yet?"

She laughed. Shaw's antics with his boots had proven popular among the crew, despite the fact that walking along the walls was, for the time being at least, slower than floating. But Shaw had claimed that once the technique was mastered, they would all be walking around the decks, boot controllers in hand.

"I'd be more worried about him learning zero-G karate."

"He is our security specialist, Kosinski. He's effectively a space cop. It's part of his job to master his environment."

Kosinski smiled. "We're like a little community in space, aren't we?"

Pierce raised an eyebrow. "So, what did he want you to tell me? He knows where my flight-seat is."

"He says that the engineers have found a secret compartment in Area Six."

"There are a lot of compartments in Area Six."

"Sure, but this one has several tons of excess mass."

"Oh?"

"Not only that, but there's an excess consumption of oxygen in that level."

"I see."

"You don't seem very surprised by this."

"Kosinski, we all have a job to do here. This mission has been carefully designed to execute a plan, and we're here to make sure that plan runs smoothly. You have your job, and I have mine. Shaw has his. He wants to know exactly what everyone is capable of on this flight. It's his job. He also needs to know what each crew member has access to. But that does not mean it's his job to second-guess our cargo! That's my responsibility. Tell him to keep his nose out of it. It doesn't concern him."

"Cargo?"

"Neither does it concern you, Kosinski! I need to make this really clear. You will both drop this! Right now! If it gets back to me that this investigation of Shaw's is on-going, then I shall take effective action." He turned to half-face her, maintaining his steady stride. "It's a long float home, soldier."

Kosinski looked at Pierce in horror. Was he serious?

His face was impassive. She suddenly lost her footing and felt the rush of air as she was swept upwards. Pierce's hand grabbed her arm, and her momentum sent her crashing into his chest.

Remarkably, he remained standing, holding her, inside the giant spinning autoclave. Shaken slightly, she held onto him with her left arm, and found her footing using the right boot's remote control in her right hand.

"Trust me, Kate. I know what I'm doing." His voice had softened considerably.

For a while at least, she felt quite sure he did.

EPILOGUE

Like a rainbow in the clouds on a rainy day was the sight of that encircling radiance; it was like the appearance of the glory of the Lord.

The green light flashed intermittently. Its strength was feeble.

Its presence was unnecessary, for there were no eyes to witness it. No hearts to run to its beat. No minds to wonder at its symbolic importance. But its solitary confinement within the vault transcended such matters. Its mechanical beat was the work of men, but the meaning of its rhythmic pulse was Divine.

If there had been *Adamu* eyes to see in this enclosed space, the *Adamu* travellers would have marvelled at the stone sarcophagus secured to what just about served as a proper floor. Their backward *Adamu* minds would have wondered at the wealth accumulated across the walls. Line upon line of gold brickwork created familiar, *Adamu* patterns of wall-building.

But the resultant structure was no mere *Adamu* house. This golden tomb paid homage to its sole Occupant. And the flashing green light was His sole worshipper. This golden tomb, sealed up within the grey, metallic walls of Area Six, was to be His home for fifteen Earth years. For this Ancient God-King of Babylon such a length of time was but a passing moment. His 12 guardians would dutifully stand watch over the sealed chamber, laying down their lives if necessary to prevent defilement by the unclean Adamu who were flying Ezekiel One.

The stone sarcophagus, which had been, until so very recently, buried beneath the foundations of Babylon, was ageless, as if hewn from primordial rock. In times gone by, it had known the interiors of spacecraft far more skilfully designed than this crude machine. In times gone by, it had dwelt in Ziggurats, faithfully constructed by armies of slaves. Slaves who had *understood* what it meant to pay homage to their God.

For Earth Millennia it had lain hidden beneath the city, as armies of soldiers had come, and armies had gone; as Empires had risen and fallen. Its precious Cargo had slowly breathed the tomb's dense, Earthly air, as if for an eternity. Its precious life had been maintained by technology supremely superior to that of the *Adamu*.

And then, suddenly, the *Adamu* had found the tomb. The Adamu from the American Continent had taken Babylon by force, and had excavated His temple, Esagila. They had discovered the secret chamber buried deep below the Ziggurat. They had found His living tomb. Unexpectedly, they had recognised its importance. A new Empire had taken Babylon, and this Empire alone, at last - after so many millennia of waiting - understood some of the Old Ways!

It had been easy to assert command, to attain dominion over the greatest *Adamu* Empire the world had ever seen. It was true that the modern *Adamu* had become resourceful, and numerous. But they were as malleable as they had always been. He remembered how Father Enki had once expressed concern to the Council of Nibiru that his greatest work was flawed. The *Adamu* were bred to work, to serve, to fight. But their inherent instinct was to *think* like a herd. Not like a hunter. Not like a *Nephilim*. Not like a Watcher.

Father Enki cared for his *Adamu* sheep, and had done so, alone, for Earth Millennia. Father Enki's Age was now passing.

Now, it was His time. He was on His way Home.

The Age of Marduk had finally begun.

Printed in the United States
140463LV00003B/61/P

9 781892 264251